THE ARKHEL
CONUNDRUM

Book Four
of
THE TEARS OF ARTAMON

Sarah Ash

Published by: Tourmalise Press

ISBN: 9781700902719

The Tears of Artamon

The Story So Far...

Portraitist Gavril Nagarian has inherited more than a distant wintry kingdom and the title of Drakhaon of Azhkendir from the father he never knew. With the title comes the curse of the Drakhaoul, a daemon-dragon spirit that inhabits his body and lends him tremendous shape-shifting powers—at a terrible cost. After Gavril and his Drakhaoul Khezef defeat the invading army of neighbouring ruler Eugene of Tielen, Eugene collects the legendary Tears of Artamon, seven rubies that enable him to summon his own Drakhaoul and make himself Emperor of the Western Quadrant. But when his rash act sets free other Drakhaouls, Eugene and Gavril must put aside their differences and make a pact to send them back through the Serpent Gate to the Ways Beyond, in a bid to restore peace to the mortal world. Gavril is helped by Kiukiu, a servant girl, a Spirit Singer who uses her songs to travel into the world of the dead—and ambitious Eugene is aided by his onetime tutor Kaspar Linnaius, the long-lived Magus, a powerful wind-mage and alchymist.

PROLOGUE

Steamy waters bubble and fizz. Clouds of mist, tinged with the acrid scent of minerals, rise to blot out the stars. And through the rising steam, eyes gleam, green as jade. A soft, sibilant voice whispers, "I can see you, Kiukirilya. Wherever you are, whatever you are doing, I shall be watching you, watching and waiting."

Kiukirilya sat bolt upright, staring into the darkened bedchamber.

"Do not forget your promise." A barb of pain, sharp as a serpent's poisoned bite, pierced her ankle.

My promise.

"What's wrong?" a sleepy voice asked from beneath the rumpled blankets beside her.

"How can *she* be here?" Kiukiu could still hear the faint bubbling of the hot springs, could still sense the serpentine eyes gazing at her.

"Who's here?" The bedclothes heaved as her husband turned over, surfacing from deep slumber.

His question jolted her fully awake. "I must have been dreaming again."

"Another nightmare?"

She nodded.

"It's all right." Gavril reached out in the darkness and pulled her to him. "I still have nightmares too. Sometimes it helps to tell."

She snuggled closer, absorbing the heat of his body, the comforting strength of his arms. She wanted to lose herself in that human warmth and forget the insistent, sibilant voice that had penetrated her dreams every night since she discovered that she was bearing his child. But she could never tell him the substance of her nightmares. Not until she had figured out a way to undo the secret bond she had entered into with Anagini, the Guardian of the Jade Springs, a bond sealed by the touch of the snake goddess's fangs on her ankle.

"Give me your firstborn child, be it boy or girl, to tend my shrine . . . And you must never tell anyone what passed between us here today or you will find yourself an old woman again."

Part One

Chapter 1

"What will the druzhina say?" Kiukiu felt tears pricking at the corners of her eyelids. "She's just a girl. They were expecting a boy. An heir to Kastel Nagarian."

"She's perfect." Gavril gazed at their newborn child. He was holding her very gingerly, as if afraid she might break. But the look in his eyes had softened to one of such tenderness that it made her heart melt. "Let the druzhina say what they will. She's my daughter—and they'll learn to love and respect her. They'll get their heir next time."

"Next time! Who assumed there's going to be a next time?" Exhausted, Kiukiu flopped back on the pillows and closed her eyes. Did Gavril have any idea what she had gone through to bring his daughter into the world? Every muscle in her body ached as if she had been stretched to breaking point.

"Look at her hair; it's coppery in the candlelight," she heard him say. "What there is of it, that is."

These moments were so important that she wanted to remember every second so she could treasure them when the time came to give up her precious firstborn.

No. She stopped herself. There must be a way to annul her contract with the Guardian of the Jade Springs.

"What's wrong?" Gavril leaned across, still cradling the baby in one arm, and stroked her face. "Are you in pain? Should I send for Sosia?" The gentleness of his touch only made the tears well up and spill down her cheeks.

"I'm all right," she said, forcing a smile as she wiped them away with the back of her hand. She was annoyed at herself for feeling so weak. "Just a little . . . weary." She reached out to tousle the baby's soft wisps of hair. "Auburn, like your mother's. Should we call her 'Elysia'?"

"What about 'Malusha', for your grandmother?"

She shook her head vehemently. "An Arkhel name for a Nagarian child? The druzhina would never allow it."

"The druzhina will do as I tell them." For a moment, the sea-blue eyes darkened and she caught a brief glimpse of the stern, ruthless clan leader he had forced himself to become to win back his kingdom. Then he said, less harshly, "But you're right, love; there's no point creating bad feeling when this little one is the first of a new generation of Nagarians, and our hope for a better future."

"Still here, Lord Gavril? Your wife needs to rest." Sosia reappeared, carrying a steaming cup of tea. "A long first labor drains a woman of her strength. Drink this, Kiukiu."

"What's in it?" Kiukiu sniffed the tea suspiciously.

"Just a few medicinal herbs," Sosia said, plumping up her pillows. "They're good for women after childbirth."

Kiukiu sipped the tea; it tasted bitter, with a strong hint of aniseed that made her pull a sour face. "Are you trying to make me feel worse, Auntie?"

"Drink it all down; you'll thank me later on," Sosia said briskly. And then she turned to Gavril. "My lord, you mustn't hold your daughter like that, you have to support her head properly!"

Kiukiu saw Gavril's mortified expression as Sosia took the baby from him and demonstrated.

"And what's this little angel's name?" Sosia asked, cooing over her great-niece.

Kiukiu exchanged a guilty glance with Gavril. "We haven't quite decided yet."

"But all the kastel are waiting to celebrate her birth," Sosia said, shocked. "Askold can't propose a toast to a nameless child."

Sosia's words made Kiukiu laugh—and then stop abruptly, sucking in her breath as her aching muscles protested.

"Besides, you know the old tales, Kiukiu, that a nameless newborn is easy prey for the Lost Souls trying to find a way back into this world."

"Yes, Auntie," Kiukiu said, handing her the empty tea cup. *And I should know more than anyone, for I've encountered them on the borders of the Ways Beyond.*

"Well, I need to go help Ilsi in the kitchens; old Oleg's drunk as a pig again. He insists that he had to sample the wine to make sure it was a good vintage to wet the baby's head." Sosia placed the baby in Gavril's arms again and bustled out.

Kiukiu lay back on the pillows. Had there been a sedative in the tea? She felt suddenly sleepy.

"I've always liked the name Larisa," Gavril said after a while. "It comes from an old Smarnan song our housekeeper Palmyre used to sing to me when I was little."

"Larisa? I like it too," she said drowsily. "And I don't think there's ever been anyone of that name in either clan, Arkhel or Nagarian."

***

Kiukiu had lapsed into sleep and Gavril sat beside her, doing his best to hold Larisa the way Sosia had shown him.

My daughter. It still seemed too extraordinary a thing to comprehend. *I'm not ready to be a father. I'm not worthy to be given this precious new life to guard and protect.* Yet the warm little bundle that he was supporting so cautiously knew nothing of who he was—or what terrible things he had done. She just lay there, lightly dozing, letting out the faintest little squeaky sound from time to time. Her vulnerability terrified him. *Do all newborn babies make such strange grunts? Is that normal? Suppose she's struggling for breath?* He tried to push all the worries and fears to the back of his mind. *How would I know what to do?*

Suddenly her lids opened and she gazed directly up at him with eyes that were the same deep sea-blue as his own. Startled by this intense scrutiny, he gazed back.

"Hallo, Larisa," he said softly, certain that she was studying him. "I'm your father." And then his view of her little face blurred and he found he was blinking away tears. "If only your grandmother Elysia could have lived to meet you. She'd have been enchanted with her first grandchild." And she'd have shown him the right way to hold the baby so that he didn't feel quite so incompetent.

***

The Elysia Summerhouse, Lord Volkh's wedding gift to Gavril's mother, had fallen into neglect again during the Tielen occupation.

But Gavril had been working steadily through the summer to repair the damage and convert it into a studio where he could paint, just as his mother Elysia had done after his own birth. And with the coming of autumn, there was a painful anniversary to be marked.

There were hardly any flowers left in the garden but he knew that the bunch of bright-berried twigs, glossy ivy, and the last soft-furred seed heads of wild clematis he had assembled would have pleased her far more than any bouquet of hothouse flowers. There were no greenhouses at Kastel Nagarian, and none of the elegant conservatories. filled with exotic plants and fragrant roses all year round, found in all the country estates in Tielen or Muscobar.

The rotting floorboards and carved woodwork balustrade had been replaced, the holes in the roof repaired, and Dunai had helped him paint the veranda a soft gray-blue. Gavril imported clear glass panes from Tielen to improve the quality of light inside and cleared the overhanging vegetation that had smothered the building: brambles, vines, and rampant wisteria hardy enough to survive the harsh winters.

A couple of easels stood inside, each one sporting canvases—but both canvases were blank. His sketchbooks lay on the floor, boxes of pastels untouched beside them.

"Can it really be a year already, Mother?" He heard the catch in his voice. She had died bravely yet recklessly trying to stop the Drakhaoul Nilaihah from abducting young Giorgi Vashteli. He had arrived too late to save her, seeing only the departing daemon's trail scoring the sky, finding her lifeless body lying sprawled on the floor. And since that time he had not once been able to bring himself to paint or draw, even though sometimes he thought he could hear her affectionately chiding him, "Why are you wasting your life and your talent? My time is over, my life's work finished, but yours has hardly begun. Stop moping around and pick up your paintbrush! Heavens, Gavril, life is short enough as it is! What kind of a son have I raised?"

He lifted his hand to wipe away a stray tear that had suddenly leaked down his cheek, defiantly blinking away the salt, stinging trickle.

"Mother, you're right and I'm sorry. It's just that I . . . I . . ." He knelt down and opened up the battered, stained artist's case that had been hers. Before he left the Villa Andara, Palmyre had thrust it into his hands, insisting, "No, you must take it, she would have wanted you to."

The pungent smell of oil paints and turpentine that issued from inside made his eyes start to water again.

Suddenly he was back in her studio, no more than five years old, sitting at her feet, watching her with wide eyes as she placed a carefully-judged brushstroke on the canvas, then stood back to assess its effect. One tiny dab of white . . . and suddenly, there was an uncannily lifelike glint in the eyes of the portrait in progress.

I felt as if I was watching a sorceress weaving spells. And I longed—more than anything I'd ever longed for before—to learn the secrets of her magic.

"You taught me so much more than any of the professors at art school," he said aloud to the empty studio.

His fingers strayed over the crushed metal tubes, crusted with bright flakes of dried paint, the latest invention that she had ordered from Francia. He remembered her telling him what a boon they were to any traveling artist, her eyes alight with enthusiasm at the new possibilities they presented.

"Don't listen to those conservative old farts at the art school who turn up their noses and say that a true artist must always grind and mix his own paints!" She had never been one to trim her language when she felt strongly about an issue. After all, she had often traveled abroad alone, fearlessly seeking out new experiences, and new commissions.

Then there was Palmyre. He had wanted to bring her back with him to Azhkendir but she had been reluctant to leave Smarna. Elysia had left her a generous legacy, more than enough to buy a small house of her own.

"But who will keep the Villa Andara ready for you when you come to visit?" Palmyre had objected. She had worked there as housekeeper and companion to Elysia for so many years that Gavril realized it would be unkind to compel her to leave. So he had agreed that she should stay on and open the house in summer to visitors who wanted to view Elysia's paintings.

The blank canvases mocked him. *You were never as good as your mother. Your career as a painter ended before it began. What's the point of starting again?* Insidious voices began to whisper in his mind once more. *A true painter paints because he has to. You're just a dilettante, a dabbler, an amateur . . .*

He clapped his hands over his ears and shouted out, "That's not true!" And then he glanced guiltily around, wondering if anyone had heard him.

I would start painting again—if only I didn't feel so . . . empty.

Chapter 2

On entering the Pump Room in Sulien, Lilias Arbelian blinked, dazzled by the glittering light radiating from the crystal chandeliers overhead. Even though it was still day, the elegant watering place was illumined by the flames of hundreds of white wax candles.

"It must cost a fortune," her maid Dysis murmured. "No wonder the entrance fee was so extortionate."

From behind her black lace fan, Lilias was carefully observing the other visitors who had come to take the healing waters of the spa. The steamy air was cloyed with heavy perfumes and lavender pomades, although she also noticed the presence of an unpleasant sulfurous odor. *A problem with the drains?* And even though the fashion for periwigs was long gone, many of the older clients tottering around with the aid of canes were wearing fanciful, curlicued confections on their heads, as though they were still the latest mode.

"Oh dear. The average age here must be sixty at least." Lilias felt her spirits sinking as she scanned the company for a glimpse of a younger, unwrinkled face.

"But remember that it's only three in the afternoon. The footman at the door told us that later on there will be cards . . . and dancing."

The faint strains of a string trio floated toward them; on a raised dais at the rear of the lofty room sat three musicians earnestly scraping away, but the guests' chatter was so loud that their efforts were all but in vain.

"So where is this famous pump dispensing the healing water we've traveled so far to sample?" Lilias asked no one in particular.

"My dear lady, let me escort you to the bar." A white-wigged gentleman was beaming down at her; one glance at his upright stance and the military cut of his coat, overlaid with a splendid gold-embroidered sash, told her that he must be a retired soldier.

"The bar? Surely they don't serve alcohol here?"

He laughed and she placed one lace-gloved hand on his outstretched arm, allowing him to lead her through the throng. As they moved across the crowded parquet floor, heads turned, undoubtedly wondering who the auburn-haired newcomer in the discreetly modish mourning dress might be. Black suited her, enhancing the pale luster of her skin and the languid green of her eyes, and she knew it. She was here to play the tragic young widow who had lost her husband. No one need know that they had never been formally married; she had borne his son and Stavy was proof of their liaison.

A buxom serving girl wearing a fetchingly ruched white cap was serving glasses of the steaming spa water from a special fountain. As they approached, Lilias noticed that the sulfurous smell grew stronger.

Her gallant companion beckoned the serving girl over and she handed Lilias a glass. Lilias took a sip and tried not to spit it out. The taste was revolting and its unpleasant bitterness was only enhanced by the warm temperature of the cloudy water.

"It's very good for you," said her companion, smiling even more broadly at her evident disgust. "It's kept me young and vigorous, I assure you!"

Lilias took a swift gulp, swallowing the tepid water yet unable to prevent herself from pulling an unbecoming face.

"Dysis; you should try some."

"No thank you," said Dysis in an undertone.

"The waters are blessed by our patron goddess," continued the gentleman, leading Lilias away to the steam-misted windows that overlooked the healing waters. Lilias saw a large public bath below, filled with rheumatic and arthritic sufferers soaking in the green mineral waters, watched over by an ancient statue of the goddess Sulien. "They certainly helped me make a good recovery after I took a bullet in the thigh in the Allegondan campaign of '67."

"I knew it!" Lilias exclaimed. "I knew you must be one of the military—and to have served your country in such a distinguished way."

"I'm retired now. My role here is to welcome visitors to the Pump Room and to ensure the young bucks don't get out of hand."

"Wait—you must be the one they call the King of Sulien. Am I right, sir?" Lilias, genuinely excited that she had made such a conquest so soon, gave him her most winning smile. "Are you Captain Montpelier, the Master of Ceremonies?"

He smiled back, evidently pleased that she had recognized him. "I had no idea my name was so well-known beyond Sulien."

"I made sure to read the Sulien Guide on the ship traveling here from Muscobar." She was certain, by now, that their conversation had attracted the attention of many of the visitors.

"Muscobar? You've traveled a long way to take the waters. Do you have acquaintances here in Tourmalise? I couldn't help noticing, my dear Mistress—erm?"

"Arkhel," Lilias said, shyly averting her gaze. "Lilias Arkhel." It said Arbelian on her papers and travel permit, but she was confident that Captain Montpelier was unlikely to ask to see them.

"Arkhel?" he repeated. "Can it be that you've come this way because—" And then he broke off, returning to his earlier unfinished question. "I couldn't help noticing that you were in mourning dress, Mistress Arkhel."

Lilias nodded. "My husband Jaromir was killed in Azhkendir. He was a ward of Emperor Eugene . . . and lost his life at the siege of Kastel Nagarian."

"My deepest condolences for your loss." The captain bowed his head. "But I wonder if you are aware, Mistress Arkhel, that there are Arkhels currently residing in Sulien?"

"In Sulien?" Lilias affected a tone of surprise. "But Jaro told me he had no living relatives. I thought his family were all massacred in the clan wars."

"It may be sheer coincidence. But it's not a common name. I will see if I can arrange an introduction. Lady Tanaisie has brought her daughters here for the season for the last two years; such charming young ladies,

Miss Fleurie and Miss Clarisse. I'm certain they would be delighted to make your acquaintance."

"So there is no Lord Arkhel?" Lilias asked slyly. "Or has he no interest in the delights of the Sulien season?"

"Far from it; Lord Ranulph is a frequent visitor at the card tables, here, and at the new Assembly Rooms."

Was that a slight note of disapproval in the captain's voice? *Does Jaromir's uncle have a taste for gaming, I wonder? How remarkably convenient.*

"Ah! I've spotted Lady Tanaisie taking tea in the alcove. Please follow me, Mistress Arkhel."

Lilias needed no further bidding, darting a swift, triumphant glance at Dysis who nodded and followed at a discreet distance.

***

"Mistress Lilias," announced Captain Montpelier, "has recently arrived from Tielen to take the waters. She asked me to arrange an introduction, my lady."

"All the way from Tielen?" Lady Tanaisie set down her tea cup and smiled welcomingly. "Won't you join us? The tea is freshly brewed; it's a special blend from Khitari that I think you'll find very light and refreshing."

"Thank you, Lady Tanaisie." Lilias smiled back and settled herself on one of the little gilt-painted chairs.

"How do you take your tea? With cream or lemon?"

"Black, with just a little sugar, thank you."

"Fleurie, pass our guest the sugar bowl and tongs."

"Yes, Mama."

Lilias took up the tongs and carefully dropped one lump into the fragrant liquid, stirring until the sugar dissolved. Then she took a sip and smiled again at the Arkhel ladies. "Delicious."

"I knew you would like it!" Lady Tanaisie clapped her plump little hands together in evident delight.

"In Muscobar we take our tea with jam to sweeten it; plum works well with a strong Serindhen blend, but apricot suits a more delicate, perfumed leaf."

"Tea with jam?" echoed Fleurie, the elder daughter, pulling a face. "How peculiar."

"Fleurie," said her mother in mild admonition, "just because people from other countries do things differently doesn't mean that their customs are 'peculiar'."

"Excuse me." Fleurie bit her underlip and blushed a becoming rosy pink.

"Your daughters are so pretty," said Lilias. "They obviously take after you, Lady Tanaisie." In fact, all three had the delicate white skin that flushes too easily, with eyes the light blue of summer speedwells. There was not a trace of the distinctive shade of dark Arkhel gold in their soft hair which had been artfully teased into curls and ringlets to frame their heart-shaped faces. *How to describe the color? Pale buttercup? Winter jasmine?*

Lady Tanaisie nodded her head in acceptance of the compliment and then looked up at Captain Montpelier who was still hovering in attendance. "Won't you join us, Captain? Or is something a little stronger more to your taste?"

The Master of Ceremonies laughed. "You know me too well, Milady. But as I'm on duty, not a single drop of the stronger stuff will pass my lips until the Pump Room clock strikes six." And then he bent down and whispered in Lady Tanaisie's ear. Lilias saw her expression change, her eyes widening as she glanced in her direction. He straightened up and bowed before taking his leave.

Lilias set down her cup and saucer, steeling herself for what might follow.

"So we share a surname," said Lady Tanaisie. Her face betrayed no emotion other than surprise. *She's either utterly lacking in guile, or supremely skilled at hiding her true thoughts.* "Fleurie, Clarisse, as you've finished your tea, perhaps you could take this opportunity to greet Mistress Hauteclere; I imagine her daughters are just as eager as you to discuss last night's ball."

"Thank you, Mama!" The girls rose, each bobbing a curtsey, and hurried away. Lilias could sense their relief at being excused.

"My sweet sylphs," Lady Tanaisie said affectionately as they vanished into the animated throng. Then she turned to face Lilias. "My dear Mistress Arkhel, the captain has just intimated that we might be related by marriage. But surely it can't be the same family; my husband was the only one to escape that shocking massacre twenty-one years ago."

As Lilias hesitated, wondering how best to frame her reply, she became aware of a swell of familiar music from the trio rising above the tinkle of tea spoons on fine porcelain: how ironic that they should be playing *October Seas* at this moment.

"The truth is that my husb— my late husband was also unaware that anyone had escaped Lord Volkh's murderous attack. Even when he became a ward of Eugene of Tielen, the prince's agents were unable to track down any blood relations."

"That would have been at the time when Ranulph thought it prudent to lie low in Tourmalise, I imagine. But you said your 'late husband'," and Lady Tanaisie's voice throbbed with sympathy. "My dear child, this is tragic. Tell me all about him."

Lilias drew in a halting breath, as though steeling herself to retread painful ground. "His name was Jaromir and he was the eldest son of Lord Stavyor. He was studying at the monastery of Saint Serzhei when Volkh Nagarian attacked Kastel Arkhel. The Drakhaon's men came looking for him but the abbot managed to spirit him safely out of Azhkendir to Tielen."

"Lord Stavyor?" Lady Tanaisie repeated softly. "You were married to my husband's nephew?"

"So your husband Ranulph is . . ." Lilias was determined to ensure that she had her facts right. It would be a disaster to make a mistake at this stage.

"The idle youngest brother of Lord Stavyor."

"But Ranulph is not a name that I've ever heard used in Azhkendir."

"He changed his name. For many reasons, as I'm sure you can imagine, but most of all to be accepted into polite Sulien society. Ranozhir has—if you'll excuse me—a rather barbaric, uncouth ring to it."

Lilias nodded.

"His idle nature saved his life. Lord Stavyor had sent him abroad on business to Tourmalise and when the terrible news leaked out from Azhkendir, he and his servants thought it wise to stay in Sulien. Not long after, we were introduced, and well," Lady Tanaisie blushed as becomingly as her daughter, "we married, Ran took over the running of my father's estate, and now we have three children of our own. But that's enough of me. Tell me—if you feel strong enough, that is—about your own husband. If he was Eugene of Tielen's ward, then you must find yourself in the Emperor's favor."

Lilias, in spite of all her skills at dissembling, felt a muscle twitch at the corner of her mouth. *The Emperor's favor! Would I even be here if Eugene had deigned to treat me with the slightest show of compassion?* She took out a little handkerchief from her reticule and dabbed at her eyes, hoping her new acquaintance would interpret her reaction as provoked by excess of emotion.

"A fresh pot of the special Khitari blend," she heard Lady Tanaisie ordering, beckoning one of the Pump Room flunkeys over. "And a plate of sandwiches. Cucumber."

Fortified by cucumber sandwiches and more tea, Lilias began to confide in Lady Tanaisie. It was strange to be unburdening herself (selectively, of course) to this sympathetic, trusting woman. She almost felt guilty for a moment. And then pushed the feeling away. *I'm the injured party here. It's taken months to raise the funds to make the journey to Sulien. I'm going to win these people over—and make Eugene regret that he stole my son from me.*

"So you met your husband by chance when your ship was forced to take shelter from autumn storms? Two lonely travelers, thrown together by the capricious elements, and unexpectedly finding love. How very romantic." Lady Tanaisie's pale blue eyes sparkled with enthusiasm.

Lilias conveniently avoided any reference to her intimate relationship with Lord Volkh, the true reason for her visit to Azhkendir, or that her brief, impulsive affair with Jaromir had nearly ruined her mission to infiltrate the Drakhaon's household to gather information for the Muscobar spymaster, Count Velemir. It was all in the past, and there was no need to over-complicate her explanation. "When Eugene of Tielen invaded Azhkendir, there was no alternative but to flee with little Stavyomir, even though he was only a few weeks old. And then—at the siege of Kastel Nagarian—Jaromir was shot as he tried to mediate between the Nagarians and the Tielens. He was killed by . . . by a Nagarian crossbowman." She dabbed at her eyes again. "It was horrible. My poor little Stavy. He's too young to remember his father."

"How very distressing for you." Lady Tanaisie leaned over and pressed Lilias's hand between her own. "And where is the dear little fellow now?"

Lilias let a sob escape from behind her handkerchief. "The Emperor Eugene has made him his ward. I'm sure it's all for the best and growing up at the imperial court will give him an excellent start in life but I—I miss him so." And she hid her face in her hands.

"But why must your child be separated from his mother? I don't understand the reasoning behind such an action?"

Lilias shook her head. "The Emperor has very strict ideas about the education of children." She improvised. "Faced with the choice of raising Stavy myself on a widow's pension or taking up the Emperor's offer, I acted in my little boy's best interests. But it's been hard for me." Eugene had not given her a choice, but Lady Tanaisie didn't need to know that.

"Fate has dealt you a cruel double blow. But you are among friends here. You must come to Serrigonde and meet my husband. We Arkhels must stick together."

"Serrigonde?" Lilias wiped her eyes.

"Our little country estate. We'll be returning next week."

"So Lord Ranulph is not in Sulien?"

Lady Tanaisie hesitated and Lilias saw a look of vexation briefly cross her pretty features. "Indeed, he is here—but he is at the card tables and would not appreciate any interruption." She let out a forced little laugh. "You know how stubborn men can be, Mistress Arkhel." She lifted the teapot. "More tea?"

***

"That went well . . . I think." Lilias sank into a threadbare chair in their lodgings as Dysis lit the lamp.

"An invitation to luncheon at Serrigonde Manor next week? I think that went very well," said Dysis, brushing the street dust from her mistress's velvet cloak before hanging it up. "And who'd have thought those rumors about the Tourmalise Arkhels were true?"

"It turned out to be all for the best." Lilias closed her eyes; her head was aching and she felt faint from lack of food; cucumber sandwiches made a delicious snack, but that was all she'd had to eat since the previous night. "Considering how low our funds are . . ."

"But how will we get there? Didn't you say the estate lies some ten miles to the west of the city?"

"Lady Tanaisie will send her carriage to pick us up," Lilias said. "She was most insistent."

"I'll see if I can make some alterations to your other dress; you can't appear in the same gown twice in Sulien society."

"How I hate being poor!" Lilias sat up. "And these dingy lodgings are costing us a fortune. They're not even in the fashionable part of the city; they're too close to the river."

"Would you mind if I removed my mask?" Dysis settled herself with her little sewing box close to the lamp. "I find it hard to do needlework with it on; it impedes my vision."

Lilias waved a hand in assent and Dysis carefully undid the ribbons, placing the black lace mask on the table, revealing the scars marring her face. Lilias still found it hard not to shudder when she looked at the terrible disfigurement her maid had suffered trying to protect baby Stavy from Gavril Nagarian. At the time he'd been possessed by the terrifying dragon-daemon, the Drakhaoul, and not in his right mind, hungering for innocent blood.

You are still at the top of my list of those whom I intend to be revenged upon, my dearest Gavril, directly below Eugene of Tielen.

"So what have we learned today?" she said as Dysis began to sew some silk violets onto the décolletage of her other gown. "That Lord Ranozhir—or Ranulph as he prefers to be called—is 'idle' and likes to play cards rather than tending to his father-in-law's estate. If he's a betting man, I imagine the prospect of the little deal I'm going to suggest to him will definitely appeal. And Lady Tanaisie seems like a dutiful loving wife who wouldn't dare to oppose her husband's will."

"But going back to Azhkendir to reclaim the Arkhel lands." Dysis looked up from her sewing, the contours of the scars slashed across her forehead and cheek harshly emphasized by the lamplight. "The Nagarian druzhina won't like it. And Lord Gavril will petition the Emperor."

"Legally that land still belongs to the Arkhels. I had Boris check it out when I was in Azhgorod."

"Lord Stoyan?" Dysis looked up again, a quizzical expression on her face. "Didn't he go back to his wife?"

Lilias gave a disdainful sniff. "The instant he suspected I was out of favor with the Emperor, he went running back to Marfa. 'Oh take me back, my beloved, forgive me and I swear I'll never stray again!'" She mimicked Lord Stoyan's deep voice, making Dysis smile. "He changed allegiances so many times I don't think he even knew what day it was. But at least I coaxed copies of the documents out of him. I thought I was doing it for Stavy, but it seems that Lord Ranulph has a son too." The knowledge that there was a rival heir to the Arkhel lands had been troubling her all day. The sylphlike daughters were not a threat to Stavy's birthright; in Azhkendir, only men could inherit. But this son, Toran, was eighteen and old enough to succeed his father. "Who is the official legal inheritor, I wonder? My Stavy, the grandson of Lord Stavyor? Or Toran, Lord Stavyor's nephew?"

"If they had any idea of the value of their lands," Dysis said softly, "after the Emperor's alchymist made that discovery at Kastel Nagarian . . ."

"That's why I must play this game with extreme caution." Lilias sat up, determined to remain resolute. "I can't afford to lose. I need the Arkhels to return to Azhkendir and stake their claim. And they need me if they're to benefit from the mineral riches—and that firedust stuff—in the Arkhel Waste. The only thing troubling me is, how to stop the Emperor from plundering the treasure for himself first. Once Eugene gets wind of what I'm planning, he's bound to intervene. He'll even maintain he's doing it for Stavy's future benefit." Lilias heard the resentment burning in her own voice and told herself to calm down. "I must be careful. When it comes to Eugene, I let my feelings show too easily. Why is that?" There was still a tremor in her voice. But before Dysis could answer, there came a tap at the door and the landlady, a bird-like old lady, popped her mob-capped head around the door. "I've brought you and your maid some supper, Mistress Arkhel. Soup, bread roll and butter. Are you sure that's all you want?"

"Oh yes, I'm on a strict diet," said Lilias, wishing she had not caught a whiff of the enticing smell of roast capon floating up the stairwell. But soup was all they could afford. "That's why I've come to Sulien, to take the waters for my health." Her empty stomach growled and she coughed, trying to conceal the sound. "That soup looks delicious."

Chapter 3

The Serpent Gate looms high above Gavril and a lurid light leaks from it, a glimmering swirl of turgid colors, like oil in muddy rainwater.

"What am I doing here?"

Clawed hands emerge, reaching out to drag him beneath the portal.

Terrified, he feels rough, scaly fingers clench his arms, his legs, and start to tug him toward the churning instability that lies beyond the Gate. Talons puncture his flesh, sharp as barbed fishhooks; he is caught, unable to break free.

He tries to cling onto the ancient stones beneath his feet, to the knotted creepers growing through the cracks of the sacrificial altar, but in vain; he finds himself sliding slowly, inexorably back toward the turbulence.

A dazzling light sears his eyes, a light so powerful that he cannot endure its burning brightness.

"The Other Gates, Khezef. Tell me where to find them." A deep voice thunders, every word piercing his racked body like a fire-tipped spear.

Through the glaze of pain, he can just make out a shimmering figure hovering above him on gilded wings, accusing eyes glittering fiery gold with anger.

"No!" he cries with all his might, although he can hardly hear his words above the roar of the winds beyond the Serpent Gate.

"Then your punishment is to live on in eternal, unendurable torment."

"Don't imprison me again. Kill me, Galizur. Destroy me. Don't—" He gasps the avenging Warrior prince's name in vain, just before the searing light is abruptly extinguished and he is sucked back into the chaotic, wind-tossed darkness of the Realm of Shadows.

***

"No, Galizur!" Gavril sat up, gasping for air. His throat burned as if he had breathed in poisonous fumes. He was drenched in a cold sweat. He could still feel taloned, scaly hands pawing obscenely at his body, could still hear that merciless voice condemning him to eternal torment.

"What did you say?" Kiukiu turned over, wheaten hair tousled, strands escaping her single bedtime plait, to peer up at him in the dim dawn light.

A sleepy wail came from the cradle beside their bed.

"And now you've woken Larisa," Kiukiu said wearily. She put out one hand and began to rock the cradle.

Gavril was still confused, still mired in the vivid horror of his dream.

Am I really here? Or is this just an illusion and I've been trapped in the darkness beyond the Serpent Gate ever since I destroyed it? Was I sucked in by the force of the explosion? There had been times in his lonely prison cell in Arnskammar, high above the storm-tossed Iron Sea, when he had sought comfort in dreams of Kiukiu until he had begun to wonder if they were nothing but fantasies conjured to console himself.

Larisa let out another wail, more insistent and disgruntled than the last. And then another, and another . . .

"I don't think she's going to go back to sleep." Kiukiu let out a sigh and swung her legs over the side of the bed, shivering, as Larisa began to cry in earnest.

"Hush, now; Mama's here, baby, it's all right, don't wake the rest of the household up."

But this seems so real. Kiukiu, our baby daughter, the bitter chill of an Azhkendi autumn morning . . .

"You were having another nightmare," Kiukiu said, yawning as she opened her nightdress and offered her breast to the furious baby. Larisa's yells quietened into snuffly suckling sounds. "She was hungry." Kiukiu stroked the baby's fine strands of auburn hair.

"This is real, isn't it?" Gavril said uncertainly.

Kiukiu looked up at him over Larisa's head, frowning. "Of course this is real. What on earth were you dreaming about this time?" There was a hint of exasperation in her voice. "I wouldn't have minded, but little Lady Larisa might have slept on for another half hour, maybe, and so would I."

"The Serpent Gate."

"Well, that's hardly surprising. It's a year, isn't it, since the Great Darkness?" And then she said, her tone softening, "We've been so busy, with rebuilding the kastel and looking after Larisa, perhaps this is the first time you've allowed yourself to remember what happened."

"He called me Khezef."

"Who did?" Kiukiu sounded distracted.

"Galizur."

She shrugged; the name evidently meant nothing to her.

" I couldn't see his face. He was so bright. So powerful." Gavril shuddered.

"Ah. Khezef may have left your body, but he's still left a trace of his memories in your mind and soul."

"Do you think so?" Gavril was not sure whether to feel reassured by Kiukiu's words or even more disturbed. "It was so vivid. As if I was there*." And I heard myself begging Galizur not to punish me again.* Was Galizur the Heavenly Guardian who had imprisoned Khezef in the Realm of Shadows? He shivered, remembering the aching cold of the lightless pit of darkness. "Suppose Khezef and his kindred didn't escape through the Rift when I destroyed the Gate. Suppose they're trapped in that terrible place again, and trying to escape?"

Kiukiu leaned across and stroked his cheek. He raised his hand to cover hers, pressing her palm against his face to reassure himself that he was not dreaming.

Larisa looked up at them both, her eyes piercingly blue in the growing light.

"Such bright eyes," Kiukiu said, lifting her onto her shoulder and rubbing her back. "I wonder if they'll stay so blue? Are all babies born with blue eyes? Or is that just puppies and kittens?"

Gavril gazed at her affectionately. Only Kiukiu could ramble on so inconsequentially and sound so charmingly naive. He wanted to hug her for bringing him back to reality from the confusion of his recurring nightmares.

"Did I say something silly? I'm only half-awake, thanks to a *certain someone.*"

"I'm sorry."

"You can hold your damp daughter while I find some clean clothes for her." Kiukiu thrust Larisa into his arms and sure enough, she was warm and wet, smelling of milk and wee. "Damp? She's sopping wet!" He pulled a face but Larisa cooed at him, smiling so winningly that he relented and smiled back.

This has to be real. No matter how vivid the nightmares, this smelly baby is no dream. He held Larisa at arm's length and said, "How can you smile so sweetly, little Risa, when you're such a stinky child?"

Kiukiu returned with a change of clothes and took Larisa from him with a resigned and pointed sigh.

"Surely a nursemaid should be doing this," Gavril said. "I can't imagine that the Empress Astasia dirties her hands cleaning up little Rostevan."

"The Empress Astasia? But she was born to that life. She probably doesn't even know how to look after a baby. When you asked me to marry you, don't you remember I told you that I could never be like her: a highborn lady? If you wanted a princess, you could have chosen from any number of eligible royal daughters."

Larisa began to wriggle violently, causing Kiukiu to let out a grunt of exasperation as she tried to ease her waving arms into sleeves.

He had said the wrong thing. "But I wanted you." Why did they always end up arguing over little things, these days? Was lack of sleep making them both short-tempered? "Can't Ninusha help out? She's still nursing Dion—" He broke off, as she shot him a furious look.

"She's our precious daughter, Gavril; I can't trust her care to anyone else."

Was it his imagination or was she protesting too forcefully? *Does she believe, as I do, that we don't deserve this happiness? That someone is waiting to snatch Larisa away from us?*

A fragment of dream-memory gusted through his mind like a tainted breath, darkening his mood. *Shadowy whirlwinds flinging stinging dust into his eyes and nostrils and mouth. Eternal torment, eternal despair.* He shivered, wanting to banish the death-tainted taste from his mouth.

"Gavril? Are you all right?"

He blinked, seeing Kiukiu staring at him with a concerned expression furrowing her brow.

"How's the painting going? Is anything finished yet? Can I come and look?"

There's no way I could show anyone what I've been painting, even you, who's seen me at my lowest, my most depraved. He could not meet her eyes.

"Had you thought of drawing Larisa? Nothing fancy. Just little sketches, showing how she's growing from week to week."

"Drawing Larisa?" he repeated, wondering why he hadn't thought of it before. The idea appealed. Concentrating on capturing the baby's expressions might block out the other disturbing images that kept darkening his mind.

"Just like that book of sketches your mother did of you that you brought back from Smarna. I love looking at those. You could use those—what are they called: pastels? I like the way you smudge the lines to get that special soft effect. "

"Pastels." He looked gratefully at her as she leant over the cradle to place Larisa back inside, realizing that she had managed yet again to draw him back from the shadows. He went over and put his arms around her as she straightened up, hugging her close. For a moment she leant against him, closing her eyes. And then she let out a little cry, pushing him away. "There's so much to be done today and it's nearly sunrise!"

"What's happening today?"

"How *could* you forget, Gavril? It's only a fortnight to your daughter's Naming Day and Abbot Yephimy is coming to discuss the ceremony. We have to give him a good meal in thanks for making the journey over here. I can't leave all the preparations to Ilsi."

***

"You're not supposed to be in the kitchens, my lady." Ilsi looked up from her mixing bowl as Kiukiu entered.

"Can't I help? Ninusha's looking after Larisa and I can't just sit around idle with visitors coming." The truth was that Kiukiu was in need of company and the only place she felt at ease in the kastel was in the kitchen.

"Well, it's not that I couldn't do with an extra pair of hands, but what will Lord Gavril say?"

Kiukiu was tying on an apron and scrubbing her hands. She pretended not to have heard Ilsi's question. "What would you like me to do?"

"You used to make passable pastry. And we're serving wild boar pie to the Abbot, flavored with juniper berries."

Kiukiu rolled up her sleeves and flexed her fingers. "Pastry it is, then."

As she was kneading the dough, Semyon came into the kitchen.

"Don't you dare tread mud in here, Semyon!" Ilsi cried, rounding on him, brandishing her rolling pin like a rapier. "Out!"

"I only came to ask," Semyon began, hastily retreating, "if you knew where Lord Gavril is. There's an urgent matter the Bogatyr needs to discuss with him."

"He's probably in the summerhouse, painting," Kiukiu said, "again." And she heard herself sigh rather more loudly than she had intended.

"What's wrong?" Ilsi said, sprinkling flour on the table top.

"There was a time when Sem wouldn't have needed to ask where to find Lord Gavril," Kiukiu said, slapping the ball of pastry down on the floured surface and reaching for the rolling pin.

"So the blood bond—?" Ilsi scraped chopped onions into a pan to sauté them.

"Hasn't worked since the Great Darkness. Lord Gavril can't summon the druzhina using the bond anymore."

"Thank goodness we're at peace, then." Ilsi shook the pan vigorously as the onions began to sizzle.

"He won't speak of it, not even to me, but I know he's still not himself," Kiukiu said, more to herself than to Ilsi as she rolled the pastry. "It's almost . . . as if he left a part of himself on Ty Nagar."

Chapter 4

"Jaromir Arkhel was like a brother to me," said the Emperor. He stopped in front of Jaromir's portrait—a faithful copy of the original in the Palace of Swanholm—and gazed pensively up at it. "The younger brother I never had."

"So you've often said, my dear," murmured the empress, dandling their baby son on her knee. She pulled a silly grimace at him and Rostevan instantly erupted into chuckles. She thought it best not to remind Eugene of the existence of his true younger half-brother, Oskar Alvborg, his father's bastard son, condemned to exile on the distant shores of Serindher with her brother, Andrei.

"And the thought—the mere thought—that *that woman* has dared to petition us to have our little Stavy returned to her is enough to make my blood boil."

"She *is* his mother," the empress reminded her husband. She made another grimace, rolling her eyes at Rostevan, and his chubby little face creased up as a peal of laughter came out.

"How poor Jaro ever came to allow himself to be seduced by that shameless adventuress, I'll never know."

"She's very attractive," said Astasia, tempted to blow a raspberry on Rostevan's tummy.

"But she used him to further her own ambitions. She planned to use Stavy too—and would have done so, if I hadn't stepped in and made him our ward."

"Perhaps she just wanted to ensure that Stavy had a secure future."

Stavy, who had been engrossed in building a tower with wooden blocks, placed one more on the wobbling pile, and the whole edifice collapsed with a clatter on the parquet floor.

"Down!" he said triumphantly. Rostevan let out a shriek of excitement and clapped his hands.

"Yes, Stavy, they all fell down." Astasia lifted her wriggling baby and placed him on the parquet floor beside Lilias and Jaromir's son. "Let's build them up again, shall we?"

Stavy lifted his face to hers, and gave her an angelic smile which almost melted her heart. *He has his father's golden hair, but his mother's bewitching green eyes. With looks like yours, I fear you're going to seduce all the ladies when you grow up, Stavy.*

The inner door in the paneling opened and Gustave appeared.

"Forgive me for interrupting, but Baron Sylvius requests an audience," he said, and Astasia did not miss the significant look he gave her husband. Gustave and Eugene had, she realized long ago, developed their own secret code of meaningful glances that allowed them to communicate without alerting others except the Emperor's most intimate inner circle.

"Pa?" Rostevan attempted to toddle after his father as Eugene disappeared through the secret doorway after his secretary and the panel slid silently shut behind them. Frustrated, he thumped his fists on the wood, crying out indignantly, "Pa! *Pa!*"

Oh dear, she found herself thinking as she retrieved their son, *what new troubles have arisen in the empire to make Gustave interrupt our precious family time together?*

***

"It seems," said Baron Sylvius, settling himself into the button-backed chair opposite Eugene, "that your lively young ward Stavyomir is not all alone in the world, after all."

Eugene gazed enquiringly at his spymaster; he had been expecting a report on some recent disquieting rumors of dissident activity in Mirom that the baron's agents had been investigating.

"But all the Arkhels perished in the Clan Wars; all, except Jaromir."

"Apparently not. My agents were following up on a quite different lead in Tourmalise when they stumbled upon some unexpected information. It seems that Jaromir's youngest uncle is still alive."

Eugene was so surprised that words deserted him as he digested the information. Eventually he said quietly, "Why were we not made aware of this earlier?"

Sylvius looked pained. "I believe you *were* made aware, Eugene."

Eugene frowned. His recall of matters of such significance was usually excellent. He was sure he would have remembered.

Am I becoming a little absent-minded as I grow older? I'm only thirty-eight; surely it's a little early for senility to set in. Or has someone at court deliberately tried to prevent me finding out about Stavy's family?

Sylvius screwed in his monocle, produced a silver-cased notebook from an inner pocket and began to read aloud. "'Ranozhir, youngest brother of Lord Stavyor Arkhel, is currently residing at the spa resort of Sulien in Tourmalise under the name Ranulph. Ranulph has amassed a considerable gambling debt at the Assembly Rooms.' At the time, I reported to your father, 'This fellow is obviously a gambler and a wastrel.' My instructions were to keep a weather eye on him. 'He seems no real threat.' That was back in '68, the year after your father defeated the Francian navy in the Straits."

"I would have been seventeen, and this Ranulph not much older at the time, I imagine. What was he doing so far from Azhkendir?"

"His brother sent him on some kind of Grand Tour. Unusual for the Arkhels to indulge in such genteel practices; their main pleasure seems to have been perpetuating their blood-feud with the Nagarians." Sylvius closed the silver notebook case with a click and slid it back into his inner pocket.

"Sulien, you say?" Eugene was pondering the information. "Perhaps the boy was sickly and they sent him to take the spa waters for his health. And while he was away, Lord Volkh massacred his clan and laid waste to the Arkhel lands. What reason was there to go home after that?"

"Indeed. And Prince Karl kept the news of Jaromir's survival a closely-guarded secret; smuggling him out of Azhkendir alive was one of the trickiest tasks your father ever set me." Sylvius nodded his elegantly-cropped white head.

"So why do you think that—having lain low for twenty years—Lord Ranulph has suddenly decided to reveal his true identity?"

"If I were to tell you that a woman calling herself Lilias Arkhel visited Sulien to take the waters this summer . . ."

"Lilias again," Eugene echoed under his breath. *If only I had found a way to stop her damned meddling once and for all.* He glanced at Sylvius, wondering if he had spoken his murderous thoughts aloud.

Sylvius merely nodded again. "She's artful—and resourceful. Sometimes I wonder if she could be persuaded to work for us, rather than against us—"

Eugene raised one hand. "She is the most duplicitous woman I've ever had the misfortune to cross. Don't even think about approaching her." He would never forgive her for treating Jaromir so callously. *Thank God the poor boy died believing she still loved him.* "I pity Lord Ranulph if he's allowed himself to fall prey to her notorious charms."

"So what would you like me to do at this stage? Continue surveillance?"

"I don't see what else we can do. But I want to know at the first opportunity if she commits the slightest transgression. If she's persuaded the Arkhels to return to Azhkendir, who knows what trouble might suddenly erupt?" And just when Gavril had lost the one advantage he possessed to keep the peace in that barbarous wintry kingdom: Khezef.

"Very well." Sylvius removed his monocle, fastidiously draping its silver chain over the front of his stylishly tailored charcoal jacket. "Oh, and there is one other piece of information from Serindher that you should be aware of. It may be nothing to concern ourselves about."

Eugene raised one brow. "Serindher? It's not to do with Prince Andrei, is it?" Astasia still missed her brother, although he knew how careful she was not to speak of her worries in his presence; Andrei had, after all, abducted their only son just days after his birth.

"Not the prince, but his fellow in exile, a certain Count Alvborg."

"Oskar." Even speaking his illegitimate brother's name aloud left Eugene with an unpleasant taste in his mouth. "So what's the information?"

"Perhaps I should rephrase that; to speak more precisely, it's the lack of information that's somewhat disconcerting."

Sylvius had a way of disguising bad news that Eugene found singularly irritating. "Baron," he said, "please be more precise."

"You may remember that he was working with the Francian missionaries to help the local people after the tidal wave swept through the Spice Islands. Well, the priest we asked to keep an eye on him has reported that he's gone missing. And as it's taking many weeks for a ship to reach Tielen from the islands—"

"Missing?" Eugene echoed. "Fallen overboard, lost in the Serindhen jungle, or absconded and on his way back to Tielen to make life difficult for us?"

"I've told all my agents to keep a watch out for him at the ports," Sylvius said calmly. "He's not difficult to spot, after all, with that distinctive white-blond hair."

"You, of all people, know how easy it is to change hair color," Eugene said dryly. "Wigs aren't so hard to come by. He might even have shaved it all off."

"Or, he's made himself a tidy little fortune in Serindher and has decided to spend it closer to home."

"That man still bears us a grudge," Eugene said, remembering the look of hatred he had seen smoldering in Oskar's eyes when he left him behind on Ty Nagar, the Serpent Isle. "I want him arrested the moment he sets foot on Tielen soil. And Sylvius, not a word of this to the empress or Princess Karila; I don't want to alarm them unnecessarily."

"We'll find him, don't worry, Imperial Majesty," said Sylvius, bowing with customary elegance as he withdrew.

"Oskar Alvborg," Eugene muttered. Oskar's Drakhaoul, Sahariel, had been the most rebellious, the most dangerous of the six servants of Nagazdiel. And he could not help but wonder exactly how much of that rebellious streak Alvborg had retained.

Chapter 5

Lilias rolled up the carriage blind so that she could get a clearer view of the Arkhels' manor house.

"What a quaintly old-fashioned place it is," she said softly to Dysis as the carriage meandered down the long drive into the valley, passing sheep cropping the lush green grass of the parkland on either side. "It must have been built at least two hundred years ago."

To Lilias's eyes, the timbered and plaster façade looked rather too rustic to suit her cultured tastes. A forest of tall chimneys rose above the mossy roof tiles, each one different from the next, with lozenge patterns, shields, and twisting ribbons worked in contrasting colored bricks.

"It's even got a moat," she exclaimed, seeing ducks swimming in a v-shaped flotilla across the dark waters. The carriage crossed over a little bridge and came to a halt on the gravel in front of the main entrance. The postilion jumped down and opened the door to help Lilias out, Dysis following.

A hollow baying sound sent a shiver through Lilias as the main door opened and a pair of shaggy wolfhounds, each the size of a small pony, bounded toward her enthusiastically. Lilias froze, certain she was about to be knocked over. Volkh had kept a pair too—and she had been terrified of the hairy brutes. She looked around for Dysis to shield her, but her maid had retreated inside the carriage.

"Cuall!" called a commanding voice as Lady Tanaisie hurried out. "Rhymni! Heel!"

The hounds hesitated and then slunk away,

"I must apologize," Lady Tanaisie reached Lilias and clasped her hands in her own. "They're really very affectionate, but they don't know their own strength. Please come in. My housekeeper will look after your maid; our servants take luncheon in the kitchen."

Lilias allowed herself to be led into the lofty hallway of the manor house, casting anxious glances as the wolfhounds followed—rather too closely for her liking.

"Ranulph, my dear," called Lady Tanaisie, firmly shooing the hounds away, "we have visitors!" She opened a door and ushered Lilias inside. "This is the young woman I told you about: Lilias, the widow of your late nephew Jaromir."

Lord Arkhel was standing gazing out through one of the mullioned windows over the parkland, his hands clasped behind his back. He turned, and Lilias, who had been steeling herself for this meeting, felt, in spite of all her careful preparation, her heart miss a beat as she saw his face. His features were strong-hewn, with a prominent aquiline nose—although his complexion had acquired a roughened, ruddy hue which told her that Jaromir's uncle was fond of hunting and strong liquor. But the eyes that gazed piercingly at her were dark and clear. And, even though his hair was cropped short in the military style made fashionable by the Emperor, she could not help noticing that, although fading to silver at the temples, it still had a hint of the distinctive burnished Arkhel gold that her little Stavy had inherited from his dead father.

"Good day to you, Mistress Arkhel," said Lord Ranulph with easy courtesy, nodding to her.

"My lord." Lilias curtseyed demurely. "It's a pleasure to meet you at last."

She cast a quick glance around her, noting that the furnishings of the Manor of Serrigonde, although spotlessly clean and neat, were showing distinct signs of age; the delicate fabrics were fading and worn and the pale sprigged patterns were some thirty years out of fashion. The current craze for richly colored Serindhen silks, imported at vast expense, had obviously yet to reach the country manors of Tourmalise. Although, she suspected that the signs of genteel dilapidation were probably a direct result of Lord Ranulph's losses at the gaming tables and Lady Tanaisie was probably desperately hoping to marry her girls off to rich suitors.

How fortunate for the "sweet sylphs" that they have such a devoted and doting mother, Lilias found herself reflecting bitterly, having had to fend for herself from the age of fourteen when her own mother's lifeless body had been dredged out of the chilly River Dniera.

"I'm at your disposal today, ladies; all my estate business is done." Lord Ranulph's words brought her abruptly back from that unpleasant memory.

Why was I thinking of Mama? I have to concentrate on the present.

"Let's take luncheon first," said Lady Tanaisie. "It's just simple fare: mutton pie from our own flock, fruit tarts made with apples and plums from the orchard, and goats' cheese. All produced from the estate."

"It sounds delicious," said Lilias, not needing to feign her enthusiasm; she was famished after the long drive.

"And after lunch, we can retire to the library . . ."

***

The library at Serrigonde exuded a distinctly masculine odor of old leather, dust, and . . . was that apple brandy? Lilias couldn't help sniffing the air as Ranulph ushered her inside, and spotted the decanter and glass on the desk. One of the wolfhounds followed faithfully at his master's heels, his claws making a sharp, tapping sound over the worn parquet floor. Ranulph offered Lilias one of two leather armchairs and sat in the other opposite her, flipping back his coat tails as he eased himself down; the wolfhound turned round a couple of times before settling at his feet, like a gray furry rug.

The walls were lined from floor to ceiling with ancient volumes, bound in brown and blood-red leather, and whose gold-tooled titles had faded so much as to be almost illegible.

"My father-in-law liked to think of himself as something of an inventor." Ranulph gestured somewhat apologetically at the stacks of books. "They're mostly scientific—or treatises on hunting and animal husbandry. Don't have much time for reading, myself; the estate keeps me too busy."

"But have you kept abreast of current affairs?" Lilias had noticed a copy of the *Tourmaline Times* lying on the blotter on the desk. "You're aware of recent events in Azhkendir?"

"Even an obscure country squire like me would find it hard to ignore the extraordinary happenings of the last two years." Did she detect an edge to his self-deprecating description of himself? She darted a glance at him and saw again the faint shadow of a frown fleetingly darken his amiable expression. *So you, too, have learned to play your new role well. But now you're growing weary of dissembling.*

"Have you ever been back?"

"Why would I? I have a new life here, a loving wife, children to raise, an estate to manage . . . Kastel Arkhel was completely obliterated by Lord Volkh and all the surrounding lands laid to waste."

She waited a moment before lowering her voice to say in her most intimate tone, "Do you give me your word, my lord, that you will keep what I'm about to reveal to you as utterly confidential—and not share it yet with anyone, not even your wife?"

He hesitated. And then he said, "I give you my word as an Arkhel."

"And no one can overhear us in here?"

He patted the wolfhound's shaggy head. "Old Cuall here would warn me if anyone decided to spy on us. Even one of my daughters!"

She'd have to be satisfied with that assurance. She paused, steeling herself to play her trump card, and said, "What if I told you that I happen to know that the Arkhel lands, the so-called Arkhel Waste, is a goldmine, waiting for the right developer to make use of its hidden riches?" She paused again, waiting for his reaction. But he was a good card-player and, whatever he might have felt on hearing her revelation, he was skilled at not letting it show on his face.

"Go on."

"When I was last in Azhkendir, the Emperor's alchymists discovered that a certain substance in the surrounding soil had extraordinary combustible potential. They call it 'firedust'."

"Firedust," he repeated, shaking his head. "Never heard of it."

"Of course you haven't; it's one of the Emperor's most closely guarded secrets!"

"And what is this volatile material?" His expression was wary, even skeptical.

"It appears, as far as I understand it, to be the product of some kind of alchymical reaction in the soil brought about by Drakhaon's Fire; it only occurs in sites that have been devastated by the Drakhaon's breath."

"It sounds somewhat fanciful."

"But only a small area on Lord Nagarian's domain has been mined so far. Just imagine the possibilities of digging up the whole Arkhel Waste!"

Ranulph Arkhel said nothing—but she was certain that he was turning over in his mind what she had just revealed to him. The wolfhound yawned widely in the silence, revealing a jawful of yellowed teeth, and went back to sleep.

"Mistress Arkhel—"

"Please call me Lilias."

"I can't help wondering why you've come to *me* with this information. There could be a conflict of interests, for a start. Who has the greater claim to the Arkhel lands: myself—or your son, Stavyomir? We would need to consult the lawyers."

"With so few of the clan left alive, I don't see why we shouldn't agree to work together and divide the proceeds equally," Lilias said in her sweetest, most persuasive tones. "I feel it's so important for Stavy to know that he's not alone—and that he has a family to support and protect him."

"And then there's the matter of the Drakhaon. Gavril Nagarian."

"He's lost his powers."

"Can you be sure?" He was regarding her warily.

"I haven't seen Lord Nagarian since he attempted to abduct Stavyomir. My poor, brave Dysis still bears the scars he inflicted on her when she tried to stop him." Lilias drew in a shuddering breath, risking a little glance at Ranulph to see what effect her tale was having upon him. "My main concern then was to take my son and get as far away from the Drakhaon as fast as possible. But since the Great Darkness last year, I have it on very good authority that he has lost all his powers and, in recognition of that fact, has even rejected the title of Drakhaon."

"The Great Darkness." Lord Ranulph seemed to be reflecting on what she had said. She wondered if she had said too much. Did he know more about the recent events in Azhkendir than he was prepared to reveal?

"And were you aware that there is still an Arkhel Guslyar living in Azhkendir?"

"A Spirit Singer?" A tremor of genuine emotion had crept into his convivial tone.

At last. I've found your weak spot, Lord Ranulph.

She leaned forward and said earnestly, "She's the granddaughter of Malusha."

"Malusha had a granddaughter? I . . . I had no idea."

"Her name is Kiukirilya. It's a little unfortunate that she also happens to be Lord Gavril's wife." She made an extra effort to modulate her own voice, as even mentioning the name of Gavril Nagarian's wife aloud still made her twitch with irritation. *Why did he choose that useless, awkward servant girl to be his bride? She's not fitted for the role of at all; she's an embarrassment.*

"An Arkhel clanswoman marrying a Nagarian?"

"Much has changed in Azhkendir, my lord, in the twenty years you've been away."

"But Gavril Nagarian is the Emperor's staunchest ally. Anyone fool enough to make a move against him would be soon be crushed."

"Then," Lilias said softly, "we must find a way to destroy that friendship. To raise doubts in the Emperor's mind. It's not so very long ago that they were bitter enemies."

"Doubts?" She was aware that Ranulph's disinterested expression had altered. She had caught his attention at last. "What kind of doubts?"

She laughed, delighted that he had taken the bait. "Have you no imagination, my lord? There are so many delightful possibilities."

He was staring at her with an intensity that made her wonder if he suspected her motives. Had she gone too far in suggesting such a ploy?

"Before I agree to anything," he began but the sound of hoofs on the gravel outside distracted his attention; he glanced toward the mullioned window and Cuall woke up, lifting his shaggy head to listen.

"Another visitor?" Lilias inquired as men's voices could faintly be heard from the courtyard, and Cuall let out a low, warning growl.

"I'm not expecting anyone," Ranulph said, a slight frown furrowing his forehead. The voices grew louder; Lilias was certain that she could hear a querulous voice repeating, "You can't see Lord Ranulph now; he has a guest."

"If you tell him Touchet is here, I'm sure my lord will make time in his busy schedule to see me." The loud reply was tinged with unmistakable sarcasm— and an accent that was far from refined.

There came a knock on the library door and a gaunt old man appeared, slightly stooped. "Forgive me, my lord, but this rude fellow calling himself Aristide Touchet insists on seeing you."

Lilias heard Ranulph sigh. "Very well. Mistress Arkhel," he said, evidently still not ready to call her by her first name, "perhaps you would like to take tea with my wife and daughters? Ryndin, please escort Mistress Arkhel to the drawing room."

Lilias had no alternative but to go after the elderly butler out into the hall. There she spotted the unwelcome visitor, Touchet, closely examining one of the family portraits. He looked up as she swept past and she could sense his gaze following her, shamelessly ogling her. She chose not to acknowledge his presence—but noted the ostentatious way he was dressed, from the bright mustard yellow of his jacket to the glittering jeweled tie-pin in his cravat and the glint of a matching gold and diamond signet ring as he raised his hand to smooth back an errant lock of hair.

"I think you already know why I've come to pay you another visit, Lord Ranulph," she heard him say as he swaggered into the library. The paneled door clicked shut behind them.

Lilias lingered, longing to eavesdrop, but heard a polite cough behind her; Lord Ranulph's elderly butler, Ryndin, was standing there, one gloved hand extended, to show her into the drawing room.

***

"Oh dear, girls," Lady Tanaisie said for the third time as she sipped her tea. "Your father's been closeted with that odious man for at least a quarter of an hour. Oh, dear me."

"You mean Touchet?" Lilias nibbled at an almond biscuit. "His taste in clothes is certainly odious; that jacket was so loud it hurt my eyes."

Lady Tanaisie sighed. "You're family, Mistress Lilias, so there's no point keeping up pretences. Although it grieves me to have to admit it, we've fallen on hard times. When Ranulph and I inherited the estate from my father, we also inherited considerable debts. We sold off some of the family treasures: pictures, silverware, my late mother's jewels, to try to keep the debtors from our doors. But the house is becoming dilapidated; it costs a small fortune to keep an old place like this from falling down. We even sold off some land, but it still wasn't enough. And with our dear daughters reaching marriageable age . . ." Fleurie and Clarisse each took hold of one of their mother's hands.

"We don't want to be a burden, Mama," said Fleurie in a trembling voice.

"How could you ever be a burden, my dears? Papa and I want to ensure that you're both happily settled, without any financial worries to inherit. And we still have to pay your brother's way through the military academy."

"We all love Serrigonde," added Clarisse staunchly.

Lilias nodded, setting down her empty tea cup on the saucer. *This is better than I could have hoped. They're impoverished . . . and they're desperate to find a way out.* "So that impertinent fellow, Touchet, is a bailiff?"

"Worse," said Lady Tanaisie with a shudder. "He's a debt collector from the Upper Rooms in Sulien. Ranulph was a little rash. In his efforts to raise funds to cover our outstanding debts, he thought he'd try his luck at the card tables."

So he's an inveterate gambler, as I suspected, and she's either a loyal wife or remarkably naïve.

"Unfortunately, luck was not on his side, and now we find ourselves worse off than before. They've even been threatening to seize the estate."

Lilias nodded, acquiescing to the "family version," doubtless created to save face. "I see."

"We could sell the town house in Sulien, Mama," said Clarisse.

The sound of men's raised voices came from the hall. Clarisse and Fleurie drew closer to their mother who rose, slipping an arm around each of her daughter's waists.

And now they're arguing? This just gets better and better.

"Temir! Iarko!" Ranulph bellowed. "Escort this fellow off the estate straight away."

"Oh, I'll be back soon enough, Lord Ranulph," came Touchet's response, "with the bailiffs."

Chapter 6

Empress Astasia shivered, drawing her soft wool shawl around her shoulders as she sipped her tea.

"The Winter Palace is full of draughts." Her husband stood up and began to pace the breakfast room, stopping every now and then to test the windows and wainscoting for leaks.

"Autumn in Mirom is always chilly," she said, wishing Eugene would sit down and finish his tea; his restlessness was making her irritable. "It's the fogs rising off the River Nieva."

"But this place was built a hundred and fifty years ago; it's archaic. No architect today would site it so close to the river. In summer the rising effluvia—and those damned mosquitoes—make it unhealthy for Karila and the boys."

Here we go again. Astasia tried to conceal a sigh. *He's plotting something.* And this was the one morning in the week they had the chance to breakfast alone without the children or Gustave arriving bearing the daily agenda. "Your tea has gone cold," she said, trying to change the subject. "Shall I ring for a fresh pot?"

"No need." He stopped in his pacing to snatch up the delicate cup and downed the tepid tea in one gulp.

"But the Orlovs have never stayed in the capital in the summer months," she said, wondering why he was suddenly so obsessed with their domestic arrangements in Mirom. "We always went to the villa in Smarna. Lots of sun and fresh sea air! And the court came too . . ."

"A pity that your father didn't think to raze the whole building after the riots and commission a new one," Eugene muttered, staring out across the Nieva. "The Kaliki Heights would make a fine position overlooking the city. Or in Brynski Park, perhaps . . ."

"Of course, I realize that a holiday in Smarna is out of the question until the political situation stabilizes." Astasia stirred her tea rather more vigorously than usual to contain her growing exasperation. "I hate to think what condition the Villa Orlova is in; we haven't been back to stay there in over three years. And given the Smarnans' rebellious nature, I don't imagine we'll be returning there soon."

Eugene turned. "If it's any consolation, we're no longer the Smarnans' most hated nation." She saw a mischievous sparkle in his keen blue-gray eyes. "That honor has gone to Francia. The two governments are still wrangling over who is in control." The sparkle faded as swiftly as it had appeared. "If only I could . . ." He let out a sigh and sat down at the breakfast table. Astasia saw that his shoulders were drooping. This dejected posture was most unlike the Eugene that she knew.

"My dearest, what's wrong?" she asked, genuinely surprised.

He heaved another sigh. "Smarna's so far away. It would take us too many days to travel there overland— or by sea. How can I be truly in control of the empire if I can't get to be where I'm needed quickly?"

Astasia stood up and went to place her hands on his shoulders; she could feel how stiff and tense they were beneath the fine wool cloth of his jacket. "You can't be everywhere at once; it's not humanly possible. That's why you choose your ministers with care—and why you trust them to carry out your instructions. You delegate wisely, Eugene."

"It wasn't always like this."

"You mean . . . when you could fly?" So he was still mourning the loss of the powers he had inherited when he had been possessed by the daemon Drakhaoul Belberith. He had become a monster, beautiful yet cruel—and unimaginably powerful. Even thinking of that terrible time made her stomach contract painfully.

"I've never experienced anything like it."

She heard the naked longing in his voice and the sense of uneasiness increased. When Eugene wanted something badly enough, he would pursue it determinedly where other less strong-willed men would abandon the quest. *That was how he won my heart, after all.*

"To go wherever I wanted, unfettered by all these clumsy mortal contraptions: leaky ships, dependent on wind and tides; bumpy carriages drawn by horses that tire and drop horseshoes . . ."

Mortal contraptions. Was that really Eugene speaking? Or was it a shadow in his mind, left by the daemon? She turned him around to face her, staring keenly into his eyes, searching for a telltale glint of emerald green.

"What is it?" He gazed at her, puzzled. "Have I a smear of jam on my face?"

"I was just checking," she said sternly. "Because I thought I heard another voice talking then, not your own."

"Ah." He had understood. He covered one of her hands with his own; she felt its dry warmth. "Belberith's. But there's no way I could ever summon him back, my dearest. Gavril and I made sure of that. And now even Ty Nagar, the gateway between our world and theirs, has sunk beneath the waves."

So he *had* been thinking about his Drakhaoul. She was not at all relieved to hear him confirm it— although, if he had flatly denied the fact, she would have been even more suspicious.

"And there's still no word from the Magus?" Not that she approved of Eugene's friendship with Kaspar Linnaius; even the mention of the elderly alchymist brought her out in goosebumps. But Eugene valued Linnaius's counsel more than any other man's and she knew that he missed *him* sorely.

Another heaving sigh confirmed it. "Vanished. Without trace."

"He was a very great age, Eugene. You have to face the possibility that he might have—"

"No. I'd know if he'd died; I'm sure of it. He's just being elusive again. If only I knew why."

"But he appointed his successor. He left Professor Kazimir all his research papers. It was as if he was going away . . . for good."

"He's still alive. I feel it in my bones, Tasia."

"Then he must have faith that you can fulfill your role as Emperor without his help any longer." She heard the words issue from her lips and felt guilty that she should be spouting such empty and meaningless words of consolation to him. She might not care for Linnaius, but to Eugene he had been more a second father than a mere mentor. And she knew that Karila missed him too. *Perhaps I'm a little jealous that I was never a part of that time in Eugene's life.*

She bent over him and kissed his cheek. "Why not ask yourself: What would Linnaius advise me to do?"

He looked at her questioningly, his brow a little furrowed. And then he leapt up, wrapping his arms around her and hugging her tightly.

"My dear girl, you're a genius! You must be prescient."

"I must be?" she gasped, struggling for air.

"There's no point sitting around moping any longer. We have some of the best brains at work in our universities and laboratories." He kissed her, then let her go. "I'll set up a competition. 'Design a Flying Machine!' The prize will be a gold medal—and enough funds to construct the winning design." He flung open the doors and strode away, calling out for his private secretary. "Gustave. Gustave!"

"Oh dear." Astasia sank back down on her chair. "What have I done?" she whispered, pouring herself another cup of tea.

***

"Professor; have you seen the Emperor's latest project?"

Altan Kazimir started guiltily as his colleague Guy Maulevrier burst into the laboratory, and slopped his coffee down his shirt. Cursing, he pulled out a handkerchief and started to blot the stains from his coat.

"Ha! Caught you taking an illicit break, did I?" Maulevrier said triumphantly, eyeing the crisp glazed cinnamon bun Kazimir had just been about to enjoy. "Hiding from your students?"

"I don't know what you mean. I was just having some coffee while I caught up with the departmental correspondence." Kazimir heard the defensive tone in his voice. "You could have some too," he said, glaring at his colleague.

"Thank you; I'd love a cup." Maulevrier poured himself one from the pot and offered Kazimir a refill which he grudgingly accepted.

"So what's all the fuss about?" Kazimir asked, perching himself back on the laboratory stool.

"This." Maulevrier placed a poster—headed with the imperial crest—on the desk in front of him.

"'Competition to Design a Flying Machine,'" Kazimir read aloud. "Good gracious. What on earth has the Emperor in mind this time?" He scanned the details. "Gold medal, finance and facilities to build the winning design . . . *here,* at Tielborg University? He passed the poster back to Maulevrier. "This is more your line of business, than mine, Maulevrier. You're an ingenieur; you should enter."

"But you're Kaspar Linnaius's successor. You have access to the great man's research papers."

In truth, Kazimir still felt a little in awe of his younger colleague; affable with staff and students alike, good-looking in a lean and smoothly chiseled way, with straight, almond-brown hair neatly tied back, he was a popular member of the faculty. But Kazimir, who had learned to be wary of such outwardly attractive individuals the hard way after his extraordinary experiences at Kastel Drakhaon in Azhkendir, thought that from time to time he caught an ambitious glint hardening the friendly light in Maulevrier's light blue eyes. And as Maulevrier said, casually enough, "the great man's research papers," there it was again, that telltale glint.

Maulevrier leaned in, conspiratorially close. "How about we collaborate, Altan? The Emperor's a generous man; if our entry wins, he won't be averse to splitting the prize and awarding two gold medals."

Kazimir instinctively drew back; such close contact made him feel uncomfortable. "But I can't see what I could usefully contribute to such a project."

"A flying machine isn't going to move through the air by the power of wind alone, is it?"

Kazimir had a brief vision of Kaspar Linnaius, twisting his fingers to summon a breeze to lift his sky-craft. He sighed, knowing that such extraordinary powers were beyond the reach of ordinary men. "No," he allowed. "But why do you think there might be some substance, chymical or alchymical, that Linnaius was working on? He had no need of such complications."

"But he was always devising new inventions to please the Emperor. I was only a research student when the firedust project was implemented—"

"And that ended in disaster when our enemies sabotaged the munitions factory." Kazimir shook his head, remembering the terrible night when the sky above Tielborg had lit up with the exploding kegs of firedust that reduced the factory to a charred heap of rubble.

"Don't tell me that single disaster would put a stop to your natural curiosity as a chymist, Altan." Maulevrier was grinning at him provocatively.

Kazimir sighed again. "Go on then; tell me your plan."

"I don't think you ever met Gerard Bernay, did you? He was the most promising student I ever taught."

Kazimir shook his head; the name was unfamiliar.

"He's gone to Tourmalise to work as a civil ingenieur. But, for his doctoral thesis, he was preparing a design for a flying craft."

"His thesis?" Kazimir was interested now, in spite of his earlier misgivings. "Did he complete it?"

"There was something of a scandal at the time. One of the undergraduates—from a rich and influential family—claimed that Bernay had," Maulevrier gave an discreet cough, "made an assault on his virtue."

"Oh dear," Kazimir said, unhappy at the mention of scandal. He would be held responsible if anything untoward were to occur in his department, in spite of the Emperor's patronage. "And was there any truth in the allegation?"

Maulevrier shrugged.

"So he never got his doctorate?" Kazimir had begun to feel a certain sympathy with the unfortunate Bernay.

"Afraid not, no. I pleaded his case, but the university board was swayed by the young man's family and threw him out. I managed to get Bernay a post far away in Paladur in an iron works; it's a waste of his talents, but it's allowed the scandal time to die down."

"You have faith in his abilities?"

"He's an exceptional young man." Was that another glint? Kazimir wondered, as Maulevrier praised his ex-student. "You might not think him anything out of the ordinary, if you passed him in the corridors here, he looks more like a laborer; rugged, completely uninterested in his appearance. But he's passionate about his work. He has a vision."

Kazimir nodded, ruefully. *I think I must have been like that once. Before I was ensnared by Lilias Arbelian.* He shuddered in spite of himself, seeing for a moment her languorous green eyes, remembering the sensuous scent of her creamy skin. *I've never really gotten over her. Beside her, all other women seem insipid.*

"So; what do you say, Professor?" Maulevrier was regarding him with his keen gaze.

Kazimir made an effort to banish Lilias from his mind. "Surely if you want to use your student's design, you have to involve him in the project?"

"Precisely so; I thought this might give him the chance to clear his name."

"Why don't you write to him and find out if he's interested first?"

"We only have six months, Professor. I thought I'd plant the seed of the idea in your mind as soon as possible. I'm sure the empire's treasuries could fund three gold medals if we win. Which, given your genius in the chymical arts, is almost a certainty."

"So you want me to concoct some kind of fuel to lift this craft into the air?" Kazimir was intrigued, in spite of his initial misgivings. "And then to propel it over a considerable distance? Without exploding or catching fire?"

"We'll need to find a volunteer to demonstrate the prototype; the competition stipulates that the winner will be the one that flies the furthest."

"I see." Kazimir had just remembered a certain battered ledger containing Linnaius's notes that he had found gathering dust on a high shelf in the Magus's laboratory at Swanholm entitled "On the Uses of the Unique Substance Commonly Known as Firedust."

"You have a distracted look," said Maulevrier. "I'm guessing that your brilliant mind is already occupied with this little project. Leave the finding of a pilot to me. I'll contact Bernay first—and if he's interested, let's work together and do our best to win the Emperor's prize."

My brilliant mind? Kazimir wondered if Maulevrier was trying to tease—or flatter—him. If his experiences had taught him anything, it was never to share the fruit of his researches with his colleagues. There had to be a way of unobtrusively consulting the Magus's notes without alerting Maulevrier to their location.

Chapter 7

"Gavril! Lord Gavril!"

The calling of distant voices gradually penetrated Gavril's thoughts. He looked up from the easel, realizing that he had been utterly lost in his work again, oblivious to everything else around him. His first reaction was one of irritation and frustration at being disturbed. The demands of the vision he was trying to capture on canvas clamored much louder than the voices of his household.

What's so urgent that Askold can't sort it out for me? If it's a household matter, then Kiukiu will deal with it.

Since the dreams had started he had felt the need to escape, to find a place where he could be alone, undisturbed, to try to depict what he had been experiencing and purge the darkness polluting his mind. Suddenly he had begun to paint again and, having started, he could not stop.

I have to rid myself of these images. How can I be around Larisa with this black mood shadowing everything I see? How can I trust myself?

"Lord Gavril!" The voices were coming nearer. He stood back from the canvas, looking critically at what he had done. He had wielded his brushes in a kind of controlled frenzy, without any preliminary sketching or planning, just trying to let out whatever had been shadowing his dreaming mind.

How can any trace of Khezef still be possessing me? He's gone from this world for good.

Yet when he looked at what he had painted—violent slashes of color daubed like freshly spilled blood over a nightscape rich in luminous blues—he felt a wave of revulsion and guilt engulf him.

I can never show this to anyone.

The Drakhaoul had forced him to seek out innocent blood to preserve their fragile symbiosis and he could never forget it. Khezef had taken control of him whenever he hunted down his prey

He would have to hide it with the others: the series of portraits that he had painted from his guiltiest memories, each canvas the image of one of his victims, a gallery of pallid dead girls, staring out accusingly from ghost-dark eyes at the viewer. He had hoped to exorcise the phantoms from his conscience by bringing them back to life in paint but all he had done was make his memories even more vivid and increase his torment.

How can I ever pay for what I did? I—Khezef—we seduced those innocent girls and left them for dead.

He snatched the painting, the oil still wet, and placed the canvas in the darkest recess of the summerhouse, face to the wall.

"My lord!" Semyon appeared outside the summerhouse, panting for breath. "A messenger. From the Emperor."

***

The imperial dispatches from Tielen were delivered by a travel-stained courier who had ridden post all the way from the new harbor at Narvazh. While Ilsi served the Emperor's trusted servant refreshments in the parlor and the stable boys were tending to his horse, Gavril retired to his study to examine the dispatch box which, the courier explained, contained new trade treaties. It seemed that the Emperor urgently required his official seal and signature to confirm Azhkendir's participation.

But Gavril knew Eugene well enough to suspect that mere trade treaties would not require delivery by a specially selected imperial agent. The instant he opened the box (using the secret cipher agreed upon between them) he detected a shimmer of Linnaius's alchymical mirror-dust, only released when the correct codes were entered. Senses set tingling by the Magus's iridescent powder, he watched as it worked its magic on the blank page, swiftly revealing the Emperor's clear, strong pen-strokes:

"My dear friend,

"Our agents in Tourmalise have alerted us to the presence of a woman calling herself Lilias Arkhel in the spa resort of Sulien. She has made contact with the family of a certain Lord Ranulph whom we have been watching for some while. Lord R's real name is Ranozhir Arkhel and he is the youngest brother of Lord Stavyor."

But I thought they were all dead. Gavril looked up from the glistening script, trying to absorb this unexpected and unwelcome information. If the druzhina came to hear that Lord Stavyor's bloodline had not been eradicated after all, all the old hatreds and grievances toward the rival clan would be reawakened.

"Lord R managed to erase his true identity so effectively that we only made a definitive identification a few months ago. He's married into the local gentry in Tourmalise and has three children. I wouldn't have bothered to warn you if *that woman* had not inveigled herself into Sulien society and, more troublingly, into his household. It seems that she is now bosom friends with Lord R's wife. She's plotting something, Gavril, I'm certain of it. And as she bears a grudge against you and your household, I wanted to warn you to be on your guard.

"It's possible, of course, that these suspicions are unfounded, and Lord R has no wish to reveal his true identity, preferring to continue to play the part of a Sulien country gentleman. But our agents have discovered that he is over-fond of the gaming tables and has—unbeknown to his wife—run up considerable debts. If his creditors are not paid soon, they will seize the estate (which he married into) and leave his son Toran and daughters without any inheritance. It doesn't take much imagination to see that such a situation might well drive him back to Azhkendir to reclaim his family lands.

"My advisors are unfamiliar with Azhkendi laws of inheritance so I cannot offer any useful advice here except to urge you to consult your lawyer as soon as possible—and to be very careful, my dear friend; *that woman* is not only a skilled manipulator but she is also extremely vindictive. She bears you and your wife a deep grudge. And now that you and I are no longer 'protected' as we once were, we must be doubly vigilant."

"Lilias." Even speaking her name aloud stirred up feelings of unease and revulsion. And guilt. Crazed by his daemon-driven thirst for blood, Gavril had attacked Lilias's maid Dysis and badly disfigured her with one wild slash of his glittering claws as she tried to protect Lilias's baby son.

He stood up, almost knocking over his chair and began to pace the little room, barely able to contain his agitation.

I must talk with Avorian about this. And keep watch at the ports for any visitors from Tourmalise; there can't be that many arriving at this time of year. But how can I do that without alerting Askold and the druzhina? He stopped pacing abruptly. *What's the matter with me? I've faced far more terrifying foes than Lilias. Why am I sweating over one woman?*

A vivid memory of Lilias surfaced; sensuously beautiful Lilias with her creamy skin and fiery hair, gazing at him with those beguiling green eyes that artfully hid her true designs. He shuddered. "Beautiful, yes," he murmured aloud, "but ambitious . . . and ruthless." Too many of his household had died because of her machinations. "She must not be allowed anywhere near Kiukiu or Larisa."

He looked back at the Emperor's letter to read the postscript.

"Astasia sends her most affectionate good wishes to you, your wife, and little daughter, as do I. She and Karila commissioned the Naming Day gift for Larisa from Paer Paersson, one of Tielen's most talented jewelers; we hope you like it.

"Eugene."

Gavril took out a little casket nestling inside the dispatch box. Opening it, he saw a necklace inside, delicately fashioned with tiny jeweled flowers, sapphire petals around pearl centers, strung on three slender chains of gold. He smiled, his heart warmed by Eugene's thoughtfulness. He took out pen, ink and paper and began to write a reply:

"The gift for Larisa is exquisite; how did you guess that her eyes are blue? I enclose a little pastel sketch I made of her last week; as you will see, she's growing fast. We cannot thank you both enough for such a delightful present."

And after penning the usual courtesies, he added as postscript:

"I will be vigilant."

Chapter 8

Song for a Naming Day

The Great Hall of Kastel Drakhaon was bustling with servants and druzhina, busily hanging garlands of ivy and rowan berries from the beams, kindling a fire of pine logs in the cavernous fireplace, and setting out the tables for Larisa's Naming Day feast. Sosia was marshalling her forces in the kitchen with the ferocity of a general in mid-campaign. Kiukiu retreated to the quiet of the bedchamber and stood at the oriel window with Larisa in her arms, looking down at the torchlit courtyard as the guests began to arrive.

"All these grand visitors coming to celebrate your Naming Day." Larisa did not seem much interested, nuzzling her little nose against her mother's shoulder, on which Kiukiu had placed a piece of linen to protect her best gown. "Aren't we lucky that the first snows are late this year?"

A group of gray-robed monks had entered the courtyard; Gavril appeared below, hurrying across the cobbles to greet them.

"There's your daddy!" Kiukiu cried delightedly. "Doesn't he look handsome? And that's Abbot Yephimy; you've got to promise me you won't cry when he blesses you with the holy water from Saint Sergius's shrine."

A horse-drawn coach turned in under the archway; the postilion leapt down to open the door and help the occupants out.

"My lady, are you ready to receive your guests?" Sosia was calling her from downstairs.

Larisa gave a little burp as Kiukiu turned away from the window. "Larisa, don't you dare be sick on your lovely lace dress. Auntie Sosia spent a long time sewing it for you." Kiukiu hastily checked her shoulder to make sure that there was no stain of regurgitated milk on the blue sheen of the hyacinth silk. Trying to quell a sudden unwelcome flutter of nerves, she set out for the Great Hall.

***

It was not so long since Kiukiu had been one of the kastel serving maids, and she felt awkward, more used to waiting on the guests than greeting them as their hostess. She hoped that her welcoming smile was not beginning to look strained.

"All you have to do is be the proud mother," Gavril had reassured her when she admitted her anxieties the night before. "That's all that anyone will expect. They'll be too busy cooing over Larisa—and enjoying the feast."

"You have a lovely daughter, my lady."

A slender woman, modestly veiled, stood before her. "Thank you," she began. "I don't think we've—"

"I come from Khitari," said the stranger, letting her veils drop away, revealing a face of exquisite beauty: almond eyes of a liquid, honey brown, fringed by long, black lashes, set in a heart-shaped face. "My name is Khulan. I bring gifts from Chinua. He sends his deepest apologies that he cannot be here with you for this special occasion."

"You're a friend of Chinua's?" Forgetting all decorum, Kiukiu reached out and shook Khulan's hand warmly. "Is he well? How is he faring?"

"This is for you, my lady: a special blend of tea that your grandmother was fond of." She handed Kiukiu a little caddy of black and scarlet lacquer. "And I am the other half of his gift."

"*You* are?"

"I am one of Khan Vachir's court singers; if it pleases you and Lord Gavril, I will entertain your guests after the feast."

"Oh, that would be wonderful!" Kiukiu turned to Gavril. "Songs from such an illustrious Khitari singer? We'd be honored, wouldn't we?" When she had been traveling across the steppes of Khitari with Chinua, she had been entranced by the wild, throbbing lilt of the ballads sung around the fireside at night.

"Lord Gavril!" The powerful voice of Lord Stoyan, the governor of Azhgorod, boomed out across the hall and Kiukiu saw him approaching at a swift stride. "We need to discuss the new harbor at Narvazh. The customs officers aren't keeping up with all the paperwork and Tielen smugglers are already taking advantage. "

"Of course; excuse me." Gavril, distracted, nodded his agreement to Kiukiu and went to join the governor.

***

Kiukiu stole a quick glance at the cradle. Larisa was sound asleep, one little hand clutching the crumpled sheet tightly to her cheek. She had yelled loudly enough when Abbot Yephimy had performed the Naming Ceremony, much to the approval of the druzhina, and her mother's acute embarrassment.

And look at you now, sleeping so peacefully in the middle of your feast.

A sudden lull in the babble of voices made Kiukiu glance up. Khulan, smiling, had settled herself, cross-legged, on the floor in the center of the hall, her slender-necked dombra balanced on her lap. The guests fell silent.

After a few moments' tuning, Khulan announced, "A song in praise of Gavril, Lord of Azhkendir, and his wife, Lady Kiukirilya, who is much honored in Khitari for her service to the khan."

A roar of approval erupted from the druzhina, raising their glasses in a toast to their lord and lady.

Blushing, Kiukiu sat back in her chair, as Khulan struck the first notes on the sonorous strings of the dombra. Yet soon her embarrassment melted into a feeling of warm contentment as she surveyed the firelit hall.

"Praise to the Dragon of Azhkendir and praise to his brave warriors . . ."

The druzhina began to sing along with the stirring refrain, stamping their feet enthusiastically in time to the music until the hall was filled with their lusty voices.

"She's no fool, this Khulan," Gavril murmured in Kiukiu's ear. "She's won the druzhina over—and that's no mean feat."

Disturbed by the rowdy singing, Larisa stirred restlessly in her cradle and let out a wail of protest. Kiukiu put her foot on the rocker of the cradle and began to press vigorously. "Hush, Larisa, not now."

"Idiots!" cried Semyon, clambering up on his bench to try to quiet his fellow druzhina and sloshing ale on his friend Dunai beside him. "You've woken the baby!"

Khulan's agile fingers instantly switched to a gentle rocking motive on the dombra. As soon as she began to sing, in a voice as sweet and cooing as a forest dove, Kiukiu realized that she had chosen a Khitari lullaby. And to her amazement, Larisa's protests subsided and one tiny thumb found its way into her mouth as the soothing melody cast its spell over the hall.

"That was magical," Kiukiu whispered to Khulan. "You must teach me that song before you leave."

Khulan nodded, then turned back to the audience. "And now, a ballad from my homeland, the tale of a water witch and a young girl."

This time there was a dark, ominous quality to the notes she drew from the dombra's deepest strings.

"She can grant your wish, the jade-haired witch of the springs. But take care. For nothing comes without a price. She never gives without taking something in return. Something you value more than life itself . . ."

Kiukiu shivered. Shadows like mountain mist were seeping into the hall, blotting out the rapt faces of the guests until all she could see was the singer, head bent intently over the strings of her instrument. The sacred snake-mark on Kiukiu's ankle began to throb.

"'If I grant your wish, you must give me your firstborn child,'" sang Khulan in a low, foreboding tone. *"But the foolish girl didn't heed the witch's warning . . ."*

The singer slowly raised her head. To Kiukiu's horror, she saw that Khulan's eyes were no longer brown but the piercing green of Anagini, Guardian of the Jade Springs. And the shadowy mists swirling around them both had taken on the viridian tinge of the steam that rose from the hidden healing waters.

"Have you forgotten, Kiukirilya? One year has passed since you made me that promise." Her words, softly sibilant, made Kiukiu's heart stop with fear.

"S-seven years," Kiukiu stammered. "You said seven years. She's only three months old."

"And if you tell a single soul of our bargain, the cure wrought by my Jade Springs will be undone, and you will become an old woman again."

"Won't you take me instead?" Kiukiu burst out. "At least let Larisa stay with her father. Let me come serve you in her place."

"The child of a Spirit Singer and a Lord Drakhaon is a unique and special being. She was conceived when your lord was still possessed by the Drakhaoul Khezef, wasn't she? There will be others who come to seek her out, Kiukirilya, others who will seek to use her for their own ends. Others who are not so kind as I."

"To use her?" Kiukiu had never thought of such a possibility. "Are you saying that she has powers? How can that be? The Drakhaouls are gone from the world—and the Serpent Gate is sealed for all eternity."

"I can protect her. I can train her to use her powers. But left unprotected, untrained, she may not live to see her seventh birthday."

"Is her life in danger? Tell me!"

"The bargain was broken," floated the singer's voice through the mists, *"and the beloved child disappeared, never to be seen again. So beware the jade-haired witch of the springs . . . she never gives without taking something in return."*

"No!" Kiukiu cried, snatching Larisa out of her cradle and clutching her close. The song halted abruptly. To Kiukiu's surprise she saw that everyone was staring at her. There was no trace of green mist swirling around the hall.

"Kiukiu?" Gavril said as Larisa began to wail. He stood up and put his arms around them both. "Khulan; could you sing us something more cheerful?"

"I apologize, my lord." Khulan bowed, and instantly began to play a lively dance melody. Semyon leapt to his feet and began clapping in time to the beat. "Come on, lads!" he shouted. "Let's show the girls our best moves!" He made a somersaulting leap from his bench into the center of the hall and launched into one of the traditional Azhkendi warriors' dances, arms crossed, stamping and kicking with muscular agility.

Thank you, Sem, Kiukiu thought gratefully as the young druzhina's prowess drew others to join him and the guests' enthusiastic clapping urged them to try wilder leaps and turns.

Gavril eased Kiukiu back down into her chair. "What was that about, love?" he murmured into her ear.

So he had sensed nothing of Anagini's presence?

"Forgive me," she said. "That song just made me feel sad."

***

Even here, in Azhkendir, Anagini is watching me. Kiukiu sat in front of the mirror, listlessly removing the pins from her hair. Her shadowy reflection, gilded by the trembling candle flames, stared back as one wheat-gold lock after another was released. *Would it be so terrible to see my youth fade away again if it meant little Risa could stay here with us?* She began to pull a comb through her hair, remembering that time a year ago when it had turned gray and her skin had wrinkled. *But what use would I be to her as a mother? The time I spent wandering in the Realm of Shadows drained so much of my lifeforce. It wasn't vanity that drove me to beg for Anagini's help. I was dying.*

Chinua's lacquer caddy caught her eye; Khulan had said it contained Malusha's favorite blend. Kiukiu removed the lid and sniffed, hoping that the aromatic fragrance would bring back happier memories. Then she noticed a little piece of paper tucked inside. Unfolding it, she read:

"I will come if you ever have need of me. Leave a message at the tea merchant's shop in Azhgorod."

"Thank you, Chinua," she whispered.

The bedchamber door opened. She stuffed the note back into the caddy and turned round to see Gavril on the threshold.

"I thought Lord Stoyan would never stop talking." He threw himself onto the bed, stretching his arms above his head. "He wants me to preside over the boyars' council in the spring. Azhkendi politics. I agreed, just to make him turn in for the night." He patted the mattress beside him. "Come here, Kiukiu."

She snuffed out the candles and went to lie beside him in the darkness.

"And yet a year ago, it seemed as if there might be no future for us at all," he said, putting his arms around her.

"Is it exactly a year ago?" She nestled closer to him.

"To the day. I found you by the shores of Lake Taigal and Khezef took us to the ruined temple on the island, remember?"

"How could I forget?" she said. She had cherished the memory of their passionate love-making, made all the more poignant by the fear that they might never see each other again. But now Anagini's warning had tarnished even that precious memory. Her heart heavy with guilt, she turned away from Gavril, feigning sleep.

Chapter 9

Tourmalise

"You still don't get it, do you, Azhkendi peasant?" The Honorable Elyot Branville looked up from the green baize of the billiards table as he aligned his next shot and fixed his dark eyes on Toran Arkhel. "You're not welcome here. This games room is for the use of the elite cadets only. So you can leave now—quietly—or I can throw you out. Your choice."

"What did you call me?" Toran said quietly.

"Come on, Toran," Lorris murmured, "don't waste your breath on this boor."

"Azhkendi peasant." Branville walked around the side of the billiards table to stare closely at Toran. "That's what you are, right? Lord knows how much money your peasant father had to pay to persuade Colonel Mouzillon to accept you as a cadet here, but that doesn't mean you're entitled to the same privileges as the rest of us."

"Is that so?" Toran stared back, determined not to be faced down by Branville, even though he was already aware of his reputation around the Military Academy. "I was born in Tourmalise. I reckon that gives me as much right to be here as any other cadet."

"'As much right?'" echoed Branville with a sneer. "From what I heard, your darling mama was obliged to marry your papa in rather a hurry."

Toran felt Lorris grip his arm, trying to hold him back. He shook off the restraining hand and advanced toward the smiling Second Year. He knew Branville was spoiling for a fight, deliberately needling him. If he landed the first punch—well-deserved though it might be—he would be the one to get into trouble. But at that moment, he really didn't care. Anger burned through him, white-hot, searing everything from his mind but one intense desire: hit the arrogant bastard hard right in the middle of that infuriating grin. *Walk away now, while you can.*

Branville suddenly brandished his cue like a rapier, aiming a jab at Toran's breastbone. Toran's right hand blocked the blow automatically, gripping hold of the cue.

"Fights like a peasant, too."

"Steady on, Branville," Toran heard Lorris say. "This has gone far enough."

"Stay out of this, Lorris." The glint in Branville's eyes hardened. "This is between the Azhkendi by-blow and me."

That was it. Toran suddenly yanked the cue from Branville's hand and threw it onto the ground. The rattle it made as it rolled across the flagstone floor caused the other cadets to look round from their games.

"You insolent little prick." Branville's eyes gleamed with the reflected flames of the firelight. Toran saw him gathering himself, fist clenched, to punch him. Branville was a good head taller than he and muscularly built. The shadow of the older cadet loomed over him. But before Branville's punch hit home, Toran was in and under his guard with a solid jab to the side of his chin. He felt the graze of stubble then the crunch of knuckle against jawbone. His whole hand throbbed as if he had hit a wall. Branville let out a grunt and then, to Toran's surprise, the loud-mouthed cadet sagged, collapsing to his knees, and then the floor.

Toran, his blood still blazing, stood over him as he lay stunned on the flagstones. A thin line of crimson trickled from the corner of Branville's mouth.

"Don't *ever* insult my mother again."

Then he turned to Lorris and said, "I'm leaving." Nursing his bruised knuckles, he set out toward the door, aware that his fellow cadets were staring at him, open-mouthed, suddenly silent, speechless.

Over the crackle of the flames in the grate he heard Branville say thickly, "I won't forget this, Toran Arkhel. I'm going to make your life hell." But he walked on, not even bothering to acknowledge Branville's threat. He half expected to be knocked to the ground with a flying tackle from Branville, but he reached the Games Room door and pushed it open, stepping out onto the central parade ground, without further interference.

The damp of the misty evening cooled his burning face, but not the rage; he kept on walking, not looking back.

Why did my father force me to enroll here? I'm never going to fit in.

"Wait up, Toran!" Lorris came hurrying out after him.

He slowed a little. "Are you sure you want to be seen with the Azhkendi peasant?"

"Branville's a bully. And a coward. He had it coming."

Toran stared up at the night sky; the eerie ghost of the crescent moon could just be glimpsed behind fast-moving clouds. "The air smells of autumn already," he said. "We always have a big bonfire back at Serrigonde this time of year. And fireworks." He kicked at a pile of fallen leaves that had drifted down from the horse chestnut trees lining the parade ground.

"Homesick?"

"It was my father's idea I should come here. I had other plans." He didn't want to talk about it, not even with the good-natured Lorris.

"I wanted to go abroad to university," Lorris said. "To Tielborg. They have the best laboratories in the Western Hemisphere. But all the men in my family join the army, so my father refused to listen."

Toran stopped, gazing in surprise at his friend. "I never took you for a scientist, Lorris. You hide it well."

"What about you, Toran?" They had crossed the wide parade ground and reached the entrance to the First Years' hall of residence.

"What about me?" Toran had a dream too, but it had nothing to do with joining the Sulien army for a military career.

He felt Lorris's hand on his shoulder. "Is it true? That your father is from Azhkendir?"

Toran sighed.

"Sorry, sorry!" The hand lifted in a placatory gesture. "Didn't mean to pry."

"It's true," Toran muttered. "But I'm not supposed to talk about it."

"Then don't," Lorris said amicably. "Anyone who can take Bully Branville down with one punch is all right by me."

***

"Brawling in the Games Room? You should be ashamed of yourselves."

Toran stood stiffly to attention as Colonel Mouzillon glowered from behind his desk; beside him, Elyot Branville, also at attention, was almost quivering, his tall frame emanating an aura of barely-repressed fury.

The colonel rose and walked around the cadets, his hands clasped behind his back. Toran stared straight ahead, concentrating on the cloudy sky that he could see through the window panes. *What's the worst punishment the colonel could inflict? A beating? Or expulsion?* He tried not to wish too hard for the latter, knowing that it would make his mother cry if he were sent home in disgrace.

"Cadet Branville; you claim you were attacked by Cadet Arkhel. Did you do anything to provoke him?"

There was a pause. Then Branville said smoothly, "We may have exchanged a few words, Colonel."

A few words? Toran bit his underlip, forcing himself to keep silent.

"I see." Colonel Mouzillon moved on to stare directly into Toran's eyes. The cold steel of his gaze transfixed him, driving all his carefully prepared words out of his head. "Cadet Arkhel; what have you got to say for yourself?"

"I broke an Academy rule, Colonel," Toran said, trying not to be distracted by Mouzillon's magnificent waxed moustaches. "I can only offer my apologies. I should not have struck Cadet Branville."

"Brawling is strictly forbidden within the Military Academy and will be severely punished."

Toran dropped his gaze, staring at the glossy sheen of the polished floorboards. "I understand." He wondered what kind of punishment the colonel would impose. A beating would be painful—but swiftly over. Unless the colonel decided to make an example of him and inflict the punishment on the parade ground, in front of the whole academy. The thought of being subjected to such a humiliation sent a cold shudder through him.

"Unless, of course, there are extenuating circumstances." Mouzillon moved a couple of steps to the right to gaze at Branville again. "Such as deliberate provocation."

Has someone told him that Branville insulted my mother?

Branville still said nothing but Toran sensed the suppressed quiver become even more intense.

"You're both confined to quarters while I decide what to do with you. Dismissed."

Both cadets saluted the colonel and turned to leave. Toran dropped back to let Branville go first and had just reached the door when the colonel said, "Arkhel. There's one more matter."

Toran turned, catching a glimpse of Branville's expression, already darkening with a look of suspicion, before the door swung shut. "Colonel?"

Mouzillon beckoned him over to the desk.

"There's nothing else you wish to add to your account?"

"No, sir."

"You have a good and loyal friend, you know. Someone who has testified in your defense. "

"I have?" This was not what Toran had expected to hear. *It must have been Lorris.* He was surprised—and moved—that the quiet and studious Lorris had gone out of his way to defend him. As long as his gallant act didn't lead to Branville singling him out too. *I'll have to find a way to thank him.*

"And because of that testimony, I've decided not to pursue this matter further. Although I'm withdrawing your privileges; consider your free time canceled until further notice. And the Games Room is obviously out of bounds for the time being."

Toran bowed his head. "Thank you, Colonel." He could live with that; it seemed remarkably lenient in the circumstances.

"And, with all that extra free time on your hands, I don't want you idling around doing nothing. So I've an errand or two for you to run for me."

Toran looked up, surprised. He'd imagined that he'd be confined to barracks, kicking his heels, or given menial tasks to do such as blacking the officers' boots or polishing their sabers.

"I want you to deliver this to Master Cardin at the Iron Works down by the canal. He's been doing some work for us." The colonel held out a folder; after a moment's hesitation, Toran took it, weighing it in his hands. "He'll probably want to send a reply; you'll have to wait and then bring it back straight away. Is that clear?"

"Yes, sir." Toran tucked the folder under one arm and saluted.

"Dismissed."

As he turned to leave, he heard the colonel say quietly, "Next time you see your mother, please remember me to her. I've known Tanaisie since childhood and anyone who dares to tarnish her reputation will have to answer to me."

Toran had no idea that Mouzillon had known his mother for so long. Perhaps he had been an admirer when she had been voted the most eligible heiress in the Sulien season, perhaps even a disappointed suitor . . .

***

The walk down the hill into Paladur helped to clear Toran's mind; the fresh wind, spattered with a few drops of rain, chased away the louring feelings of resentment that he had been harboring since the Branville incident. But the sight of the distant hills rising beyond the roofs of the garrison town, the trees tinged with shades of copper and gold, reminded him of the parkland at Serrigonde.

But there's no point feeling homesick. If I'm ever to achieve my ambition, I have to leave Serrigonde behind. I don't want to end up like my father, frittering away my days as an impoverished country squire.

Even though he could see dark plumes of smoke rising from the tall Iron Works chimneys, it took longer than Toran expected to make his way there; the canal tow-path had seemed the most direct route but he soon discovered he was mistaken. Fortunately, a bargee was leading his horse and coal-laden barge toward him, so he stopped to ask him for directions. Having retraced his steps, he heard the clank and clatter of the great machinery and found himself at last in front of tall iron gates that proclaimed in intricately wrought gilded letters: Cardin's Iron Works.

Venturing inside, he looked around for someone to ask. Spotting an open door in the closest building, he went inside—and instantly his ears were assaulted by the pounding of a vast and gleaming machine. Toran stared in amazement, overwhelmed by its size and power, feeling his whole body vibrate and the ground shake beneath his feet.

A workman passed by and spotted Toran, beckoning him outside, away from the thunderous racket of the great engine.

"A letter for Master Cardin?" The workman pushed back his leather cap and scratched his head; Toran could not help noticing that he left a smear of oil on his forehead. "You won't find him here today, lad; he's gone up to the mines. How about I take you to the site office and works superintendant, Ingenieur Bernay? Maybe he'll be able to help you."

The colonel had said there would be a reply; Toran hoped that Ingenieur Bernay had enough authority to deal with the matter, "Thank you," he said, following the workman away from the deafening rhythmic pounding of the pumping engine driving the machinery. His ears were buzzing, assaulted by the noise, but his heart was singing with excitement. *I've never seen modern machinery this close before. I wish I could stay longer and watch.*

Everything intrigued him: the searing heat from the furnaces; the smell of smoke and molten metal. *Has the colonel found out my secret passion? Is that why he sent me?* Toran had concealed his well-thumbed treatises on the mechanical arts in the trunk beneath his bed. Only Lorris, his room-mate, knew of Toran's dream to study to become an ingenieur.

He followed the workman across the cobbled yard, passing a couple of workers unloading coal. A separate small building stood at the far end, close to the high wall that separated the works from the street beyond.

"See that blue door? Go through there and you'll find the superintendant's office on the right."

Toran, ears still ringing, knocked.

"It's open."

Toran went in. One wall was lined with shelves stuffed full of ledgers and document boxes. A desk stood next to the stove on which a kettle was softly singing, a wisp of steam issuing from its spout. The desktop was covered in more ledgers and stacks of papers. Tall windows cast a clear light onto a long table at which a man sat, his back to Toran, leaning over his work, pen and rule in hand.

"Yes?" he said, not looking up.

Toran cleared his throat. He felt embarrassed to be disturbing the superintendant. "Are you Ingenieur Bernay? I—I've brought this from Colonel Mouzillon. He said there would be a reply."

Toran heard a slight sigh; the man laid down his pen and rule and turned around on his stool.

He's young. Somehow I'd imagined a superintendant to be a much older man . . . about my father's age.

Toran became aware that he must be staring at the ingenieur and, lowering his head to hide his confusion, handed the folder to him. But as Bernay opened it and scanned its contents, Toran could not help stealing another glance: clean-shaven, with his brown hair tied back, the ingenieur sported an impressive scar across his forehead, above his left eyebrow. *Did he get that working here? It looks more like a dueling scar. I wonder ...*

"It'll take a half hour or so to assemble the necessary information for the colonel." Ingenieur Bernay said, looking up.

"What information?" Toran heard himself asking.

Clear gray eyes pierced him through, keen as a steel blade, and he shivered.

There's something different about this man. For a moment I felt I was standing on a hillside on a stormy day, buffeted by the raw power of the wind.

"Did the colonel not explain? This is a foundry; and, among other products, we forge cannon and artillery guns for the military."

Toran blinked, forcing himself to concentrate on what he was being told.

"The Master of the Works has an arrangement with your colonel; the cadets test the new cannon for us up on Berse Heath as part of their training."

"Ah." Toran nodded. "I'm only in the first year; I haven't been trained how to fire a cannon yet."

"Then it looks like your chance is coming; the colonel is proposing that we hold the trials next week." Ingenieur Bernay stood up, stretching, as though he had been seated at his desk for too long. "Do you want to wait in here? Or to take a tour of the works?"

"A tour of the works? Really?" Toran could not disguise his excitement at the prospect. He dearly wanted to see what was going on in the foundry halls and get a closer look at the pumping engine. *This must be my lucky day!*

"I'll get one of the men." Bernay disappeared, reappearing with a workman whose face was red and shiny with perspiration. "This is our foreman, Mahieu. He'll show you around."

"So what d'you make of our young inventor?" The foreman winked at Toran as they went back out into the yard.

"Inventor? You mean Ingenieur Bernay?" *Was he working on an invention? And I disturbed him.* All of a sudden Toran longed to go back to see what Bernay was designing.

"He's made all manner of improvements in the short time he's been here. He's got a mechanical mind; we call him the Professor behind his back. Saved a few of the men's lives too. If it weren't for him and his modifications to the main pumping engine, I'd have lost this arm, my livelihood—and my family would have gone hungry."

***

Dusk brought drizzle down on Paladur as Toran left the Iron Works carrying the documents for the colonel. He turned up the collar of his cadet's uniform and tucked the folder beneath his jacket so it wouldn't get damp, glowering at the dreary sky which still bore a few faint streaks of dirty red where the sun was setting in the far west.

Yet even the dismal twilight couldn't dampen his spirits; his mind was buzzing with ideas and his ears were still filled with the rhythmic clamor of the machinery. That single visit had re-kindled his passion for the power and potential of the mechanical arts, an enthusiasm first fired and encouraged by his grandfather.

Yet when he signed back in at the academy, he found Colonel Mouzillon's adjutant waiting for him.

"The colonel wants to see you," he said, setting off at such a brisk stride across the parade ground that Toran had to run to keep up.

"I came straight back from the Iron Works," he said. "It took the superintendant a while to assemble all the necessary documents."

"You can give those to me." The adjutant led the way into the colonel's quarters and gave a brusque salute to the two cadets standing guard outside. "This is a personal matter. Your father's here."

"My father?" Toran fumbled a salute and hurried up the main stairs after the adjutant. He could not imagine anything but that the colonel had summoned his father because he was so displeased with his conduct.

At least then I could go to university and study to become an ingenieur.

"Cadet Arkhel," announced the adjutant, beckoning Toran to enter.

Toran swallowed hard and went in. A coal fire crackled in the grate; the two men were seated on either side in the glossy leather-upholstered chairs the colonel reserved for entertaining visitors. As Toran entered, his father rose, gazing earnestly at him.

"Toran, my boy, it's good to see you," cried Ranulph. "I'll wager you've grown again; you'll overtake me soon!"

Embarrassed, Toran saluted the colonel, and then bowed formally to Lord Ranulph; for one moment he had feared his father had been about to fling his arms around him.

His eyes are shining and his cheeks look even redder than usual; is it the autumn wind or has he been drinking?

"If you would like some time in private with your son—" began the colonel.

"No, no, Colonel—you need to hear what I have to say too."

Toran swallowed, steeling himself for a lecture on his unruly behavior and dishonoring the family name.

"I'm returning to Azhkendir," announced Lord Ranulph.

"Azhkendir?" Toran could only stare in disbelief at his father. "But why?"

"It's a new business venture. An enterprise. An opportunity that's too good to miss."

My father going into business? Toran shook his head, certain he must have misheard. "But you said you would never go back. You said that everything was destroyed by Lord Volkh, that there was nothing to go back to."

"Which is true. But Lord Volkh has been dead for several years and his son, Gavril, is generally reported to be more interested in his painting than politics, let alone reviving old clan rivalries. And since the Great Darkness, there have been no more . . . *unnatural* events in Azhkendir."

"May I enquire what this enterprise entails?" asked the colonel.

"Mining, Colonel. Now that the new harbor has opened in Narvazh, there's a direct route to Tielen; and the New Rossiyan Empire is hungry for all kinds of mineral resources."

There's more to this than my father's letting on. Toran's suspicions were multiplying. *Something must have happened. Something bad.*

"Which is why I wanted to reassure you, Colonel, that Toran's fees will be covered. And, contrary to any malicious rumors you may have heard about my financial situation—"

"Wait a moment." Toran was trying to make sense of his father's plan. "It's autumn. And from the little you've told me about Azhkendir, I remember that once the winter sets in, the sea freezes over, the trade routes shut down—and for two to three months no one can get in or out. Why go now?"

"Because if I wait any longer, others may beat me to it." Lord Ranulph's eyes gleamed more brightly.

"And how are you funding this trip?" *Once my father gets an idea in his head, he's obsessive about seeing it through.* Toran's mind was racing. *This could be disastrous. He could ruin us as a family.*

"I've sold off the town house in Sulien."

Mother really loved that house. She must be very sad to be forced to let it go. "Who's going to look after mother while you're gone?"

"Your mother's a practical, sensible woman who would be disappointed to hear her son ask such a question; she's more than capable of looking after herself. But I wondered, Colonel," and Lord Ranulph turned to the colonel, "if you would permit Toran to ride over to Serrigonde every month or so to check on my wife and daughters? He'll have to be the man of the house in my absence."

"These are exceptional circumstances, Lord Ranulph, so I suppose I can't object. As long as these absences don't affect his studies," and Colonel Mouzillon stared piercingly at Toran. "And I, of course, will also do all I can to support Lady Tanaisie," he added gallantly.

"Then it's settled!" Lord Ranulph cried and before Toran could evade him, he flung his arms around him, hugging him tightly. "This is goodbye, my boy. Take good care of your mother and sisters while I'm away." His breath smelled strongly of apple brandy.

"Wait." Toran tried to extricate himself from his father's bearlike embrace. "How can we contact you? Where shall we send letters?"

"You can write to me in the capital Azhgorod, *poste restante.* But don't use our family name; use your grandfather's. We don't want to arouse unwelcome suspicions." Lord Ranulph let Toran go and turned to shake hands with the colonel.

"Permission to accompany my father to the lodge, Colonel?" This was all happening too fast and Toran wanted to speak with his father alone.

"Permission granted."

Once outside on the dark parade ground, Toran turned on his father. "What's the real reason for this, Father? Is it the bailiffs again?"

Lord Ranulph stopped. His shoulders slumped and, as a sickly moon appeared briefly from behind scudding clouds, Toran saw that he looked much older and more vulnerable, the optimistic gleam in his eyes dulled.

"I can't hide the truth from you, Toran; we're practically ruined."

"Ruined?" Toran echoed warily, wondering if his father was exaggerating.

"I made some ill-judged investments in the Serindhen Spice Trade. No one could have predicted the spice plantations would be washed away by that terrible tidal wave! But I don't want the slightest whisper of scandal to harm your mother or sisters."

"Is there anything I can do to help?"

Ranulph placed a hand on Toran's shoulder and gazed intently into his eyes. "I want you to carry on here as if nothing were wrong. Keep up the pretence. Malicious tongues won't begin to wag if you continue your training here, and the girls take part in the winter season at Sulien."

"But Father—"

"My lord; we must go."

Toran started as a man stepped out from the shadows; a shimmer of moonlight revealed the lean, sharp-boned features of Iarko, his father's valet.

"I'm in excellent hands with Iarko and Temir to protect me; don't worry, my boy, this little venture is going to change our fortunes!" Ranulph let go of Toran. "Oh, I almost forgot; this is from your mother." He fumbled inside his jacket pocket and brought out a crumpled envelope, placing it in Toran's hand. "I'll send word when we arrive."

With a nonchalant wave, he turned and followed Iarko towards the lodge. Toran, clutching his mother's letter, stood watching, bewildered, wondering if he would ever see his father again.

Chapter 10

'By order of his Imperial Majesty, Eugene of New Rossiya, a competition to design a flying craft capable of sustained aerial travel over many leagues is announced. The winner must be able to demonstrate that their design is airworthy and safe. The prize: a gold medal, and a lectureship awarded by the University of Tielborg, as well as the establishment of a new department dedicated to the development of mechanical flying craft.'

Gerard Bernay unfolded the letter accompanying the announcement, trying to control a tremor in his normally steady hands at the sight of the familiar handwriting. He moved to the office window to read more it easily:

"My dear Gerard,

"I thought I should bring this to your attention. I imagine you've had little time to devote to your research since you started to work for Master Cardin but, even if you don't win, entering this competition could bring your talents to the attention of a wealthy patron. Imagine being given the opportunity to develop your ideas in your own workshop without having to worry about the cost of the materials; surely any young inventor's dream? As you were one of my most promising students, I'd be happy to endorse your application. But don't think about this for too long; the closing date is next month.

"Your friend, Guy Maulevrier, Doctor of Mechanical Arts"

Gerard read the letter a second time. Entering the competition could place him in a very tricky situation. Tourmalise, like its larger neighbor Allegonde, had stayed neutral in the recent conflicts that had led to the establishment of the empire of New Rossiya. If he agreed to work for the Emperor, could that be seen as betraying his own principles—or worse, his adopted country, Tourmalise? The letter was couched in the vaguest of terms, implying that the project had no military connections, yet everything Eugene of Tielen had achieved in his rapid ascendancy involved deploying his armies and naval forces to invade and conquer his neighbors.

And then there was the matter of his own disgrace and unfinished doctorate. He had been forced to flee Tielborg in such a hurry that he had left most of his research material behind in the university laboratories.

I owe you a considerable debt, Doctor Maulevrier. If you hadn't come to my rescue, I would have been forced to answer Edvin Stenmark's charges before a university court.

Even now, far away from Tielen in sleepy Paladur, the shame of his disgrace still tormented him. He was still furious with himself for throwing away such a promising academic career over an affair with a younger student.

Edvin Stenmark's face appeared yet again in his mind's eye, his handsome features distorted with rage and fear, as he pointed accusingly at him over the laboratory bench and cried out, "That's him! He's the one who violated me."

Every time he remembered that moment, Gerard still felt physically sick, the memory rising like a surge of bile in his throat, even though hundreds of leagues separated them. Because Edvin had been the one to lead him on, pursuing him relentlessly. Flaxen-haired Edvin, blessed with the face of an angel, the willful, indulged elder son of a wealthy Tielen noble family, who had never been denied anything he wanted.

And God knows I denied him enough times. Why I was so foolish as to give in that last time, why I did allow myself to believe he really meant what he said? I must have been flattered that such a beautiful creature was so interested in me.

He shook his head, unwilling to admit it even now. *No, not just flattered. I fell for him.* In unguarded moments, he would find himself recalling the way Edvin used to sit on the laboratory bench, idly swinging his elegantly slender legs as he watched him at work, lips curving in a mysterious, alluring little smile whenever he glanced up and caught his eye. The smile that always made his heart miss a beat, so intimate and affectionate that he found it hard to concentrate.

Why? Time and again he had asked the same question on the long journey to Tourmalise. *Why did you denounce me, Edvin? Why did you lie? Was it all just a warped game for you, toying with the affections of a poor scholarship student, only to ruin his reputation? Or did you do it to assuage your guilt at falling for another man? Was I your last fling before a prestigious aristocratic wedding? Did you blame me to avert a scandal? Would your father have disinherited you if he once believed you'd been a willing partner, let alone initiated the affair? I'd never have betrayed you—but perhaps there were others, observing us from the shadows, who tried to blackmail you.*

Gerard gazed at the letter again, the mere sight of Guy Maulevrier's strong, distinctive hand bringing back his dreams of a distinguished academic career at the most prestigious university in New Rossiya . . . dreams that had been so rudely shattered by that single night's indiscretion.

And at least Guy hasn't lost faith in me. If it hadn't been for his help, spiriting me out of Tielborg so swiftly, I'd have been forced to face those threats of litigation. Edvin's father would have stopped at nothing to bring me down. The post of supervising ingenieur at the new Iron Works had been ideal as a bolt-hole. "Rasse Cardin's an old friend of mine; you'll get on well with him." The little republic of Tourmalise was independent, and, like its larger neighbor Allegonde, it lay outside the constraints of the empire. Thanks to the enlightened attitude of its government, free-thinking and scientific endeavors were openly encouraged.

In spite of his initial resistance, Gerard found himself clambering up on his chair to reach the top shelf above the stacks of Works ledgers where he kept a folder of his ideas. He placed it on the draughtsman's table and opened it up, frowning as he turned the pages which were filled with his sketches, dashed off in rare idle moments in the office. Even though his research had been so brutally terminated, his ideas had continued to multiply; since his days as an undergraduate, he had been obsessed with the concept of manned flight.

If my project won the Emperor's approval and patronage, there's nothing that Edvin or his family could do to touch me. I would be reinstated at Tielborg University and continue my research.

That desire alone was almost enough to quell the bitterness that Edvin's betrayal had left in his heart, tarnishing every new relationship, making him wary, unwilling to get close to anyone.

It's just too risky to have close friends, let alone a lover. Thank heaven that I can lose myself in my work here in Paladur.

Gerard folded the letter and stuffed it into the inside pocket of his greatcoat. Extinguishing the lamp on his desk, he left the office and called out into the echoing hall of the main Pump House to ensure that the workmen and apprentices had all gone home. Satisfied that none were left, he locked up for the night.

It was drizzling again outside; he turned up the collar of his coat and set off through the dreary light over the wet cobblestones. *I could do with a decent hot dinner tonight. Shall I call in at the Tollhouse Tavern to join Rasse and the foundry lads for a glass of ale? Or go straight to the chop-house by the bridge?*

He had just entered the alleyway that led away from the canal, debating with himself the relative merits of a good piece of beef over liver and bacon, when he heard raised voices. Turning the corner, he saw, highlighted by the rain-streaked light of the lantern, three men attacking a fourth. They had wrestled their victim to the ground and were subjecting him to a violent kicking.

Thieves? Forgetting that he was alone and unarmed, Gerard shouted out, "Hey! What's going on?" and launched himself toward them. Something about the sight of three laying into one triggered bitter memories from grammar school days and the vicious bullying he'd had to endure because of his scholarly nature and his Francian father.

He clamped his hands onto the shoulders of the one who was doing most of the kicking and caught hold of his right arm, twisting it and forcing it up behind his back in a lock he'd learned in the wrestling club at university. To his satisfaction he heard the man give a grunt of pain. *Not so brave now, huh?* But at these close quarters, he saw that this was no shabbily-dressed robber; the assailant was wearing the navy blue serge jacket of the military academy with the distinctive silver cord piping decorating the stand collar.

"Academy cadets?" He twisted the young man's arm more tightly. "You should be ashamed, causing a public disturbance in town. I'm calling the watch."

"Scram!" he heard one shout. The two holding down their victim let him drop, and made off into the darkness, the sound of their receding footfall echoing dully off the high brick walls on either side.

"Let me go, damn you!" His prisoner suddenly drove his head upward into his chin, wrenching his twisted arm free. Gerard's jaw juddered with the shock of the blow; he tasted blood. The cadet staggered free and went running after his accomplices, slipping on the wet cobbles in his haste.

"Ouch." Gerard rubbed his tingling jaw. "That hurt." He had already decided not to give chase. He bent down over the cadets' victim and put one hand on his shoulder. "Here; take my hand. Can you get up?"

It was only then that he recognized the dark bronzed gold of the boy's hair.

"Toran?"

A sound issued from Toran's mouth that was halfway between a sigh and a groan. *Is he fully conscious?* Gerard forgot the ache of his own jaw and slipped his arm underneath the boy's arms and heaved him upright. Toran lashed out wildly.

"Steady on." Gerard ducked Toran's punch, catching him again as he staggered. "It's me. Gerard Bernay."

Toran suddenly gave a heaving cough and threw up on the cobbles.

"Can you walk?" Gerard asked when Toran had finished. "It's not far back to the Foundry. Lean on me. I'll get you cleaned up there."

"Mm-mm."

Gerard took the mumble as a sign of assent and set off at a slow pace, supporting Toran's weight against him. Toran could hardly put one foot in front of the other and it was all Gerard could to half-drag, half-carry him to the works office. He propped the half-conscious boy up against the wall, holding him upright with his left hand whilst he fumbled with the key to unlock the door. Then he managed to get him inside the unlit entrance hall and maneuver him onto a chair while he went to light a lamp.

The ingenieurs kept a box filled with medical supplies on site as a matter of necessity and Gerard had already learned how to treat a wide variety of minor injuries incurred by the workers. He retrieved the box and hurried back to Toran who had slumped sideways in the chair where he had left him.

Is he concussed? Should I call a doctor? He bent over him and gently touched his shoulder. "Toran," he said, "do you recognize me?" He couldn't help but notice the way the lamp flame had caught fiery glints in the bronzed gold of Toran's hair. *Such an unusual, distinctive shade.*

Toran slowly raised his head, blinking in the warm glow. "Bernay," he said thickly; his lower lip was swollen and a trickle of blood had dripped down his chin onto his shirt.

"I'm going to clean those cuts; this stuff may sting a little but it's an effective antiseptic." Gerard unstoppered the green glass bottle and the pungent smell of the cleansing tincture made his nose prickle as he poured some onto a pad of clean cloth. "We use this on any open wounds the workmen sustain; it's an old local herbal remedy but it works a treat." He dabbed at Toran's grazed face and the boy sucked in his breath sharply as the tincture began to bite.

"What's in that bottle? It burns like—hellfire."

Gerard chuckled. "A powerful alcohol; local firewater, distilled up in the foothills. But it contains healing herbs, too. Lucky I happened by when I did, though. You took quite a beating."

Toran nodded, wincing as he moved his head.

"Friends of yours?"

Toran swore under his breath.

"I see." Gerard carried on dabbing, cleaning the blood from the boy's swollen mouth. "If you want to talk about it anytime, I'm here to listen. I took more than a few beatings in my time at school—and not all from the masters."

"You did?" He heard a note of surprise in Toran's voice. "But you hauled Branville off of me so easily." The words came out rather distortedly; the damage done to his mouth must be making it hard to speak.

"Branville—is that the name of that big lout?"

"The Honorable Elyot B-B-Branville." Toran's teeth had begun to chatter. Gerard took a step back. *The lad's in shock. No surprise, really. Lucky we're well prepared for casualties here.* He fetched a blanket from the infirmary and wrapped it around Toran's shoulders. "I'll brew up some tea," he said. "A mug of strong, sweet tea. That'll warm you up."

"I'm f-f-fine," said Toran, pulling the blanket closer around him.

Gerard ignored him, shoveling fresh coal onto the glowing embers in the iron stove in the corner and setting the filled kettle on the top. The workers at the Iron Works liked their tea and there was always a brew on the hob. The truth was that he needed the hot sweet tea as much as Toran; now that the fury that had flooded his body had died down, he felt weak and a little shaky. Taking on a big bully like the Honorable Branville on an empty stomach had used up more energy than he had realized.

"So, what did you do to upset the Honorable Elyot Branville?" The kettle began to sing on the hob as he lifted Toran's hair to clean a clump of congealing blood from a gash to the side of his forehead. Such soft, luxuriant hair, he found himself thinking as he gently freed the matted strands, more like a girl's than a military cadet's. He was surprised that no officer had yet ordered the boy to have it cropped short.

"I knocked him out. Cold."

Gerard stopped, stepping back to look his patient in the eyes. He was met with a glare of such intense and stubborn defiance that he didn't doubt for one moment the truth of the blunt reply. "So that's why he brought along those other two: for self-protection."

"He insulted my mother. And my family."

The kettle had begun to rattle on the hob; the water was nearly boiling.

"I see. You were defending your mother's good name." As steam began to issue from the spout, Gerard went over, picked up the worn potholder, and set about making the tea. "We've only got black Serindhen tea," he said as he poured the boiling water onto the leaves in the teapot, releasing their powerfully aromatic, malty scent. "It's not a subtle blend, but it keeps us alert when we're working the machinery. Can't afford to be inattentive or nod off in this job." He gave the leaves a brisk stir and went to find two clean tin mugs. Then he poured out the tea; a robust, brown liquid that needed several chips off of the loaf sugar to sweeten its strong malty flavor. "Here," he said, passing a full mug to Toran, "this should help."

Toran gripped the mug with both hands and took a sip. "Ow," he said.

Of course, the hot tea must make his injured mouth sting like hell. Gerard could not help reaching out and tousling the bronze-gold hair in sympathy. "I'll put some cold water in," he said. "It's from the spring, so it's clean. But wait till it cools a little," he added, "or you'll burn your tongue."

After Toran had taken a few more sips, Gerard saw the color begin to return to his pallid face and the hunched shoulders relaxed a little.

"It's a long walk back uphill to the Academy," Gerard said. "How about I call you a cab? I'll just step outside; you rest here."

***

Alone, Toran tried to sip another mouthful of the hot, sugary tea. The soft, sensitive tissue in his mouth and his cut, swollen lip began to smart as the liquid flowed down his throat.

Why is he being so nice to me? I'm not that badly hurt. He felt the prick of tears and blinked fast to try to dispel them before Bernay returned. Blows and harsh words he could deal with. He wasn't used to anyone showing him any sympathy. That wasn't the way at the academy, which prided itself on turning boys into military officers and openly discouraged any show of feelings as unmanly.

He looked around for somewhere to put the mug down; plans were spread out on Bernay's table and he took care not to place it on the neatly inked sketches. And then he leaned closer, intrigued by what he saw. Toran had read enough in his grandfather's books to know that he was not looking at a design to pump water, although there were a few similarities: pistons and cylinders he recognized, but not the elaborate way they were arranged in a circle, fanning out from a central hub. He was so absorbed in trying to figure out how it worked and what it might be for that when Bernay came back in, he jumped, guilty at being found snooping.

"I've found a cab—" Bernay began.

"I didn't mean to spy," Toran blurted out. "But it's fascinating. What's it for?"

A strange expression fleetingly crossed Bernay's face. "That? Oh just some ideas I was playing with," he said dismissively.

"Are you going to build it? Are you making a demonstration model? If you are, could I help?" Toran couldn't disguise his enthusiasm—or his longing to get involved.

"Better not keep the cab driver waiting," Bernay said. "Lean on me; I'll help you to the door."

"I'll do any task, I don't mind how menial." Toran allowed himself to be steered into the hall and toward the door; there was something comforting about the strong, sturdy arm that was supporting him.

"And what about your studies at the academy?" Bernay reminded him as they went out into the night; it was drizzling again and Toran found himself shivering after the warmth of the ingenieur's office as he climbed up into the back of the cab.

"I'll come in my free time. Please say yes."

"Good night, Toran." Bernay closed the door and handed the fare to the driver; as the horse trotted away, Toran saw Bernay turn back into the works without a backward glance. Toran sat back against the worn leather seat and closed his eyes, suddenly aware how tired and battered he felt. But that brief glimpse of the intricate drawings on Bernay's desk had stirred his curiosity and his imagination.

I'll find a way.

***

The moment Gerard returned to his lodgings, he hurried to dig out his notebooks from the bottom of the trunk beneath his bed where they had been gathering dust since his arrival in Paladur.

At the time he'd been too bitter, too confused, to ever want to look at his doctoral thesis again. All he knew was the hurt and humiliation of Edvin's betrayal—and the inescapable fact that by that single indiscretion he had destroyed all his hopes of pursuing an academic career. In his mind, Edvin and his researches had become inextricably entwined, so that he couldn't even bring himself to think about his work without a cloud of self-loathing and resentment enshrouding him.

But now I know that Guy Maulevrier hasn't forgotten me. He still has faith in my ideas. This letter is proof. And the Emperor's competition . . . If I entered, might there be some chance of restoring my reputation and returning to the university?

Dangerous as it was to raise his hopes, only to have them dashed again, he couldn't quell the growing sense of excitement he felt as he took out the notebooks and began to turn over page after page of sketches and designs.

Whatever was I thinking of when I drew these? Some were so ridiculously fanciful that he felt embarrassed to look at them. *I can't have been much older than Toran at the time.*

He had infiltrated the Natural History Department, meticulously examining and drawing bird skeletons, studying the wing structure of albatross and osprey. He had spent days trapping insects with smears of honey and jam in large glass bell jars to observe how they flew. He had been especially fascinated by the way beetles and bumblebees lifted their heavy bodies into the air, but had been forced to conclude that the massive amount of energy they expended in beating their wings to achieve any kind of lift would be difficult to replicate in a machine powerful enough to carry a man.

And then the dragon sightings began.

Gerard considered himself to be a man of science and in his scientific opinion dragons were mythical creatures. So when reports started to appear in the Tielen journals—even the reputable *Tielborg Courier*—that dragons had been spotted at sea and flying over the Palace of Swanholm, his first instinct had been to dismiss them as natural phenomena. His second had been that he wanted to see one of these "dragons" with his own eyes. He had obsessively collected amateur drawings done by those who had witnessed the creatures at first hand. And then, as dragon fever mounted in the capital, came the Great Darkness. The astronomers at the university were thrown into disarray, having not predicted an eclipse. When it was discovered that the phenomenon was not caused by an eclipse, the panic began. It had been extraordinary to see rational and highly educated minds giving way to fear as the debate raged as to whether this was indeed the end of the world.

Which was when Edvin had flung open the door of his room.

"They say we're all going to die, Gerard. I'm afraid. I'm so afraid." Edvin's soft blue eyes had gazed so imploringly into his that he could not help himself; he had crossed the study and taken Edvin in his arms, holding him tightly to stop him trembling. His heart had been overwhelmed with a single thought: *If it is the end of everything, Edvin has chosen to spend his last moments with me—and me alone.*

Before he had been wholly aware of what he was doing, he had found himself tipping Edvin's face upward, brushing his cold lips with his own.

The sketches dropped from Gerard's hands as the memory overwhelmed him. First love, first betrayal. The bitterness still affected him physically; he could feel it rising in his throat like a wash of searing acid. Would it be better to ignore Maulevrier's letter? *I've made a new life for myself here. Do I really want to stir up all the old resentments? Am I man enough to put them behind me and stand up for my rights?*

Gerard abandoned the contents of the first sketchbook as mere juvenile scribblings and began to leaf through the second. This was the project he had been working on for his doctoral thesis: "Designs for a Flying Craft Capable of Safely Transporting a Man through the Air."

"Here they are," he murmured.

He had made models of winged machines that glided on air currents and launched them from the university clock tower, to the cheers of his fellow students. He had tested a design based on winged sycamore seeds; that had been an utter failure, spiraling dizzily round and round before smashing on the flagstones far below. "Bernay's Experiments" became a regular event in the university, attracting crowds of student supporters who began to lay bets on which models would fly and which would crash. The university chancellor was eventually obliged to put a stop to the riotous behavior which was disrupting lectures. But by then Gerard had found a staunch ally in Doctor Maulevrier.

"And that was about the time I made my breakthrough."

He turned the page slowly, almost reluctantly, to look at the last design he had been working on when Edvin had made his accusation. It had been a windy day. The moment he launched the craft from the bell tower, he knew it was a success.

It was as if something buried deep within me awoke and connected with the flyer, keeping it aloft.

He saw it glide above the crowd of upturned faces, over mouths gaping open with a general cry of amazement toward the target: Guy Maulevrier, waiting on the far side of the quad, with hands raised, arms outstretched, to catch it. The flyer, having gained momentum on the way down, didn't merely float gently into his grasp; it knocked him to his knees as he tried to grab hold of it.

What was different about that one? Was it the method I used to launch it?

That was the last time he had seen his prototype. Forced to flee that same night with just a traveling bag, he had bidden a hasty farewell to Maulevrier who promised to send his books on to him when the fuss died down. The books had eventually arrived in a trunk—but, unsurprisingly, none of his models.

I'll just have to make a new working model. He would need wood, canvas, leather, strong glue—and some precision tools. And payday was still two weeks away, at the end of the month. The cab fare for Toran had taken the last of his cash; perhaps Master Cardin would make him an advance.

***

"Next time we'll finish what we started," said Morsan, thumping his fist onto the tavern table.

"Make it a lesson the barbarian boy never forgets," added Aubin, with a laugh.

"Spoil that pretty face of his." Morsan turned to Branville. "Ruin him."

Branville was staring into his half-finished mug of cider, seeing again Toran's blood-stained face, eyes still blazing defiance from the muddy cobbles where he lay, even as he swung in for another punch. Those eyes: hazel flecked with gold, fringed with lashes of darker gold . . . eyes you could drown in.

"Ruin," he repeated dully.

"Send him crying home to his mama," said Morsan, giggling tipsily. "We don't want bad blood polluting the cream of the academy. We don't want his foreign st-stink-stinking – "

"You're drunk, Morsan." Branville, in spite of the alcohol he'd swallowed, felt extraordinarily sober, as if he'd just experienced a revelation. He cuffed Morsan over the head. "Go and sleep it off."

Morsan staggered to his feet, knocking over his chair.

Aubin shook his head. "Morsan can't hold his liquor. What are the odds we'll find him puking his guts up on the parade ground?"

"Not even worth betting on."

"What about that civilian you hit? He threatened to call the watch."

"He won't bother. It was too dark to see." Branville dismissed the idea with one careless wave of the hand.

"But if Arkhel reports us to the colonel—"

"He's too proud. He won't want to admit we beat the shit out of him." But even as he heard himself saying the words, Branville found himself realizing that the matter between himself and Toran Arkhel was far from over.

***

Branville lay in the darkness of the room he shared with Aubin and Morsan, listening to their drunken snoring, watching a brief gleam of moonlight penetrate the slits in the shutters and then slowly fade.

Every time he closed his eyes, he saw Toran's face again as his fist smashed home, distorted with pain and defiance. And every time he saw it, a shiver ran through him, each shiver kindling a slow-burning fire in his loins.

"Ruin him," Morsan had said. *Is that what I really want? To see those gold-flecked eyes glazed with pain . . . or desire? To torment him till he begs for release? To hurt him, humiliate him—break him?* Branville could feel his own breathing quickening at the thought. And the image of his hated rival lying helpless and disheveled on the ground, shirt torn, breeches gaping open, was exciting him in ways he had never imagined possible.

And now I'm hard, damn it.

Toran lay asleep only a short distance away in the First Year Wing. He could go there right now and force him to suck him off.

"Look what you've done to me. This is your fault; take responsibility."

What was he thinking? Such an admission sounded more like a confession of love.

But for some godforsaken reason it only excited him more and there was no ignoring the throb of hard, engorged flesh between his thighs that demanded to be assuaged.

"No, Elyot, don't hurt me. I—I can't."

His hands slid down to touch himself, gripping harder, harder as he imagined his hated rival moaning and writhing beneath him with each thrust until he came, suddenly and with a shuddering intensity that utterly took him aback. Wretched and confused, he curled in on himself, the sticky wetness of his own semen slicking his hands and thighs, telling himself angrily that it was nothing but a drunken delusion.

***

Toran wasn't entirely sure why he felt it necessary to thank his rescuer in person; his father would probably have advised in his usual casual way, "Just send a note with the cab-fare. Nothing too grateful in tone; always remember that you're the heir to Serrigonde."

Toran winced as Lord Ranulph's lazy drawl echoed in his memory; he knew that it wasn't his father's true voice, just one that he affected so often around the Sulien gentry that it had almost erased his original accent.

That might be your way, Father, but I'm not like you; I pay my debts.

Besides, there was something else that was drawing him back to Cardin's Iron Works. Curiosity? A sense of awe at seeing the vast machinery in action? No, it was an insatiable desire to understand the mystery that made the pistons pump and the wheels and cogs turn. The heat, the noise, the raw smell of molten metal . . . he was utterly seduced.

The persistent rain of the past few days had cleared, leaving a clear autumnal sky, smirched only by the plumes of smoke rising from the tall chimneys at the Iron Works. And as Toran approached, the rhythmic pounding of the engines and the mechanical forge hammers made the ground judder beneath his feet. The sound and vibration sent a thrill of anticipation through him but, as he turned the corner, the machinery shuddered to a stop.

"I'm looking for Ingenieur Bernay," he told the watchman at the gate.

"He's over in the boiler house. He's helping them fix a broken valve." The watchman pointed the way and Toran set out across the yard. But before he reached the boiler house, the door opened and Bernay came out, wiping the oil from his hands on a rag.

"My lord." He looked up in surprise as he recognized Toran. "You didn't have to come all the way down here again."

Toran glowered at him. He hated to be made to feel different. "Please don't call me that. I told you: my name's Toran. And I came because I wanted to." He held out the cab fee in an envelope. "Thank you. I didn't want you to be out of pocket. I-I pay my debts." Why was he stammering like a schoolboy? The words that he had rehearsed so carefully sounded stilted and awkward. He felt sure that his face was flaming—and not just with the heat from the furnaces.

Bernay took the envelope. "Thank you," he said. "That was thoughtful of you, Toran, and I appreciate it."

He's accepted it and without any fuss. Toran felt as if a weight had lifted from his shoulders.

"I see the bruising's come out." Bernay lifted his hand as if to tilt Toran's head toward the daylight but Toran instinctively flinched away. "That's quite an impressive shiner you've got there. Did anyone make any comment at the academy?"

"I told them I'd slipped on mud and fallen." Toran was embarrassed by Bernay's concern. "Lorris covered for me. He made some joke about the inevitable consequences of drinking too much of the local cider."

Bernay's look of concern darkened to a frown which made the deep scar over his left brow stand out more starkly. "Is that really what you wanted? For Cadet Branville and his cronies to get away—without even an official reprimand—with what they did to you?"

I thought you understood. Toran said nothing, turning his face away so that Bernay could not see his disappointment. And then he felt Bernay's hand on his shoulder.

"Then I'll make a report."

"No!"

"Branville headbutted me. I'm a civilian, a citizen of Tielen. Does the academy want its reputation sullied by the loutish behavior of three of its cadets?"

"Or does the academy value the generous donations made by Branville's wealthy father more than its reputation?" Toran said sourly.

Bernay opened his mouth to reply—and then closed it again. In the moment's silence Toran heard the clack and hum of the great pistons as the machinery of the Iron Works started up again. Another thrill went through him. *The mighty engine.* He longed to go back into the Rolling Mill and watch the mechanical marvel in action again.

"Very well." Bernay said, raising his voice above the clatter. "If that's what you want, I'll respect your wishes." Then, to Toran's annoyance, he bowed and said formally, "And now, if you'll excuse me, my lord, I must get back to my work."

Why is he so cold today? Toran stood watching Bernay walk away. *Did I offend him? Or am I just being a nuisance?*

Chapter 11

"Today you will be testing the new cannon," announced Colonel Mouzillon, waxed moustache-tips trembling in the autumn breeze as he paced up and down the lines of cadets assembled for roll call. "First Years; this is your chance to impress me and show me your mettle. And don't forget: you will be assisting Master Cardin by ensuring that these splendid new cannon are ready for use in protecting our country."

"Didn't you say that most of 'em are being exported to Tielen?" murmured Lorris to Toran, as they stood, straight-backed, the prickly silver piping on their stiff stand collars irritating their necks.

Toran nodded, reflecting that Lorris was too astute for his own good. *Nothing gets past Lorris.*

"The testing ground is half a mile from here; we'll be using Berse Heath as usual. One detachment will go on ahead to make sure the area is clear of livestock and civilians. The second detachment will accompany the carts transporting the cannon and the third will guard the black powder carts." The colonel stopped in front of Branville and added brusquely, "Second Years: you will instruct the new cadets and demonstrate the correct procedures. This exercise will be conducted exactly as if you were on the field of battle. Any cadet who is incapable of taking it seriously will find himself in danger of immediate expulsion. Dismiss!"

As the cadets scattered to their appointed muster points, Toran found himself silently praying that he had not been assigned to the same detachment as Elyot Branville. But as he approached the group assembling to accompany the gunpowder carts, he saw with a sinking heart that Branville was loudly asserting his authority as a Second Year and already ordering the First Years around.

Is the colonel testing us to see whether we can work alongside each other without coming to blows again?

"You and Branville? An explosive combination," Lorris said and sped off to join the second detachment.

"Ha ha, very funny," Toran called after him. "Change places?"

"Not a chance."

"Cadet Arkhel!" A deep, irritated voice called out. "Get over here. Don't make us all wait."

Toran hurried to join the other cadets in Branville's group. *I have to go through with this.* He noticed that Colonel Mouzillon was watching them, slowly tapping his baton of office against his palm. He hoped that Branville was also aware that he was being closely observed.

"We're in charge of the munitions carts." Branville pointed to the two carts behind him. "Barrels of black powder go in the first cart. Cannon balls, ramrods, fuses, and wadding go in the second. Start loading— and be careful with the powder kegs or we'll all be blown sly-high."

As Toran and another cadet carefully rolled a barrel of black powder up a sturdy plank and onto the back of the cart, he sensed that Branville's gaze was fixed on him. *He's waiting for me to make a mistake. Well, I'm sorry to disappoint you, Elyot Branville, but I don't intend for that to happen today.* He straightened up and, shielding his eyes against the low autumn sun, gazed across the parade ground, suddenly catching sight of a familiar lean figure in a long brown greatcoat overseeing the cannon carts as they set off.

Ingenieur Bernay.

A pang of strong emotion vibrated through him. *If only I could have been placed in the second detachment instead of Lorris.*

"You're in the way, Arkhel!" came a harsh shout. Branville was glaring at him. "Get down and carry on loading."

***

As Gerard Bernay clambered up beside the cart driver of the second cart, weighed down with its load of cannon balls, he caught sight of Toran Arkhel laboring to push a powder barrel up onto the third cart, while a tall, arrogant-looking older cadet looked on, arms folded, shouting orders at him.

I recognize you. You're the bastard who sprung that attack on Toran. What idiot put Toran under your command?

"Ready to leave, sir?" asked the carter.

"Ready when you are." Gerard sat down beside him, grabbing hold of the side of the seat as the cart lurched away. He could not help looking back over his shoulder to see how Toran was faring as the sturdy cart horses lumbered across the parade ground toward the road.

Toran's proud, too proud to accept any help; he won't thank me if I intervene. Best to let the boy fight his own battles.

***

Berse Heath, a bleak, windswept stretch of common ground, lay at the top of the hill above the Academy, affording views to the west over the damp, misty valley in which Paladur nestled. Thistles, nettles, and willow herb grew there in abundance, making it a favorite grazing ground for goats and donkeys, hence the need for the first detachment to clear the area before the trials began.

Gerard watched, coat collar turned up against a cold wind that had begun to spatter a few drops of rain across the heath. Not the best weather for testing cannon, he thought wryly, and yet the wild wind made him feel strangely exhilarated, as if each fresh gust was charging him with renewed energy.

The cadets he was supervising had managed to unload the new cannon and set them up. All that remained now was for the third detachment, under Branville, to pack them with shot and then the trials would begin in earnest. But, as Gerard knew all too well, the loading and firing of cannon was a delicate and tricky procedure, in which the slightest error could result in an expensive and bloody disaster. These young men were the flower of Tourmalise's most influential families; any injury, no matter how it was incurred, would cost the supervising officers their posts and reputations.

"Careful with that powder keg, Arkhel!" shouted Branville. "One slip and you could blow us all to bits."

Gerard clenched his fists, which he had thrust into the pockets of his greatcoat, resisting the urge to go to Toran's aid as he and a fellow First Year struggled to roll the heavy barrel down the ramp to the ground. A faint breath of relief escaped his lips as the task was successfully accomplished.

"Teams of six." Branville was giving out his instructions. "Second Years: you're Number One, the gun captains. You're responsible for priming, aiming and firing. Line up your teams and give each cadet a number."

Branville might be a braggart and a bully, but he knows how to command the cadets' attention.

"Arkhel; you're Number Six? That means you're the powder monkey. What're you waiting for? Fetch the powder!"

Gerard forced himself to turn away from Toran's team to observe the other cadets as they went through the drill.

"All cannon primed and ready to fire, Colonel." Branville saluted Mouzillon. Watching him, Gerard had to grudgingly admit that the tall cadet cut an impressive figure; he exuded an air of aggressive self-confidence which had earned the respect of his fellow cadets to the extent that they had followed his orders with exemplary efficiency. He was also astonished that Toran had managed to stun him with a single punch. *There's no point worrying about that boy; he can look after himself.*

Checking his pocket watch, Gerard also noted that the teams had performed the preparatory tasks in record time.

"Very good, Cadet Branville. If the firing ground is clear, then you may proceed."

Branville called out across the waste ground to a fellow Second Year who had been overseeing the sweep of the heath. "Morsan! All clear?"

"All clear!" came back the faint reply as the cadets under Morsan's command waved green flags from their stations in the undergrowth.

"Detachment One; take cover." Branville turned to teams behind him, waiting for their orders. "Detachment Three; prepare to fire the cannon. On my mark; Cannon One."

"Cover your ears," Gerard called out, preparing to take his own advice. He had learned the hard way that omitting to do so resulted in days of aural fog and ringing. "And stand well back to avoid the rebound."

**

The first cannon was fired successfully. Toran had followed Bernay's instructions, but he still felt the full force of the explosion, a powerful vibration that rippled through his whole body. The cannon ball fell with a thud in a patch of brambles well beyond the target line and one of Morsan's cadets hurried out to place a flag beside it.

"On my mark: Cannon Two," rang out Branville's voice.

It was only then that Toran thought he caught a brief suggestion of movement in the scrubby bushes.

Is someone hiding over there? Why hasn't Detachment One noticed?

"Wait!" he called, but it was too late; Branville's white-gloved hand had come down, giving the order to fire and the second team captain was about to apply the match to the quill fuse. He launched himself forward at a run.

If they see me, they'll abort the next shot . . . I hope.

***

It all happened so swiftly. One moment, the second team captain was lighting the fuse, the next, Gerard saw Toran dashing into the field of fire.

What on earth is he—? Has he lost his mind?

"Toran!" he yelled. The acrid smell of the fast-burning fuse, the cannon-mouth pointing on the intended line of fire directly toward Toran. The other cadets were shouting out to Toran to get out of the way but Toran kept on running.

Extinguish the fuse. But there was no water to fling over the lighted powder quill. Panic and desperation clashed in Gerard's mind, sending a rush of fear from his brain to his fast-beating heart.

He'll be blown sky-high.

In that single instant, Gerard felt as if a gust of wind had invaded his mind, sweeping aside all other thoughts but one*: Divert that cannon ball.*

***

"Get down, you bloody idiot!" Toran vaguely heard Branville's cry carried on a sudden violent gust that swept across the heath, almost toppling him over. At the same moment a little white goat burst, terrified, from the brambles and, bleating, ran across in front of the cannon mouths, pursued by a ragged child.

Toran threw himself at the child, bringing her to ground on the rough tussocks of grass even as the cannon went off and the ball veered over their heads and smashed, off-target, into the bracken nearby where Morsan's detachment were standing watching. As the cadets scattered in alarm, the goat continued its wayward skedaddle across the heath, still bleating.

***

Gerard blinked. He was standing, one arm outstretched, forefinger pointing across the heath toward the place where the cannon ball had fallen.

What happened there?

His mind felt as if it had been scored clean by the tremendous blast of wind that had torn across the heath.

How come I'm still standing? Why didn't it topple me over?

Colonel Mouzillon's cockaded hat had been blown off and several of the cadets were running to recover it.

"Toran? Where's Toran?"

As the cloudy film that had veiled his vision cleared, he saw Toran lying where he had flung himself headlong to avoid the cannonball.

He's not moving.

For a moment Gerard's heart stopped beating. And then he saw Toran roll over, revealing a tatter-coated child that he had been sheltering beneath him.

He saved the little goatherd. Gerard let out a grunt of relief. "Halt the trial!" he shouted. And then he found himself running across the heath toward the student as fast as his legs would carry him, silently offering up a desperate prayer to whichever god might be listening. *Let them both be unharmed.*

***

"Get off, mister!" said a shrill, aggrieved voice and the little goatherd delivered a sharp kick to Toran's shin. He rolled aside, cursing, but managed to shoot out one hand to catch hold of her by the bony wrist.

"Didn't you see the warning flags? Didn't you hear the cannon? You could've been killed."

Big brown eyes, welling tears, stared up at him from a grimy face. "Pa would've killed me if I hadn't gone after Blondine. And now she's run off."

"Arkhel!" The voices of the other cadets began to penetrate Toran's blast-damaged hearing. He knew he was in trouble.

He dug in his breeches pocket and pulled out a coin, pressing it into her hand. "Get out of here. Scram."

"Are you all right, Toran?" Gerard Bernay was hurrying toward him over the rough ground. Others were following but Bernay reached him first, offering his hand to pull him to his feet.

Toran, looking dazedly up at Bernay, caught a brief glitter of crystalline light, clear as drops of rain, illumining the gray eyes that were staring concernedly into his. It sent a shiver through his whole body, as if a storm was about to break overhead.

What's happened to him? He's . . . different.

And then a shadow loomed over them both and he saw Branville's face glowering down at him. "You fuckwit," he said, voice hoarse from running and Toran heard the hint of a tremor—though whether it was fury or concern, he had no idea. "Do you have a death wish? Because, if so, right now I'd be only too happy to make it come true for you."

"Shouldn't you be saving that speech for the First Detachment, Cadet Branville?" Bernay said coldly. "They failed to clear the testing ground of civilians and livestock."

Even as Bernay was speaking, Morsan came stumbling over the tussocks of coarse grass toward them, followed by some of the younger cadets.

"I'm sorry, Branville," he said, with an embarrassed grin. "Deuced lucky for you, Arkhel, that the cannon misfired, eh?"

Branville swung around to face him, dark eyes ablaze with anger. "The cadets in your detachment were careless, Morsan—and that reflects badly on their leader. You'd better conduct another sweep before we proceed any further." Morsan began to stammer an apology but Branville had turned away, ignoring him, to focus the full force of his anger on Toran.

"Cadet Arkhel; get back to your team immediately. You'll be punished for going against orders—even if you did it to save a civilian." And with that he strode back toward the line of cannon.

Toran realized only then that Bernay's hand was still resting on his shoulder in what felt at that moment very much like a protective gesture. Bernay seemed to realize at the same moment, for he withdrew it, briefly giving Toran a reassuring clap on the back, before setting out after Branville.

"I'm sorry, Ingenieur," Toran called, following, realizing that what he had done had not only interrupted the trials but must have inconvenienced Bernay's busy schedule.

"You acted rashly," Bernay said, "but bravely. Morsan's cadets were at fault."

"What will you do about the cannon that misfired?" Toran, hurrying to keep up with Bernay's swift pace, realized that his legs felt as if they were filled with jelly. Delayed shock?

"Test it again," Bernay called back over his shoulder. "One misfire doesn't warrant the expense of melting it down and re-forging it."

"Too expensive?" Toran's legs gave way and he almost tripped headlong over a molehill. Strong hands shot out and grabbed him, holding him upright. He found himself staring into Bernay's gray eyes again— but this time all he saw in them was concern; the earlier shivery glitter was gone. *I must have imagined it; it could have just been a gleam of sunlight through the clouds.*

"Steady there, Toran," Bernay said quietly. "You just cheated death; don't push yourself too hard."

"Ingenieur Bernay." Colonel Mouzillon had retrieved his hat. "I really must apologize for the impulsive behavior of our boys."

"No problem, sir, I assure you." The warm, steadying grip was relaxed as Bernay let Toran go and went over to confer with the colonel. "I'm just relieved that no one was injured."

Toran continued slowly back toward his team, aware that his fellow cadets were watching him in awed silence. Lorris broke ranks and hurried across to greet him.

"Are you all right? You saved that girl's life! Imagine the fuss if she'd been hit by a cannonball."

Other First Years surrounded him, slapping him on the back and mussing his hair. Toran allowed himself to bask in the warmth of their congratulations. *Am I really all right?* he wondered shakily. *I just reacted to what I saw; I didn't even stop to think.*

"Cadets! Who gave you permission to leave your posts?" Branville roared, eyes dark as a thundery sky. "Get back to your detachments!" The boys scattered and Toran saw Bernay signaling to the team leaders.

"The trials will continue," announced the colonel, "exactly as planned."

***

A troubled sunset bruised the western sky, dirty gray cloud, blotched with stains of red, like dried blood. The tired cadets pushed and heaved the cannon back up onto the carts and the slow, cumbersome procession back down the hill began. The wind had dropped and rain was threatening again; they would be lucky to reach the academy without a soaking.

Gerard caught the occasional glimpse of Toran's bronze-gold hair (difficult to miss among the darker heads of his fellow Tourmaline cadets) as the boy dutifully followed Branville's orders. Since the incident, he had been too busy noting the results of the trials for Maistre Cardin and measuring how far the cannonballs had been propelled to take stock of what had just happened. He was aware from time to time of a faint, chill tingling in his head but he forced himself to ignore it; there was work to be done first. But as he went back to the carts, he couldn't resist a last glance to check that Toran was all right. Branville was overseeing the covering of the powder barrels with thick tarpaulin to protect them from the coming storm. *Let's hope that Branville doesn't have a go at him on the way down.* For a moment he wondered whether to abandon the cannon and hitch a ride on the munitions cart to ensure that the two cadets didn't come to blows again.

As the carts carrying the cadets left the darkening heath, Gerard took his place on the first of heavier wagons that were transporting the cannon back to the Iron Works. The carter spoke softly to his dray horses, coaxing them over the stony ground toward the winding road that led down into Paladur. Gerard suddenly felt a sense of numbing weariness settle over him. He was so tired that every bone, every sinew in his body ached. *What's up with me? Am I coming down with a fever? It was cold up on the heath, but I'm well used to such weather.*

"Are you all right, Ingenieur?" he heard the carter asking as if from a great way off. "You don't look too good."

"Just a little weary," Gerard said, forcing a laugh. "It's been a long—and eventful—day."

"Shall I drop you near your lodgings?"

"And then who would ensure that the cannon are safely locked up? Master Cardin wouldn't be best pleased if thieves stole the Emperor's new cannon in the night." Gerard tried to make a joke of it but his temples had begun to throb; he leaned back against the seat and closed his eyes as the cart lurched and juddered back down the hill.

***

Toran was ravenously hungry by the time they turned into the academy grounds—but above the rattle of wheels over cobblestones, he could hear Branville telling his cadets that no one would be allowed to enter the mess hall until the powder casks were securely stowed away in the magazine.

"And before you all start griping that it's unfair, let me remind you that I'm the one obliged to lock up, so I'll be the last to get my dinner."

Night had fallen and covered lanterns had to be lit well away from the munitions so that the cadets could see their way safely into the pitch-dark vaults. But at last the final cask was rolled inside, Branville cast a last critical glance over the cadets' efforts, and the lanterns were removed.

Toran climbed the steps from the cool vault of the magazine and came out into the night to see Elyot

Branville leaning against a column in the lantern-lit colonnade.

"You've got some explaining to do, Arkhel," he said, straightening up. "What on earth possessed you to take such a risk today?"

Toran glared at him. "Why are you wasting your time with me? Shouldn't you be reprimanding Morsan?"

"That's Cadet Morsan to you, Arkhel." Branville came closer. Uncomfortably close. "For a First Year, you don't show much respect for your elders and betters."

Toran took a step back. *Where exactly is this leading?* The feeling of unease increased in intensity as he became aware that the others had gone on ahead to the mess hall and he was alone with Branville.

"That ingenieur; Bernay. He spoke to you very familiarly. Called you 'Toran'. Friend of yours?"

"What if he is?"

"I'm just surprised that Lord Toran Arkhel allows a commoner to call him by his first name."

Toran took another step back, realizing— rather belatedly—that he had allowed himself to be maneuvered into a corner. His only means of escape would be to make a run for it between the columns, which meant darting straight past Branville. And though his first thought was that Branville was intent on giving him another thrashing, he sensed another far more disturbing aura emanating from the older cadet.

"Bernay's tutoring me." It wasn't exactly a lie.

Branville suddenly lunged, his palm hitting the wall just above Toran's head as he leaned further in toward him. Toran felt a slick of sweat break out on his forehead.

"Tutoring you? In what, precisely?" Branville was regarding him with an unreadable look in his dark eyes.

"It's none of your damned busin—"

"Toran!" Lorris's voice rang out across the courtyard as he and a couple of the other First Years came running up. "We've been waiting for you. The mess hall's going to finish serving in five minutes."

Toran heard Branville sigh. The imprisoning arm dropped back to his side as he moved aside to let Toran go. "You'd better not keep your friends waiting," he said dryly. "Scram."

"What was that about?" Lorris said to Toran as they made their way toward the noisy mess hall.

"I have no idea," said Toran, sniffing the savory aroma of beef and peppercorn stew wafting out into the misty night. His empty stomach rumbled. He cuffed Lorris amicably. "Thanks for coming to rescue me. I'm starving! Let's go and eat."

***

Afterward, Gerard could not even remember how he made his way back to his lodgings, or climbed the creaking stair.

Sleep. I need to sleep. In the darkness, he stumbled across the room, stubbing his toe on the table leg, wanting only to feel his way to his bed and collapse onto it. But before he reached the bed, he caught a glimpse of two faint points of light glittering in the shadows in front of him. *Cat's eyes?* he thought stupidly. *Is one of the landlady's cats sitting on the mantelpiece, staring at me?*

Exhausted as he was, he forced himself to take a second look—and found himself staring at his own reflection in the mirror above the fireplace.

My eyes. What's wrong with my eyes? He rubbed his aching lids, blinking, and peered again.

Twin silvered stars glimmered back at him . . . no, not so much silver as the translucence of falling rain when a brief shaft of sun pierces the windblown clouds.

What am I babbling about? Rain, clouds, wind . . .

He shakily raised one hand to cover the growing ache behind his eyes. *It must just be a migraine, brought on by the stress of the day.* Gerard had occasionally been brought to bed with crippling headaches in the past and each one had been preceded by the appearance of whirling pinwheels of flickering light; perhaps this was another manifestation of the same warning symptom. *If I sleep it off, all should be back to normal by the morning. As long as I don't get the nausea too.*

He staggered back toward his bed and collapsed onto it, clutching his throbbing temples, inwardly praying for sleep and oblivion.

Something happened to me up on Berse Heath.

Chapter 12

"'By order of his Imperial Majesty, Eugene of New Rossiya, a competition to design a flying craft capable of sustained aerial travel is announced.'" Colonel Mouzillon adjusted his monocle as he read the Emperor's proclamation to the assembled cadets. "'The winner must be able to demonstrate that his design is airworthy and safe for the pilot. The prize: a gold medal, and a lectureship awarded by the University of Tielborg, as well as the establishment of a new department dedicated to the development of mechanical flying craft.'"

A flying craft. Toran felt his heart beat faster. He exchanged glances with Lorris whose attention had evidently been caught by the words: University of Tielborg.

"Even though Tourmalise is not part of the Rossiyan Empire, the Emperor has sent details of this competition to all academies and universities in the Western Quadrant," continued the colonel. "And we have decided that Paladur Military Academy will enter. Major Bauldry will lead the project; anyone wishing to volunteer should stay behind after the daily inspection to sign up."

A flying craft. Toran's mind was racing with possibilities. *A chance at last to develop Grandpa Denys's designs.*

"Are you going to sign up?" Lorris whispered.

"You bet!" Toran whispered back. He was squinting into the over-bright morning sun to try to get a better look at Major Bauldry's face; the major taught classes in battle strategy and weaponry to the older cadets but didn't deign to instruct the First Years. Even though the major walked with a limp (a bullet through the knee, sustained in the last Allegondan campaign) his chestnut hair had only silvered on temples and neatly-trimmed sideburns and he exuded an air of fiercely keen intelligence. *He won't suffer fools gladly; I'll really have to prove myself to be accepted.*

About a dozen cadets from all three years stayed behind to volunteer, forming a line to sign up with the major. Toran found himself at the back of the queue, uneasily shifting from foot to foot as he tried to make out who else was interested enough to risk Major Bauldry's scrutiny.

"You there, first volunteer; you can be my adjutant and write down each candidate's details. I want to see neat handwriting—or you're off the project."

As Toran drew closer to the front of the queue, he heard the brusque questions the major was firing at each applicant and began to work out his own answers in advance. So it was only as the volunteer ahead of him saluted and withdrew that he saw Major Bauldry's "secretary" was none other than Elyot Branville.

"Name and year," barked Major Bauldry.

"Toran Arkhel, First Year, sir," Toran said, gazing straight ahead, yet only too aware of Branville's stare that seemed to bore straight through him.

"You're the only First Year to apply, Cadet Arkhel. What makes you think you already know enough to compete with your elders and betters?"

Toran swallowed hard, sensing Branville's stare hardening. Branville wanted him to make a fool of himself in front of the others. *Well, I'm not going to give you that pleasure, Elyot Branville.* "I wouldn't dare to presume, sir," he said boldly, "but I was trained in elementary mechanics by my grandfather. If such skills would be useful on the project, I'd be happy to offer them."

Major Bauldry gave a noncommittal grunt. "Exactly how elementary?"

"I helped him maintain the pumping works on his estate."

"Didn't he have servants to perform such tasks?"

"Indeed he did—but as he designed the machinery, he preferred to look after it himself."

"Hmmph. You might be useful to us. But you're on probation, Arkhel; if you're not up to the job, you're off the project. Now get back to your class; you're late."

"Thank you, sir." Toran saluted and hurried away, heart singing that he had been selected.

***

Gerard awoke from a turbulence of troubled dreams. His head still churned with rushing wind and storm-driven clouds. But at least the crippling headache had gone. A wan daylight penetrated the cracks in the ill-fitting shutters.

How long have I been asleep?

And then he heard the distant chiming of the clock above Paladur's Guild Hall.

Eight strokes? *Damn it all, I overslept.* He threw back the blanket, forgetting until that moment that he had collapsed into bed fully clothed the night before.

I need a good hot bath and clean clothes. He drew one hand over his stubbled cheeks. *And a shave. Not to mention I'm empty as a drum; no supper last night and only a hunk of bread and cheese at midday yesterday.*

The notebook in which he'd carefully jotted down the results of the trials lay on the table; he picked it up, flicking through the pages in the dim light. The figures were more than acceptable, they were exceptionally good. But Maistre Cardin would be waiting for the information so that he could release the cannon for transportation to the port and thence on to Tielen. He grinned wryly as he remembered the colonel's inspirational speech to his cadets in which he had informed them that the cannon were to be used to defend Tourmalise; the Emperor's coffers had paid for this shipment. *Cardin's cannon must be the best in the western quadrant for Emperor Eugene to come to us above any other manufacturer.*

"If I deliver the results first, then I can ask Maistre Cardin to release me to get some breakfast. What I'd give now for a strong cup of coffee." He went to open the shutters but had to shade his eyes as the pale morning light poured in. *Perhaps I'm not yet rid of the damned migraine.* Dazzled as he was by the daylight, the disturbing ripples distorting his vision from the previous evening had gone; nevertheless he went over to the mirror above the mantel to check.

Above the shadow of stubble darkening his unshaven face, alien eyes stared back at him, still gray, but touched with an unmistakable glimmer of silvery translucence.

What's happened to me? He passed a hand across his eyes and checked again, leaning in to the mirror until his breath fogged the glass. *Did some of the powder sear my sight? No, I would have been rolling around in agony if that had happened.* Gerard had once seen a gunner caught by a misfiring fuse quill and he had never forgotten the wretched man's screams—or the terrible damage done to his face and eyes.

He sat down, trying to order his wildly careering thoughts. *All was going well until Toran ran out to save the goatherd girl. After that . . .* There was a hole in his memory. The next thing he remembered was bending over Toran to help him to his feet.

Am I sick? Is this some kind of disease that affects the eyes? Should I consult a physician? Will Master Cardin grant me an hour or two's leave to find an oculist? I'm late already . . .

***

It was not until the end of a long day filled with classes and weapons drills that Toran had the opportunity to return to the room he shared with Lorris and dig under his bed for the trunk he had brought from Serrigonde. Delving beneath his neatly folded civilian clothes, his fingers closed on the worn leather binding of Grandpa Denys's notebook. He went to his desk and, by the weak flame of the single oil lamp, began to read. The sight of his grandfather's strong handwriting gradually becoming spindly and increasingly illegible as illness and age caused his mind to deteriorate filled him with sadness.

Yet these were the designs Lord Denys had been convinced would restore the family fortunes and save the manor from the bailiffs. As Toran turned the pages, memories flooded his mind: hours spent in the stable his grandfather had converted into a workshop, sawing, measuring, gluing, to make working models. He could still smell the fishy odor of the glue, mingled with fresh sawdust, and still hear his grandfather's deep voice, reminiscing about his last campaign, chuckling to himself. "Of course, if we'd had flyers like this one, we could have swooped in over the Allegondans' heads and taken the pass. I'd love to have seen the looks on their faces!"

The door quietly opened; Toran looked up and saw that Lorris was back from a debate of the academy Humanities Society. His face was flushed; Toran caught a whiff of claret on his breath.

"Still working?" Lorris said, stretching out on his bed. "It's past midnight."

"Looking through my grandfather's designs. He was convinced he'd made a breakthrough . . . but then he suffered an apoplexy and died soon after."

"I'm sorry," Lorris said, sitting up. "It sounds as if you were close."

"He was an inspiring man." Toran swallowed to clear the tightness in his throat; he had often felt closer to his grandfather than his own father and remembering the way he had died left him bereft all over again. "I promised him I'd carry on with his work. He couldn't speak by then . . . but he lifted his hand. I think he understood."

"Look, Toran, if I were you, I'd do all I could to find a safe place to keep this notebook."

"Because of Branville?"

"Now he knows that you're rivals, I wouldn't put it past him to set one of his cronies to spy on you."

"But I never imagined that the Honorable Elyot Branville would have had the talent—or the interest—for entering a contest like this."

"He may act the bully, but I heard that he came top of his year in the academy examinations. He doesn't like to lose. You're a threat to him in more ways than one."

***

Dusk brought down a dismal drizzle on the garrison town. Toran stuck his hands in his pockets, glowering at the dreary sky which still bore a few faint streaks of angry red where the sun was setting in the far west.

Why is it always so damp in Paladur? The buildings are constantly streaked with rain and there's moss growing between the cobbles.

A lamplighter was lighting the lamp posts at the corner of the street; the faint glow was reflected on the wet pavements, like a slick of oil.

"Spare a coin, mister." The thin voice took him by surprise; looking down, he saw a ragged boy holding out a tin cup. Dark, sunken eyes stared hopefully at him from out of a dirt-smeared face. So even prosperous Paladur had its beggars. *"It's not their fault they were born to poverty,"* he heard his mother's voice saying, as she gently chided him for ignoring a poor woman begging from door to door. *'We, the more fortunate ones, must always be generous."*

Soon we could find ourselves out on the streets too if my father's mad venture doesn't pay off.

He dug in his pocket and found a coin which he flipped into the cup. The boy stared at his prize and let out a wail of disapproval. "Here, mister, can't you spare a bit more? That's hardly the price of a pasty."

Toran glared at him and the child took off at high speed, almost colliding at the end of the street with a man who came around the corner, head down, clutching a broad-brimmed hat to his head.

"Oi! Are you blind? Look where you're going!" shrilled the boy indignantly, swerving.

"Ingenieur Bernay?" Toran called out, surprised to see his mentor walking back toward the Iron Works from the town, rather than coming away. "I need to talk with you. There's this competition and the academy is going to enter, so I thought—"

"Toran?" The man stopped and peered at Toran in the gloom. Toran saw, to his surprise, that Bernay was wearing spectacles. "You mean the Emperor's competition? This makes us rival entrants, so don't say another word."

"*You're* going to enter as well?"

"That was my intention." The gathering gloom and the broad brim of Bernay's hat made it hard for Toran to make out his expression.

"Does that mean you can't tutor me any longer?" It hadn't occurred to him that they might find themselves competing for the same prize.

"It could make things difficult." Toran detected a distinctly reserved, distant note in the ingenieur's voice. "I imagine the academy would not approve."

"I see." Toran's head drooped. He had never imagined that in volunteering to be part of the team at the academy he would be placing himself in direct rivalry with Bernay. "So?"

"I believe the correct protocol is to wish each other good luck," said Bernay gently, "and may the best design win." With this, he nodded farewell to Toran and continued on his way toward the Iron Works. Toran, so disappointed that he could not even find the words to reply, just stood in the drizzle until the sound of Bernay's footfall died away into the night.

Chapter 13

"I've narrowed down the entries for the Emperor's competition to the two most promising: Branville's and Arkhel's," announced Major Bauldry, tapping each drawing in turn with the tip of his cane as the cadets crowded around.

Toran felt a swell of pride that his work was still in contention—until he looked up and saw that Branville had fixed him with a smoldering stare.

It's just between Branville and me? Not good.

"Branville has devised the most practical and elegant solution to the flying craft itself—but I fear, my boy, that your design won't get very far without a more viable means to lift and propel it successfully through the air than with gas-filled balloons. Unless, of course, you've found a way to control the winds?"

Branville's dark brows drew together in a scowl at the playful jibe, but, to Toran's surprise, the older cadet didn't arrogantly challenge the major's judgment.

"Arkhel."

Toran started, realizing that the major had moved on from Branville to give his verdict on his entry.

"Your design is far too fanciful; dragonflies may use double wings to stay aloft, but a man-made double-winged craft is almost certainly doomed to fail." Smothered snorts of laughter greeted the major's judgment; Toran, eyes fixed on the floor, forced himself to endure the others' amusement at his expense. "However, your design for an engine is extremely original." The laughter died away. "Is it based on your grandfather's research?"

"Yes, sir." Toran looked up and saw that the major was nodding approvingly.

"Then I propose that we combine the best elements from each design; we'll build Arkhel's engine, place it in Branville's craft, and compete with the best ingenieurs of the empire!"

The other cadets applauded the major's verdict.

"But we'll need new drawings to work from to build our prototype. Branville and Arkhel, you'll have to get to work straight away."

"Together?" Toran heard himself ask, all his pleasure at being selected fast melting away. *Is this just another scheme devised by Colonel Mouzillon to make Branville and me cooperate?* Branville had said nothing so far but his louring expression told Toran only too well how he felt about the project.

"And the rest of the team will assemble the materials to construct a scale model. Although where we'll go to get the metal parts made for your machine, Arkhel . . ."

"A clockmaker?" Toran suggested. And then he had an inspiration. "How about Master Cardin's foundry?"

"They forge bloody great cannon down there, you idiot," he heard Branville mutter scornfully, "not fiddly little pieces of metalwork."

"I could ask Ingenieur Bernay if he knows anyone with the necessary skills." *Then I'll have the ideal excuse to go to see him again.* Toran was delighted with his plan. *I know he told me we were rivals, but . . .*

***

"So your design's been selected to represent the academy for the Emperor's competition? Well done." Gerard Bernay smiled at Toran as they crossed the yard, Toran hurrying to keep up with the ingenieur's brisk stride.

"My design for an engine." Toran corrected him. "The major's combining it with Branville's craft."

Bernay stopped. "Branville? Not that dark-haired bully?" Bernay's smile had faded. "How do you feel about having to collaborate with him?"

Toran wasn't sure he knew. "We'll be supervised by Major Bauldry," he said, shrugging Bernay's concern aside. "And that's why the major gave me permission to come to ask for your help."

"*My* help?"

"We have to make a scaled-down version of the craft to test it. And the major was wondering if you could help us forge the parts for the engine. The academy will pay for the materials." Toran looked anxiously at Bernay, fervently hoping that he would agree. But Bernay's expression was hard to read.

"I told you before, Toran," he said, "that I'm also a competitor. It really wouldn't be ethical for me to assist the academy."

"Surely if you're just helping us by making the parts to our specifications, it wouldn't be seen as unethical?"

"And if I were to secretly incorporate some of your ideas into my own work?"

"But you wouldn't—" Toran began and then stopped.

"*I* wouldn't, but there are others who wouldn't be so scrupulous."

Toran caught a chill glint in Bernay's gray eyes behind the thick lenses of his new spectacles. He could not help staring, distracted by a thought that had been bothering him for some while. "Forgive me, Ingenieur," he began awkwardly, "but I can't help noticing that you're wearing spectacles. Your eyes—um—you didn't suffer an injury to your sight up on Berse Heath?"

"An injury? No, no . . ." Bernay said, a little too hastily, Toran reckoned. "Eyestrain, headaches, caused by too much close work in poor light, that's all." He put a hand on Toran's shoulder. "Make sure you don't make the same mistake when you're studying."

"I'll do my best," said Toran, gazing up into the ingenieur's face. Suddenly he was very aware of the warm, firm pressure of Bernay's hand on his shoulder. *He's talking to me like an equal, a fellow ingenieur.* The realization sent heat flooding through him and he looked swiftly away, conscious that he was blushing like a girl. In the same instant, Bernay withdrew his hand. "I think it best that I don't help you out this time," he said, his remote, professional self again. "I'm sorry, Toran. However," and he fished inside his greatcoat pocket and brought out a little card, handing it to Toran, "this clockmaker is a genius. Tell him I sent you."

Toran read, "Gieffroy Ferrant, Horlogier: Clocks and Watches Mended."

"I'd much rather it was you," he said accusingly, not caring what Bernay thought. But the ingenieur merely laughed and walked off, one hand raised in a nonchalant farewell wave.

***

Toran walked slowly back along the canal path, desultorily kicking at a stray pebble.

Why did Bernay send me away again? There's so much I want to learn from him. Why do we have to be rivals in this competition?

A rather too forceful kick propelled the pebble into the murky water where the splash disturbed a moorhen in the rushes, sending it squawking across the canal in a disgruntled flurry of ruffled black feathers.

Or is it because of what happened up on the heath? Yes, I was reckless. But if I hadn't, that child could have been killed.

Yet the memories that lingered so vividly were not of his furious dash across the tussocky heath, or of flinging the child to the ground just as the cannon ball whistled so close overhead. What haunted his dreams was the reassuring sound of Bernay's voice, the firm pressure of his hand on his shoulder, that

inexplicable sensation—just as a few minutes ago—
that his presence made everything all right.

A heavily-laden barge was sailing toward him, the
bargee leading his plodding horse. Toran stood back
to let them pass, nodding a greeting to the bargee.

Bernay's come to my rescue twice now. Toran was
suddenly overwhelmed by the realization that he must
seem nothing more than a liability to the ingenieur: a
callow, over-privileged youth, too impulsive to be of
any real use. *God, what a brainless idiot I must look to
him.* He felt his face flaming again, and even though
there was no one but the bargee in sight on the weed-
overgrown tow-path, he wanted to crawl into the
bushes and hide.

*But I really want him to help us. How can I make him
change his mind? What would Grandpa Denys have said
to me? "Have you no backbone, boy? Go for it! Have
faith in yourself."* The old soldier's gruff tones rumbled
through his memory—and next moment, he found he
had turned right around and was heading back toward
the Iron Works, his pace increasing with every step.

***

Gerard Bernay was so absorbed in his calculations
that it was a moment before he became aware that
someone had entered the office.

"Yes?" he said absently.

"I don't want a clockmaker; I want *you.*"

The pencil dropped from Gerard's fingers; he
spun around on the draughtsman's stool to see Toran
standing there, red-faced and breathless. Had he run
all the way back?

Gerard's first reaction was one of irritation at being interrupted. But then the irritation inexplicably evaporated.

"Damn, but you're persistent."

"So you'll do it?" Toran said between gasps.

"I have no idea why you should trust me this much. What happens if I steal your ideas? Or sabotage your model?"

"But you won't. You're not that kind of man."

Gerard let out a slow, resigned sigh. "Very well; I'll help you—but you'll do the work, under my supervision. Otherwise you'll learn nothing and I'll have wasted my time." In spite of his misgivings, he was touched by the way Toran had blurted out such a vehement declaration. *I suppose I must see something of my younger self in him . . .*

"But that—that's wonderful!" Toran was gazing at him, hazel eyes brimming with emotion. Gerard looked away, dazzled.

"And you'll work hard. Precision molding on a small scale takes a great deal of concentration and skill." *I mustn't get carried away by his enthusiasm; someone has to keep a cool head or we'll risk making errors.*

"I told you before; I'm not afraid of hard work." Toran drew himself up to his full height. "When can we start?"

"Just don't bring Elyot Branville down here, understand?"

Toran laughed. "Don't worry; I won't let him anywhere near your inner sanctum."

"Then it's agreed." Gerard held out his hand. "Now show me those plans."

***

The great pistons and wheels in the Engine Hall slowly shuddered to a halt; the men secured them for the night and extinguished any lights or fires still burning in the works and went home, leaving only the night watchman on duty.

Gerard came back to his office from his nightly tour of the silent works to see a faint light still burning. *Is Toran still here? He should have gone back to the academy over an hour ago.*

"Toran?" he called as he opened the door. There was no reply. By the guttering wick in the oil lamp, he saw that Toran had fallen asleep over his drawings, his head resting on his arm, still gripping his pencil as if he was so immersed in his designs that he was determined to battle on to get the corrections done.

Gerard leant forward and gently pried the pencil from his fingers; Toran let out a soft, halting little sigh but did not wake. *He must be exhausted.* Gerard could not restrain a wistful smile. *Was I like this too when I was eighteen? He's certainly dedicated. No, more than that—obsessed.* The little diagrams beneath Toran's arm, onto which a loose lock of bronze hair had strayed, were meticulously drawn, displaying a draftsman's skill well beyond his years. *Obsessed . . . and gifted.* He felt a sudden dark shiver of pain around his heart. *And it's hard to develop that gift when others around you, jealous of your talent, set out to belittle and crush you.*

His hand stole out and tucked the straying lock of hair back in place. "Time to wake up, Toran," he said, lips close to the young man's ear. For a moment, all self control melted away and he was unable to stop himself from gently kissing the nape of his neck, just below the hairline where the odd bronze tendril had escaped the academy barber's rough shears.

Toran stirred and sat up, blinking, eyes unfocused.

Guilty, ashamed, Gerard stepped back, his heart thudding so loud he was sure Toran must be able to hear it. "You fell asleep," he said.

"I? Oh, hell." Toran leapt up. "What time is it?"

Gerard pointed to the works clock on the wall.

"Past eight!" Toran grabbed his jacket and began pulling it on, doing the gilt buttons up in the wrong order in his haste. "I'll be gated—and I haven't got an exeat."

"But Major Bauldry gave you a special permission, didn't he?" Gerard, turned away to hide his confusion which was as great as Toran's, although for entirely different reasons. "Don't worry; this project is all for the glory of the academy. I'm sure the good major will speak up in your defense if you tell him where you've been and—"

But Toran had already fled, the door banging shut behind him.

How could I? Gerard sank down on the chair, furious with himself for giving way to temptation.

***

"So where are the parts for this famous engine of yours?" Branville gazed up from the work bench on which he and his team were busily constructing the frame of the prototype.

Toran heard the sneering hostility in his voice but merely said, "They'll be ready soon."

But Branville was not so easily appeased. He put down the brush which he had been using to glue sailcloth to one of the wing frames. "Soon?" He placed himself in front of Toran, blocking his way. "This is only the prototype. If your engine doesn't work, you're going to have to make modifications before we build the competition entry."

Toran sighed. *Why do we have to collaborate? He'll find fault with everything I do. I can almost smell the hatred on his breath.* "I'm going back to collect them tomorrow. It takes time to craft them to scale. And Ingenieur Bernay—"

"Ingenieur Bernay again, eh?" repeated Branville. "You seem to like spending your time with this Bernay fellow, Arkhel. Just what's the attraction? Is it his . . . equipment? Perhaps he possesses a *tool* superior to any *tool* to be found here at the academy."

Morsan let out a snort of laughter.

"He happens to have the expertise to help us. Us," Toran repeated, glaring at Branville, then at Morsan. He didn't like the way Branville was twisting his words, making lewd insinuations about his mentor.

"What are you calling this craft?" Major Bauldry picked up the frame, weighing it in his hands, examining it with a critical eye. "It must have a name."

"The *Eagle*," said Branville without hesitation.

"Really? More of a buzzard in size, I'd say, than an eagle."

Some of the cadets sniggered at the major's observation. Toran saw Branville's face flush dark red.

He can't take a joke. Yet Eagle *is a good name . . . a surprisingly apt one.* "How about *Eaglet,* then?" he heard himself suggesting. "Or *Aiglon,* in the old tongue? When we make the craft full-size, we can call it *Eagle.*"

In the ensuing silence, he became aware that Branville was staring at him, stumped, for once, for words.

"*Aiglon* sounds good to me," said the major. "Branville?"

Branville curtly nodded his assent.

***

"Damn." Gerard had been so caught up in his own thoughts that it was only the slip of the chisel and the sharp pain as it sliced into his finger that brought him back to himself with a jolt. "Idiot; what am I doing, day-dreaming when I should be paying attention?" Blood dripped into the molten metal, making it sizzle and hiss. Cursing, he drew out his clean handkerchief to wrap around the gash. And as he pressed the edges of the cut together, he had an unexpected moment of *déjà vu.*

I've done this before. He had been in the university laboratory, toiling into the small hours to finish making the working parts for his sky-craft and, in his sleep-starved clumsiness, he had cut his hand, mingling his blood with the molten metal he was pouring into the molds he had fashioned.

His face seared by the intense heat, Gerard stood back, watching as the steam cleared and the contents of the molds began to cool. *It didn't cause a problem then, in spite of my concerns, so I just have to trust that it'll be all right this time.*

"You all right over there, Ingenieur?" Mahieu, who had been assisting him (persuaded to stay late by the promise of a steak and porter supper at Pobjoy's chop house afterwards) glanced up.

"Nicked myself," Gerard said, grimacing.

Mahieu shrugged. "Never remove your gauntlets till the work's done. Isn't that what Maistre Cardin insists on?"

"Guilty, as charged."

Mahieu grinned. "Not like you to be careless, Ingenieur. But why did you take on this extra work for the academy when you've been so busy?"

"A favor for a friend." Gerard was staring at the contents of the molds, hoping that he wouldn't have to cast them again; Toran would be back in the morning, eager to start assembling his engine and he didn't want to disappoint him.

"I'll finish off here while you get that cut cleaned up."

***

"*Génie,*" Toran murmured as he stared in wonder at all individual parts of his engine laid out on Bernay's table, each piece placed upon the detailed drawing the ingenieur had used as a template. "They're so small." He picked one up and began to examine it minutely. "But perfect."

"They'll need some fine-tuning before they're ready to be assembled," said Bernay. "I've brought files and machine oil. If you like I'll give you a hand."

158

"I don't know how to thank you—" Toran began but Bernay shook his head.

"No need for thanks. Frankly, I enjoyed the exercise; I haven't had so much fun since I was a student." He grinned at Toran and Toran found himself grinning back, surprised to see how much younger Bernay looked when he smiled.

"Let's get started, then," he said, picking up a file.

***

"My grandfather had a theory." Toran had never shared Grandpa's Denys's philosophy with anyone else before. He had come to look forward to these sessions with Gerard Bernay which reminded him of the times he had spent helping his grandfather in his workshop. He felt so at ease with Bernay that he had begun to chat away quite unselfconsciously.

"Oh?" Bernay glanced up from the tiny cog he was carefully filing. "About what?"

"He used to say that a gifted ingenieur was born, not made. He said that any project they touched would be instilled with a special quality. He called it '*Génie.*'"

"*Génie*?"Bernay laid down the file, smiling. "An apt name. Did he believe he was born with the gift?"

Toran shook his head. "No. But he thought I might have been."

"I wish I could have met your grandfather."

"You would've got on well. I really miss him." Toran was so busy concentrating on making two of little cogs fit together that it was only as the mechanism began to move that he realized what he had said. He looked up gratefully at Bernay over the mechanism, unashamedly blinking away the tears that had filled his eyes. He had known instinctively that Bernay would understand where others, even Lorris, made fun of his obsession.

"How did you do that?" Bernay was staring at the whirring machine. "What's powering it?"

"I—I don't know." Toran stared too. Bernay came closer. The intricate little mechanism whirred faster. "Move further off." Bernay slowly backed away, not taking his eyes from the little engine. As he retreated, the moving parts slowed again.

"It wasn't me," Toran said. "It seems to be you."

Gerard shook his head in disbelief. "It must be some residual momentum that we created when we were assembling the parts."

It was only much later when Toran had returned to the academy that Gerard remembered that his own blood had mingled with the molten metal from which the parts had been forged, exactly as had happened in the university laboratory.

Something in my blood sets the mechanism in motion?

But the thought was so irrational and unscientific that he almost laughed out loud. A mere coincidence; any ingenieur worth his salt would find a credible reason for the puzzling phenomenon.

Chapter 14

The cadets of the Paladur Military Academy marched briskly onto the frosty parade ground and lined up for inspection, chins jutting up over their stiff collars, gilt buttons gleaming in the pale winter morning sun, boots freshly polished.

Colonel Mouzillon, followed by Major Bauldry and the other staff, walked slowly along the rows, adjusting an epaulette here, tutting over a scuffed boot there, finally climbing onto the raised platform from which he usually dismissed his charges. But, instead, Major Bauldry barked, "At ease!" and the colonel removed a letter from his pocket which he raised high so that the imperial seal could be glimpsed.

"I have just been informed that the academy's design has made it through to the next round of the Emperor's competition."

Toran, whose thoughts had been miles away, heard the words "design" and "competition".

"Colonel Nils Lindgren, the Emperor's representative, will be paying us a visit to assess whether our entry will be selected for the final shortlist."

Toran felt a sudden tightness in his chest; he was so excited at the news that he could hardly breathe. He heard as if from very far away the other cadets raising a rowdy cheer—and it wasn't until someone clapped him heartily on the back that he woke up.

"Well done, Toran!" Lorris was beaming at him.

"The working scale model must be ready by the end of the month when Colonel Lindgren arrives," Colonel Mouzillon announced. "So, as a special concession, Major Bauldry's design team will be excused from weapons training in the following weeks to concentrate on their competition entry."

"You lucky dogs," whispered Lorris.

"There can be no slacking off now," continued Colonel Mouzillon. "It's an honor that the academy has been selected; it would be an even greater honor if our students' design was chosen for the final round of the competition to be held at Tielborg University."

"A trip to Tielen." Lorris nudged Toran. "Isn't that where you want to study after the academy?"

The Department of the Mechanical Arts at Tielborg University . . .

Toran nodded. Behind Lorris he saw that Branville was staring directly at him. But the instant their gazes intersected, Branville looked away. Toran scowled, in spite of himself.

"Cheer up," said Lorris. "Why the glum face? Anyone would think you'd just been disqualified."

If only I didn't have to work with Branville. Something in that glare of his tells me he's going to make every moment of this competition difficult for me.

***

162

As Gerard came out of the foundry, his ears ringing with the pounding of the machinery, he passed Mahieu the foreman.

"Letter's just come for you, Ingenieur!" Mahieu called, his breath steaming on the frosty air. "Looks important. I've left it on your desk."

Gerard nodded his thanks and quickened his pace toward the works office, wondering who had written to him; since the scandal at the university, his father had all but disowned him, never putting pen to paper.

So unless the old man's suffered a change of heart . . .

The warmth from the stove in the office was stifling after the freezing chill outside. Gerard unwrapped his woolen scarf and shrugged off his greatcoat, then searched for the letter. Mahieu had left it propped up on the Works ledger where he could hardly miss it. But this was not personal correspondence; the creamy paper bore the imperial seal.

The competition.

Gerard seized it and eagerly cracked open the seal:

"To Ingenieur Gerard Bernay:

"It is with the greatest regret that I write on behalf of the judges to inform you that your entry for the imperial competition to design a Flying Machine has been disqualified."

"*What*?" Gerard checked the wording again, just to be sure that he had not misread the stark message written in some obscure imperial secretary's fussily neat handwriting. The second paragraph was even harder to digest.

"The judges declared that your design was too similar to another entry from a well-known and established ingenieur and, rather than insist that you undergo a cross-examination to defend yourself, they thought it best to avoid any kind of unfortunate scandal which would reflect unfavorably on your professional reputation."

For a moment the perfectly scribed letters blurred. The letter dropped from his hands to the floor. He tore off his glasses, knuckling the wetness from his eyes. Tears of frustration almost spilled out as he furiously blinked them away. He had not realized until then how much he'd been pinning on the outcome of this competition—or how much he'd been hoping to return to Tielborg and reinstate his good name.

"Damn it all to hell." He brought his clenched fist down on the desk, setting the pens rattling. "An 'established ingenieur?' Someone must have stolen my work. Someone at Tielborg University. Someone who—"

And then the realization that he had been set up sank in.

"Guy Maulevrier. Only you knew . . ." Even saying his tutor's name aloud left a bitter taste souring his mouth. "Why did I trust you?" He had been played for a fool. "How could I have been so gullible?" It would be almost impossible to prove that he was the first to do the research and the designs; everything had been undertaken in Maulevrier's department, under his supervision. Only one other student had watched him working on his drawings late into the night and that had been Edvin Stenmark.

The one person in the whole empire Maulevrier knows damn well I could never ask to testify on my behalf.

Chapter 15

Azhkendir

The neat columns of figures in the estate accounts grew ever more indistinct before Gavril's eyes. He looked up, realizing that his sight wasn't failing, but that the sky had darkened and flakes of snow were drifting past the windows of his study.

"Here comes winter," he said aloud, reaching for the tinder to light the oil lamp on his desk. Winter was harsh this far north and the prospect of the long months of gloom ahead only made him regret being so far from his other home, sun-warmed Smarna with its temperate climate. As he gazed out over the gardens which were rapidly disappearing in snow mist, he heard men's voices raised, coming from the courtyard below, loud and agitated.

The druzhina—probably arguing over some trivial matter again. Since the weather began to turn, there had been frequent disagreements over the daily duties.

Surely Askold can deal with the issue and leave me in peace to wrestle with these accounts.

"Lord Gavril!"

Apparently not.

Gavril sighed and laid down his pen. "Enter."

Askold came in, only to be elbowed out of the way by his burly lieutenant, Gorian, whose fur-lined jacket was damp with fast-melting snow.

"Forgive us, my lord—" Askold began.

"It's my boys, Lord Gavril." Gorian, always blunt to the point of rudeness in his manner of speaking, cut in. He was out of breath as if he had just ridden back through the falling snow; his cheeks glowed red from the cold. "They've not returned. I've scoured the demesne for them but there's no trace and—"

Gavril raised one hand to halt Gorian's impassioned flow. "Your sons were out on patrol, Lieutenant? Perhaps they were forced to take shelter when the snow started."

"Shelter? From a few flakes of snow?" Gorian let out a snort of disgust at the suggestion. "I've brought my lads up to handle all kinds of weather, like true druzhina."

Askold cleared his throat. "There were reports of strangers on the northern edge of the forest. So I sent Radakh and Tarakh out to investigate. With strict orders to report straight back to me." He shot a stern look at Gorian. "And they should have been back by noon."

"Are you implying that my lads were malingering?" Gorian turned on his commanding officer.

"Strangers in Kerjhenezh Forest?" Gavril leaned forward, all attention now. "At this time of year? Why was I not told of this earlier?"

"Be on your guard," the Emperor had written. *"That woman . . . bears you and your wife a deep grudge. And now that you and I are no longer 'protected' as we once were, we must be doubly vigilant."* He found

himself wondering if this might be some new mischief orchestrated by Lilias Arbelian.

"We didn't want to disturb you, my lord, until we'd gathered more information. They could have been pilgrims who'd got lost on their way to Saint Serzhei's monastery."

"But you suspect they might not have been pilgrims at all?" Gavril said. There had been "pilgrims" before who turned out to be members of the Francian Commanderie, on a mission to steal the holy relics from the monastery shrine.

"Send me back out with a patrol, my lord," said Gorian. "The sun will set soon and the snow's setting in."

"Very well." Gavril slammed the ledger shut and stood up. He was weary of poring over figures. "But I'm coming too."

A look of alarm flickered across Askold's face. "Suppose these strangers are here to cause trouble, my lord?"

"I assume you're not proposing we ride out to meet them unarmed?" Gavril could not resist a barbed dig at Askold. Askold shook his head and stood back to let him lead the way.

***

"It's still snowing," said Ninusha, reaching up to close the winter parlor shutters and draw the heavy velvet curtains. "If it continues like this all night, we'll be cut off by dawn."

Larisa gave a gurgle and slid slowly sideways onto the rug at Kiukiu's feet.

"Time to get the sleighs ready, then," Kiukiu said, clutching her shawl closer to her as she bent down to sit Larisa upright again. "I hope your daddy will be back before nightfall, little one." Why had Gavril insisted on accompanying the patrol? *Sometimes he forgets that he's not invulnerable any more . . .*

Little Kion made a grab for Larisa's red woolen ball; the two babies tussled amicably for a while before Kiukiu thought it was wise to distract them with the little wooden horse Semyon had carved for Larisa. Soon they were both chuckling as she made silly horse-like noises to amuse them, moving it up and down while they grabbed at its legs.

Kiukiu saw the adoring expression softening Ninusha's eyes as she watched her baby son. And then the maid started, as if remembering something vital, and asked, "Would you like some tea, my lady?"

"Yes, but you really don't have to call me 'my lady'."

"Ilsi says I must."

"Only if we have guests, then, to keep Ilsi satisfied. But when we're here with the children, we can be as relaxed as we please. I'm so happy that Larisa has a playmate of her own age. Her little face lights up whenever she sees Kion."

The wind began to rattle the shutters and a fierce draught gusted down the chimney, making the flames flicker in the grate.

"Lady Morozhka's woken up," Ninusha said, making the sign to avert evil as she went to pour the tea.

Kiukiu felt a shiver run through her body, setting the fine golden hairs on her arms on end. "And so have her Snow Spirits." She had never forgotten the time she nearly died, lost in a blizzard on the moors . . . nor the eerily seductive song of the Snow Spirits, Morozhka's Daughters, as they lured her away from the path . . .

"I've heard the Snow Spirits singing," Ninusha handed her a cup of steaming tea, "but I've never seen them."

"You don't ever want to, believe me." Kiukiu stared into the clear dark liquid; she had chosen one of Chinua's most fragrant black blends from Khitari for today's treat. "I would have died if Grandma Malusha hadn't come to my rescue. Their song was so sweet . . ."

"Then the old tales are true?" Ninusha's brown eyes widened. "The Snow Spirits sing to charm travelers off the road—and then they suck out their souls and leave them to freeze to death? Or if they find a handsome young man, they take him to Lady Morozhka to be her new lover. And when the thaw comes, his body is found, frozen in ice—"

Larisa suddenly dropped the horse with a clatter that made both mothers jump, and then she crawled off determinedly toward the woolen ball. Gavril had inserted a bell from off of one of the sleigh harnesses so that it made a bright jingling sound when rolled or shaken. Instantly Kion set off too and soon the two babies were tussling again.

"They really love playing with that ball," Kiukiu said, scooping Larisa up, ignoring her squawk of indignation. "I must ask Gavril to help me make another." She'd been surprised—but pleased—when Gavril had begun to make little toys for Larisa; at first he'd seemed so much at a loss around the baby that she'd feared he was feeling elbowed out and neglected.

There came a tap at the door and Sosia came in carrying a laden plate; the delicious scent of freshly-baked poppy seed cakes wafted into the parlor as she offered them to Kiukiu.

"And how's Larisa today?" Sosia held out her arms to her grand-niece who smiled broadly at her and let out a little squeal of welcome. "Come to Auntie Sosia, then, and let your mama eat her cake in peace."

Kiukiu nodded gratefully to Sosia and bit into the warm cake. "Mm; these are delicious, Auntie."

Sosia was too absorbed in talking to Larisa to hear the compliment. "What's this red cheek? And all this dribble? Are you teething, little one?" She popped her finger in Larisa's mouth and then hastily withdrew it. "Don't chew on me; I don't taste so good!"

"Teething already?" Kiukiu said, wiping crumbs from her lips. "Trying to catch up to Kion Two-Teeth?"

"Kion Two-Teeth." Ninusha giggled.

"I'll bake some more rusks for our little ones," Sosia said, sitting down on the other side of the fire. "Better chewing on a good, hard bread rusk than my rheumaticky old fingers."

The wind howled in the chimney again, setting the sparks spinning from the sweet-burning log of old apple wood. Sosia shivered as she dandled Larisa on her knee.

"It's a real blizzard out there this evening."

"Are the men back yet?" Kiukiu asked, trying not to sound too anxious.

"Your husband's in safe hands; Askold knows where the winter shelters are. If the snow's too fierce, they'll make for one of the old watchtowers and wait till morning. Don't you worry; the druzhina won't let the Snow Spirits come anywhere near Lord Gavril."

***

The last blood-red streaks were fading from the darkening sky when a biting wind began to blow off the mountains. Suddenly Gavril found himself half-blinded by a blizzard, scarcely able to make out the form of Askold ahead of him as they rode in single file.

"Your orders, my lord?" Askold turned around in the saddle.

Gavril reined his roan mare Krasa to a halt. "Abandon the search." He had to shout to make himself heard above the howling of the wind.

Why didn't we turn back sooner? We saw the snow clouds massing over the Kharzhgylls.

"There's shelter up ahead!" Askold called. "Follow me."

Gavril turned Krasa's head to go after Askold and Gorian. And then as the blizzard's first fury began to abate, he realized that they were riding between the thick trunks of tall pines and firs. The branches acted as a filter, although as they swayed in the violent gusts, they occasionally deposited clumps of wet snow onto the bent heads of the horsemen.

Kerjhenezh Forest.

"Not much further now," came back Askold's voice faintly.

Gavril could hardly see in front of him for the swirling of the wind-driven snow. His feet and hands were frozen, in spite of the warmth of the thick, fur-lined coat he was wearing (one of his father's) and his sturdy leather boots. He had lost all sense of direction. *I must get Askold to teach me how to find my way in a blizzard.*

The bitter chill was growing stronger, seeping through every pore of his body. He felt as if his blood was freezing in his veins, turning his body to ice.

He blinked away the snowflakes encrusting his lashes as Krasa slowed to a stop and swiveled around in the saddle to look for the other druzhina who had been riding behind him.

There was no one there.

How could we have become separated so easily?

"Askold!" Gavril shouted but the thickly falling snow soaked up the sound of his voice. "Gorian!" His throat burned with the cold as he drew in another breath to shout again.

Krasa suddenly gave a shudder and whinnied, baring her teeth.

"What's the matter, girl?" Gavril whispered in her ear. "Easy, now." The mare began to jitter about nervously and he hoped that she hadn't scented wolves. *This is one time when I need the blood-bond between me and my* druzhina. Yet since Khezef had left him, he had not once been able to reawaken the link the Drakhaoul had forged between the Drakhaon and his bodyguard.

"Why are you trespassing in my domain, Drakhaon?" The voice throbbed through him, piercing as the whine of the wintry blast around the peaks of the Kharzhgylls.

"*Your* domain?" Gavril peered through the blizzard. A cloaked woman was standing before him, staring challengingly at him from silvery eyes as cold as shards of translucent ice. *Eyes like the Magus's . . . or the Drakhaoul Za'afiel, the Spinner of Winds.* But there the resemblance ended; she was tall, with long white-blond locks that sparkled dully as if they had been dusted with hoarfrost. Her hooded cloak was the color of snow clouds.

"Drakhaon was the title I inherited from Volkh, my father." Gavril found his voice and was ashamed to hear how weak it sounded against the whine of the wind. "But I have a new title now: High Steward of Azhkendir."

The woman let out a scornful laugh that made the snow-laden branches shiver. "All the new titles in the world won't bring back your dragon-daemon familiar, Drakhaon."

Gavril began to feel the stirrings of a dark and visceral fear as he stared into the woman's ice-silvered eyes. *She knows I've lost my powers. She knows I'm defenseless.* His instincts told him that he was in the presence of some ancient, implacable force of nature and he had no idea how he could escape her clutches.

"Who are you?" he demanded, trying to control the tremor in his voice. "And what do you want with me?"

"My name is Morozhka."

Krasa's ears went back as she gave a whicker of fear.

"I was here long before the Drakhaoul. And now the Drakhaoul is gone from this world, I'm here to make a pact with you."

Morozhka? I've heard that name before. She must be one of the Elder Ones. "A pact?"

"Strangers. They've entered the old sacred places in the mountains: my sanctuary and my refuge. Did you let them in? Are they here with your permission?"

"N-no." Gavril's teeth had begun to chatter. The bitter chill was slowing his brain. "I'm just searching for two of my men."

Morozhka made a sweeping gesture toward the sky, the snow stopped falling and the clouds parted to reveal a crescent moon. By its pale light, Gavril saw, frozen in the act of crying out in surprise, the two youngest druzhina: Radakh and Tarakh, Gorian's twin sons. There was no sign of their horses.

"What have you done to them?" Were they under some kind of enchantment? Or had Morozhka turned them to ice? The anguished look on their contorted faces made him feel sick with guilt. "Release them at once!" *And if she's turned them to ice, will they die? How long can a man stay frozen until his heart stops?*

"Lend these boys to me."

"*Lend* them to you?" Gorian's face, distorted with fury, arose in Gavril's mind. *I have to protect them.* He dismounted, stumbling through the snow toward the twins to see for himself if they showed any sign of life.

But Morozhka placed herself in front of the frozen druzhina and Gavril felt the air grow colder still as she approached, as if her slender body was exuding a shimmer of frost.

"I'll set your men free, Drakhaon, if you agree to lend them to me to guard the mountain."

"I don't know that I can—"

"The longer you hesitate, the harder it'll be to revive them."

Gavril knew he was outmanoeuvred. "Name your price."

"A pact between us. Sealed in blood."

"In b-blood?"he managed to stammer through frozen lips.

The woman drew a knife from her belt; its slender curved blade was as translucent as glass. "Your blood for their lives. Just a drop or two to seal the pact."

"You give me your word that they'll be set free? Unharmed?"

Morozhka suddenly pounced, seizing Gavril's left arm. Gavril tried to twist free but the Elder One's grip was so powerful that he found himself unable to move. With one swift slash, the ice-glass knife sliced through the thick sleeve of Gavril's coat, the woolen jacket and linen shirt beneath, and punctured his skin beneath, leaving a thin, dark line of blood welling up. Gavril was so cold that he felt no pain, only shock that he had been attacked so swiftly that he had been unable to defend himself. Before he could recover, his attacker lowered her white head and, to Gavril's revulsion, licked the wound with an ice-cold tongue.

"For God's sake—" Gavril cried out, jerking his arm away. The silvered eyes stared piercingly at him as Morozhka licked her lips.

"Your blood still burns," she said. "It must be *his* legacy."

"What do you mean?" How could Khezef have left any kind of legacy? Gavril had seen him pass into another dimension, through a gateway so bright it had seared his eyes, leaving him dazzled for days afterward.

"Once you've been possessed by a daemon of such tremendous aethyrial power, you can never return to being wholly human. As you will find out, Drakhaon."

"Not wholly human?" Gavril repeated, his mind churning with disturbing possibilities. "But there're no outward signs left. My hair, my eyes, even my nails—"

"No outward signs, true. But your blood, your mind, your soul . . . Have you been having strange dreams?" One frosted eyebrow quirked inquiringly.

Strange dreams . . .

Morozhka reached out, pressing one hand to Gavril's brow. The Elder One's fingertips sent icy splinters into his mind, spreading like frost flowers to penetrate the deepest recesses of his brain. The sudden invasion caught him off-guard and, as she let him go, he dropped to his knees in the snow, his head filled with a swirl of incoherent images.

"I thought as much," she murmured. "Your Drakhaoul has left you a trail to follow. But only you can decipher the clues."

"Clues?" The frosty filaments began to thaw and with them the snowmist clouding his brain.

"So that you can be reunited."

Then that wasn't the final farewell on Ty Nagar? Khezef left me a trail to follow so we could meet again? The realization stirred up so many unresolved feelings Gavril had tried to ignore: love and loss; anger at abandonment . . .

"Now that I've unlocked those memories, your task is to make sense of them." The Elder One reached down to pull him to his feet. Gavril felt her preternatural strength resonating through his whole body. "And now our pact is sealed. Drakhaon. Sealed with your burning blood."

"Pact?" Gavril pressed one hand to his frozen temples, still dizzied by the images Morozhka had stirred up from the clouded sediment of his memories. "I never—"

"We'll meet again, Drakhaon. Soon." Morozhka turned on her heel and as she began to walk away, the snow started drifting down again, as if the pale disc of the moon was shedding soft white petals.

"What about my druzhina?" Gavril cried. "Set them free! You gave me your word."

"Give them what you gave me." Her voice floated back to him. "But do it now—or they'll die."

Gavril hurried over to the two frozen figures. The moon's light was rapidly disappearing behind a veil of fresh-falling snow and he could barely make out the faces of the young druzhina in the darkness.

"Hang in there, Radakh." He lifted his left arm and, steeling himself, pressed the edges of the fresh wound to try to squeeze out some more blood. In his desperation, he tore off his gloves and forced himself to touch the raw wound with his forefinger, smearing some of the blood onto Radakh's icy lips, and then Tarakh's.

"Radakh," he said urgently, gripping the young man's shoulder. The icy leather burned his hand. But he heard Radakh take a long, wheezing indrawn breath and what had been a frozen statue shuddered back into life. Beside him, Tarakh began to cough and then to shiver, as life brought colour flooding back into his blue face.

"Lord Gavril?" whispered Radakh.

"Thank God." Gavril put out his arms to hug both young men to him. "You're still alive."

"Where—where are the horses?" asked Tarakh, staring around him dazedly.

If my blood still burns, does that mean the blood-bond still works too?

"Bogatyr Askold said there's shelter nearby."

Radakh sank to his knees in the snow. "What's the matter with me? I can hardly put one foot in front of the other."

"Call the horses, brother," urged Tarakh, heaving him to his feet. "Lean on me."

Radakh put two fingers to his lips and blew. But the piercing whistle made Krasa shake her head and jitter around in the snow; before Gavril could grab the bridle and try to calm her, she set off like a crazed creature into the darkness between the trees.

"Krasa!" Gavril yelled, setting off after her. Suddenly weak and light-headed, he found himself losing his balance.

Loss of blood? he wondered as he pitched forward into a snowdrift. *Or did Morozhka lay some kind of enchantment on me too?*

Chapter 16

"Your Drakhaoul has left you a trail to follow. But only you can decipher the clues."

As Gavril pushed himself to his feet, Morozhka's words still echoed through his mind.

"I'm sorry, my lord," Tarakh gasped out. "Krasa's not easily spooked. I never thought she'd bolt—"

"Lord Gavril . . ."

Gavril's head jerked up a distant voice called his name. "Did you hear that?"

"I can't hear anything but the wind, my lord."

"Where are you, my lord?" The distant voice came again.

The blood-bond between me and my druzhina. Gavril began to realize that only he could hear the reply. *Has Morozhka reawakened the link between us?* "We have to keep moving." He pressed on the fresh wound with frozen fingers. *"I'm here. Gorian's boys are with me. Tell me where you are."*

"At the old watchtower on the edge of the ridge. Your horses have found their way here." The reply was clearer this time; he recognized Askold. *"Can you follow the sound of my voice?"*

"This way." Gavril set off, gesturing to the twins to follow.

***

"More logs for the fire, my lady." Dunai limped in, and the flames leapt higher in the grate as another gust swept in.

"For heaven's sakes, don't leave the door wide open," scolded Sosia, "the babies'll catch cold in that draught!"

"I'll help you, Dunai." Ninusha hurried to help the young steward whose face, Kiukiu noticed, had flushed a dark red at Sosia's tart reprimand. "You pass me the logs; I'll put them on the hearth."

That was an act of kindness that would never even have occurred to the old, air-headed Ninusha. Kiukiu nodded her silent approval as Ninusha knelt down by the fireside and piled the logs neatly one by one as Dunai handed them to her. *She knows that the damp snow air must be making Dunai's legs ache.* And even though his crushed bones had set better than anyone could have hoped, Dunai had been pronounced lame for life. Gavril made him steward of the kastel, hoping that the dashing young warrior would heal faster if he had plenty to occupy his mind. But sometimes she caught a sad, hopeless look dulling Dunai's clear blue eyes—and she knew that there could be no easy or swift recovery from such terrible injuries.

And it must be especially hard for him to stay behind with the women while his brother and Sem are out with Lord Gavril.

"Any word from the Bogatyr, Dunai?" she asked, trying not to sound too anxious.

"No, my lady," he said and then added swiftly, "but I'm sure that he's taken Lord Gavril to shelter till the storm blows o—" He broke off, his eyes losing focus.

"Dunai?" Kiukiu leapt up, alarmed. "What is it?" He stood still, as though listening intently to some distant voice. Ninusha stood up, dusting the bark from her hands, and laid one hand on his arm. He started, as though waking from a trance.

"I heard him," he said. "I heard Lord Gavril calling."

"You *heard* him? Have you lost your wits, Dunai?" said Sosia.

"The blood-bond."

Kiukiu's heart skipped a beat; she pressed a hand to her chest to calm its sudden pounding. "But—but the blood-bond was destroyed when the Drakhaoul passed into the Ways Beyond."

"It was Lord Gavril," said Dunai stubbornly. "I heard him here," he touched his forehead, "and here." His hand moved smartly to his left breast as if he were saluting his master.

"Is he in danger?" Kiukiu was not just worried now; she was genuinely frightened, wondering what this unexpected reawakening could mean. "Dunai—was he calling for help?"

***

Mustn't leave Kiukiu alone for too long . . . she'll be worried. And I promised I'd be home by nightfall . . .

Gavril stumbled doggedly on through the darkness, guided only by the distant voices of his druzhina.

It took all his willpower to lift one booted foot out of the knee-high snowdrifts and put it down in front of the other. But the thought of Kiukiu furious with him for being so foolish gave him new energy. *"Whatever possessed you to go out in such weather?"* he could hear her saying, her voice throbbing with fury. *"Have you forgotten you have a daughter to look after now?"*

Behind him, Radakh was supporting his flagging brother, one arm around his waist, both following in Gavril's wake.

"Where is she?" Gavril heard Tarakh mumble. "That lady. We can't leave her out here alone . . . in the snow."

"What lady?" Gavril stopped, turning around. The frail silver light of the crescent moon shone though once more as the snow clouds drifted apart.

"So pretty." Tarakh's words came out muzzily as if he was drunk or feverish. "Said she was . . . lost."

"What did she look like?"

Tarakh let out a secretive little laugh. "She kissed me."

"Idiot. It was me she kissed," Radakh said indignantly.

"So you both saw her?" Gavril began to suspect that Morozhka and the twin's "lost" lady were one and the same. He set off again, wading on through the moonlit drifts. "What was she like?"

"Hair as white as Dunai's," Tarakh said dreamily.

"But prettier."

"She said she had a special reward for us."

"I'll set your men free, Drakhaon, if you agree to lend them to me to guard the mountain."

What fate had he consigned these two young men to? He had agreed to Morozhka's terms to save their lives—but now he wondered if he had unwittingly condemned them to a lifetime of service to the cold-hearted Elder One.

"Look," he heard Tarakh say. "It's the old western tower."

"The one Da calls the Pepper-pot?" Radakh said. "Who knew we'd come so far west in the dark?"

Gavril realized that they were right. A crooked pepper-pot roof loomed ahead out of the moonlit darkness. It must be one of the outer watchtowers; during the Clan Wars with the Arkhels, Gavril's Nagarian ancestors had built several such defenses around the inner and outer boundaries of the kastel estate so that they could keep an eye on the activities of their enemies and defend their borders.

"Lord Gavril!" A full-throated roar startled him as Gorian charged out from beneath the ivy-choked archway. "Come on in out of the cold."

Warmth greeted them as they entered the round tower; a log fire crackled and sputtered in the ancient, soot-stained hearth, its glow lighting the faces of the druzhina as they rose to welcome them. The chamber smelt pungently of cinders, damp horses, and a savory steam that was rising from an iron cooking pot suspended over the blaze.

"My boys!" Gorian cuffed them in turn and then hugged them. Semyon hurried over to help him support the twins over to the fire.

"Does anyone have any aquavit?" Gavril asked. Askold handed him his flask and he took a good swig of the fiery liquor, hoping it would steady his nerves.

"I've made soup," said Vartik, looking up from stirring the pot. "Dried meat, berries, snow melt; it'll warm you up, my lord."

The horses were tethered at the far side of the round chamber; Gavril went over to check on his mare. She gave a welcoming whinny when she sensed him approach and he was glad to see that she was calm again after her panicked flight had left him stranded in the forest.

A little while later, thawing his frozen toes and fingers near the fire, Gavril sat drinking his soup from a tin mug and listening to his druzhina arguing companionably. The color had returned to Tarakh's cheeks. And when he saw Radakh throw back his head and laugh at one of Vasili's jokes, he began to wonder if the encounter with Morozhka had been nothing but a snow mirage. Then he looked down at his left forearm and saw the gash her icy blade had made. Drying blood had stained his sleeve where her ice blade had slashed through the material and now he was out of the cold, he could feel the raw ache of the wound. She had been no mirage.

"Lady Morozhka would never have dare enter Nagarian territory in the old days." Gorian said with a grunt, tapping out the residue from his clay pipe and stuffing a fresh wad of tobacco into the bowl.

The other druzhina fell silent, staring at Gorian.

Gavril broke the awkward silence. "You mean: when the Drakhaoul was here?"

"Too right, my lord. Morozhka and her Snow Spirits showed proper respect." Gorian held a glowing taper to the tobacco, puffing as he spoke from one side of his mouth, teeth gritted around the pipe stem. Gavril nodded. He sensed that the druzhina were waiting for him to reprimand Gorian for his bluntness. But all he said was, "Tell me more about her."

"Morozhka was here long before the Drakhaoul." Gorian blew a smoke ring into the flickering firelight. "She's one of the Elder Ones. They were here when the world was first made. And they're still here, even if no one pays them much respect anymore."

"So did people used to worship Morozhka?"

Gorian shrugged. "There're ruins up in the mountains: a broken stone circle on one of the high plateaus. It's called Morozhka's Round. My father told me never to go there; he said the place was cursed."

"With reason!" said Askold with a harsh laugh. "The only way to Morozhka's Round was through Arkhel territory. You'd have never have made it out alive. Those bastards would have skinned you alive and hung you up as fresh meat to feed their cursed owls!"

Gavril saw the younger druzhina eye each other uneasily; all three were too young to remember what it was like before Lord Volkh destroyed the Arkhel clan.

"My granddad used to say there was treasure buried up there," said Vartik. "Lady Morozhka's Hoard, he called it. But no one who went looking for it ever came back."

"Your granddad could've been right," said Gorian, nodding. "There used to be copper and gold mining up there until the Arkhels claimed the land as their own and drove everyone else away."

"Arkhel gold?" Askold said darkly. "The only Arkhel gold I ever saw was the hair on their cursed heads—and the light of battle in their eyes when they attacked the kastel. Owl eyes. Mad and gold and bright as stars."

"That's a color you won't see again," Gorian said, jabbing the stem of his pipe at the Bogatyr to emphasize his point. "Kostya made sure of that when he shot Jaromir Arkhel."

Gavril stared at the dirt floor. There was no point defending Jaromir Arkhel, the enemy whom he had come to love as a friend; the older druzhina would never understand.

"And he was the last of that cursed line," said Askold, nodding.

The wind gusted fiercely around the tower, rattling the roof tiles above; the horses shifted from hoof to hoof uneasily, startled by the noise.

"What we didn't tell you, my lord," said Askold, "was that someone was sheltering here before us."

"Recently?" Gavril looked up.

"We found evidence of a fire. Someone was sheltering in here last night."

The druzhina were exchanging glances. "The trespassers who were sighted on the edge of the Waste?" Gorian suggested.

"Could have been fur trappers," said Vasili.

"Or pilgrims," added Semyon.

Gavril had been trying the gauge the right moment to tell Gorian and his sons of the pact he had been forced to make with Morozhka.

"Listen," he said. "Morozhka told me that strangers passed through her sanctuary yesterday."

"The same ones?" said Askold.

Gavril steeled himself. "She made me enter into a pact." He gazed at Radakh and Tarakh who were beginning to nod off, drowsed by the warmth and the aquavit. "I gave my word that, in exchange for your lives, you would protect her sanctuary."

"You did *what*?" Gorian, eyes blazing, rose up as if he was going to swing a punch at him. Vasili and Vartik caught hold of him, pulling him back down.

"Gorian! Apologize to Lord Gavril!" Askold's rebuke rang out, sharp as a whip-crack. "Didn't you hear what he said? He saved your boys' lives."

"Only to condemn them to spending all winter up here on the mountain."

"It's all right, Da." Tarakh looked ashamed of his father's outburst. "Radakh and me, we're fine with it."

"It's just another patrol," Radakh said with a shrug. "We can make this tower our base; if we bring plenty of supplies and firewood, it won't be so bad."

"But who are these strangers? Treasure hunters?" Gorian was not so easily appeased. "Or bandits from Khitari," Semyon said under his breath, "sneaking across the border before the high passes are blocked with snow."

Gavril stifled a yawn; the warmth of the fire and the potency of Askold's aquavit were making him sleepy.

"You must be tired, my lord." Askold rose and went to put another log on the fire; the snow-damp wood made the flames spit sparks up the wide chimney. "Get some rest; we'll keep watch."

Gavril did not argue. He wrapped his coat around him and lay down, and in spite of the hardness of the dirt floor, his lids began to close.

***

"Abbot!" Brother Cosmas strode into Abbot Yephimy's candlelit study. "Some pilgrims have made it through the blizzard; they're asking to speak with you."

Yephimy looked up from the yellowed codex he was attempting to transcribe and laid down his pen. He was thankful to be interrupted; his eyes were beginning to ache with the strain of deciphering the ancient script. "Pilgrims arriving in this snowstorm?" He was surprised that anyone was rash enough to brave the snows at night, unless they were foreigners, and unaccustomed to the vagaries of the Azhkendi winter. "How far have they come?" he asked as he snuffed out the candles on his desk and followed Cosmas into the dark, draughty passageway.

"From Tourmalise."

"Tourmalise?" Yephimy repeated in astonishment. The last time a large number of "pilgrims" had arrived, they had turned out to be the most unwelcome of visitors: Guerriers of the Francian Commanderie. Their visit had ended in bloodshed and the theft of the monastery's most precious relic: Saint Serzhei's golden crook. Since then he had felt obliged to mount a guard on the gate and to search all visitors to the monastery, confiscating any weapons they were carrying. "Does anyone in Tourmalise even know of Saint Serzhei's existence?"

They crossed the snowy courtyard and entered the refectory. Yephimy saw four cloaked men warming their hands at the fire.

"Welcome to our monastery," he cried, striding down past the tables which were already laid with bowls and spoons for the morning. "My name is Yephimy. I hear you've traveled far. What brings you all the way to Azhkendir?"

They turned on hearing his voice and the foremost among them shook off his fur-rimmed hood, revealing his face. Yephimy stopped, staring. The firelight burnished his hair, catching red glints in its distinctive shade of dark gold, tempered with strands of gray. *That color . . ._*

"Thank you for your hospitality, Abbot," the pilgrim said in perfect Azhkendi. "It's been a long time since we last met."

Yephimy peered at him in the flickering light.

"Over twenty years," said the pilgrim. "These days I'm known as Ranulph, Baronet of Serrigonde. But you may remember me by the name your predecessor gave me here some forty-two years ago on my Naming Day: Ranozhir."

"Ranozhir?" Yephimy echoed, coming closer. The strong features, the aristocratic nose, and that distinctive rich-colored hair; there could be no doubt. "Ranozhir Arkhel!"

Chapter 17

"The men are back!" The shout went up from the gatehouse and was soon passed around the kastel from servant to servant. Kiukiu, who had hardly slept all night, rushed to the window that overlooked the courtyard, anxiously scanning the cloaked, hooded figures hunched over their horses' heads for a glimpse of Gavril.

"I've waited long enough; let's go find your daddy," she said, bending over Larisa's cradle. Larisa let out an indignant squawk as Kiukiu grabbed her and hastened down the stairs toward the door that led to the stable-yard.

Something happened to them out on the Waste. I'm certain of it.

"Give the babe to me," called Sosia. "You can't take her out in all that snow without wrapping her up properly. She'll catch her death of cold."

Kiukiu hastily thrust her daughter into Sosia's outstretched arms and hurried on, snatching a cloak from those left hanging up outside the pantry. As she ran along the narrow passageway toward the outer door, the moist chill of the snowy morning enveloped her.

In the courtyard, the druzhina had already dismounted and the air was filled with clouds of steaming breath from the horses. Kiukiu scanned the returning faces anxiously, searching for Gavril. Then she spotted tow-haired Ivar leading Krasa by the reins toward her stall.

"He's over there, my lady." She glanced round, recognizing Bogatyr Askold's voice. "Don't worry; we took good care of him."

"Gavril!" Forgetting how a lady should behave, ignoring the frozen slush underfoot, she flew across the courtyard to fling her arms around him and hug him tightly.

He kissed her and she felt the roughness of dark stubble grazing her cheek.

"It was only a night away," he said with a quiet laugh. "We found shelter in the watchtower on the edge of the forest."

Gazing up into his face, she saw instantly that, in spite of his reassuring smile, there was a haunted look in his sunken eyes as if he had not quite woken fully from a nightmare. But practical needs had to be addressed first. She slipped her arm through his, steering him toward the open door. "You must all be famished. Come into the kitchen and get warm."

"You go on ahead, my lord," Askold said, "I'll make sure the morning watch are briefed."

The meaningful look that passed between the two men did not escape Kiukiu. *I was right; something has happened!* But she had learned that it paid to be patient with Gavril and not to press him with questions too soon, so she guided him inside and waited while he and the other druzhina spooned down bowlfuls of hot porridge, sweetened with bitter-sweet heather honey, and drank spiced, mulled ale.

"What happened out there?" Kiukiu had waited long enough; she wanted to know. "Did you find anyone trespassing in the Waste?"

Again she saw a look pass between Askold and Gavril; the other men stared fixedly at their bowls or drained their ale mugs.

"We met Lady Morozhka," Gavril said in the silence.

Ilsi dropped the porridge ladle with a clang. "Lady Frost?" she said, making the sign against evil. "It's a wonder she didn't freeze you all to death."

I sensed Morozhka and her Snow Spirits were about last night. Kiukiu, remembering her encounter with the Snow Spirits, wrapped her arms more tightly around herself. *They lull you to sleep with their cold, clear lullabies . . . and you never wake up again.* It terrified her to think how close Gavril had come to succumbing to their chill embrace. She watched him as he pensively scraped the last of the porridge from his bowl and realized how vulnerable he was; no longer protected by his daemon Drakhaoul, he looked as tired and careworn as his druzhina.

But it was not until Gavril returned from the bathhouse, clean shaven again and skin glowing from the heat, that she drew him into their bedchamber.

"Tell me what really happened," she said, sitting him down on the bed and toweling the last of the moisture from his damp hair. *Such soft hair for a man. Darker auburn than our daughter's, with coppered glints in the firelight . . . but not a single trace of daemon blue anymore.*

Gavril picked up his comb.

"Let me do that for you. Your hair's all tangled." She knelt up beside him and took the comb from him. "Mmm. You smell of birch bark; you must have been using Sosia's special soap."

"What would I do without you?" he said softly. "Don't ever leave me, Kiukiu. I don't think I could go on without you."

"Silly," she said, although his words made her heart ache. "I'm not going anywhere. My place is here, at your side."

***

"Old Mother Winter is plucking her geese. White feathers come tumbling down, tumbling down . . ."

Kiukiu heard the distant strains of the old children's song, sung in a sweet, husky woman's voice.

"Who's singing?" She went to get up but saw that Larisa's eyes had closed and her little head drooped against Kiukiu's shoulder. As the baby's breathing grew slow and regular, Kiukiu gently placed her back in the cradle and pulled the woolen blanket around her, loosely tucking it in. *If we're lucky she'll sleep through now until dawn.*

Suddenly she felt the fine hairs prickling at the back of her neck as a cold sensation, light as a flurry of snow, settled over her.

Someone's watching me.

Slowly she raised her head from Larisa's cradle and stared at the oriel window. A woman's face was pressed up against the glass panes, barely visible in the mauve light of the snowy dusk. For a brief second, Kiukiu's gaze connected with hers—and then Kiukiu heard the door open behind her and Gavril came in.

"Gavril," she whispered, clutching at his arm, "someone's at the window. Looking in. I saw a face."

"At the window?" he repeated. "But we're on the first floor. There's no balcony outside. How could anyone look in? Who did you see?"

"A woman . . . I think. Dark eyes, pale skin, a strange look on her face, curious, yet somehow . . ." *Hungry.* She didn't want to say the word aloud, but hunger was the emotion she had sensed emanating from the apparition at the window; hunger and longing.

"There's no one there." Gavril had gone directly to the window and was gazing out onto the twilit garden below.

Just like a man; needing physical proof before he'll believe anything.

"Perhaps you dreamt it? Or it could have been a trick of the light, casting shadows on the frosted glass?"

"It'd better not be one of the Drakhaon's Brides come back to haunt you." The words were out of her mouth before she could bite them back and she saw him flinch. *There are things he still hasn't been able to bring himself to tell me. But he wouldn't still be alive now if he hadn't drunk innocent blood.* But she couldn't bear to think—even if he had been under the Drakhaoul's influence—of her man talking so intimately with these other girls, touching, kissing, *biting*—

Gavril was gazing at her, a look of puzzled hurt dulling his eyes.

"That was unfair of me," she said, annoyed with herself for speaking out thoughtlessly. "I've just felt so . . ." She hesitated, searching for the right word, "So unsettled since you told me about those strangers."

"And still no one knows who they were or where they were headed."

"Why would anyone try to cross the Arkhel Waste at this time of year?" Kiukiu had a sudden disturbing thought that made her reach out to seize Gavril's hand. "Suppose it's assassins, Gavril? You know you made enemies when you were Drakhaon. Only a well-paid assassin would be motivated enough to venture out under cover of winter to try to take down his—or her—target."

"But an assassin who climbs up walls and lurks outside windows in the freezing cold?" Gavril shook his head, mouth creasing in a smile of incredulity.

"We heard tales in Khan Vachir's caravan of subtle killers from the islands of Cipangu, who can slip past the best bodyguards unnoticed." Why would Gavril not take her worries seriously? "Shino something, they're called. And they use magical shadow skills to infiltrate their victims' houses—"

"Kiukiu." He put his hands on her shoulders, drawing her close. "Why would anyone go to the trouble of sending assassins all the way from Cipangu to kill me? Besides," and he stroked a stray lock from her forehead and gazed into her eyes, "Eugene's agents are looking after us. If someone had put a price on my head, the Emperor's spies would have warned us long before now."

The warmth of his fingers caressing her face, her hair, moving down to her shoulders, sliding off the soft folds of her nightgown so that it fell in a whisper of cloth to her bare feet, drove all worries from her mind—but one. Naked, she pressed herself against him, seeking his heat, and they sank back together onto the bed.

"What about Risa?" she whispered, longing to give in to her desires yet still aware that they were not alone.

"She's sound asleep," he said, his lips moving against her throat, her breasts, kissing the scars that would never fade, deep-scored by his teeth and sapphire claws when he had been daemon-possessed. "We must take advantage while we can."

***

Kiukiu lay lost in dreams, one hand clutching a lock of her own hair, like a little child. After they made love, Gavril usually drifted effortlessly into deep slumber. But tonight, that much-desired repose was eluding him and all he could think about was the pallid face she had glimpsed at the window.

Is there a revenant haunting the kastel? Or could it be Lady Morozhka?

He had sensed nothing. Well, maybe a slight chill but that could have just been the bitter cold seeping in from the snowy gardens beyond. The oriel window was encrusted in jagged icicles, some as long as a rapier blade, its panes frosted over.

Kiukiu's a Spirit Singer, after all. She's more sensitive than the rest of us to the presence of troubled ghosts.

Spirit Singer. All day he had been remembering Eugene's warning, and wondering whether to tell Kiukiu about Ranozhir Arkhel. *Heaven knows, we have worries enough of our own without the Arkhels returning to claim their lands. And suppose Lord Ranozhir wants not just his lands but his Spirit Singer too?* Kiukiu had confessed, the night before they were married, that she had made a vow of allegiance to the Arkhel Clan. At the time he had told her not to worry about what she had done. *But then I truly believed that all the Arkhels were dead.*

What shall I do if Lord Ranozhir comes back and demands that Kiukiu returns to his clan to serve him? How binding is the vow of allegiance she made to his father?

***

Kiukiu woke to find Larisa sitting up, grumbling in a low ominous voice that promised to grow into a full-throated yell if no one took any notice. Accustomed by years in service to rising before dawn to clear the kastel grates, Kiukiu swept her daughter up and out of the cradle, whispering, "Who's awake bright and early again? Let's not disturb your daddy; let him sleep a little longer." She wrapped a soft shawl around them both, then tiptoed out of the bedchamber and down the stairs, heading for the warmth of the kitchen.

Ninusha was already up, warming some milk over the fire for Kion. The little boy was safely confined in one of the wooden baby chairs Semyon had carpentered, enthusiastically beating a spoon on the tray. Larisa's eyes lit up at the sight of Kion and the grumbling instantly ceased, replaced by excited wriggling so that Kiukiu had to use all her strength to secure her in the other chair.

When the babies had been fed and were contentedly chewing on rusks of hard-baked bread, Kiukiu looked down at Larisa and sighed. "There's almost as much porridge on your face and hair as in your tummy."

"And all over the kitchen table," muttered Ilsi, tying her hair back in her embroidered headscarf before she began to clean up after the little ones.

"Let's take them both to the bath-house," suggested Ninusha.

"Yes, please do," said Ilsi pointedly as Dunai came into the kitchen.

A deep blush spread over Ninusha's face as the young estate steward greeted them. Ever since Dunai had endured excruciating torture at the hands of the Francian Inquisition, he had been making a slow recovery from the injuries that had left him lame.

"Just in time, Dunai," said Ilsi, shoving a pile of bowls into his hands. "Set these out, will you?"

"How are you feeling today, Dunai?" Ninusha ventured in an uncharacteristically shy voice. "This cold weather must make it harder for you to get around."

"A good soak in the bath-house helps," Dunai said, grinning at her as he laid the table—although his face had also turned red.

What's going on here? Has Ninusha fallen for Dunai? Kiukiu wondered, gazing from one bashful expression to the other. *He may not be one of the druzhina anymore, but with his white-blond hair and blue eyes, he's still the best-looking man in the kastel—after Gavril, of course.*

"Ah, Dunai; the very man I was hoping to find."
Gavril came in just as Kiukiu was about to pick up
their messy baby. Larisa let out a happy shout at the
sight of her father and shot out both hands, inviting
him to hold her. After one glance at the lumps of
porridge in her hair, Gavril hastily retreated. "I see
you enjoyed your breakfast, Risa."

"Coward," Kiukiu whispered as she whisked
Larisa out of the kitchen, wishing that the baby hadn't
decided to hang on to her hair with one sticky hand. As
she followed Ninusha and Kion down the passageway,
she heard Gavril saying to Dunai, "Since we can't do
much today except clear the snow from the courtyards
and make sure there's enough firewood, I suppose it's
an ideal day to start on the year's accounts."

*Poor Gavril. He hates anything to do with accounting
and figures.*

"Serves your daddy right," she said to Larisa as
a drift of steam from the bath-house wafted out.
Several of the druzhina came tramping in, greeting
her as they stamped the snow from their boots. The
fears stirred up by the ghostly face she had glimpsed
the night before melted away like the frozen snow on
the floor tiles, banished by the banal but reassuring
morning routines.

I must have imagined it.

***

When Gavril and Dunai didn't appear for the midday
meal, Kiukiu went to the study to ask if they wanted
their food brought to them.

She found them almost hidden from view by towering piles of estate ledgers which lay open on the desk in front of them.

"Why the long faces?" she asked, turning from one to the other; Dunai exchanged an uncomfortable look with Gavril. Gavril gestured to the open ledger in front of him and she saw several columns of figures etched in red ink. "Oh dear. But I thought that Avorian said your father had set aside funds to see us through difficult times."

"These have been exceptionally difficult times, my lady," said Dunai. "The rebuilding of the kastel after the siege exhausted most of the reserves."

"But didn't we make any money from the firedust?" Kiukiu turned to Gavril. "Did all the revenue go into the Tielen coffers?"

"The Emperor promised us a percentage of the profits—but the final shipment was destroyed at sea, so . . ."

"Is any money coming in from the estates at all?"

"The tenant farmers are barely making enough to live on," said Dunai, "let alone to pay us their rents. And it's been a poor harvest again."

"Are we in debt?" It would bring shame on the clan if the news were to leak out that they were penniless. "Then there must be something we can sell." Kiukiu stared pointedly at Gavril.

"Lilias made off with what little jewelry was left; she claimed my father had given it to her and who are we to disbelieve her?" Gavril said, suppressing a sigh. Kiukiu could see that he was longing to be elsewhere: in his studio, most likely.

"We're going to have to find some income soon." Dunai looked down at the columns of figures and shook his head, like a physician called too late, Kiukiu thought, to tend to a dying patient.

"I can't ask Eugene for a percentage of profits he never made. And Tielen is still recovering from the collapse of the Spice Trade. There must be something on our lands that we can sell to generate some funds." Gavril sat back in his chair, stretching his arms wide above his head in a gesture of bored frustration.

"Firedust," said Dunai bluntly.

"Too risky." Gavril said, with equal bluntness. "It's volatile, it's difficult to mine—and it's disrespectful to all those who died in the siege."

"The Emperor was not as fastidious as you, my lord, and his countrymen died here in their hundreds."

Gavril closed the ledger with a bang; Kiukiu shook her head at Dunai. Gavril did not like to be reminded of the acts of slaughter he had committed when he was possessed by the Drakhaoul.

"What else have we got?" he asked. "Timber in the forest? Minerals, precious stones, ores in the mountain foothills? How did my father maintain the estates?"

Dunai looked down, as if unwilling to meet Gavril's keen gaze.

"He was Drakhaon," he said softly.

A floorboard creaked as a tall figure appeared in the doorway. "What my son is unwilling to say out loud," said Askold, "is that the local landowners paid a yearly sum into your father's coffers on the understanding that he would leave them in peace."

"My father was extorting money?"

Kiukiu heard the shock in Gavril's voice and placed her hands on the back of his chair, wanting to protect him from any more painful revelations.

"Your father was a good ruler. But he was also an embittered man, tormented by the role he was forced to assume as Drakhaon. I was only third in rank in the druzhina; I didn't know him as well as old Kostya or Jushko did, but I do know that the tradition of tribute stretched way back through the centuries."

"Tribute? You don't mean—"

"I realize it must sound barbaric to your ears, my lord, with your Smarnan upbringing, but the local families used to offer up their daughters to the Drakhaon in return for his favor. All your father did was to change the virgin bride barter to a sum of money. And that money, I believe, he sent to Avorian to be put in trust for you, when you came of age."

"But what did my father do in return for that money?" Gavril's voice was stifled and his words were hardly audible; Kiukiu saw that he was struggling to contain his feelings. Almost without realizing she was doing so, she moved her hands to rest on Gavril's shoulders.

"A few drops of Drakhaon's Blood bought them some protection."

Gavril closed his eyes. "I remember," he said distantly. "The first time I set foot on Azhkendi soil at Arkhelskoye as Drakhaon, I was mobbed by the crowd. Kostya forced me to 'give them proof' of my birthright. They fought over the snow where the drops of blood had fallen. Of course, I didn't understand then what it meant. And now that the Drakhaoul is gone—"

In the awkward silence that fell in the draughty study, Kiukiu left his side to place more wood on the fire, wishing with all her heart that there was some way to share this burden of responsibility with her husband.

"Bogatyr," Gavril said, "how long is it since the Nagarians mined for precious metals in the Kharzhgylls?"

Kiukiu dropped the poker with a clang in the grate. "Sorry," she whispered, retrieving it.

"That's how the last Clan War began, my lord," said Askold heavily. "A dispute over the mining rights."

"Join us." Gavril gestured to the chair next to Dunai's and Askold sat down beside his elder son. "Suppose we opened a mine of our own. There's a great demand for metal ores in the new empire." Kiukiu could hear the earnestness in Gavril's voice. *He's trying to think of new ways to raise money. Surely Askold will listen to him?* "Emperor Eugene is building a new fleet; his shipyards will need iron and copper. I'm sure he'd be interested in establishing a trade treaty. We could invest in the latest mining expertise from abroad and employ ingenieurs to train our men."

"The druzhina are warriors, my lord," said Askold in affronted tones. "They were only forced into the mines against their will when they were Tielen prisoners of war. It would insult their honor as fighting men to return to such menial labor."

Gavril let out another sigh. Kiukiu sensed his frustration building again; trying to persuade the druzhina to change from their old ways was a fruitless task. *If they insist on staying stuck in the past, we'll soon find ourselves penniless.*

"If only there was some way to communicate directly with the Emperor again." Gavril pointed at the Vox Aethyria on his desk, its crystal facets dull in the snowy light. "Ironic, isn't it?" he said with a regretful little smile. "It survived the bombardment of the kastel only to break down completely after the Second Darkness."

"So what's become of that old Magus, the one who invented it?" said Askold, scratching his head. "Why hasn't the Emperor sent him to fix it?"

"Kaspar Linnaius?" Gavril said and Kiukiu twitched at the sound of his name in spite of herself. "He's vanished. The Emperor's had his men searching for him throughout the Western Quadrant. But no one knows where he's gone. Perhaps he's trying to find a way to make the Vox work again. For now, there's nothing for it but to send a letter to Eugene the old-fashioned way: by courier. "

***

As Kiukiu wearily climbed the stair, she could hear Ninusha happily chattering to the two babies, as she prepared them for bed.

"Who's a pretty girl, Larisa? Look, Kion, Risa's showing you her new teeth. How many teeth have you got now, Ki—" Ninusha broke off suddenly, letting out a shrill scream. Kiukiu grabbed her skirts and ran up the last of the stairs, bursting into the room to see Ninusha clutching the two babies to her.

"What's wrong?"

"Someone's outside," gasped Ninusha as both Larisa and Kion began to cry.

Kiukiu went straight to the window as Sosia came in, followed by two of the druzhina on duty .

"How can there possibly be someone outside?" chided Sosia, taking the wailing Larisa from Ninusha. "We're on the first floor—and the balcony is covered in snow and icicles."

"We'll go and check the gardens, my lady." The druzhina went clattering back down the stair, their booted footsteps echoing hollowly around the lofty hallway.

"Who did you see?" Kiukiu, her heart thumping, turned to Ninusha who was trying to hush Kion.

"A woman. I'm sure it was a woman," Ninusha hugged Kion to her, stroking his fair hair to calm him down.

"Now you've frightened the babies." Sosia jiggled Larisa up and down until the sobs subsided. "You must have been seeing things, Ninusha. Are you sure you didn't add a dash of Oleg's aquavit to your tea?"

Kiukiu tried to calm the rapid beating of her own heart. "The other night," she said quietly, "I thought I saw a white-haired woman outside our bedchamber window."

"A ghost," said Ninusha, wide-eyed. "It has to be a ghost."

"Don't say we're being haunted again," said Sosia, fishing out the little golden crook of Saint Serzhei she wore around her neck and kissing it fervently. "Abbot Yephimy won't want to come over from the monastery to perform an exorcism in all this snow."

"And she only appears when Risa's there." New anxieties had begun to ferment in Kiukiu's mind. *What does she want with my daughter? Is it one of the Drakhaon's Brides come back from beyond the grave for revenge?*

Or has she been sent by Anagini?

Chapter 18

Since the winter solstice feast, fresh snow had been falling steadily on Kastel Nagarian for five days and nights, covering the last ragged russet bracken on the moors with its chill, white purity.

Beware the jade-haired witch of the spring. Kiukiu stood at the bedchamber window, gazing out at the falling flakes. The ominous refrain from Khulan's song had begun to wreathe round and round her mind again. Before she realized what she was doing, she had begun to sing softly, "She never gives without taking something in return—"

She stopped, clapping one hand over her mouth to stifle the mocking words. "How can I protect Larisa?" she whispered, her breath frosting the diamond panes.

If only you were still alive, Grandma, you'd tell me what to do.

"Something in return," echoed a man's voice.

She started, turning around to see Gavril watching her. She'd been so wrapped up in her own thoughts that she hadn't even heard him enter.

"Ever since that singer came, you've been so . . . quiet." He placed his hands on her shoulders, gazing searchingly into her eyes. "Did something happen in

Khitari last year that you haven't told me about? Does Khulan have some hold over you?"

She had never hidden anything from him before. It made her heart ache to know that she could never share this burden. *A wound leaking life's blood that never heals . . .* She must lie and go on lying until she could fathom out a way to save Larisa from a lifetime of service bound to Anagini. And she hated to deceive the one she loved so dearly.

"No hold," she said, forcing herself to smile.

"Or was it the song? You never did tell me exactly what happened at the Jade Springs."

"Lady Anagini healed me. She restored my lost youth." Kiukiu couldn't look at him directly. She would have to dissemble better than this if she were to allay his suspicions.

"Yet in Khulan's song, the refrain said that the witch never gives without taking something in return. What did *you* have to give her, Kiukiu?" His grip tightened.

"It's just an old song, a fanciful superstition." She tried to make light of it. "The Guardian of the Springs had a grudge of her own against Prince Nagazdiel. She wanted us to make sure he was never set free from the Realm of Shadows. She knew that if my powers as a Spirit Singer were restored, I could help you and the Emperor defeat him." There was a grain of truth in the explanation.

His grip loosened but he did not let go of her. "So that was the bargain?"

"Why?" She forced a laugh. "What did you think?"

"Oh, all kind of crazy jealous stuff. The product of an overheated imagination."

"Such as?"

Now he was the one to look away. "You're the last of the Spirit Singers. I thought maybe that you had been forced to sleep with Khan Vachir to infuse his bloodline with your powers. Or—"

Kiukiu let out a snort of derision. "Do you remember how old and hideous I was then? The Khan was surrounded by women, each one as beautiful as Khulan. He hardly even noticed me." Then, as the full impact of his words sank in, she cried, "Now wait a moment! Were you suggesting that Larisa isn't your child, my lord? That I deceived you?"

He retreated, hands raised appeasingly. "I should never have said it. I—"

A piercing wail arose from Larisa's crib. Kiukiu shot Gavril a resentful look and went to pick up the baby. When she turned around, Gavril had left the room.

***

The snow-covered garden was icily chill yet Gavril hardly noticed, walking stubbornly on, shivering, toward the summerhouse.

What on earth possessed me to make such a crass accusation? He opened the door, ducking as a small avalanche slid off the sloping roof. *How could I be so insensitive?*

Inside, his breath fogged the cold air. *Too cold to paint until I get a fire going.* He'd had a little wood-burning stove installed for winter days but had neglected to clean it out since his last visit. He squatted to scrape the cold ashes into a pail, and then laid fresh wood inside, using the tinder box and dry kindling to start a blaze. He stamped his feet as he waited for the logs to catch alight, blowing on his frozen fingers. At least these practical tasks were keeping his mind occupied. His conscience was pricking him, urging him to return to Kiukiu and apologize for his hasty and irrational words. But something held him back: pride, maybe, mingled with guilt at having acted with such insensitivity.

And yet I'm sure she's hiding something from me. Sometimes I catch a strange look in her eyes: distracted, almost desperate.

He stopped in front of the little self-portrait of his mother that he had brought from the Villa Andara; Elysia had dashed it off one day when he was about twelve "in an idle moment" and then lightly flavored it with a dash or two of watercolors. That "idle moment" had resulted in a remarkably honest piece of work; she had not flattered herself in any way, showing her rich auburn hair touched with the first streaks of silver, and the little worry lines between her brows. But what Gavril loved most about the sketch was the way she had captured something of her indomitable zest for life: the ghost of a smile curving her full, generous mouth upward as she gazed at, through, beyond her own reflection into an unknowable future. They had been living off her earnings as a portrait painter in her ramshackle family villa, poor yet carefree, untroubled by the distant shadow of the Drakhaoul.

"What would you have advised, Mother? You'd have just laughed and said, 'You'll have to work it out, the two of you. If you love each other, you'll find a way.'"

Yet just as he was basking in the warmth of his cherished childhood memories, a sudden cold stab of pain shot through his wrist, so intense that it made him suck in his breath. Peeling back his cuff and sleeve to expose the bare skin, he saw that the place where Morozhka had slashed his flesh with her ice-blade was still raw.

It's not healing. If Kiukiu had secrets she was not ready to share, so had he. Thus far he had avoided telling her what drove him back to the studio, day after day, to paint like one possessed. He had not mentioned the hold that Lady Morozhka had over him.

He gritted his teeth as he tried to bind the wound with his clean handkerchief. *What poison did Morozhka inject into me? Is this her way of keeping track of me, insuring that I don't renege on our bargain?*

There was no way out of the deal but to keep painting.

He removed the cloth that he'd slung over the current work in progress and shuddered as the unsettling sensations were reawakened.

It was almost as if the very act of dipping a brush in a dark, oily gray or daubing vivid shafts of stormy light only served to enhance the disorienting dream images until they bled into his waking life, tainting everything he did. The quiet domestic routine that he had longed for was fast slipping away from him as the compulsion to keep working dominated his waking hours.

There's been no peace since I met Morozhka. It must be her doing.

At first he had been reluctant to commit these visions to canvas but now he had started, he could not stop.

"What do they mean, Khezef? Why did you leave these images with me?" He took a step back to assess the latest bleak landscape, absently rubbing his forehead as he peered at it, leaving a smear of ultramarine behind and hastily wiping it off on his sleeve. "One clue. Just one clue, that's all I need."

The building pressure in his head made his temples throb; he reached for the mug of tea he'd brought with him, only to find it had gone stone-cold.

How long have I been out here? The light's fading.

The temperature was dropping fast too; the glass panes in the windows were icing over with a sugary tracery of frost flowers. The gash in his left wrist began to tingle.

"Good day, Drakhaon."

He turned around and saw that a woman had silently entered his studio; the dusky light lent her white hair a faint crystalline shimmer.

"Lady Morozhka?" His heart was beating too fast; her unexpected appearance had spooked him. She smiled at him and the smile sent a shiver through him.

"I've come to see what you've done since we last met. Show me."

***

The warm scent of cinnamon and ginger filled the kitchen.

Gavril's avoiding me. Kiukiu had tried to concentrate on other tasks all day since they had argued: helping Ninusha with the washing; baking spiced biscuits and generally getting in Ilsi's way.

"For heaven's sakes, Kiukiu, go to the parlor and I'll bring you some tea," Ilsi cried. "I've got to prepare dinner and the oven's full of half-cooked biscuits."

If she hadn't felt so unhappy, Kiukiu would have given Ilsi a tart answer back, but she was too downhearted to bother.

She gathered up Larisa and went to the parlor where she set the baby down on the rug at a safe distance from the hearth and went to draw the curtains. A single light burned at the far end of the garden, casting a streak of yellow light over the darkening snow. *So that's where Gavril's been hiding; he's painting again in the summerhouse.* She sighed. *He doesn't want to talk to me. He's still furious and I can't really blame him.* She tugged the worn blue velvet curtains closed, shutting out the lonely sight of the solitary lamp-flame.

There's no one here I can confide in. No one who understands me, as Grandma did. If only I could talk to her one more time.

Ninusha appeared in the doorway, holding a wriggling Kion in her arms. "I'm just going to give Kion his bath; shall I bathe Larisa at the same time?"

Kiukiu sniffed; the air in the parlor was tainted by an unmistakably ripe odor of smelly baby. "Please do," she said, grimacing as she passed her cheerfully squawking daughter to Ninusha. "I think she must be teething again."

No sooner had she sat down than a pine log in the grate spat noisily, releasing a cloud of sparks. Kiukiu got up hastily to seize the poker and push the wildly-flaring log to the back of the chimney-place before any damage was done.

But I could go to look for Grandma in the Ways Beyond. The thought sneaked its way into her mind before she could suppress it. "No," she said aloud. "I promised Grandma I'd never go back there again. I promised I'd only perform the Soul-Sending rites for the dead, not Soul-Seeking Songs." She drank her tea, listening to the crackle of the pine-scented logs and the snow-muffled silence beyond the kastel walls.

"But this is different. Larisa's future is at stake. And my marriage. If I just ventured in for a few moments . . ."

As she made her way to the bedchamber, she heard the sound of splashing and happily gurgling babies issuing from the nursery. "Here comes Mister Duck," Ninusha was singing, and the babies joined in with the chorus, "Quack, quack, quack . . ."

Kiukiu's gusly lay beneath the bed, gathering dust. She dragged it out and wiped it clean, dampening the strings to mute their dissonant twang. She felt guilty to have let it lie there neglected for so long. This was, after all, the precious instrument that had once belonged to her grandmother and that had been left behind in Kaspar Linnaius's rooms at Swanholm. The Emperor himself had arranged for it to be sent back to her, carefully wrapped in fine cloth and sealed in a metal casket.

So long since I played, even to please myself. She began to tune, plucking very softly. *Babies take up so much time and energy.* The gusly was a Spirit Singer's pathway to the Ways Beyond but finding the right sequence of notes to open up a gateway that would let her pass safely through was always a considerable challenge. Her fingertips had grown soft and she was badly out of practice. Soon, even though she was wearing the special plectra, she was wincing as she gently plucked the sonorous strings and felt the twisted metal bite into her flesh.

Forget the pain. Concentrate. She closed her eyes, letting each deep pitch resonate through her whole body, letting it take her drifting consciousness and carry it far out into the winter night and beyond.

"Grandma, can you hear me? Where are you?"

Grandma and I were walking through a grove of silvered birch trees. The light was soft, like the spring sun glimpsed through drifting clouds, with the shimmer of a great lake in the distance.

Her fingers instinctively begun to pick out notes that she had not played in a long while: a praise song written by Malkh, her father, to honor his clan lord, Stavyor Arkhel. Out of the insubstantial gray mists swirling around her she saw slender tree trunks appearing, mottled white and gray. She paused, and heard someone continue with the next phrase.

Who else would know that song?

A woman was singing nearby, in a low, throaty voice that sounded like the purring coo of a wood dove. Each phrase was accompanied by a swirl of reverberant notes from a gusly.

Kiukiu hastened eagerly onward, letting the music guide her. The last trails of mists melted away and she saw the form of a woman sitting with her back against the papery bark of a silver birch tree, holding a gusly in her lap. But this was not the gray-haired, stooped Malusha she remembered; this singer was straight-backed, her brown hair plaited in braids threaded through with colored cords of red and blue, and her eyes were clear and piercing as crystal.

"Grandma?" Kiukiu cried. "Oh, Grandma, it *is* you."

The shaman woman set down her gusly. "What are you doing here, child? Go back. Go back now while you still can."

"But Grandma—" Kiukiu began, then stopped, her voice choked by sudden tears. "I've missed you so much."

"Didn't I warn you before?" Malusha said sharply. "If you get lost in the Ways Beyond, I won't be there to call you back into the world of the living. And what would become of my great-grandchild if her mother couldn't take care of her?"

Great-grandchild? Kiukiu gazed at her grandmother through tear-blurred ideas. "How did you know?"

"It's written all over your face." Malusha's stern tone softened a little. "Such happiness in your eyes, it does my heart good to see it. What name have you given the baby?"

"Larisa," Kiukiu said. And then, overcome by emotion again, she burst out, "I wish you could see her, she's so beautiful, with dark sea-blue eyes just like her daddy's."

"So why have you taken such a risk coming here, Kiukiu?"

"I badly need your advice. I promised never to tell a living soul, so you're the only one I can turn to." Kiukiu hung her head, unable to meet Malusha's penetrating stare any longer.

"Never to tell what precisely?"

"I made a promise to Lady Anagini. In exchange for restoring my youth I promised—I promised to—"

"Give her your firstborn child?"

Kiukiu nodded, too miserable to say the words aloud, as if in saying them—even here—she was sealing her child's fate forever.

Malusha let out a sigh. "This wouldn't be the first time that Anagini has exacted such a harsh price. And what does Lord Gavril think about this bargain?"

Kiukiu winced. Malusha had guessed.

"You haven't told him."

"How *could* I, Grandma? She said if I tell, I'll lose my youth and become an old woman once more."

Malusha let out a slow sigh.

"I don't want to be old again before my time, Grandma." The desperation that had been building within her since Larisa's birth began to pour out. "But Gavril's already guessed that something's wrong. He knows I'm hiding something from him. And it's driving us apart. What can I do?"

"You've endured so many hardships together—and come through, thanks to your love for each other." Malusha nodded encouragingly. "You'll find a way."

"Should I go back to Anagini and ask her to spare our baby? Suppose I offered myself in her place?"

"And how would that make matters any better for your child—or for your husband?" A breeze shivered through the golden leaves of the birches overhead and Kiukiu suddenly felt uneasy, as if others might be listening to their conversation.

"Can you tell him?"

Malusha laughed. "And how would I do that? I refuse to take over some poor living soul's body as a conduit; it's messy and it'd be risky for the both of us."

"Couldn't you speak to him in a dream, then? There has to be some way to warn him."

"And even if I could, what good would it do? There's no way the snake goddess is going to change her mind. You sealed a bond with her; she marked your ankle with her forked tongue, didn't she, as proof? It's written on your skin and in your blood."

Even as Malusha reminded her, Kiukiu felt as though the mark had begun to burn, like the envenomed sting of a wasp or a bee. *How is that, when I'm only here in spirit? It's as if Anagini put her mark on my soul as well as my body.* The thought filled her with dread and despair; there seemed no way to escape this impossible contract. "Is there no one else who can help me?" she heard herself asking.

"If I were a callous woman, I'd say to you: Have more children. Accept that you've borne Larisa for Lady Anagini; she's always been the snake goddess's child and you're merely acting as her nursemaid until she's old enough to go back to her mother."

"How can you even suggest such a thing?" Kiukiu felt tears filling her eyes. "I—I love Larisa. She's our firstborn. I can't just give her away. It would break Gavril's heart."

Malusha shrugged and a breath of breeze stirred the strings of her gusly, making them give off a metallic whisper of notes. "And suppose Lady Anagini has looked into the future and foresees a better life for your little one if she stays in her care?"

Kiukiu shook her head vehemently. "How could Larisa have a better life apart from her parents?" Unless Anagini had foreseen a terrible event that was yet to occur. Was someone coming after Gavril for revenge? *He's made many enemies.* The possibilities made her brain ache. *The future's not graven in stone. No point worrying about what might happen.*

"You said that Lady Anagini has done this before. What happened then?"

"I only heard snips and snaps of rumors. But they all concerned Kaspar Linnaius."

"The Magus? He had a child?" This thought was so astonishing to Kiukiu that she could hardly imagine one as old and cold-hearted as Linnaius ever falling in love, let alone siring children. But then she remembered his younger spirit-self, encountered once before in the Ways, tall, and well-favored in a lean, scholarly fashion, with hair the light brown of alder bark. *He must have had many women sighing over him in his time.* "I could go to seek him out and ask for his help. But . . ." She shuddered. "It was his fault I lost my youth in the first place. How could I ever trust him not to trick me again?"

The breeze stirring the gilded birch leaves began to gust in earnest; Kiukiu sensed—with a sudden chill of foreboding—that she had outstayed her time in the Ways. Mist was seeping in between the silvered trunks, drifting between her and her grandmother so that Malusha's beloved, familiar face was already becoming indistinct.

"Don't linger, child," she heard her grandmother say, her voice harsh with warning. "I sense *Others* are watching us."

219

Others. Lost Souls wandered the margins of the Ways Beyond, seeking to suck the life force out of unwary Spirit Singers who were trespassing in the lands of the dead—or to return to the mortal world as revenants to trouble the living. They usually gave off a disturbing, unwholesome aura that made Kiukiu's senses crawl. But this felt different.

Malusha leaned in close and whispered, "Remember the Golden Scale?"

Kiukiu remembered. "But the Heavenly Guardians warned us never to use it again. When they threw us out of the Second Heaven."

"Use it. But only when all else fails." The mist came rolling in so swiftly that Kiukiu could hardly make out her grandmother's face any longer. But the urgency of her words reached her even through the shifting veils. " Now go back home straight away."

"What are you doing here, trespassing in the Ways Beyond?" The voice rang out like a trumpet call: clear and commanding.

Kiukiu fled.

***

Lady Morozhka came closer to the easel and Gavril placed first one canvas, then another and another for her to look at.

"As I hoped," she said softly. "These may well be gates between this world and that other realm where your daemon and his kin have gone." She seemed mesmerized by his work, gazing intently at each image in turn.

"So you recognize these places?"

"This one." Morozhka pointed to the most recent landscape he had finished; a green-grassed plateau, high among mountain peaks. "This is the way I first came into this world. But then *they* appeared and sealed the gate. And I was trapped here."

"Who appeared?" Gavril asked warily.

"The Gatekeepers. From the Ways Beyond. They drove us out, us Elder Ones. And then they forced us into hiding."

"From the Ways Beyond?" Gavril repeated under his breath. Her words stirred something at the back of his mind. "Do you mean the Heavenly Guardians?"

"'Heavenly'?" Morozhka's voice hardened with contempt. "They punished all our followers, all those who clung to the old beliefs. And without followers, us Elder Ones, we fade and eventually cease to exist. It's a slow, cruel way to die."

Gavril's teeth had begun to chatter uncontrollably; the intense cold was slowing his thoughts and he was struggling to make sense of what Lady Morozhka was saying. It sounded like a warning. "Have you seen the Heavenly Guardians? Here, in Azhkendir?"

"Not yet. But they've been watching us." She wound her arms across her breast as if in self-defence. "I can sense them."

"But why did Khezef leave these memories with me?" He was troubled by her words. "Does he want me to follow him?" What had Khezef foreseen in his future? "Are they coming to punish me?"

She turned to gaze at him and the frosty glitter of her eyes made him shiver. "Maybe so."

"Even if we could find one of these gates, how could it be opened?" He'd have no truck with any resort to child sacrifice; no innocent blood would be shed or innocent souls stolen this time, no matter what it cost him. The blood-imbued rubies that once adorned Artamon's crown and divided his sons and the empire were gone.

"Didn't your daemon tell you?"

Gavril shook his head.

"Perhaps," she said, her breath cold against his cheek as she leaned in toward him, "you need me to help you remember." And before he could turn away, she kissed him, the touch of her icy lips flooding his mind with a riot of images and sensations.

He took a step back. There was a bitter tang of snow on her breath that sent fresh chills through him.

"Without my help, you would not have been able to paint these, would you? I've helped you. I unsealed the memories Khezef left in your mind—" She gave a sudden start, turning away to stare in the direction of the kastel.

"Your wife is in danger."

"Danger?" Gavril echoed, caught off-guard.

"Go to her. Now." The urgency in her voice propelled him toward the door. "We'll talk again." Her words carried after him across the snowy garden as he hurried, slipping and sliding up the frozen path in his haste.

***

"Halt!"

The clarion command brought Kiukiu to a sudden stop.

A radiance, pure as a cloudless morning sky lit the birch trunks, melting away the wisping mist, growing in brilliance until she was so dazzled it hurt her eyes to gaze at it and she raised her hands to shield her face.

This brightness—I've seen it before.

Eyes, pale as the blue waters of Lake Taigal, fixed her with a challenging stare, as the light-riven mists parted to reveal a tall Warrior, his great wings furled, armed with a spear whose translucent head glittered as if it had been carved from ice.

"Why are you here?"

Definitely not a Lost Soul, this one.

"Answer me." His long hair shimmered with the sheen of sunlight seen through rain, as he came toward her. She tried to run, but found herself unable to move.

He's one of the Heavenly Guardians. "Beautiful, yet terrible to behold." *This is how Khezef must have looked before he rebelled and was imprisoned in the Realm of Shadows .*

"The living are forbidden to enter the Ways Beyond." He leveled the tip of the crystalline spearhead at her breast. "How did you find your way?"

Kiukiu could feel powerful vibrations emanating from the spear. Terrified, she could only shake her head. *If he attacks me with that weapon—even in my spirit form—what will it do to me?*

The young Warrior's stern expression showed no sign of softening. "You must be one of those rebellious Spirit Singers I've been warned to look out for."

She nodded, wondering if he was going to punish her. *Or suppose he punishes Grandma for speaking with me?* "Please," she managed to whisper, "don't hurt my grandmother. I came looking for her—she didn't ask to be found."

The pale, stern eyes stared at her, unblinking, as the Warrior raised his spear, pointing it toward her forehead. A bolt of pure energy, keen and cold as a sliver of ice, pierced her consciousness.

Everything was obliterated in a sheen of frost.

When her vision cleared, she was alone. There was no sign of the young Winged Warrior or Malusha. The familiar birch grove had melted away. Mists were swirling around her, stirring up little puffs of a fine, grimy dust.

Out of the corner of her eye Kiukiu glimpsed shadowy forms materializing in the swirling mist, heard a dry whispering on the breeze that began to form words.

"Help us, Spirit Singer."

Wavering figures, dust gray, insubstantial as skeletal leaves, reached out with long spindle fingers to paw at her. Lifeless, hungry eyes gleamed through the billowing mist.

"Take us back with you."

Chapter 19

Don't look at them. Don't look into their eyes.

Kiukiu shrank away from the clustering shadows as they surrounded her, swarming closer and closer. If a Spirit Singer gazed into the dead eyes of a Lost Soul, they were lost. Sucked into the miasmic aura of decaying memories and bitter regrets, they were easy prey for the Lost Ones who would gorge on their spirit energy, leaving their victims' physical bodies soulless and inanimate, locked in a deathlike trance until the last glimmerings of life faded, and nothing remained but an empty husk.

The sickly smell of moldering charnel breath made her want to retch.

How do I get home? Her mind had gone blank. The mists were swirling around her and stirring up clouds of dust. *Not good. I must have strayed too close to the Realm of Shadows. Or did that Warrior send me here?*

"Kiukiu!"

Gavril's voice . . . calling her name.

But that was impossible. Without Khezef to be his guide and protector, the Ways Beyond were inaccessible to him. She struggled onward through the choking dust clouds toward the sound of the voice, eyes closed, straining to hear it again above the ominous roar of the infernal winds.

"Kiukiu. Wake up, Kiukiu."

Someone was shaking her.

"Please wake up!"

She felt a warm hand encircle her own, pressing it firmly, dragging her out of the dream.

She surfaced, wheezing, gasping for air, to see eyes of deepest sea-blue staring at her. She clutched at Gavril like a drowning woman.

"Don't scare me like that, Kiukiu." His arms went round her and she clung to him, trying to reassure herself that he was real, flesh and bone and warm blood. "You were lying there in a deep trance. And I couldn't reach you."

Kiukiu blinked. The lamps were lit; it was night. "How long was I—?"

"Too long. What on earth were you trying to do?"

"I wanted to see Malusha. I wanted to tell her about Larisa."

"But you promised me you wouldn't risk going back to the Ways Beyond." He gazed at her sternly. "You've got a daughter to think of now. Larisa needs you."

She turned her face away from his. How could he know how much those words hurt her? Larisa was the only reason she had ventured back to that strange and unknowable place. *And it's all my fault, I should never have agreed to Anagini's bond. But I was so desperate, I hadn't the wits or the strength to argue with her.*

And then she remembered what Malusha had told her. "The Magus," she said, thinking aloud. "Where can I find him, I wonder?"

Gavril held her at arm's length, gazing at her quizzically. "Did you leave your wits in the Ways Beyond? Why on earth would you seek him out after he used you so callously?"

"He owes me—and you too. You saved his life."

Gavril sighed and his hands fell away from her shoulders. "I could write to Eugene and ask for his advice. But the last I heard was that Linnaius has been replaced by Altan Kazimir as the Imperial Artificier."

The wind whined outside the window, setting the shutters rattling. Kiukiu went very still, listening intently. Was that a faint whisper of song, sung by a high, eerie voice, borne on the icy wind?

"White feathers come tumbling down . . ."

"What is it?"

"Tumbling down . . ."

"Can't you hear it?" The strange, haunting refrain sent snow-cold shivers down Kiukiu's spine.

"I can hear the wind."

"Someone's singing out there." She went to the window, opening the shutters to try to peer out through the frosted panes.

"It must be one of the servants."

"I've never heard one of our girls sing that old song." Kiukiu closed her eyes as she strained to catch the elusive strains but a fresh gust of wind drowned the plaintive melody. When it died down, there was no trace left behind, as if the wind had blown it far away.

Gavril caught hold of her hand in a firm reassuring grip and pulled her close. "Come to bed," he said. It was a command she could not refuse.

***

"You've been painting again." Kiukiu sniffed, wrinkling her nose at the strong odors of turpentine and oil paint that seemed to exude from every pore and hair of her husband's body. "Can I see what you've been working on? Please?"

Gavril hesitated, his gaze becoming distant. "I'm out of practice. Nothing's ready yet."

"You said you were painting a portrait of Larisa. I'd love to see the sketches." She rolled over onto her stomach, propping her chin on her hands to gaze at him.

"I can show you my sketchbook. But it's freezing in the summerhouse; I'm still clearing up, making paints, cleaning brushes." Was he being evasive for a reason?

"Gavril Nagarian, anyone would think you were keeping a mistress out there," she said, half jesting, half in earnest.

"Well, if so, she'd be a frozen mistress by now." Was that a glint of teasing humor in his eyes? "Sometimes you say the silliest things, Kiukiu."

She opened her mouth to protest but he made a grab for her, catching her in his arms, rolling her over onto her back and stifling her objection with a long and deep kiss. When she surfaced for air, he said, "Why would I need a mistress when I have you?" and she felt her earlier suspicions begin to melt away as his roving hands slipped beneath her night gown, exploring, caressing. "Stop! That tickles!" she cried, giggling uncontrollably, but her protests soon subsided and she surrendered to his desires.

***

Do I really know you, Gavril Nagarian?

By the dying light from the embers in the grate Kiukiu could just make out the outline of his sleeping face, his soft, dark lashes, the firm arch of his brows. He looked much younger asleep, the frown lines of responsibility and worry smoothed away. There had been a desperate intensity to his lovemaking, as if he were trying to lose himself in the act, or exorcise the fears he still would not, could not talk about. *But then, how well can anyone really know another person?* She couldn't resist gently stroking a straying lock of hair from his forehead; he was so deeply, trustingly asleep that he didn't even stir.

He's changed. Perhaps he's changed more than I realized—more than I wanted to accept. He went through so much at the Serpent Gate; maybe he can never be the same Gavril I fell in love with.

Never the same . . . That thought sent an ache of desolation throughout her whole being. *No, he's making a good recovery. It was never going to be easy for him, learning to survive without Khezef's powers. I mustn't expect too much of him too soon.*

Another niggling worry surfaced again, one that had been troubling her for many months. *We were apart for so long. Maybe he met another woman—in Francia, or back home in Smarna—and now he's having regrets at having settled down with me. After all, artists are said to be free spirits, so . . .* But the thought of Gavril being unfaithful was intolerable and she pushed it from her mind.

We were destined for each other. I couldn't bear it if he fell in love with someone else.

***

Ilsi was serving up her winter soup, a hearty herb-flavored bacon broth filled with barley, chunks of turnip and carrot. All the staff had gathered in the kitchen for the midday meal as it was the warmest room in the kastel but, to Kiukiu's exasperation, Gavril was absent—again.

"He's the lord of the kastel," Ilsi said on seeing Kiukiu's sour expression, "he can do as he pleases. He must be busy with official work."

Kiukiu shook her head; she had gone to call him, only to find his study empty, except for a daunting pile of official documents piled up on his desk awaiting his approval. "He's probably in his studio again."

"Shall I keep some soup hot for him?"

"I'll take him some in a canteen. The fresh air will do me good."

"Fresh?" Ilsi repeated. "It's cold enough to freeze your ears off out there today."

Kiukiu wrapped herself up in a shawl and hooded cloak, pulled on her mittens, and set off through the garden over the fresh skim of snow that had fallen in the night. Her boots crunched over the frozen crystals as she carefully carried Ilsi's soup toward the summerhouse. It was a day of brilliant clarity; she could see as far as the Kharzhgylls, whose craggy peaks glittered white against the peerless blue of the sky. The sun might be shining overhead but the wind off the moors was bitingly chill, rattling the bare branches like skeletal fingers and making the tip of her nose tingle.

She reached the summerhouse and set the canteen of soup down to tap at the door.

"Gavril," she called, "I've brought your lunch." When there was no reply, she sighed and said, "I'm coming in!" *Too engrossed in his painting to even hear his wife's voice.*

It was warm enough inside the summerhouse for Kiukiu to be able to push back her hood as she gazed around. She could feel a faint glow emanating from the stove in the corner and the strong odor of the oil paints made her wind-stung eyes water. But there was no sign of her husband.

"Gavril?" She gazed around her, noting all the signs of work in progress: the brushes lying on the paint-smeared table; the charcoal sketches strewn across the floor; the canvas propped up on the easel with just a detail or two already filled in. *This soup will go cold. Where can he have got to?*

Several of his mother Elysia's paintings hung on the wall: watercolors of the villa garden in Colchise, vibrant with the sun-burned tones of the hot Smarnan summer. Kiukiu loved to look at these intimate domestic pictures, knowing that the dark-haired boy sketched fishing in the rock pools on the shore, sitting high in the gnarled branches of an old peach tree or helping dig the kitchen garden, was Gavril, captured by his doting mother at the age of nine, ten, eleven . . .

I hope he's keeping a record of Larisa too. I'd love to see his latest drawings. She set the soup on top of the iron stove and popped another log inside, stoking the dying fire. *I'll bet he's just being a perfectionist, not wanting to let me see his work in progress.. .*

And then curiosity overcame any other considerations and she found herself going to the stack of canvases in the darkest corner of the summerhouse, kneeling down to steal a quick, illicit glance.

Landscapes . . . places she had never seen before, each one more strange than the one before, culminating in one painting that made her gasp out loud.

A crazed daub of lurid colors, compelling yet utterly incomprehensible: swirls of intense, luminous blues and morbid purples, lit with star-splatters of white and yellow.

Is Gavril losing his mind? She sat back on her heels, her heart pounding, as it stirred distant yet familiar sensations deep within her. The more she looked at it, the more disturbed it made her feel. *This reminds me of the Ways Beyond.* She sensed that there was a faint skim of shadow overlaying the image, as though the scene were glimpsed through other eyes. Drakhaoul eyes?

Are these Gavril's memories—or Khezef's?

Khezef, always suffering in the role imposed upon him by his fellow Winged Warriors, forced—until he rebelled—to be Heaven's Avenger: the Bringer of Death.

"Kiukiu?" Gavril stood in the open doorway, stamping the snow from his boots. He was carrying a battered leather-bound volume.

She started guiltily, caught in the act of snooping. "I—I brought you soup . . ." On seeing the distraught expression on his face, her voice died away.

He crossed the summerhouse floor and placed himself in front of the canvases, as if to shield her from further exposure to their malign influence.

"You shouldn't have looked." His voice was hoarse from the intense cold outside.

"I'm sorry." She hung her head, feeling like a naughty child caught dipping a finger in the honey jar. And then, defiantly, she rose and gripped him by the arms. "Gavril, are these your memories? Or Khezef's?"

He did not meet her eyes, looking beyond her. "Does it matter?"

"But why should you bear the burden of his guilt? Why should you go on suffering? I know you still have nightmares." Her fingers pressed harder into the worn leather of his greatcoat.

Still he said nothing. Undeterred, she tried a different tack. "You're a portraitist. When did you start to paint landscapes?"

His gaze, still centered on some far-distant point, clouded over.

"Ever since you met Lady Morozhka in the forest, you've been . . . different."

He blinked as she said Morozhka's name. Had she guessed correctly? Determined to learn the truth, she asked, "What did she do to you?"

A sigh escaped him, a slow release of pent-up breath, almost as though he was relieved that she'd guessed his secret. "She told me Khezef had left memories with me. And I don't know how else to make sense of them. Night after night I see these places in my dreams. Places I'm certain I've never visited."

She let go of him and went back to the stack of canvases. "Don't you recognize any of them?"

A confused frown flickered across his face. And then he squatted down to pull out one that showed a stark moonlit mountain ravine with a rugged peak towering behind. "This reminds me of Mount Diktra.

It's the tallest peak in the Larani range that marks the border between Smarna and Muscobar."

"Smarna? So you *have* been there."

He gave a terse nod; the memory was evidently not a pleasant one. If creating these images was meant to be therapeutic, then the therapy was not proving very effective. She pulled out another canvas. "And this?" His blue eyes narrowed as he peered at the landscape which portrayed a mountain lake surrounded by crags from which a white waterfall tumbled into the gray waters.

"This one I don't recognize at all."

"And this?" The third canvas was completely different from the others; it showed a vast expanse of sand, an arid golden desert from which arose strangely twisted rocky towers.

He shook his head. "No idea. Although I read in my father's diaries that he and Khezef once traveled to visit the Arkhan of Enhirre. And Enhirre is mostly desert. There may be a connection." He opened the leather-bound volume he had brought from the kastel, placing it flat on the floor so that she could see it was an old atlas.

"My father's. One of the books I rescued from his study after the Tielen bombardment."

She squinted at it, getting down on hands and knees to take a closer look. The yellowed pages showed a map whose ornately lettered title she slowly spelled out. "'The Western Quadrant'. Is that Azhkendir?" she asked, tracing the outline of the country, lingering over the place where the Kharzhgyll Mountains met Kerjhenezh Forest.

"And Tielen is over there, to the west." He took up a small paint brush, dipped the slender tip in some scarlet paint and—to her horror—marked a little cross on the map, and then another.

"What are you doing?"

"I'm marking the places in the paintings that I can identify. Morozhka's Round in Azhkendir. Mount Diktra in Smarna." His brush hovered above the southern lands of Enhirre and Djihan-Djihar, darting down to make another neat cross. "Ondhessar. That's the name my father mentioned in his diary. An ancient fortress in the desert."

"Places that Khezef knew?"

"Places that were gateways," he said, staring at the pattern of crosses he had made.

"Between this world and the Ways Beyond? Or that Gate beyond the Serpent Gate?" Kiukiu had helped to open a doorway to the distant aethyrial realm, using a Sending Song to dispatch the Drakhaouls beyond the mortal world once and for all. "Did he mean you to follow him? Or does Morozhka want to go there too? Surely it's too late."

"She said it was for me. Does that mean that anyone who's been possessed by a Drakhaoul falls apart once the Drakhaoul has left their body?" He seemed to be talking to himself. "Eugene, Prince Andrei, Oskar Alvborg . . ." Had these worries been troubling him since the dreams began? She reached out to touch his hand and he looked up at her, his eyes dark with concern. "You'd tell me, wouldn't you, Kiukiu? If I began to behave irrationally?"

She reached out to hug him to her, stroking his hair. "You'll be all right, Gavril. Morozhka's been putting ideas in your head. She's using you. She wants to find the Gate for herself."

Chapter 20

"Come at me again, my lord," Bogatyr Askold ordered, raising his wooden blade to a defensive position across his body.

Gavril wiped away the sweat dripping into his eyes with his sleeve and gripped his practice sword. Askold had blocked every move he made, repelling him with ease, sending him stumbling backward across the hall.

I'm not going to be beaten. There must be a way to get under his guard.

Day after day, since his encounter with Morozhka, Gavril had sparred with Askold in the kastel hall, beneath the stern gaze of his father's portrait. Determined to learn something of the druzhina's fighting skills, he put on padded practice armor and began to learn the training rituals the Bogatyr put his men through daily.

If I make as if I'm going to attack his right side but lunge upward at the last moment to the left . . .

Gavril launched himself forward, putting all his strength into a two-handed thrust. Askold parried so swiftly that Gavril forgot to plant both feet firmly and Askold's wooden blade struck his aside. The blow sent judders up both arms and Gavril's sword fell from his grip, rattling away across the tiled floor as he sank to one knee, humiliated and gasping for breath.

"Not bad," said Askold, "for a novice."

Gavril looked up and saw that Askold had extended his hand to him to help him up. He shook his head. "You don't catch me that way so easily," he wheezed. "You're going to do one of your wrestling moves on me, aren't you, and pin me to the ground with one arm behind my back."

Askold grinned. "Very good, my lord, you're learning fast. But you're still at my mercy." He slid his wooden blade-tip beneath Gavril's chin. "On the battlefield, I'd have slit your throat by now." He mimed, the sword pressing painfully against Gavril's throat. Gavril swiveled around and pointed his index finger at Askold's head. "Bang! The closer you get, the easier it is for me to take out my new Tielen pistol and shoot you."

"Ah, but you have only one shot. And if your powder gets damp or the pistol misfires . . ."

"So teach me how to get out of this situation. Without a pistol."

"If you're wearing gloves, you could grab the blade and twist it aside; that's a desperate measure. Simpler to roll away, reach for the throwing knives in your boot, and hurl those at your attacker."

"And if I've run out of throwing knives?" Gavril didn't wait for Askold's answer. "I'm dead, aren't I?" His hands were chafed and sore from gripping the wooden hilt and his padded jacket was soaked with sweat. He felt demoralized. "I'd just be a liability if we were attacked."

"You're faster on your feet than when we started." Askold squatted down beside him. "But you need to practice every day."

"Or we need to buy more pistols and muskets."

"And how are you going to afford to arm all the druzhina with such expensive weapons?"

Trust Askold to pinpoint the fatal flaw in his plan. "I'll ask the Emperor."

Askold raised one eyebrow in an all-too familiar expression of weary skepticism. Gavril knew the Bogatyr had little faith that Eugene would expend vital funds on equipping the druzhina.

"As part of New Rossiya, we need to be ready to defend the empire at all times." But even as Gavril said the words, he knew how hollow they must sound to Askold.

Askold merely saluted him with his wooden blade, indicating that the practice session was at an end.

"Go and take a hot bath, my lord, before you start to stiffen up, or you'll be walking like an old man by nightfall."

***

The Golden Scale.

Kiukiu stared down at the strings of the gusly, fingertips poised, ready to play—and paused. *"Use it. But only when all else fails."* Malusha's warning, hastily whispered before the Heavenly Guardian appeared to drive them apart, had been troubling her. "When all else fails?" she repeated under her breath. What had her grandmother meant?

The Heavenly Guardians had warned Kiukiu and her grandmother never to play it again. So even to quietly tap the strings to remind herself of the complicated sequence of notes was a very risky undertaking. If the secret Guslyars' chant could still open a way to the Second Heaven, the ever-vigilant Guardians might become aware of what she was doing—and intervene.

Larisa let out a soft little sigh beside her. After a fractious early morning start with much dribbling and a hot red cheek, she had fallen fast asleep on the bed. Which meant that she would be lively later on that evening when her usual bedtime came around, demanding songs and cuddles when Kiukiu was too tired to indulge her.

"White feathers come tumbling down . . ."

Kiukiu went very still, listening intently. There it was again, the eerie singing she had heard before, that made her go chill and cold.

"Tumbling down . . ."

***

In the heat of the bath-house, Gavril lay back in the water, hoping that the steamy warmth would soak out the worst of his aches. But by the fiery light from the coals, he saw as he dried himself briskly, that his body was covered in bruises: mottled purplish contusions on his arms and shoulders where Askold's wooden sword had struck home.

Are you trying to toughen me up, Askold, or tenderize me for roasting?

For a moment he had mistaken the bruises for fresh traces of Khezef's possession. But all signs of the daemonic fusion had fast faded after the Drakhaoul left his body.

What was he doing, wishing he was still possessed by the Drakhaoul? Yet the harsh truth was, as he and Askold knew but could not admit to one another, that if any enemy were to launch an attack on the kastel, they would not be able to defend themselves. The druzhina would fight to the death, but without Khezef's destructive powers, they were vulnerable.

A stab of ice pierced his left wrist, so sharp that it made him draw in his breath. He stared at the gash Morozhka had inflicted which had still not completely knitted over. Whenever it tingled, it was a warning that *she* was close by. Was she waiting for him in the studio?

***

The kastel women had gathered in the kitchen to warm themselves by the roaring fire as Kiukiu carried her sleepy daughter in, seeking company.

"I said I'd bring you tea upstairs, my lady." Ninusha stirred the tea and laid out a plate of honey cakes. Kion was playing contentedly at her feet with a little wooden horse that Semyon had whittled for him; Ilsi was making pastry.

Kiukiu shook her head, settling herself next to Auntie Sosia near the blaze. "It's too cold in the parlor tonight. And . . . I heard that singing again. It gave me the shivers."

Ninusha glanced up. "It must be Morozhka. Or one of her Snow Spirits."

"How can you be sure it's Morozhka?" Kiukiu wanted to know.

"I only ever heard her singing once," Sosia said, pulling her shawl around her. "And I never want to hear that song again."

"Why, Auntie?"

"Because it's sweet enough to lure you out into the snow and to your death."

"Like the Snow Spirits?"

Kiukiu fell silent, remembering how she had nearly become one of the Snow Spirits out on the snowy moors. *If Grandma hadn't come to my rescue . . .* She held Larisa more tightly, seeking comfort in the warmth of her sleeping daughter.

"Some say the Spirits are the ghosts of the travelers she lures to their death," put in Ilsi, wiping her floury hands on her apron. "But my mother told me that Lady Frost steals babies' souls. She sings a lullaby that sends mothers and grandmothers to sleep and then she slips into the house and hugs the babies in her ice-cold embrace until they die."

"Why would she do that?" Ninusha cried in alarm.

"I don't remember ever hearing her singing before," Kiukiu said. "Why didn't she show up at the kastel when Lilias had her baby son two winters back?"

"Because Lord Gavril was here and he had his full Drakhaon powers back then. She never appeared when the Drakhaoul was around. Too scared, probably."

Ilsi stretched the pastry over her pin and then carefully laid it over the top of the big pie dish she had filled with chopped egg and rice, trimming the edges and crimping them with a fork.

"Why does she need an innocent baby's soul?" Kiukiu persisted.

Sosia gave a little shrug. "Who knows? Some say that she's trying to become mortal but what would be the point of that? Others say she needs the lifeforce of a little baby to prolong her own life. It's like nourishment to her. Without it, she'd wither away and die."

"Just because some woman's been heard singing around the kastel," Kiukiu said, determined to calm everyone's fears, including her own, "doesn't mean that she's Morozhka."

"We need to protect the babies." Ninusha gazed around her in alarm, as if expecting Morozhka to make an appearance. "Is there any way to stop her getting in?"

"You'll be safe by the hearth, that's for sure," Sosia said. "They also say that if Morozhka gets too close to fire, she melts away." And then she sniffed loudly, her face puckering up into an expression of pained disgust. "Which one of these two needs fresh linen?"

Kiukiu realized as a strong waft reached her that Larisa was the culprit and swept her up. "I'm sorry," she said, wincing as the aroma grew stronger. "I'll go and change her."

"Teething," Sosia said. "Don't forget to put some of that witch hazel salve I gave you on her little bottom or she'll be sore."

"I won't forget, Auntie." Kiukiu hastily retreated upstairs.

The bedchamber was chilly; no one had come to relight the fire in the grate. After putting her reeking baby in the crib, Kiukiu turned to the pile of linen squares—only to find there were none left. She paused a moment, wondering whether to relight the fire or get Larisa cleaned up first. It would only take a moment to slip out to the chest on the landing to fetch clean baby linen.

***

"White feathers come tumbling down . . ."

As Kiukiu shut the lid of the linen chest, she heard a woman singing the old song she had come to dread—and realized to her horror that the singing was coming from the bedchamber.

"Larisa!" She dropped the basket of clean nappies and tore back down the passageway, flinging open the door.

The singer stopped in mid-phrase. A breath of chill air drifted from the open balcony window. A woman was leaning over Larisa's cradle, her hair unbound, like a skein of white silk.

Lady Frost.

Even as Kiukiu ran into the room, the woman picked up Larisa and turned toward the open window.

"No!" Kiukiu screamed in fury. She launched herself at the woman, grabbing at her with all her strength to hold her back. Her fingers clutched skin and flesh as cold as firm-pressed snow.

Risa will freeze to death.

Kiukiu steeled herself, hanging on even though the snow-cold flesh was burning her fingertips.

Larisa let out a sleepy cry.

"Give her back!" Kiukiu gripped hold of her daughter and tugged. "Give me back my daughter!"

Suddenly Lady Frost let go. Larisa gave a louder yell. She thumped fists against Kiukiu's body as Kiukiu backed away, clutching her tightly to her.

Eyes black as a starless winter's night stared at her over the baby's head.

"What are you doing in here, Morozhka?" Kiukiu heard her voice trembling as she confronted the intruder. "Why were you singing to Risa?"

"Your daughter called to me."

Larisa stretched out one chubby hand to Lady Frost. To Kiukiu's confusion, she cooed, her way of expressing approval and friendly feelings.

"I meant her no harm."

"But you steal babies' souls." Kiukiu backed another step away, reaching the doorway. She could hear a distant commotion downstairs coming nearer; her scream must have alerted the household that something was wrong.

"My lady, is all well?" Ninusha's voice echoed in the stairwell.

In that instant, Lady Frost turned and stepped out through the open window into the night.

"It's freezing cold up here." Ninusha reached the top of the stairs. "Why is the window open, my lady? Let me shut it for you."

"No; you take Risa. I'll shut it." Kiukiu did not want Ninusha to see how frightened she was; there was no point needlessly alarming anyone else until she had checked that the intruder had fled. She handed Larisa over and gazed out over the white gardens below. There was no sign of anyone below, just the eerie glimmer of snow under starlight.

"Let me light a fresh fire," Ninusha said as Kiukiu closed the window and drew the heavy curtain. "A good blaze should warm the room up in no time."

Kiukiu nodded, whispering under her breath what Auntie Sosia had said earlier, "If Morozhka gets too close to fire, she melts away."

***

"Morozhka was here?" Gavril came up the stairs from the bath-house to find Kiukiu agitatedly pacing their room. "In the kastel?" That, at least, explained the tingling ache in his wrist.

"In our bedchamber, about to steal our daughter!" Kiukiu's teeth were chattering even though the fire in the grate was blazing away, pine cones spitting and cracking as they released their resinous scent. "She said that Risa called out to her."

"Risa knew she was there?" Gavril swept Risa up from the crib and she let out a chuckle of delight. "So she's inherited your gift?" To his eyes, their daughter looked like any other baby with no outwardly discernible signs of unusual abilities. But why had Morozhka entered the kastel uninvited and tried to steal Larisa away?

He felt guilty now at not having told Kiukiu about Morozhka's visits to his studio. He hadn't wanted to worry her; she had quite enough to occupy her with caring for Larisa and overseeing the running of the household. But now didn't seem the right time to reveal that she had been visiting him . . . or why.

"We can't stay here." Kiukiu began to pace again. "We have to get Larisa away from Morozhka."

"Where else can we go?"

"The town house. In Azhgorod."

"But we can't go till the thaw sets in. It's too dangerous. We could get caught in a blizzard on the moors. We'd be at Lady Frost's mercy out there— isolated and helpless. It's not long to wait now; the days are getting longer."

She crossed her arms defensively across her chest, a gesture he recognized as meaning that she was not prepared to abandon her plan without a fight.

***

Gavril had tied his scarf in a double knot about his throat. And even though his hands were protected by old woolen gloves, he could hardly feel the paintbrush between his numbed fingers and thumb anymore.

He became aware of a faint shiver of sound, thin and high, an icy vibration in the air that set his teeth tingling. And the gash in his wrist began to tingle as well, as if in response to the one who had sliced his flesh with her blade of ice. So she had returned.

I have questions for you, Lady Frost.

Morozhka appeared in the studio doorway. But this time she was not alone. Two men followed her into the studio: Tarakh and Radakh.

Gavril set down his brush. "I thought you were out on patrol today," he said to the twins and saw that same distant look in their eyes he had seen when Morozhka had first bound them to her in the forest. "What are you doing here?"

They did not respond.

"You promised these two to me, Lord Drakhaon," Morozhka said. "Or had you forgotten?" There was a slight edge to her voice.

"They're still my druzhina," Gavril held her gaze, determined not to be outfaced. "They have duties to carry out." Still no flicker of a response from either of the twins. He had underestimated the strength of her hold over them. "And what did you want with my daughter, Lady Morozhka?"

"I was curious to see if Khezef had left any memories with her."

Her reply both infuriated and terrified him. If Kiukiu hadn't acted so swiftly the previous night, what would have become of Risa? "How could he have done? She's *my* child. Kiukiu's and my child. And there was no need to scare Kiukiu like that. If you had wanted to see Larisa, you could have asked me—"

"But winter will soon be drawing to a close. The hours of sunlight are growing longer. It's time for me to sleep until the coming of autumn." She came closer and suddenly leaned in to stroke his cheek. "You made me a promise, Drakhaon," she said in a low, intimate voice. "When I wake again with the falling of the leaves, I expect answers from you. You won't disappoint me, will you?"

At least while she slept through the long summer days, he and Kiukiu would have no reason to fear that she would try to steal Larisa away again. He endured her chill touch even though it had set the gash in his wrist aching more agonizingly than before.

"I'll do the best I can," he said, even though he had no idea how he would be able to make sense of the paintings.

"Don't forget our agreement, Lord Drakhaon. Set your men to watch over me while I sleep." She turned, first to Radakh and then to Tarakh, and they gazed back at her adoringly, as if mesmerized by her presence. "My beautiful, brave bodyguards. You'll protect me, won't you?"

"We won't let anyone disturb you," Radakh said fervently.

"You can count on us," Tarakh added with equal ardor.

"You will escort me to the Round," she said, slipping her hands between their arms. As they went back into the garden, she turned her white head and said over her shoulder, "Till the autumn, then. Use the summertime well, Lord Gavril."

Gavril watched them until they were out of sight. Then he stretched out his right hand to take up his paintbrush once more, automatically dipped it into a blob of cobalt, raised it to the canvas—and saw, to his concern, that it was shaking so much that little drops of blue paint were spattering everywhere.

Chapter 21

Khitari

Kaspar Linnaius drew the fur-lined coat more tightly about him as he made his way carefully up the slippery mountain path. It was a long time since he had visited the Jade Springs in winter and, although he had landed his sky-craft on a ridge near the hidden entrance to the sacred pool, a thick, icy layer of snow encrusted the rocks, making the approach treacherous underfoot.

Leaning on a sturdy walking stick, he headed toward the clouds of steam rising from the volcanic hot springs. High above the misty atmosphere, the Khitari sky was a pale wintry blue; no snow would fall today.

"Papa, why have you brought me here?" The whisper of a child's voice, long buried in his memory, drove him on, upward. *"It's so cold. So lonely. Why didn't Mama come too?"*

"Does *she* already know I'm here, I wonder," he murmured as, breathless from exerting himself in the thin, keen air, he reached the stone archway that led into the shrine watched over by the Guardian of the Springs. Passing through, he was enveloped in a thick

251

fog. The sound of bubbling grew louder, as well as the serpent-like hiss of the rising fumes.

A dark shape suddenly reared up out of the warm water in front of him. Water streamed from the emerald coils of a great snake as it rose from the springs, looming over him. Taken by surprise, he only just managed to stop, teetering on the edge, almost falling in.

"Kaspar Linnaius," hissed the Guardian, "I was not expecting to see you again so soon. Why have you come?"

"Lady Anagini." Linnaius recovered himself and bowed. "I want you to answer a question."

The jeweled coils shimmered in the dim light, wavering, reforming themselves into the figure of a tall, slender woman whose long, sleek hair falling in fronds over her full breasts was the dark green of water weed.

"I cannot tell if I can answer until I know what the question might be, Magus."

If Linnaius had not been so eager for information, he would have smiled at her predictably oblique reply. But he had been following a long and frustratingly fruitless trail and Anagini was his last, most desperate hope.

"When you first healed me, many years ago, we made a bargain. You took something from me in exchange for repairing my damaged body and extending my life force. Something very precious to me. And you forbade me to talk of our bargain with anyone. It was a very cruel exchange."

"But you agreed to it," said Anagini, her serpent's eyes glinting with a shrewd and inhuman coldness.

"Did you think you could break our bond? Did you think, Magus, that the wiles you've used to deceive others would work on me?"

Linnaius sighed. He had learned over many years to endure the heartache, to immure himself from all personal attachments, save his loyalty to the royal house of Tielen. "Whatever I thought, you proved me wrong. I hoped you might have relented. To take a seven-year-old child from her mother and family was a heartless act."

"You knew the conditions. If you cared that much about your daughter, you could have withdrawn from the agreement."

Linnaius bowed his head in assent. There was no arguing with the Snake Woman's logic. He had sacrificed his only child—and his marriage—to repay his debt to Anagini. "But why did you take away my memories of what I'd done?"

"Because," and she reached out to stroke his face from brow to chin, "you would have done all you could to take her back. And I needed her. She was such a special child; it's so rare to find a girl with mage blood inherited from both her parents. So, when did you remember?"

Little Eliane's eyes, soft black, like her mother Ilona's, dusted with silvered flecks, legacy of his wind mage blood, gazing uncomprehendingly up into his . . .

"When you healed me the second time. Not everything came back at once; fragments of memory began to surface and piece themselves together. By the time of the Second Darkness, it all fell into place."

"And now you've returned to ask me where she is."

"You must know!" She was toying with him, playing with his emotions for her own amusement, and it infuriated him to feel so helpless.

"Don't leave me, Papa. Please don't leave me here alone. I'll be good, I promise." Those plaintive words that had been erased from his memory now echoed through his mind, each one piercing his conscience like a rain-shower of poisoned barbs.

"It's all a very long time ago, my dear Kaspar. Your daughter left me. She grew into a clever, artful young woman and, at twenty-one, she found a way to elude me and escape. Are you truly surprised that she made no attempt to find her father after that? She had hardened her heart to the man who exchanged her for a new lease of life."

Linnaius felt a tremor of fury run through him at the callousness of her words. *Of course, she's an Elder Spirit, she has no feelings. She's lived for so many centuries that it merely amuses her to toy with us mortals.*

"So you never made any effort to find out what became of her?" he asked. "Even though she'd served you faithfully for fourteen years?"

Anagini gave a little shrug. "I may have whispered to her once or twice in dreams, but she devised ways to block out my voice. She wanted things I could not give her here: music; lovers; admiration . . . even children of her own."

"She wanted children?" Linnaius said, his voice suddenly hoarse. "So . . ."

"Even though—in spite of her mage blood—she must be dead by now, Kaspar, her descendants might well still be alive."

She must be dead. Those simple words tore at his heart like claws. He stared at her, hating her for her unfeeling cruelty. "If you hadn't taken my memories from me," he said, hearing a tremble of loathing making his voice unsteady, "I might have had the chance to repair some of the damage I'd done her, at the least to tell her how sorry I—"

A ripple of dazzling light pierced the rising mists. He tensed, bracing himself, sensing the sudden appearance of a keen, yet unfamiliar power nearby. Glancing at Anagini, he saw that her body had stiffened and her eyes had narrowed to jade slits as though trying to scry through the surrounding rocks and beyond .

"Who—or *what*—is that?" he asked softly.

"Whatever it is," she said, "it is powerful enough to penetrate the barriers I weave to protect the Springs. Could it be—"

Before she could finish, a tall figure materialized out of the steam. At first Linnaius could only make out a shadowy outline coming toward them at a swift, purposeful pace; then the gleam of the newcomer's eyes pierced the drifting mists, fiery gold, staring at them both like a hunter seeking out his prey.

"Who dares enter my sanctuary without asking my permission?" Anagini demanded. "Identify yourself."

The intruder came on steadily until he faced them across the pool. An aura of raw power emanating from his body shimmered like a haze of heat. His hair was the colour of flame and the feathers on the great wings furled at his back flickered scarlet, blue and gold, like a blazing furnace. And in his right hand he carried a gleaming sword from which gouts of flame dropped onto the frozen ground, melting the ice into hissing steam.

Linnaius stared, speechless. *A Winged Warrior—in the mortal world?*

"My name is Ardarel, Lord of Heavenly Fire," the Warrior said, "and I have been sent to punish you both."

"Let me guess," Anagini said, drawing herself to her full imposing height. "That young upstart Galizur sent you."

Ardarel frowned. "How dare you speak so rudely of his highness, Prince Galizur?"

"Because I am old enough to be his mother," she said, "and for all you know, I might indeed be his mother."

Linnaius glanced anxiously at Anagini, wondering why she was rash enough to speak so provocatively to Ardarel.

"Prince Galizur has reason to believe that you are protecting a mortal child born of a forbidden union."

Linnaius felt his heart begin to beat painfully fast against his ribs.

"And what if I am?" Anagini said."That child did not choose its parents. It has committed no crime. I thought that you Warriors were sworn to protect the innocent, not slaughter innocent babies."

So that's her plan; she's trying to trick him into revealing more than he should about his mission.

"Even so, we know that the Drakhaoul Khezef passed on some of his aethyric powers before he left the mortal world. And that child cannot be allowed to live."

"Why? Why would a mere child pose such a threat to the mighty prince Galizur?" The naked contempt in her question made Linnaius flinch, fearing

"Because the child is a Key. A Key that unlocks the Hidden Gates between this world and the Ways Beyond. And you, Magus," Ardarel turned his burning gaze on Linnaius who suddenly felt very vulnerable and helpless. "When the Serpent Gate was destroyed, we believed that was the end of the magi's meddling— but no, they had to go and set Nagazdiel free from the Realm of Shadows."

Linnaius's legs began to buckle as the Winged Warrior's accusing stare bored into him; he sank to one knee, wondering how long he could manage to stay conscious beneath such a pitiless, powerful scrutiny. "But I and my protégé Rieuk sealed Nagazdiel away again. The feat almost killed us both. But we closed that Gate forever—"

"Your kindred will not escape the purge this time," Ardarel said, advancing on him. "Others will follow me soon and they will be ruthless in carrying out their mission. Galizur has issued a decree: all magi with the blood of Nagazdiel and his daughter Azilis in their veins must be destroyed."

"And if I could tell you where this Key Child is to be found," said Anagini suddenly. Ardarel swung around to face her again. "What would you do, Ardarel? Could you give me your word not to harm her?"

"I am only accountable to Prince Galizur."

"If you can't assure me of her safety, then why would I tell you where she is?"

Her? She? Which child are they talking about?
Linnaius racked his brains for a clue. *Surely not little
Princess Karila? She was brought back to life by Khezef
at the Serpent Gate but as far as I know she's no different
from any of the other descendants of Artamon . . .*

"You will tell me all you know. Or I will force the
information from you."

Anagini threw back her head and laughed.
Linnaius stared, aghast. Ardarel did not move for a
second, as though baffled by her reaction. And then
he thrust his flaming sword at her.

Anagini sidestepped and plunged deep into the
pool to avoid the fiery blade. As it made contact with
the green water, the flames were extinguished in a
plume of sizzling steam.

"Go, Kaspar!" Anagini cried, surfacing a little way
off. Linnaius needed no further bidding. As he hurried
toward the rocky arch through which he had come,
he saw from the corner of his eye, that Ardarel was
following him. Passing one hand along the keen edge
of his sword blade, the Warrior' s blood dripped and
caught alight in a thin streak of fresh flame.

Is this the end for me? Linnaius had faced many
dangers in his long life, but this stern-faced Warrior
with fire-tipped wings might turn out to be his final
adversary. *I can't die yet—not without finding out what
became of my daughter.*

The clouds of steam rising from the Jade Springs
had turned as thick and impenetrable as a winter fog.
Was Anagini doing this to help him escape? He pressed
one hand to his temples, sending out a desperate plea
for help to his oldest ally.

"Izkael! Come now. I need you."

A red glow seared the drifting fogs; Ardarel was on his tail and catching up fast. Linnaius stumbled beneath the archway and found himself shivering in the bitter winter chill of the open mountainside. Overhead the stars burned cruel and clear in the moonless black Khitari night.

And then he saw Izkael, a streak of quicksilver against the jet sky, his eyes gleaming like shooting stars, as he dived down from the heavens straight toward him, uncoiling like a stretched spring. There was no time to find the sky-craft; he would have to ride the wouivre bareback as he had done as a boy.

"Get me out of here, Izkael." Linnaius hitched up his robes, grasped hold of the great creature's neck and clambered onto the silky-scaled back.

"Where now, Kaspar?" Izkael's voice vibrated through him as they skimmed upward into the chill air, deep as the bass notes of the great organ in Saint Meriadec's in Lutèce.

"Anywhere." Linnaius just about managed to say the word as he clung on to Izkael's body, his breath knocked from his body by the swiftness of the ascent.

Ardarel came through the archway and Linnaius saw him far below, his sword dripping gouts of bloody fire onto the snow. The Warrior gazed up at them and, unfurling his vast wings, leapt into the night, each powerful wing-beat propelling him closer to them.

"He's persistent, this one," Linnaius muttered. "Can you outfly him, Izkael?"

"I'll do my best. Hold on tight!" The wouivre shot off, a translucent arrow darting through the darkness.

"Stop!" Ardarel's command rang out above the whistle of Izkael's swift flight. Linnaius did not dare look back for fear of losing his grip on Izkael's back but he could sense a current of heat growing in intensity behind him.

He called himself Lord of Heavenly Fire. Does that mean his powers increase in the air?

Another bolt of flame seared past them; Linnaius felt Izkael flinch and his speed begin to decrease.

"Izkael? Are you all right?"

"Kaspar . . . I'm sorry . . ."

They came slowly spiraling downward toward the land far below, Linnaius, gripping hold with all his might, willing his own life force into the injured wouivre.

Izkael landed awkwardly, and came to a slithering, bumping halt, on a vast and empty snow-covered plain, with only the stars overhead for light.

"Izkael. Speak to me." Linnaius rolled off onto the grass, gasping the icy air into his lungs to regain his breath. After a moment's dizziness, he forced himself up and began to check the wouivre's long, translucent-scaled body for injuries. "Where did he get you? Tell me."

Izkael merely laid his great head down on the snow and let out a rippling sigh. And before Linnaius's astonished eyes, his long serpentine body began to shrink and alter, changing to his mortal form: a horned man whose hair and eyes were silver as the starlight overhead. He had not undergone this drastic transformation in over a hundred years and Linnaius, distressed to see it, knew that he must be badly hurt to be forced to resort to this life-preserving tactic.

"Come on, old friend, don't leave me now." Linnaius knelt beside him, lifting the wouivre's head onto his lap. "We've been through so much together." His heart was still beating too fast from the terrifying flight. He and Izkael had been partnered since he was a boy.

A sudden rushing sound made Linnaius look up; Ardarel had caught up with them and was hovering overhead, his flaming sword, blazing like a comet in the frozen night.

"What have you done to Izkael?" Linnaius cried.

"Take me to Khezef's child," Ardarel replied, "and I will spare your wouivre."

"Khezef's child? I have no idea what you're talking about." *And there's no way I would ever betray Eugene by giving Karila into your hands—if she's the really one you're seeking . . .*

"Then you are of no use to me." Ardarel came swooping down toward Linnaius, sword raised.

If this is the end, Izkael, at least we'll leave this world together. Linnaius tightened his hold on his wouivre and closed his eyes, waiting for the flaming sword to pierce his heart.

The blow did not come. Instead, Linnaius heard the sound of a body falling onto the plain. He opened his eyes and saw that Ardarel had crashed to earth and was lying face-down in the snow, his wings splayed wide, like a feathered cloak across his body. The flames on his fiery sword had been extinguished, leaving only the glimmer of starlight overhead to light the scene.

Is this some kind of trick to lure me away from Izkael? Linnaius, shaken, wary, watched the shadowy form for any hint of movement. After what seemed a very long time, he heard a groan and saw the fire-tipped wings twitch, their lustre dimmed.

"What's wrong?" Ardarel's halting words were slurred. "Why . . . am I . . . so weak?" He tried to force himself to his knees, only to collapse again. "Help me, Magus." And he began to retch, coughing up a tarry sludge that sizzled as it touched the snowy ground.

"Me? Help you?" Linnaius could hardly believe what he was hearing. "When you just nearly killed me and my wouivre? How gullible do you think I am, Ardarel?"

"I'll . . . spare you . . . Just help me." All the earlier pride and righteous fury had gone from Ardarel's voice and another long, aching groan issued from his throat as if he was in agony.

"*His aethyric body,*" Izkael said in a faint voice, "*is not adapted for the mortal world.*"

"Just like the Drakhaouls, when they were first summoned through the Serpent Gate?" Linnaius stroked Izkael's head in mute gratitude. "Thank you, old friend." He looked up and saw that Ardarel was trying to force himself up onto one knee again. *At least the sword's blade is still dull and dark; the flames seem to be linked to Ardarel's inner strength.*

"You need to find a way to alter your physical body to survive for long in the mortal world, Ardarel," he said. "Khezef and his kindred were driven to seek out mortal hosts and fuse with them. So unless you're planning to fuse your body with mine—"

"Never. I'd never commit such a sacrilegious act."

Linnaius almost smiled to himself. As he'd anticipated, Ardarel had rejected his suggestion outright, not even bothering to listen to the rest of what he had to say. *And now I know your weakness.* "Then you have no alternative," he said, "but to return to the Ways Beyond—or cease to exist here, alone."

"I will not fail," Ardarel forced the words out between gritted teeth. "I cannot fail." And to Linnaius's alarm, a faint flicker of fire suddenly shot along the length of his dulled blade.

The Heavenly Guardian could still do him considerable damage, even in this weakened state. Where were Izkael's kin? They must have heard his call for help.

A chill, dry wind began to gust across the dark steppe. Linnaius raised his head, listening with all his wind mage skills. Izkael felt it too, for he half-opened his eyes. "Asamkis," he whispered. "Brother."

Ardarel must have sensed the change in the air, for Linnaius saw him push himself to a standing position, bracing himself, struggling to lift his sword.

"Go back, while you can, Ardarel!" Linnaius cried out. "Your body can't take much more."

Ardarel slowly raised his sword, both hands gripping the hilt, until the tip was pointing up into the heavens.

A jagged rent ripped the night sky open and blinding light poured through.

Dazzled, Linnaius raised his arm to protect his eyes. He could just make out the outline of another Guardian, an indistinct form, etched against the searing brightness, bending down to offer his hand to Ardarel. With one tug, he pulled Ardarel through the rent which instantly closed.

"This isn't finished, Magus," he heard Ardarel call back. "We'll be back."

And then the steppe was plunged once more into the dark of the freezing Khitari winter. Linnaius gazed down in desperation at Izkael whose faint glimmer was fading.

"Stay with me, Izkael," he whispered, holding him close. "Help's on its way."

They came snaking through the sky, at first thin, silvery streaks, like translucent ribbons blown on the keen wind, then, as they drew closer, Linnaius could make out their familiar forms: Izkael's kin, the wouivres he had known since boyhood: Asamkis, Auphiel, Nahaliel and Serapiel, and his heart swelled with relief as he recognized them.

But before the wouivres reached them, an eerie yipping barking pierced the silence of the night.

"Wolves?" Linnaius's head went up. Bounding toward them across the snow, eyes luminously golden, came a pack of steppe wolves. *First an angel with a fiery sword, now ravening predators . . .*

The foremost wolf, a big, vigorous male with piercing orange eyes, approached and bowed his head.

Linnaius's reactions, slowed by exhaustion and the bitter cold, realized that the wolf looked—and felt—familiar.

Don't be afraid, my friend. We've come to help.

"Ch-Chinua?" Linnaius stammered, teeth chattering. "Is that really you?"

Chapter 22

"It's been a while, Magus." Chinua appeared, back in his human form, smiling. He took the kettle from off the little iron stove and poured steaming water onto tea leaves, releasing a balm-like, soothing scent.

"How did you know where to find me? Khitari is such a vast place." Now that Linnaius was inside the shaman's yurt and the immediate need to stay alert and on the defensive was gone, exhaustion washed through his body.

"Lady Anagini warned me that you would need help. She must have guided your wouivres towards my yurt too."

"But Izkael was hurt protecting me." They had dragged the unconscious wouivre inside, rolling him over to lie on his right side, exposing the blackened patch on his left shoulder and back where Ardarel's fire had seared him. To Linnaius's concern he could see that little drops of silvery ichor were oozing from the burned skin.

"That may be part of Izkael's self-healing process," Chinua said. "Best to let him be for now."

"This has happened before." Seeing Izkael lying insensible in his mortal form stirred up more long-forgotten memories from the murky sediment of Linnaius's past. "My mentor nursed him back to health." Wise, strict, yet kindly, Eliane of . . . He had not thought of her in many years, but she was the one who had first trained him and he had given her name to his only child. "But she is long dead."

Aromatic fumes awoke him from his reverie; he blinked, seeing the shaman holding out a bowl of fragrant tea.

"Drink this; it'll ease your aches and pains."

As Linnaius lay back on a soft straw mattress, he let his jangled senses slowly surrender to the smoky warmth. He felt safe within Chinua's wards, with his own wouivres circling and keeping watch overhead. His body still ached from head to toes; sharp, arthritic twinges reminded him that he was far too old to go riding on a wouivre's back. And in spite of the discomfort, sleep overwhelmed him.

But his troubled mind would not let him rest and long-buried memories began to invade his dreams: elusive, beloved faces flashed in and out of sight as he chased after them through a mist-washed mountainous landscape that felt tantalizingly familiar.

Baume . . . where I grew up? In Sapaudia?

***

"Ardarel?" Chinua placed a bowl of creamy curds before Linnaius who realized—only then—that he could not remember the last time he had eaten. "I don't recall the name."

"One of Galizur's lieutenants; arrogant, young and ardent, like his name," Linnaius said, picking up a horn spoon to eat the curds. "But the real puzzle we need to solve is the identity of this child Galizur is looking for: a little girl, it seems, gifted with aethyric powers by Khezef. A 'Key Child'."

"That sounds like your young Tielen princess, Karila."

"Perhaps." Linnaius considered this suggestion, wondering if he should warn Eugene to be on his guard. "Fortunately for me, at any rate, Galizur's Warriors don't yet seem to have discovered a way to successfully maintain their physical forms here for more than a few minutes. But once they overcome that problem, there'll be no holding them back. So we haven't long to find this Key Child and devise a way to protect her."

Chinua sat down, cross-legged, opposite Linnaius on the worn rug. "How long have you been away on your travels, Magus?"

Linnaius blinked, not quite grasping what the shaman meant. "How long?"

"Have you made contact recently with your old friend and patron, Eugene? Or Gavril Nagarian?"

Linnaius shook his head. "It must be many months since I last saw them. I've lost track of the time."

"So you haven't been able to congratulate Lord Gavril and his wife on the birth of their daughter?" Chinua asked slyly.

"They've had a daughter?" Linnaius was all attention now. He set down the bowl of curds, half eaten. "The Drakhaon and the Spirit Singer?" He had been fearing for Karila's safety, when another innocent child's life might be at stake.

"Born in the late summer and named Larisa; I hear she's a precocious, lively little thing."

"How are we going to protect her, if she's the one?"

"Unless . . ."

"Unless what?" Linnaius knew that the wolf shaman rarely made suggestions unless he had something of importance to say.

"Where exactly have you been all these months, Magus?"

Linnaius did not reply straight away, weighing up the risks of revealing—even to an old and trusted friend—exactly what he had been doing. Eventually he sighed and said, "When we sealed Prince Nagazdiel and Azilis back in the Rift, something happened to me. I don't know whether I was affected by the timeless magic within the Rift or by the wandering, restless spirits of the dead set free when the Rift became unstable, but I regained memories that Anagini had taken from me."

"Memories?" Chinua echoed softly.

"The seven-year-old daughter I gave to Anagini in payment for her rejuvenating skills. The wife I betrayed and who never forgave me for spiriting away our only child. The misery we both endured, trying to make new lives for ourselves." Even speaking of these matters—so long ago and yet so raw and fresh now in his restored memory—made his voice tremble. *I have inured myself for so long to living alone, without personal attachments, even though the original reason for doing so—to spare myself further pain—was locked away, deep in my memories.*

"So where is she? Your lost daughter?"

"Anagini could not tell me. It turns out that Eliane ran away." The irony of the situation was not lost on him. "Or maybe she had served her purpose and Anagini let her go. Certainly, Eliane made no effort to find me. And why would she? The father who took her away from her mother and left her with a stranger in that lonely place, hundreds of leagues from home."

"Eliane? Pretty name." Chinua got up to put more sticks on the fire which was burning low.

"She was a pretty child, with soft dark unruly hair, just like her mother's." Linnaius found himself smiling at the long-forgotten memory of Ilona struggling to pull a brush through their daughter's tangled hair as the little girl wriggled free and ran off, shrieking loudly in protest.

"And her mother had mage-blood too?"

"Inherited from her father, another wind mage like myself." Linnaius glanced up at Chinua. "Are you suggesting Eliane might be in danger too?"

"She might—if she's still alive, that is. What did Ardarel tell you? 'All magi must be destroyed.'"

Linnaius shuddered; the truth was brutal but he had to accept that so many years had passed since he had said farewell to little Eliane that she must be at least ninety by now. And the rare gift-curse of mage blood often skipped a generation or two. "She might have had children— my grandchildren—of her own. But how do I begin to find them? To warn them too?"

"I take it you've been searching?"

"But so much time has passed. Even the little kingdom where I was born has been swallowed up by its bigger neighbor. People move away, go to the prosperous cities in search of work . . ." Linnaius's words trailed away into silence as he remembered standing in puzzlement in front of the house in which he had once lived with his beloved Ilona.

"That, my friend, is one of the disadvantages of living as long as we do," Chinua said, nodding in agreement.

"But why has Galizur ordered this purge? That's what I don't understand."

Chinua leaned forward and said in a low voice, "They're keeping close watch over the Ways Beyond. I've traveled freely there ever since my master initiated me into the shamanic rites and rarely caught sight of one of Galizur's Warriors. But the last time I went to consult Master Oyugun, one of the Warriors appeared before me and told me to get out. And never return."

"Intriguing. And when was this?" Linnaius asked, although he suspected he already knew the answer.

"After the Second Darkness. After you sealed Prince Nagazdiel and his daughter back within the Rift."

"Even though we magi did all we could to restore the balance between this world and the Ways Beyond."

"But in doing so, you reminded Galizur of your existence."

"We have to warn Lord Gavril. Is there any way you can reach him? Through Kiukirilya?"

Chinua fell silent for a while, pensively stroking his broad chin. "If I try to contact her," he said at length, "whether through the Ways Beyond, or in dreams, I risk showing Galizur exactly where to find Larisa."

"You're right," Linnaius said; he had been swiftly assessing all the information he had gathered so far. "But we have one significant advantage: the Warriors have not yet learned how to adapt their bodies to the mortal world. Until they devise a way to conserve their strength and powers, they will only be able to appear briefly." The sight of Ardarel, crashing to earth from the sky, had been burned into his memory. "Even now, I can't imagine that Ardarel, for all his fierce talk, is ready to return."

"Unless," Chinua said, his habitually placid expression creasing into a frown, "they seek out mortal hosts, as the Drakhaouls did."

"Ha!" Linnaius was almost amused, remembering Ardarel's outraged reaction to his suggestion. "There's little danger of that; the only mortals alive with bodies strong enough to contain them are those whom the Drakhaouls used as hosts and they would never . . ." He realized that Chinua was staring at him. "You don't think that Galizur would stoop so low?" The possibility that Eugene, the master he had sworn to protect and defend, might be in danger of being possessed against his will appalled him. "No," he went on, partly to reassure himself, "such a bond would go against everything Galizur and his followers were created to protect. It would be sacrilege. Galizur will find others to do his will— just as he once persuaded Serzhei of Azhkendir." Although it pained him to say so, remembering how he and his fellow magi had suffered much at the hands of the devout followers of the Blessed Serzhei in Francia.

"I'll think of a way to warn Kiukirilya," Chinua said. "But what will you do about Izkael?"

Linnaius rose and went to where his wouivre lay, still in human form. The black burns searing his back and shoulder were all crusted over with the silvery ichor that had oozed out.

"I'll consult his brother Asamkis." He took up his coat, wrapped it around himself, and ventured outside. The keen air almost took his breath away; the white of the snow-covered steppes was so bright after the firelit yurt that his dazzled eyes ached as he scanned the skies, calling for Asamkis.

A whistling rush of air, sharp with the glitter of frost, brought the wouivre snaking down from the high clouds to circle above Linnaius.

"How is my brother?" Asamkis, as gentle-natured and kindly as Izkael was wild and impetuous, hovered low enough for Linnaius to reach up and pat his noble head.

"Could you take a look at him?"

Asamkis nodded. "Although I haven't assumed my mortal form in a long while." He alighted on the ground in a whirl of spinning cloud, emerging from the misty spiral as a slender, silver-skinned youth, two dragon horns protruding from his long locks of feathery hair.

Linnaius held open the flap of the yurt for him to enter and saw Chinua—well used to extraordinary sights—blink in astonishment.

"Chinua, this is Asamkis."

Asamkis bowed his head but said nothing, going directly toward where his brother was lying. A soft radiance followed him, like the rain-washed light when the sun shines through the clouds. As Linnaius and Chinua looked on, awed, he gently placed his translucent fingers on his brother's head. Izkael let out a soft, deep sigh.

Asamkis rose and turned to Linnaius. "He might still have a chance if we can take him back home to Sapaudia. To our mountains."

"Sapaudia?" Chinua echoed, as if the name were unfamiliar.

"It's part of Allegonde now . . . but it's where I was born. Where I grew up," Linnaius said. "Perhaps if I go too, I'll be able to find out what became of my daughter."

"Kaspar." Asamkis fixed Linnaius with his frost-gray eyes. "We mustn't delay. He's very weak."

"Can you carry him as well as me?"

"Nahaliel, Serapiel and Auphiel have gone to retrieve your sky-craft. They'll be here soon," Asamkis said, rising from his brother's side.

"Be careful," Linnaius said. "The Winged Guardian who attacked us may come back. There may be others lying in wait for you." The possibility that all his faithful wouivres might crash to earth like Izkael, seared by the Guardians' flaming swords, was almost too distressing to contemplate. He had promised his beloved mentor as she lay dying that he would protect Izkael and his kin to the end of his days. *Am I too old to be able to keep that promise any longer? I need to find an heir . . . and soon. Someone younger and stronger, who'll watch over them in my stead.*

***

A thin sunlight broke through the whey-pale skim of clouds as Linnaius, Chinua and Asamkis settled the unconscious Izkael inside the sky-craft. Behind the yurt, Chinua's sturdy brown ponies were munching at a bale of hay. The snowy steppes stretched into the frost-hazed distance, white and empty.

"Thank you, Chinua." Linnaius shook the shaman by the hand. "I owe you my life. What little's left of it, that is."

"I can only wish you luck with your search," Chinua said, bowing his head in farewell. "Perhaps it will bring you unexpected happiness."

"Happiness? For me?" Linnaius climbed into the sky-craft and settled himself down beside Izkael, one hand on the tiller. "It's too late for that." And with his free hand, he twisted his fingers in the air, summoning a breeze that gusted in across the plain, stirring the ponies' manes and tails, making them glance up, startled.

The sail of the sky-craft filled with the breeze and the wouivres came darting down to lift it into the air.

"Where now, Kaspar?" cried the foremost, turning his head and fixing him with frost-gray eyes.

"Home, Asamkis," said Linnaius. The word had a strangely comforting ring to it. "Home . . . to Sapaudia."

Part Two

Chapter 23

Tourmalise
Spring

Toran Arkhel gazed down at the cadets assembled far below on the parade ground. From the roof of the crenellated square tower of the academy he could hear the animated buzz of conversation; none of the instructor officers had called their students to order yet as the final preparations were made for the first trial.

"So where's the Emperor's representative?" Branville loomed close behind him. "What was his name again?"

"Colonel Nils Lindgren," Toran turned back to the *Aiglon*.

"Is he an ingenieur? Or just another military bigwig?" Branville sounded unimpressed. But Toran paid him scant heed. He was so keyed up that his hands were trembling as he prepared the little engine. On Bernay's advice he had already tested it outside the frame many times. *An ingenious fusion of clockwork and steam.* Bernay's description had pleased him and yet he was still not convinced that all his calculations were right. The downscaled wheels and cogs turned, the pistons went up and down—but could they produce enough power to lift the craft and then keep it airborne? The rules of the competition stated that, to win, the flying machine must stay aloft for up to five minutes and travel a distance of at least five hundred yards.

The cadets below suddenly fell silent; Lorris, who was acting as lookout and liaison officer, called excitedly, "The colonels have arrived."

"Ready, boys?" Major Bauldry, a little out of breath after climbing the steep stair to the tower roof, emerged onto the lead, followed—to Toran's surprise—by Gerard Bernay.

"What's *he* doing here?" Branville glowered at Bernay.

"I invited Ingenieur Bernay to thank him for helping us out."

"Are you mad? He's a rival competitor."

"Not any longer. He—" and Toran hesitated, not wanting to betray the ingenieur's confidence and make matters worse than they already were. "He decided to withdraw his entry."

"Oh, he did, did he?" Branville gave Toran a contemptuous look. "Do you really expect me to believe that?"

"Shouldn't you be helping Cadet Arkhel with the *Aiglon*?" Bernay said pointedly.

"Off you go, Branville," Major Bauldry said, "to the finishing post."

Branville turned on his heel and went down the stair. A minute or so later he appeared on the far side of the parade ground where the other members of the design team were waving flags. They had painted a white circle on the ground.

"Is that your target?" Bernay asked Toran. Toran nodded.

"And is the wind in your favor?"

"We didn't have much choice." Toran glanced up at the flagpole behind him on which the Academy's flag was flying, billowing in a stiff breeze that was blowing across the parade ground from the north. If the wind direction could just change to ENE . . .

He offered up a quiet prayer to his grandfather and set the *Aiglon*'s engine in motion. Standing with the craft in both hands, feeling its mechanical heart beating, chugging, like a living creature straining to be free from his grasp, he lifted it high, pointing its nose toward Branville far below.

He let go.

Far below there was an audible gasp as all the cadets strained to watch the *Aiglon*'s first flight. Toran felt every beat of its tiny engine as if it were his own heart, thrumming in his chest.

It skimmed like a white bird across the heads of the spectators below.

It flies! It really flies!

And then a gust of wind caught the craft, tilting it in the wrong direction. A groan of disappointment arose from the watchers below. Toran watched, unable to look away, gripping the rough stone of the crenellations, forgetting to breathe.

It's going to crash.

***

The white flyer soars through the air, high above the upturned faces of the black-gowned students.

Gerard blinked, trying to remind himself that he was not on the bell tower roof at Tielborg University launching his own model craft. And the *Aiglon*, Toran's pride and joy, was caught in a sudden northerly gust, in danger of being blown off course and crashing onto the dais where the Emperor's representative was standing.

He took off his spectacles. For the fraction of a second, he could actually see the wind streaking past, silvery, translucent traces scored on the clear air. Instinctively, he raised his right hand, almost like the conductor of an orchestra shaping a phrase with the curve of his fingers, subtly nudging the breeze in a different direction.

The *Aiglon* juddered slightly as the breeze lifted it—but then steadied and continued downward toward the painted circle where the waiting cadets were shouting out their excitement and Branville was waiting, his arms raised high to catch it.

Toran let out a cry of exultation, punching the air with his clenched fist.

From down below a roar of approval arose from the ranks of cadets. Gerard hastily put on his spectacles again, just as Toran turned to him, his eyes shining.

"We did it," he said. "The *Aiglon* flew. But we couldn't have done it without your help."

For a moment, the sight of Toran's ecstatic expression, radiant with pride and gratitude, almost took Gerard's breath away. *So bright.* "No," he said quietly. "You deserve the acclaim: you, Branville, and your team."

"Come and meet Colonel Lindgren, Arkhel," said Major Bauldry, steering Toran toward the stairs. Toran gave Gerard an apologetic grin and disappeared into the stairwell. Gerard stayed where he was, trying to find a logical explanation for what had just happened—and failing.

Those silvery translucent wisps of breeze . . .

He shook his head. It must have been a trick of the sunlight—or another manifestation of the problems with his eyes. There was no way that he could have manipulated the breeze to change the flight path of the little craft.

Far below on the parade ground he could see Colonel Mouzillon presenting Toran, Branville and the other cadets of the Aiglon team to the Emperor's representative who was neatly dressed in the distinctive pale gray uniform of the Tielen army.

It was a while since Gerard had seen that uniform and it brought back bitter-sweet memories of his home city. Not that he had ever felt the slightest desire to enter the Tielen army or the navy, but he still entertained a genuine admiration for the Emperor and his passionate interest in the sciences. Disappointment overwhelmed him. He had not realized until then how much he had hoped to win the chance to return to Tielen.

If only he had not been disqualified from entering the Emperor's competition, he could have requested to be reinstated at Tielborg University. And though he had tried to suppress his desire to spend his days developing his designs, working with Toran had reignited his passion for invention.

"You've earned your success, Toran," he said softly, turning up his coat collar and heading for the stair. "But now I have to find another path and make a new life for myself."

***

Rasse Cardin owned a grand town house, built on fashionable Halcyon Hill in Paladur, high above the pall of smoke and steam exuding from the chimneys of his Iron Works. Gerard had been there once before when Master Cardin had invited him to dinner and had been surprised to find that the other guests included an architect, a popular operatic soprano, a portrait painter, and the prelate of Paladur Abbey; he had never imagined till then that his employer kept such distinguished company. As Gerard trudged up the steep hill past other fine houses, their candlelit windows illuminating the rain-slicked pavements, he wondered if he had been summoned to attend another such genteel gathering. He was not in the mood for making polite small talk.

But on arriving, he was shown into Cardin's study. The works owner looked up from his paper-strewn desk and smiled, laying down his pen. "Gerard; do sit down. Will you take a glass of burnt wine with me?"

"Thank you." Gerard was glad of the refreshment; it had been a long and testing day and he relished the warming glow of the rich fortified wine after the chill damp of the Paladur evening.

"How do you feel about managing a project of your own?" Cardin asked. "I've been asked to supply and install pumps and drainage for a new mining development. I'm getting too old for such ventures, but it's an ideal opportunity for a young man like you. I'll supply the equipment and you supervise the installation, then train the miners to use it themselves."

"It sounds . . . interesting. Is it close to Paladur?"

Cardin's smile broadened. "A little further afield. It's in Azhkendir."

Gerard choked on the burnt wine. "A little further?" he said when he could speak clearly again.

"All the details and travel documents are in this folder," said Cardin, patting a fat leather wallet on the desk. "And money, of course, to cover your expenses."

"I don't speak Azhkendi."

"Our client is from Tourmalise, so that shouldn't be a problem. He's agreed to set you up with a translator."

"When do I leave?" Gerard took the heavy folder, glancing at the contents.

"The ship we've hired will sail for Narvazh in two days' time. Can you be ready by then?"

Two days. Gerard hesitated. But perhaps a challenging assignment was just what he needed to shake him out of the dark, dull mood he'd lapsed into since his design had been disqualified. "Very well," he said, nodding his assent.

"Have you been having trouble with your eyes, Gerard?" Cardin asked, bringing the decanter to refill his glass. "I noticed you've taken to wearing spectacles lately."

"Just a little difficulty with close work," said Gerard, hoping the excuse sounded convincing.

"At your age?" Cardin clapped him on the shoulder, laughing heartily. And then he added, serious again,

"As long as you haven't incurred any injury in the foundry; you must take care of yourself, my boy."

"I'm sure the fresh mountain air of Azhkendir will do me good."

"The foundry lads will miss you. But it's only a temporary assignment; you'll be back by autumn. Unless you're tempted to stay on in Azhkendir."

Even though he had accepted the posting without any thought as to the consequences, Gerard felt oddly relieved as he stepped back out into the evening drizzle, almost as if he was observing himself and approving his decision. Hadn't he wished for a new opportunity that would allow him to distance himself from Toran and the Emperor's competition?

But a small, dry voice whispered at the back of his mind, *'Coward. You're running away, just as you did before. One day you're going to have to stop running— and face the consequences.'*

***

Toran found the ingenieur in the works office.

"Major Bauldry wished me to convey his thanks to you for helping us." He held out the letter he had been sent to deliver; Bernay took it and placed it unopened on his desk. "He's almost certain that we'll be invited to Tielen as Colonel Lindgren confided in him that ours was the best entry he had seen so far. And this letter is from the major inviting you to continue to mentor us—"

Toran paused a moment to draw breath, realizing that, in his excitement, he had been rattling on without giving Bernay a chance to comment.

But Bernay had turned away and seemed to be unaccountably busy shuffling through some papers on the desk. "I'm afraid there's been a change of plan," he said, his back to Toran. "I won't be able to help you with the final round of the competition after all. Maistre Cardin is sending me abroad on urgent business for the Iron Works."

"You're going away?" Toran had been so full of elation; suddenly those few words cast a shadow over his sunny mood. There would be no more of the sessions at the Iron Works which he had come to look forward to so much. No more poring together over pages of intricate drawings and mathematical equations. No more sharing of discoveries and ideas with a mind so like his own: enquiring and ingenious, obsessed with finding the solutions to seemingly insoluble problems in the mechanical arts. "B-but why?" he stammered. "Where?"

"Maistre Cardin needs an ingenieur to install a pumping mechanism at a new mine works." For some reason Bernay was not looking at him directly. "In Azhkendir."

"Azhkendir?" For a moment Toran was baffled and then he made the connection. "For my father?"

"It seems I'm the only ingenieur employed at the works with the relevant experience to oversee the installation." Still Bernay did not meet his eyes.

"But what about the *Aiglon*? How will we manage without your guidance? You're the only one in Paladur who has the expertise to advise us. I thought you'd accompany us to the competition in Tielen. You deserve it." Toran had tried to disguise his bitter disappointment but it welled up, spilling out.

"Me? No; you've done the work yourselves; you deserve to take the credit, you and Branville. All I've done is act as facilitator." Bernay looked at him at last. "Have faith in your abilities, Toran."

"But we'd never have got this far without you." Toran couldn't stop himself; he knew he must sound like a child who desperately hopes to talk an adult round to doing what he wants, all the time knowing that his case is hopeless. "How long will you be gone?"

"Well, the journey by sea to Narvazh takes about a month once the winter sea ice melts. And then I have to get the equipment transported inland to the Caradas Mining Company headquarters."

"Caradas Mining Company?" Toran echoed, caught off-guard. "Is that what my father's called it?"

"Didn't he tell you?" Bernay looked surprised.

"So he's used my grandfather's family name." Toran's voice had gone hoarse; he cleared his throat, ashamed that he had let his feelings show in front of Bernay. "I wonder if my mother approves? I suppose if he'd called it the Arkhel Mining Company, the Nagarians would have point blank refused him mining rights and thrown him out."

Bernay raised one eyebrow in silent enquiry.

"So you've never heard about the clan wars?" Toran didn't know how best to explain. "The Arkhels and the Nagarians have been at each other's throats for as long as anyone can remember."

"Clan wars? Wonderful," Bernay said with a dry laugh. "This assignment gets better and better."

Toran became aware that maybe he had an ulterior motive that he had not, until now, fully acknowledged.

I wanted to spend more time with Bernay, not less. And now he's going away and I won't be able to see him at all. And with that awareness came a sense of imminent loss so powerful that he felt winded, as if someone had punched him in the gut. "Don't go," he heard himself say. "Ask Maistre Cardin to send someone else."

"There is no one else," Bernay said quietly.

"When do you leave?" Toran managed to ask.

"Tomorrow. Mahieu and I have to be up before dawn to supervise the loading of the machinery onto canal barges."

The office door opened and Mahieu appeared, grinning.

"Did I hear my name?" he said cheerily. "Master Cardin wants a moment of your time, Ingenieur, over in the fettling shop."

Toran realized that he would only be in Bernay's way if he lingered; he'd carried out his mission in delivering the major's letter. As the ingenieur bent to pick up his ledger and stuck a pencil behind his ear, Toran slipped out of the open door, head down so that Mahieu could not see his troubled expression and ask him what the matter was.

***

Why, on this of all mornings, had Colonel Mouzillon called a full drill? Toran fretted as the colonel slowly walked along the rows of cadets, taking his time to reprimand those whose boots were not polished to perfection. The rattle of the drummers beating out a martial marching rhythm and the squeaky fifes only increased his frustration.

The instant the cadets were dismissed, Toran broke ranks, speeding off toward the academy gates.

"Arkhel!" He heard Branville's irate shout ring out across the parade ground but kept going without a backward glance. He would have to deal with Branville's fury when he returned to the workshop later; he reckoned, as he tore down the hill, that the team could manage without him for an hour or so.

Bernay said they would set sail early. Suppose I'm too late and he's already gone?

As Toran neared the canal, he hastened his pace, even though he could feel a stitch burning in his left side, forcing himself to keep going along the muddy tow path.

There were three barges lined up outside Cardin's Iron Works, the pump machinery destined for the Caradas mining venture was already covered in tarpaulins, but to Toran's relief, he spotted the ingenieur on the tow path, ticking off items in a small ledger.

"Gerard!" He stumbled on a loose stone, righting himself.

Bernay turned around. "Toran? Has the major sent you?"

Toran was so out of breath that he was obliged to bend double, heaving and spluttering. It was not the way he had planned to say farewell.

"Perhaps you have a letter for your father?"

Toran shook his head, aware now that he had arrived that he was in the way and impeding Bernay's schedule. "I just came to wish you God speed and a safe journey," he managed to say at last.

"You'll be setting sail for the finals of the Emperor's contest before too long, I imagine," Bernay said.

Toran nodded, tongue-tied, unable to find the words he'd wanted to thank Bernay for helping him to achieve his ambition.

"A word of warning." Bernay drew closer, his expression suddenly earnest, intense. "When you get to Tielen, stay well away from Guy Maulevrier. He's a man who doesn't like to lose. If he offers help—even in the most charming of ways—just don't accept."

"Maulevrier?" Toran repeated, catching an uncharacteristic undertone of anger in Bernay's voice. "Is he the one who stole—"

"Doctor Guy Maulevrier of Tielborg University. Avoid him. At all costs."

It made Toran furious to think how Bernay had been cheated out of his rightful place in the competition by his one-time tutor. "But it's so unjust!"

"What's done is done." Bernay gave a shrug. "Let's not spoil a fair morning by thinking on what might have been."

The bargees had begun to rope their sturdy tow-horses to the laden barges.

"Imagine," Toran said, wanting to change the subject, "how much swifter those barges would move with a little steam engine inside to propel them along the waterways."

"But then those noble beasts of burden would be put out to pasture."

Toran shot Bernay an affectionate glance; it was so like him to consider the consequences of changing the old ways where others would blindly insist that progress must sweep aside everything in its path. He realized how much he had valued his discussions with Bernay—and how much he would miss him. He reached out blindly and flung his arms around the ingenieur.

"Gerard," he said, his voice choked, his face half-buried in his shoulder. He expected Bernay to disentangle himself, to gently but firmly push him away. But instead, his arms enfolded him, holding him so tightly that Toran could feel his heart thudding fast.

"Ingenieur!" Mahieu popped up from the deck of the nearest barge. "We're done here. D'you want to come and check everything's been safely stowed on board?"

"I'm on my way!" Bernay called. He placed his hands on Toran's shoulders, looking directly into his eyes. "The *Aiglon* is a fine design. You deserve to win the Emperor's prize." And then he gently but firmly pushed Toran away from him. Before Toran could react, he had stepped on board the barge, putting a barrier of wood and water between them.

"God speed," Toran said, blinking away tears.

Chapter 24

Azhkendir

"Is it much further, Master Ryndin?" Gerard asked, stopping to mop his forehead. He had been toiling up the steep mountain track for hours behind Lord Ranulph's elderly retainer and, although the air was fresh, with a nip of snow in it from the white peaks towering above, the strong spring sunshine was making him sweat.

"Not far now," replied Ryndin, "I think . . ."

"You think?" puffed Kartavoi, the stoutly-built foreman of works, whose face had turned a deep shade of red as he climbed. "How long is it you've been away, old man?"

"Twenty years, but I've trodden these paths many times in my dreams." Ryndin might be gray-haired and stooped, but he was still much more sure-footed on the stony path than Gerard or Kartavoi. *Like an old mountain goat; wiry and nimble,* Gerard thought wryly.

They had left their horses to graze in a green valley below and continued on foot. And as they walked, Gerard found himself assessing how difficult it would be to transport heavy mining equipment up and down the mountain. *The first task will be to widen this track and make it safe for wagons. We'll need to bring timbers to strengthen the surface; the soil is far too friable to support the weight.*

He was so absorbed in his calculations that it wasn't until he looked up that he realized that Ryndin had disappeared from view.

"Where's the old fellow gone now?" wheezed Kartavoi.

"Through here, Ingenieur!" came back Ryndin's reedy voice. Gerard scrambled on up the treacherous path, rounding the corner to find himself on a wide ridge. On his left was a vertiginous drop. To his right he saw Ryndin waving jubilantly, pointing to the wall of rock towering over their heads. The empty shells of miners' shacks huddled in the shelter of the cliff, all fallen into ruin, with only the stark broken tower of a tall chimney left to give any hint of what had gone on there before.

"I'd no idea we'd climbed so high." Gerard shaded his eyes, impressed by the panoramic view. Above him shimmered the snow-encrusted peaks of the Kharzhgyll Mountains. To his left lay a vast sea of somber green pines, the forest of Kerjhenezh, and below, the softer greens and heathery purples of the moorlands stretched far into the misty distance. Only the Arkhel Waste stood out, a grim, gray gash lying between the verdant mountain foothills and the moorlands.

The air smelt icily clean, yet strangely sweet, as if the honeyed pollen from the wayside spring flowers were scenting the breeze. Gerard drew in a deep lungful, feeling it flow like a cleansing draught through his body. *So much healthier than the smoke-tainted damp of Paladur.*

A harsh, high cry of a bird of prey rang out high above and, gazing upward, Gerard saw the wide serrated wingspan of a snow eagle circling overhead.

If only Toran could see his father's homeland as I'm seeing it now. He couldn't fail to fall in love with this wild, windswept landscape.

"Over here, Ingenieur."

Gerard followed the sound of Ryndin's voice and found the old man behind the ruined shacks, staring up at an ivy-covered expanse of rock face.

Kartavoi, who had been sitting on a boulder, taking a long drink from his water bottle, got to his feet and lumbered after Gerard.

"This is the mine entrance." Ryndin was holding back a curtain of old man's beard and creeper. A breath of cold, dank air issued from the lightless cavern beyond. Gerard knelt down to open his backpack and took out the lantern he had brought and tinder to kindle a flame; Kartavoi did the same. Then they went in under the leafy green curtain, lifting their lanterns high to illuminate what lay beyond.

Kartavoi let out a low whistle. "Impressive."

The unsteady lantern flames revealed a lofty cavern with two tunnels leading off into ink-black darkness. The tunnels were obviously man-made, for the openings had been widened to form roughly rectangular archways, strengthened and supported by thick props of seasoned timber. Shelves had been carved into the rock wall; useful places for the miners to store their supplies and tools, Gerard guessed. But most noticeable of all was the sound of water; not just a slow drip, or an intermittent trickle, but the persistent sound of a stream flowing somewhere in the impenetrable darkness beyond.

"This one." Kartavoi called from the left-hand tunnel; Gerard and Ryndin joined him, soon forced to stoop by the low ceiling.

"Did the mine flood in your time, Ryndin?" Gerard asked, as the sound of water grew louder and with it the oppressive feeling that they could be walking into trouble.

"A couple of times," Ryndin said. His voice sounded muffled in the confined space. Gerard began to feel oppressed by the low ceiling, the lack of light and the damp chill.

Are we crazy, venturing so far underground? If the roof caves in, we'll be crushed, and there's no one to hear us call for help.

The tunnel opened out into a chamber. The splash of water was so loud here that Gerard went to investigate, taking care to check where he placed his feet on the rough cavern floor.

"What do you think, Master Kartavoi?" asked Gerard, noticing that the foreman had been examining the cavern walls with great attention, carefully chipping out little fragments and pocketing them.

"There's evidence of a rich seam of copper here." Kartavoi said and Gerard heard an undisguised hint of greed in his voice.

"Enough to warrant the expense of installing a pump?"

"If there's this much ore here, I'll wager there's much more beyond. Lord Ranulph will be most encouraged when he hears what we've found today." Kartavoi grinned at Gerard. "This mine could make us all rich men."

***

All the way back down the scree-slippery path, Kartavoi talked about rebuilding the shacks, digging a well, blasting a third tunnel . . . And Gerard half-listened, calculating the cost of setting up a working pump to empty the mine of water. They had almost reached the place where they had left their horses when he looked up—and rubbed his eyes, not quite believing what had appeared further along the way.

Two horsemen blocked the entrance to the little valley. As they drew nearer, Gerard saw that they were no ordinary riders but warriors, armed with axes and swords, who seemed to have emerged from the engravings in his boyhood book of hero legends. Both wore their long crow-black hair in tight braids and even from a distance Gerard could tell that their faces were tattooed with blue and blood-red clan-marks. But most disturbing of all was Ryndin's reaction; the old man instantly reached for his pistol and drew it, pointing it unsteadily at the strangers.

"Wait," Gerard cautioned, placing one hand on Ryndin's arm.

"What are you doing here?" called the foremost warrior in the common tongue. "Who are you?" He rode several paces closer, staring down at them with cold suspicion. "Identify yourselves."

"Just travelers from Tourmalise," Gerard replied, "taking the mountain air." He could feel Ryndin trembling beneath his restraining grip; the old man slowly lowered the pistol. "We mean no harm."

"Tourmalise?" repeated the warrior, glancing blankly at his companion.

"We're not trespassing into Nagarian territory," rasped Ryndin. "This is Arkhel land."

"Was Arkhel land," corrected the warrior with a chilling smile. "And if you value your life, old man, you'll not mention that accursed name around here again."

Ryndin stiffened, causing Gerard to tighten his grip. "Stay calm," he murmured in Tourmaline. "Don't rise to their bait." The warriors must be members of Lord Nagarian's ferocious bodyguard, the infamous druzhina that he'd been warned about. And if Ryndin blurted out his Arkhel heritage and allegiance, Gerard had no doubt that the Nagarian warriors would not hesitate to cut them down and leave their bodies as food for the mountain crows.

"Answer my question." The warrior stared directly at Gerard, ignoring Ryndin and Kartavoi. "What is your business here?"

"To re-open the old copper mines." Gerard could see no point in denying it. "We have all the legal documentation, officially approved by Lord Stoyan, if you care to come down to the camp and see for yourselves. We're contracted to export copper to the Emperor's shipyards in Tielen." Gerard stared back at the tattooed warrior, determined not to be intimidated.

"You're too close to Lord Gavril's domain. You'd better make sure that your miners don't stray into

Nagarian territory." The warrior grinned at them, baring his teeth. "If they do—" He mimed throat-slitting, with one brutal slash of his index finger. "Who knows? Lady Morozhka might appreciate a human sacrifice or two. It's been a while."

"Go back to Tourmalise," added the second warrior. "You're not welcome here."

With that the first turned his horse's head around and set off across the grassy valley. The other followed.

Gerard stood motionless, watching until they were out of sight and the dull thud of their horses' hooves over the grassy turf could no longer be heard. He realized that he was trembling. He had not thought twice about confronting bullying cadets back in Paladur, but these young warriors—who looked so alike they must surely be twins—had shaken him.

Such raw aggression. There's no negotiating with savages like that.

Ryndin suddenly hawked and spat. Gerard turned to him and saw that the old retainer's lean face was contorted with an expression of virulent disgust. He sagged and Gerard only just managed to catch hold of him before he fell. He eased the old man onto a nearby boulder and took the pistol from him.

"Here, Master Ryndin, have a swig of my aquavit." Kartavoi handed him the flask and Ryndin silently took a mouthful. "That'll restore you." When Ryndin had finished, Kartavoi took a long swig himself. "So that's what we're up against," he said to Gerard. "They're out to stir up trouble. We'll need armed guards patrolling the mine at all times."

"But I heard that their new lord, Gavril Nagarian, is a good friend of the Emperor's. Surely he won't let his men ride roughshod over our—"

"The only Nagarian's a dead Nagarian." Ryndin said, each word bitter as bile. Color had returned to his wan face, two spots of hectic red on both cheeks; Gerard wondered if he was well enough to ride back to the camp.

"Who's this 'Lady Morozhka' they referred to? Another Nagarian noble?" he asked.

Ryndin let out a dry bark of laughter. "You foreigners; you know nothing of our ways here. Morozhka, Lady Frost, she's been the goddess of the mountains since time began."

"One of the local deities, then." Gerard was beginning to lose patience with the old man. "Do the Azhkendi still worship the old gods? I thought Saint Serzhei was the patron saint of Azhkendir."

"You don't want to anger Lady Frost up here in the mountains," Ryndin said. "She'll send her Snow Spirits to sing your soul out of your body."

As they rode back down towards the camp, Gerard could not help but recall Toran's passionate outburst. *"Branville thinks it's amusing to call me an Azhkendi peasant. But I've never even been to Azhkendir."* He remembered how Toran's eyes had blazed with the intensity of his emotions. *"Where do I fit in? I'm an 'Azhkendi peasant' here in Tourmalise, but I have no connections with my father's homeland; I can't even speak the Azhkendi tongue."*

No wonder Toran's father had wanted to keep his children away from this place. The landscape might be breathtakingly beautiful, but the mountain people were little better than savages. It was in no way a suitable environment for a gently bred young man, educated in the civilized, cultured atmosphere of Tourmalise, to advance his career.

***

"You met two of Lord Nagarian's druzhina?" Lord Ranulph's cheerful expression suddenly faded.

"Arrogant young thugs." Kartavoi, who had been giving his report on the trip, had saved the least promising part till last. "I thought they were going to rob us at knifepoint. Don't you agree, Bernay?"

Gerard looked up from the legal documents he had been consulting. "They weren't very welcoming," he said. "But, as long as we don't trespass onto Nagarian land, they can't stop us. That copper mine belonged to your father, my lord, and according to these deeds you have every right to re-open it."

"So, in your expert opinion, Ingenieur, we can go ahead? Excellent," Lord Ranulph said. "And now that we've been paid for the first shipment of firedust to Tielen, we have funds in hand to purchase more equipment for the mine."

"I say we should use some of those funds to pay for bodyguards." Kartavoi still sounded shaken by the encounter. "I wouldn't put it past those Nagarian druzhina to try to ambush us. It's so remote up there that no one would hear our cries for help—or come to our aid until it was too late. I don't want to put my men's lives needlessly at risk; opening up that old mine is going to be dangerous enough as it is."

Lord Ranulph nodded. "Very well, Kartavoi; I'll get Iarko onto it. Three or four armed men should be more than enough to guard the site."

Gerard thought it best not to make further comment.

"Let me guess what you're thinking, Ingenieur." Lord Ranulph poured himself a glass of aquavit and drank it down in one gulp. "'What am I doing, stuck on the furthest frontier in this barbaric outpost of the New Rossiyan Empire?'"

Gerard merely raised one eyebrow in reply. Lord Ranulph might give the outward impression that he was a jovial aristocrat dabbling for fun in an industrial endeavor, but he had come to realize that he was much more shrewd than he let people think.

Lord Ranulph laughed. "But when you get that copper mine up and working for me and the money starts rolling in, you'll forget all your misgivings." He clapped Gerard amicably on the shoulder. Gerard, gritting a smile, found himself wondering, *Can Toran really be this man's son? He must take after his mother's side of the family.*

Yet as he opened the door to the hut that served as home, he took out his notebook and looked through the latest drawings he had been working on: wings. He had agreed to come as a favour for Master Cardin—and if he made a little profit from the copper mine, he could put that money into developing his flyer himself—without any interference from Guy Maulevrier.

Chapter 25

Tielen

The Emperor was bored.

He had just returned from a visit to the imperial dockyards where he had inspected the newly commissioned warships under construction in dry dock. He had listened to assurances from his naval architects that copper was on order from a new mine that had opened in Azhkendir and that all new ships would be copper-bottomed to give them added protection. It pleased him to think that he was supporting Azhkendir's weak economy by importing minerals and ore; Gavril Nagarian would surely appreciate imperial investment in the stagnant Azhkendi mining industry.

But only one of his projects really excited him: the competition to design and build a flying craft. He had pored over Colonel Lindgren's reports on the finalists; he had even summoned Lindgren to give him his personal opinion on the individual merits of the designs. And then there was the matter of the proposed methods of propulsion. Professor Kazimir had been at work in his university laboratory all winter, pursuing his researches based on Kaspar Linnaius's secret notebooks. But each time Eugene enquired as to his progress, he was frustrated by Kazimir's evasive answers. The latest letter had just arrived, delivered by Gustave on a silver tray, and Eugene ripped it open, tearing the paper in his impatience for positive news.

"Dear God," he said aloud, flinging the paper down, "the man is a genius—at delivering ambiguous reports. What am I supposed to make of this, Gustave?"

Gustave picked up the discarded letter and read, "'The distillation process, while still relatively crude, is beginning to deliver more efficient results.'" He looked up, one eyebrow raised in a skeptical manner. Gustave could, by merely raising one eyebrow, express a remarkable range of reactions, most of them unfavorable. "By which he means he's far from completing his experiments."

"The competition finalists have been selected. We need this propulsive fuel to be ready for the final round. Or we'll look like fools. I think it's time to pay Professor Kazimir a surprise visit. How do you fancy a nostalgic outing to your alma mater, Gustave?"

Gustave flinched. "As long as I don't happen to bump into my old history professor, majesty; I'm afraid I wasn't the most attentive of his pupils and may even have been thrown out of his lectures on a couple of occasions."

"What? You, Gustave? But I'd always assumed you were the perfect student!" Eugene saw that the memory had made his imperturbable secretary appear distinctly uncomfortable and laughed out loud. He was already feeling in a much more jovial mood at the prospect of going to see Kazimir incognito—and was looking forward to seeing what effect his unexpected visit would provoke.

***

Gustave led the way through quad after quad of Tielborg University and Eugene followed, passing black-gowned undergraduates hurrying off to attend a lecture. Gustave had insisted that a bodyguard should accompany them and Eugene had only relented when Gustave assured him that the three handpicked men would not be in imperial uniform but civilian clothes.

But as they approached the School of Chymical Sciences—set at a suitably safe distance from the older buildings—a sudden explosion split the air. Jackdaws perched on the gabled roofs took off, letting out puttering cries of fright as they circled above them.

Eugene's bodyguards instantly surrounded him and pulled him into the shelter of a doorway. But, apart from a thin trail of smoke issuing from a broken-paned window in the chymistry school, nothing else ensued.

"Sounded like firedust to me," Eugene said when the ringing in his ears had cleared. "So Professor Kazimir is still encountering some difficulties with the task I set him."

"Let me go on ahead to warn the professor that he has visitors," said Gustave. "Otherwise we might walk in just as he sets off another explosion."

***

The sound of frantic sweeping and the tinkle of glass fragments greeted Eugene as he followed Gustave into Kazimir's laboratory. At first he could see no sign of the professor but the frantic brush strokes ceased and Altan Kazimir popped up from behind a laboratory bench, much flustered, his hair standing on end and dark smuts staining his face and coat.

"Y-your imperial majesty, this is an unexpected honor, if I had known—"

"Calm yourself, Professor." Eugene affected his most reassuring tone. "I see we have caught you at an inopportune moment. "

"N-not exactly. I just made a slight error in my calculations and this is the result." Kazimir gestured apologetically to the disorder in the laboratory. "If you would care to step into my office . . ."

The office was only a little less disordered than the laboratory; folders and notebooks were piled on every available surface, some spilling papers covered in calculations onto the floor. Kazimir swept up armfuls of his work and deposited them in a corner, clearing a chair by the desk so that the Emperor could sit down.

"I'm content to stand, Professor," said Gustave, nodding to the bodyguards who placed themselves outside to guard the doorway.

"You must be aware that the grand finale of the Flyer Competition is drawing near," Eugene said as Kazimir attempted to smooth down his wildly disordered hair and rub the smuts from his face.

Kazimir nodded. "Very aware, because Doctor Maulevrier's flying machine has the honor to be one of the two chosen to compete. He often comes by the laboratory to encourage me in my work."

Eugene could not help but frown at this. "I'm not sure the other finalists would be too happy to learn that Doctor Maulevrier has such an advantage."

"Oh, I can assure your majesty that I would never allow anyone, even my esteemed colleague, to cheat."

Kazimir looked so shocked at the suggestion that Eugene was almost sorry he had made it. He leaned forward and said in his most confidential voice, "Tell me, Professor, just between you and me, is this really a viable project? Will this miraculous explosive fuel you've been concocting be able to lift a heavy craft into the air and propel it forward?"

Kazimir leaned closer. "Every detail I've been able to decipher from Kaspar Linnaius's secret notebooks suggests that such a thing is possible, given the right combination of a subtle mechanism, a well-designed craft, and . . ."

"And?" Eugene beamed encouragingly at him.

Kazimir squirmed. "Frankly, I'm still baffled, majesty. Everything I've tried so far has resulted in a hazardously explosive mix. I've blown several model flyers to bits already. I just can't risk using this fuel in a full-sized flyer and killing the aviator—and maybe spectators too."

"I see." Eugene let out a sigh, unable to conceal his disappointment. "So we should postpone the finals?"

Kazimir hesitated. "There is one other possibility," he began.

"There is?" Eugene leaned forward across the desk, all attention. Kazimir might appear timid, maybe even something of a coward, but Eugene also knew him to be a gifted man of science.

Kazimir turned the open treatise around to show him. "I have reason to believe that Kaspar Linnaius had made a significant discovery: but, being unable to test it out for himself, he left a trail of ciphered clues."

"So like him," Eugene said fondly. "He loved to play games with us; it amused him to see us struggling to work out his little conundrums."

"Conundrum?" Kazimir said. "Precisely the word he has used here." He pointed at the page.

Eugene leaned closer, peering, but then, to his irritation, was obliged to fish inside his greatcoat pocket for his new pair of pince-nez spectacles. "'Some say the answer lies in the Arkhel Conundrum'," he read and felt a sudden delicious frisson of excitement. *No doubt about it; this is one of your devilish intellectual challenges, dear Kaspar. But are we clever enough to solve it?*

"Were all the books from the Magus's library at Swanholm brought here?" he asked.

"Only the notebooks and journals."

There was no point in prevaricating; Eugene paused a second or so before making his move on the unsuspecting professor. "How soon can you be ready to leave for Swanholm?"

"Swanholm? But my research here, my lectures?"

"As you're coming at my invitation, I'm sure the chancellor won't object to granting you a brief sabbatical." Eugene stood up, eager to get preparations underway. "Astasia and I are returning to Swanholm tomorrow for a few days; the country air is so invigorating. Gustave; make arrangements for the professor to accompany us."

Gustave nodded and Eugene smiled genially at Kazimir as he made his exit, aware that the professor was staring at him open-mouthed, whatever protest he had been about to make, still lodged in his throat.

"It's just too much fun to tease the good professor," Eugene confessed to Gustave as they came out into the quad, the bodyguards following in his wake.

"But do you think he can solve this 'Conundrum'?"

"I have faith in Altan Kazimir. Behind that timid scholarly front he shows to the world lies a rather remarkable brain. If anyone can work out Linnaius's puzzles, he can." He turned to Gustave. "Shall we make a wager?" he asked innocently.

Gustave laughed. "I wouldn't dare; you always win!"

Chapter 26

Swanholm Palace

Altan Kazimir stopped to catch his breath after climbing the winding stair and stared warily at the door to Linnaius's laboratory. He had unpleasant memories of the first time he had been brought to Swanholm Palace to meet the Magus. But there was no sign of the sinister iron door-knocker, the puff-cheeked wind god, which Linnaius had once used to entrap and poison him. Even so, he glanced around uneasily, convinced that the Magus must have left some invisible alarm to catch the unwary.

"The Emperor mentioned that the laboratory used to be protected by powerful wards." He looked down at the ornate key Eugene had given him, saying cheerily aloud, "But I'm sure Linnaius removed them all before he entrusted me with this key. No one's been allowed inside since he left. I imagine it's all rather dusty by now."

Trying to stop his hand from shaking, Kazimir inserted the key in the lock and turned it. To his surprise, the mechanism worked smoothly and the door opened, revealing the laboratory and private study beyond, dimly illuminated by light seeping in through the cracks in the shutters. For a moment, Kazimir thought he saw the old Magus turning to greet him, his white wisps of hair and frail, bent figure belied by the keen glitter in his silver-gray eyes.

He blinked. *There's nothing here but shadows.* Annoyed with himself for giving way to his own imaginings, he made his way across the room and flung open the shutters, letting the clear daylight stream in.

The Emperor had certainly been right about the dust; a thin film had settled on every surface; even the glass phials on the shelves had lost their sheen. And there was a strangely bitter tang to the mote-filled air, redolent of chymical residues.

Let's just hope Linnaius didn't booby-trap the place with some poisonous, airborne powder and I haven't just inhaled something that's started to eat through my lungs or make me hallucinate and throw myself out the window.

Even though Linnaius's papers had all been safely re-housed in his university study, Kazimir was haunted by the fact that the Magus's notes on firedust referred several times to "the Arkhel Conundrum". He was certain that the wily old man had left yet another puzzle behind for him to solve; he could almost imagine him smiling to himself as he concealed the vital pieces of information. The Arkhels had been the first ruling family in Azhkendir until—centuries ago—the first of the Nagarian princes, Volkhar, had seized power, leading to a long and bitter clan war.

An intriguing collection of old books still lined the walls of the study and Kazimir found himself gazing at the gold-tooled titles, wondering if any of them might contain a clue. He was surprised that so many were written in Francian, but then, he had heard rumors that Linnaius had been born in Francia and studied there.

"Arkhels . . . Arkhels . . ." he muttered, running his index finger along the spines of Linnaius's abandoned library. Eventually he pulled out a large tome entitled: "A Genealogy of the Clans of Azhkendir" and laid it on the desk. As he had anticipated, the contents were sealed with a curious metal lock which, on closer examination, proved to be a dial which could be turned to several different positions, none of which unlocked the book.

"A coded sequence, no doubt." Kazimir sighed and sat down at Linnaius's desk to try to puzzle out the possible configurations.

"Magus? Is that you?"

A child's voice rang out in the stairwell and moments later, a slender, fair-haired girl ran into the laboratory. On seeing him there, she stopped and her expression which had been bright with eagerness, dulled in disappointment.

"Only me, your highness, I'm afraid." Kazimir, recognizing Princess Karila, rose and bowed.

"Why are you in his rooms, Professor?" Eyes as blue and clear as her father the Emperor's challenged him.

"I'm doing research for your father," he said. "You may remember that the Magus asked me to continue his researches in his absence . . . and," he ended lamely, "here I am."

She began to wander around the laboratory. "It's very dirty," she said and sneezed. "He was going to teach me how to make mirror-dust. He promised."

"Your highness could still start to learn the basic principles of chymistry," Kazimir ventured, not wanting to disappoint the princess. "Would you like me to find a book for you to study?"

She swung around to face him. "With experiments?" she asked eagerly. "I so want to do experiments."

He raised his hands. "Experiments must only be done in a laboratory with a trained chymist to ensure nothing goes wrong." *The last thing I need is for the princess to set off an explosion.*

She came closer, staring up at him appealingly. "Will you teach me, Professor?"

"I'd be honored, highness, but I'm very busy working on a project for your father right now—"

"Princess!" A woman's voice shrilled from the courtyard. "Where are you hiding? It's time for your deportment lesson!"

Karila pulled a face. "Can't I stay here?" she whispered.

Footsteps pattered up the stairs and as Karila slipped into the study, Countess Marta, Karila's governess, appeared.

"Professor Kazimir, I'm so sorry to trouble you, but I have reason to believe that my charge has been disturbing your work." And Marta strode determinedly past Kazimir and into the study. "This is no time to play hide-and-seek, Princess. The dancing master is waiting to instruct you."

Karila let out a little sigh of irritation. "Very well, Marta," she said. "But I don't see why I shouldn't be allowed to study the sciences as well as the arts." And then she paused and said to Kazimir, "What's in that big old book?"

"I wish I could tell you, Princess," he said and then, seized with a sudden inspiration, added, "but you may be able to help me. The Magus has left us a puzzle; if you can solve it, we can open it and find out." Linnaius had been very fond of Princess Karila, he remembered, and might even have taught her a trick or two.

"May I, Marta?" Karila cried, hands clasped together in fervent appeal.

"Well, if it's to help the professor . . ." Marta began reluctantly. Before she had finished, Karila shot back to the book of genealogy and began to examine the intricately fashioned metal dial.

"There are letters here," she said. "It must be a code. Perhaps it spells out a name."

"Linnaius called it 'The Arkhel Conundrum'," Kazimir said as Marta looked questioningly at him over Karila's bent head, her smooth forehead creasing into a frown.

"Are you sure that it's safe for the princess?" she asked in worried tones. "This *is* the Magus's conceit, after all."

Karila's fingers were expertly spinning the little dial. "Jaromir Arkhel," she spelled out. There came a little click and the catch sprang open.

"You're a genius, Princess!" cried Kazimir, genuinely impressed. "How did you guess?"

"I loved Jaro like a brother," she said. "And when he went back to Azhkendir to try to rebuild his clan's fortunes, Papa asked the Magus to watch over him. There had to be a link."

"Nevertheless, perhaps you'd both better stand well back when I open the book," Kazimir said, gingerly lifting the heavy leather-bound cover. "With the Magus you can never be too sure what little traps he might have concealed."

A glint of phosphorescent light leaked out.

"Ooh," said Karila softly, "how pretty!"

A hole had been neatly cut through the pages, forming a square recess at the center of the text. Nestled within the recess and emitting a dull ocher glow, lay a crystalline rock, about the size of a goose egg.

"What is it?" Countess Marta said. "Why is it glowing? Is it safe?"

The eerie glow reflected back at Kazimir in the princess's eyes as she slowly raised her head to stare at him, through him.

Kazimir saw Marta glance at him in shock over Karila's head. "Time we were going," she said firmly. "We mustn't disturb the professor's work any longer."

"Oh, Marta . . ." Karila began but her governess steered her toward the door.

"Thank you for your help, highness," Kazimir said distractedly, his gaze drawn inexorably back to the Arkhel Conundrum. "Well, Magus," he muttered when they had gone, "have you left me any clues as to how to solve this mystery?"

And then he noticed that certain words on the page in the "Genealogy of the Clans" that lay uppermost in the open volume seemed to glint subtly in the sun, making them stand out from the others, as if the rays had activated some alchymical substance carefully painted over the original text:

'Sviatomir married Kiraana, the Youngest Child of Tomas Rytsarev, Boyar, thus ensuring the continuation of the Arkhel line. For although Teshemir, their Firstborn son, Underwent training for the priesthood and Entered the Monastery of St Serzhei, his brother Stavyor became Lord Arkhel on their father's death.'

"S - K- Y." Kazimir spelled out, "C-R-A-F-T-F-U-E-L. Sky craft fuel!" He let out a shout of triumph at having solved Linnaius's riddle. "But . . . how? How can this pretty egg power a sky craft ?" He stared at the phosphorescent crystal, all his initial enthusiasm fast draining away. As far as he could recall, Linnaius had only ever relied on his powers as a wind mage to lift his own craft into the air and propel it through the skies, a fact that he, a rationalist and scholar of science had been obliged to accept, even though it defied everything he had ever learned. *Can this little crystal really emit energy strong enough to set a mechanism in motion?*

"Sky craft fuel?" echoed a man's voice. Startled, Kazimir shot off his seat and bowed as the Emperor came in, his face glowing with an expression as eager as his daughter's had been earlier. Kazimir's elation melted away; Eugene was obviously expecting results and he only had more questions.

"Karila told me she helped you solve one of the Magus's little puzzles," Eugene said, rubbing his hands together.

"Indeed she did and without her help, I'd still be scratching my head over it," Kazimir was forced to admit.

"And this is the hidden treasure." Eugene leaned over the crystal and Kazimir noticed that, just as when Karila had come closer to it, the amber radiance it exuded glowed with greater intensity, warming the Emperor's face. "It's giving off quite a powerful energy," Eugene said, retreating a step or two.

"With respect, majesty," Kazimir said, "it only seems to respond to you and the princess."

"And the reason for that would be . . . ?"

Kazimir hesitated, not certain how the Emperor would react to his theory. "Your connection to the Drakhaouls," he ventured.

One imperial eyebrow shot up questioningly. "So how can this be converted to fuel? Surely it can't be burned like a coal? Are you supposed to grind it up?"

"I'm certain that some of its unique qualities reside in its crystalline construction," Kazimir said, squinting at their discovery, "as with the crystals used in the Vox Aethyria. But that was a kind of sympathetic resonance. Perhaps this stone emits a similar kind of aethyric energy that could turn the cogs and pistons of a mechanical device."

"Such as a clock?" The Emperor raised his hand in a little gesture that said, "*Leave this to me*," and went outside. Kazimir heard a brief conversation taking place and a few minutes later, a flunkey in the palace servants' gray and blue livery appeared, carefully carrying a clock in a glass case.

"And you're certain that this clock has stopped?" Eugene asked.

"Yes, majesty; we were awaiting the clockmaker to make some adjustments to the escapement."

"Excellent." As soon as the flunkey had gone, Eugene carefully lifted out the clock (one of the modish skeleton types with all its mechanism, wheels and cogs, exposed), set it down on the desk and turned to Kazimir. "Over to you, Professor." His excitement was infectious.

Kazimir, flustered as always when under pressure, gazed around for a pair of thick leather gloves or chymical tongs, having no wish to touch the glowing stone with bare hands. He found tongs and a couple of leather face masks with clear isinglass panels to protect the eyes, one of which he handed to the Emperor.

"Who knows what effect this crystal may produce," he said nervously. "I advise your majesty to stand well back."

He removed the clock from its glass case and then, trying to keep his hands steady, lifted out the softly glowing crystal with the tongs. He carried it at arm's length to the desk and placed it below the static clock mechanism. A gentle whirring issued from the delicately cast wheels as they began to rotate.

"Fascinating," breathed Eugene, going closer.

"Please take care, majesty." Kazimir heard the tremble in his voice but suspected that he was more nervous about protecting the Emperor than his own safety. "We don't know why this reaction is taking place yet—where it may lead or how it will progress . . ." Yet in spite of his concerns, he found himself moving forward to get a clearer view.

As the pendulum began to move, the clock started to emit a steady tick.

"Is it my eyesight," said the Emperor, leaning in closer, "or is that crystal emitting a regular pulse of light?"

"Yes—and there seems to be a correlation between the frequency of the pulsation and the ticking of the clock." Kazimir scribbled down his observations, determined to maintain a scientific approach to this unorthodox experiment. As they watched, the pulsations increased in frequency and the whirring of the escapement started to speed up. The minute hand on the clock began to move around the dial, gaining momentum until it was whizzing so fast, dragging the hour hand behind it, that something snapped. With a metallic twang, the hands flew off, causing Kazimir to jump out of the way as they embedded themselves, like tiny darts, in the wood of the cabinet behind him. The cogs, with a grinding sound, slowly wound down as the pulse of light emitted by the crystal ceased.

"Extraordinary," the Emperor said in the ensuing silence, raising his mask. And then he grinned conspiratorially at Kazimir. "If we can harness this power and put it to good use, imagine the possibilities."

Kazimir was less optimistic. "It's too early to risk, majesty."

"But the Arkhel connection?" continued the Emperor. "You know the Magus well enough, Professor. When he calls this the Arkhel Conundrum, it doesn't just refer to the cipher he's devised to protect his research."

Kazimir nodded. Just like Kaspar Linnaius to leave a convoluted trail of clues to baffle him. His thoughts were spinning as fast as the little cogs in the clock mechanism a few seconds ago.

"Did Linnaius intend us to use this crystalline distillation of firedust as the basis for a sky craft fuel?" The Emperor was musing aloud. "Or did he intend us to power the engine with one of these crystals?"

"But that would mean asking the competitors to redesign their engines," Kazimir said. "From Colonel Lindgren's report, it seems that all the entrants have created machines that work with liquid fuel."

"Then that must be what Kaspar intended." Eugene punched his fist into his palm, startling Kazimir. "Can you reverse the process?"

"What? Convert this crystal into liquid fuel?" Put on the spot, Kazimir floundered.

"The Magus knew how rare true firedust is." Eugene began to pace, expounding on his theory. "So he created this highly concentrated crystalline form, anticipating that you would know how to transmute it."

"But he left no instructions."

"Because he knew you have the intelligence and the chymical knowledge to complete the task." Eugene stopped in front of Kazimir and placed his hand on his shoulder. "He had faith in you. As do I."

Kazimir, dazzled by the intense gaze, knew he was being flattered but, as always, found it difficult to resist Eugene's persuasive charm. "If," he said slowly, thinking aloud, "if I were to create such a fuel, we would need to test it before releasing it to the contestants."

"How about using it to power the pleasure craft here at Swanholm?"

"The swan boats?" Kazimir realized that the Emperor was referring to the painted craft he had commissioned to ferry courtiers and guests around the ornamental lakes and canals in the palace gardens. "So if I were to install a little engine in one and power it with the fuel . . ."

"Bring your best students here from Tielborg," Eugene said. "And experiment to your heart's content! Just give Count Gustave a list of names."

As the Emperor left with a smile and a wave of the hand, Kazimir found himself nodding his assent, even though he was assailed by doubts and questions.

"Swans?" he muttered, reaching for his notebook and a pencil. "Will I be remembered by posterity as the man who invented the mechanical swan and gave pleasure to all those who sailed in it?"

Chapter 27

The constant hammering coming from the men at work rebuilding the East Wing had given Astasia a headache. As she dabbed lavender water on her throbbing temples, she began to wish that she had stayed behind in the relative calm of the Winter Palace in Mirom, in spite of the constant draughts and the damp chill rising from the River Nieva.

Pulling down a linen blind to protect her eyes from the clear sunlight streaming in, she wondered if she should try to lie down and sleep until the headache had gone. She opened the double doors into the bedchamber—but the insistent sound of hammering pursued her inside, even penetrating the wood of the soft-gray-painted paneled walls.

I can't ask them to stop just because my head hurts . . . and the project is already far behind schedule thanks to the harsh winter we've just endured.

She pulled the brocade bell rope to summon her maid and slipped off her shoes, pushing aside the heavy bed curtains and lying down, closing her eyes.

"What's all this? Back in bed already, majesty?" Nadezhda's voice, tart with surprise, made her open one eye. "I only helped you get dressed an hour or so ago."

"I have a terrible headache." Astasia closed the eye again. "I need you to tell Gustave to cancel my engagements today."

"Weren't you going to receive Countess Lovisa for lunch? She'll be so disappointed. How about I mix you an infusion of some willow bark? That should help."

Astasia pulled a face. "Willow bark tastes disgusting."

"I'll put in some elderflower cordial to sweeten it."

"Somehow that only makes it taste worse."

"If your headache is very bad," Nadezhda said, drawing the heavy cream and blue curtains to darken the room, "you won't want to see the letter that arrived for you today. All the way from Serindher."

Astasia opened both eyes. "From Serindher? You mean from my brother?"

"But you're feeling too poorly to read it. Not to worry; it's taken many weeks to get here, so I'm sure Prince Andrei's news can wait a little longer."

Astasia sat up. "Stop being such a tease, Nadezhda, and bring me Andrei's letter." Her head still throbbed but her excitement at the prospect of news from her exiled brother after so many months was strong enough to make her ignore the pain.

**

"Doctor Maulevrier?"

Startled, Guy Maulevrier looked up from the lecture notes he was preparing.

The newcomer was tall and bearded with long hair of a walnut brown. Pale eyes glittered in a face weathered by sun and wind to a deep coppery tan.

"I heard you were looking for volunteer pilots for the Emperor's flying contraption competition."

"And what makes you think you're suitable to apply?" Maulevrier heard the disdainful drawl in the newcomer's pronunciation of the word "contraption".

"I've had some experience in the field."

"Flying?" Maulevrier could not quite disguise his skepticism. "Even though the science is in its infancy?"

"In Tielen, yes. But I've just come back from the other side of the world. I've seen and experienced things there you would not believe, not in your wildest dreams, Doctor Maulevrier."

"The other side of the world?" Maulevrier was beginning to wonder if the man was toying with him for his own amusement. "Yet you speak our language like a native."

"Not surprising, really. I *am* a Tielen. Although we're all Rossiyans now, aren't we, in the new empire?" There was an edge to the stranger's use of the word "we" but when Maulevrier eyed him keenly, he merely smiled, showing white teeth in his sun-browned face. "I've been out in the colonies," he continued. "In the Spice Islands. Got marooned there for quite a while."

That would explain the tan and the nautical beard. "So you were in the spice trade?"

"Something of the sort." The stranger smiled again without a trace of warmth. "Helping the locals after the tidal wave hit the islands."

"Your family must be very relieved to see you safely home after so long away."

A brief, careless shake of the head. "My family are all dead."

Maulevrier had been testing to what kind of reaction he could provoke. But the stranger was expert at revealing no more than he wished to disclose about himself—which seemed to be next to nothing. Maulevrier's suspicions were in no way allayed.

"This is a singularly dangerous assignment," he said. "I can't pretend otherwise. If the machine crashes, there's no guarantee that you'll survive. On the other hand, we'll pay you generously. And, if our flyer wins, then there'll be guaranteed employment— should you choose to accept it, of course. We'll need the winning pilot to train others."

"Sounds good to me. When do I start?"

For a fleeting moment, Maulevrier wondered whether he was being rather rash in agreeing to take this man on without papers or any kind of personal recommendation.

"I'll need you to sign a contract."

"Didn't you hear me? I've no relations. No one to come demanding compensation if I crash. But if you prefer to have everything officially signed and sealed . . ."

As the stranger took up the pen, scanned the terms of employment in a mere blink and signed his name with a flourish, Maulevrier took back the contract to read his name.

"Karl Lorens?"The name sounded Tielen enough— although it was not beyond the bounds of possibility that his team's new pilot had taken the name from a fellow Tielen sailor on his voyage home from the Spice Islands. He made a mental note to have a few questions asked at the port as he leaned across the bench to offer his hand to Lorens.

"Welcome to the Tielborg University team, Karl. I'll take you to meet the students and show you our craft, the *Svala;* we're rather proud of her."

***

"How are you feeling, my dear?" Eugene sat beside Astasia and took her hand in his. Astasia was still clutching Andrei's letter which she had read and re-read several times, in spite of her headache. How would Eugene react to the news? He seemed in a good mood, exuding such an energetic aura, that she was reluctant to dampen his spirits.

"Andrei has written to warn us," she said, waving the paper. "He says that Oskar Alvborg has gone missing."

"Oh, that?" Eugene said airily. "Baron Sylvius received word late last year that Alvborg had disappeared."

"You knew? Why didn't you tell me!" Astasia grimaced; her outburst had only made her temples throb more painfully. She pressed the handkerchief soaked in ice water to her forehead.

"I didn't want to alarm you unnecessarily. Besides, it was suspected that he had suffered an accident and fallen overboard."

"Do you mean an accident?" Astasia gave her husband a stern look. "Or an 'accident'?"

"I can't pretend that the option hasn't tempted me more than once." Eugene got up and began to pace the bedchamber. "And Sylvius would see it was carried out in the blink of an eye." He stopped, gazing at her. "But since I discovered that Oskar is my brother—"

"Your illegitimate brother," she said softly.

"That was no fault of his."

"And it was no fault of yours, dear Eugene," Astasia said, seeing how conflicted he still felt, "that the truth about his birth was concealed from you both. Your father chose not to acknowledge him."

"There's no way I can ever make it up to him."

"He doesn't deserve your sympathy," she said. "He abducted Kari. I can never forgive him for that."

"Yet you forgave Andrei after he abducted little Rostevan."

Astasia shuddered. The memory was still raw in her memory. "He was under the control of a Drakhaoul."

"As was I. And Lord Gavril. And Oskar. And now we're all free."

"Free?" She glanced up at him, even though it hurt her pounding head to do so. "Are you truly free, Eugene? Or has that daemon left some trace?"

He stopped pacing abruptly and sat beside her again, cupping her face in his hands, gently forcing her to look at him. "You know me better than anyone, Tasia," he said, his voice quiet yet intense. "You'd tell me, wouldn't you? If any sign of Belberith's influence began to show?"

She stared searchingly into his eyes. There was not even the faintest emerald glint of daemonic possession—although the keen intensity of his stare was difficult to endure for long, especially with a headache.

"It's you," she said, relieved. "I can't sense anyone else." But then the hammering started up again and she winced involuntarily.

"My poor girl," he said, relaxing his grip, the probing stare softening to a look of remorse. "I forgot you weren't feeling well. Shall I have Nadezhda fetch Doctor Amandel?"

"No need to bother the good doctor . . ." She lay back, feebly waving one hand. "A little quiet would help."

"Shall I order the workmen to take an early break for lunch? I've placed them on a rather tight deadline to complete the work before the competition."

"The competition?" She saw the gleam of excitement in his eyes and felt guilty for hampering his plans; whenever he mentioned them, she caught a glimpse of the Eugene who had won her heart, the ambitious, idealistic prince with the determination to make his dreams of empire come true.

"And you must take a ride with me in Kazimir's steam-powered swan craft on the canal when you're feeling better. It's a marvel."

"So it works?" The thought of sailing in such a strange contraption made Astasia feel a tad nervous.

"After a few failed attempts," Eugene said breezily. "Now that our good professor has perfected his calculations, I can't wait to see what the flying craft will do on Dievona's Night."

Chapter 28

Azhkendir

The last snows of the bitter Azhkendi winter had thawed at last and there was a sweet tang of whitethorn blossom on the fresh breeze. The Nagarian coach trundled across the moors toward Azhgorod. Kiukiu sat inside with Larisa on her lap and Sosia for company, all three well wrapped in furs, whilst Gavril, Semyon and Vasili, Dunai's younger brother, rode alongside. State business brought them to the capital; the first meeting of the boyars' council necessitated the High Steward of Azhkendir's presence.

No sooner had they arrived in the city, than Lord Stoyan insisted that Gavril meet with him to discuss an urgent matter, so Kiukiu was left with the servants to supervise the unpacking. Unused to having others doing the tasks she was used to performing herself, she busied herself with feeding and cleaning Larisa, whilst Sosia and Taina, the mansion housekeeper, removed the clothes from the trunk.

"What are all these paintings?" she heard Taina ask in the hallway. "Where am I supposed to put these?"

"Hush," Sosia replied, "they're Lord Gavril's hobby. He insisted on bringing them with him. They're not to everyone's taste but . . ."

"Then they can go in Lord Gavril's study. They can't stay here in the hallway, cluttering up the place. And what about my lady's linen? And little Larisa's clothes?"

I'm sure Taina is tutting to herself over the way everything was folded and packed.

"Have you not employed a nurse for the baby yet, Lady Kiukirilya?" enquired Taina pointedly as Kiukiu settled Larisa in her cradle.

And now she's disapproving of my child-rearing practices.

"There's no need, really," Kiukiu said, forcing a smile. She shivered; the main rooms had been shuttered up all winter and even though Taina had lit a fire, the atmosphere was chill and a little musty. "Auntie Sosia and Ninusha help me out at the kastel."

"What a pretty box, my lady." Taina held up the little lacquer tea chest that Chinua had sent as a gift for Larisa's Naming Day. "Is that Khitari craftsmanship?"

"You're right; it's a tea caddy," said Kiukiu, pulling her shawl about her. "A present from an old friend."

"You look cold, my lady; shall I make you some tea?"

Kiukiu nodded. "That would be very welcome." She had been saving Chinua's gift for a special occasion but one had not yet presented itself. *And when I visit his shop, he's sure to ask me if we enjoyed his gift, so I'd better sample it.*

She moved restlessly about the bedchamber, stiff from sitting so long in the bumpy coach, wishing she could leave the mansion and walk freely. But twilight was falling and the first lady of Azhkendir would not be expected to go out alone at night; such an unseemly show of independence would only reflect badly on Gavril. She let out a sigh of frustration.

"You're very pale, Kiukiu," Sosia said, closing the door of the armoire. "Are you sure you're feeling all right?"

"A tad tired after the long journey." There was little point, Kiukiu knew, in telling her how cooped up she felt; she would never understand.

"Hm."

Taina came back carrying a tea tray which she set down on a little table near the fire and drew up a chair. "Warm yourself over here, my lady." She poured some of the tea into a delicate gold-rimmed porcelain cup and the aromatic fragrance wafted into the room.

"Will you join me, Auntie?" Kiukiu turned to Sosia.

Sosia sniffed the tea suspiciously. "You know that fancy scented tea isn't to my taste," she said. "Dried jasmine flowers, indeed. I'll go join Taina in the kitchen for a proper cup of Serindhen blend. With bilberry jam."

They just want a good gossip together. Kiukiu smiled to herself, settling down in the chair by the fire. The bitter-sweet odor of the hot steam was stronger than she had anticipated and made her nostrils prickle. She risked a sip and nodded, relishing the subtle flavor. *It's delicious. We used to drink tea like this in Khitari all the time. The taste brings back memories . . .*

Kiukiu took another sip. The perfumed tea fumes drew out buried images and emotions. Her lids felt heavy, drooping lower . . .

She closed her eyes, letting the tide of half-forgotten Khitari impressions wash over her: the hazy green of the vast grasslands, the haunting songs of the herdsmen following in the wake of the khan's caravan, the lonely cry of the steppe eagles wheeling high overhead, the bubbling hiss of the healing waters of the Jade Springs . . .

Kiukiu opened her eyes with a start. Fragments of melody whispered at the back of her mind. Words attached themselves to the notes.

"*She can grant your wish, the jade-haired witch of the springs.*"

Khulan's ballad again. Kiukiu shuddered at the memory—and yet still the song refrain insisted on replaying itself until she was desperate for a means of exorcising it.

Why now, of all times? She lifted her gusly from the bottom of the trunk. A swift test of the strings confirmed that they needed tightening to correct the pitches. She took out the tuning key and set to work, plucking softly so as not to disturb the sleeping baby, until she was satisfied.

As Kiukiu picked out the first notes of Khulan's ballad, she began to shiver uncontrollably. Each sonorous pitch was creating a portal into that shadowy aethyrial dimension where even the most skilled shamans trod the paths of the dead at considerable risk.

The way that had opened up before her was mountainous, hazed in ever-shifting mists.

Suppose I get trapped again?

Kiukiu's fingers slowed and instantly the pathway started to disintegrate.

But this isn't the Realm of Shadows. And now that I've come this far, I have to see it through.

She picked up the broken thread of the melody and continued to play, sending her spirit out along the mist-wreathed path. And the further she went, the more familiar the mountainous landscape became. Passing beneath a rocky archway, she saw the bubbling waters of the Jade Springs.

"Lady Anagini!" she called into the mists. "Why have you brought me back here?"

"Look into the waters," breathed a woman's voice behind her. "But don't stop playing. The instant you stop, the image will disappear and you'll never be able to recapture it."

Kiukiu nodded. The bubbles stilled as she gazed down into the pool and the waters became glassy clear. A distant murmur of voices superimposed themselves over the notes of the melody. It was hard to listen to what was being said without losing the sense of the tune but she forced herself to concentrate.

Two radiant figures appeared, their faces so bright that she could hardly distinguish their features. She had glimpsed such radiance once before when she and Malusha had dared to use the Golden Scale, travelling deep along the Forbidden Ways into the Second Heaven in search of Saint Serzhei—and that same light had emanated from the gilded wings of the Heavenly Warriors dispatched to drive them from the saint's garden.

"Angels?" she whispered.

"So it's happened again. The forbidden union. Just as it did with Nagazdiel." The speaker was a tall, powerfully built warrior with a long mane of golden hair. "The Drakhaoul Khezef has sired a mortal child."

"But can you be sure, Galizur, that the child has inherited any of Khezef's powers?" asked his companion in gentler tones.

Galizur. The name Gavril cries out in his nightmares. Kiukiu forced herself to concentrate on playing, desperate now to hear more.

"This child is a girl, Sehibiel."

Kiukiu struck a wrong note and the image wavered. Was he referring to Larisa?

"A girl? Like Azilis, Nagazdiel's daughter?" Sehibiel, the softly-spoken Guardian, shook his head; his hair was a silvery gray, shot through with strands of rose. *Like a sunset sky.*

"Even if she's inherited a fraction of her father's abilities, she'll prove a threat to the balance between the worlds. So I'm sending Taliahad to take care of it."

Take care of it? Kiukiu's fingers began to tremble. She forced herself to keep playing, even though Galizur's words had shaken her to the core.

The air thrummed and a third Winged Warrior alighted and went down on one knee before the other two; his eyes and hair shimmered with the wintry blue of the icy waters off Azhkendir's shores.

"You summoned me, Prince Galizur." His voice sounded young and fervent. "What is your will?"

"I'm sending you to the mortal world. I want you to find a child with Drakhaoul blood in her veins— and destroy her."

Kiukiu's hands flew up to her face in shock. Too late she realized that she had broken the thread of melody—and the dazzling image shattered into a thousand ripples.

"What shall I do?" She turned to Anagini. "They want to kill Larisa. How can I save her? Tell me what to do. I'll do anything. Anything!"

"You already know what to do." Anagini's voice soothed her. "Bring her to me. I will protect her."

"But what should I tell Gavril?"

"Nothing. No one must know where she is."

"It'll break his heart." Kiukiu could hardly say the words. "He adores her. How can I take her away from him?" Only then did the full import of Galizur's words hit her. *The forbidden union.* So Khezef was as much Larisa's true father as Gavril. The Drakhaoul had used them both as his mortal surrogates to ensure the continuation of his line.

***

Kiukiu pushed open the door to the tea shop, hearing the little bell tinkle overhead. Inside, the dusty, aromatic smell tickled her nostrils.

"Is anyone there?" she called. Larisa, snugly wrapped in her shawl, let out a little sneeze. The Khitari rug covering the doorway at the rear of the shop was raised and a man appeared, smiling in welcome as he beckoned her into the back room.

"Chinua!" Kiukiu cried, hurrying toward him. "I need to go to the Jade Springs. Can you take us there?"

"The Guardian warned me that you might need my help. Hallo there, little one—aren't you pretty?"

Larisa beamed and stretched out her chubby hands to him, gurgling a greeting in return.

"I see she has her father's eyes." Chinua let her grasp his finger in hers.

"And that's not all she's inherited from her father," Kiukiu heard herself say, her words salted with bitterness. *Why did Khezef use us both? What was his true design?* "When can we leave?"

"As soon as you like. But did anyone see you come in here?"

Kiukiu shook her head. "I made sure the coast was clear."

"Then I'll just shutter up the shop and we'll be on our way."

***

Gavril would not return home till late from the boyars' council. By then the gates of Azhgorod would be shut till morning and the tea merchant's little cart would be on the other side of the city walls, trundling towards the border with Khitari. No guard would think to question Chinua the tea merchant, about his passengers; he often gave lifts to villagers on his way back through the mountains.

Larisa, snuggled close beneath the cloak, lulled to sleep by the jolting of the cart, murmured in her sleep. But as Kiukiu huddled in the back of Chinua's cart, hood pulled down over her brow to hide her face, she felt an aching void in her heart as she imagined Gavril running from room to room, searching the empty mansion for them, interrogating the servants, the druzhina, all in vain.

Why had she been forced to choose between the two she loved most dearly in the whole world? And the words of Khulan's ballad returned to torment her, echoing through her mind as each jolt of the tea merchant's cart took them further away from Azhkendir.

Beware the jade-haired witch of the springs . . . she never gives without taking something in return. Something you value more than life itself.

"Gavril." But her heartbroken whisper was drowned by the rattle of the cart wheels over the stony tracks.

Chapter 29

"And now we come to the final matter on today's agenda," the clerk of the boyars' council announced, adjusting his spectacles, "the application by the Caradas Company to begin mining in the area currently known as the Arkhel Waste."

Several of the boyars were nodding off in the stuffy warmth of the council chamber; even Gavril felt his lids growing heavier, especially after another disturbed night with Larisa. But hearing the name "Arkhel" acted as effectively in waking them as opening the window and letting in a blast of cold evening air.

"The Caradas Company?" echoed Lord Stoyan. "Who the hell are they? Never heard the name before! And what claim do they have to the land?"

Gavril turned to Oris Avorian, his lawyer, who was sitting on his left.

"It seems," Avorian said, "that Caradas is also the name of an old, established noble family in Tourmalise. I've traced a Brigadier, Lord Denys of Caradas, who distinguished himself in the Allegondan campaign twenty years ago."

"So why would he want to come prospecting this far north? What possible connection does this Lord Caradas have with Azhkendir?"

"The Brigadier died five years ago. The claim has been filed in the name of his daughter, Lady Tanaisie."

"And what rights do these Tourmalise foreigners have to mine the Arkhels' lands?" demanded a tetchy voice from the end of the council table as Vsebor, the eldest boyar, glared at the others. "Surely they belong to Lord Gavril now."

Gavril was thinking about the letter Eugene had sent, warning him about Lilias and a certain Ranulph Arkhel, currently residing in Tourmalise, who had married into the "local gentry". He shifted uncomfortably in his seat, unwilling to mention Lilias who had been, until not so long ago, Lord Stoyan's mistress. "Is that so, Avorian?" he said, aware that all the boyars were staring at him.

"Legally speaking," said Avorian, "the Arkhel lands still belong to the Arkhel Clan. The only living claimant that I'm aware of is Stavyomir Arkhel, the Emperor's ward. And he's only two years old."

"Claimant? Doesn't Stavyomir inherit automatically?" Gavril asked, wondering if they'd come up against some complex Azhkendi law of birthright.

Avorian cleared his throat. "Stavyomir was born out of wedlock. Unless his mother can provide us with proof that she and Jaromir Arkhel were married, their son is a bastard in the eyes of the law, and has no automatic rights of inheritance."

"I see." Gavril sat back in the uncomfortable carved chair of office, wishing he had thought to bring a cushion or two. He would have asked, but suspected that such a request would be frowned on as betraying his soft Smarnan upbringing; sitting through an interminable meeting on a wooden chair would be seen as a luxury for an Azhkendi man raised to endure the hardships of the long northern winters without complaint. "And the Caradas Company? What are their plans?"

"They've been recruiting miners already," said Lord Pereneg, a boyar whose estates lay to the west of Azhgorod, on the main road to the port of Narvazh. "They set up an office as soon as the thaw began. A dour, sallow-faced fellow's running it; he's called Iarko, if I recall correctly. And he's offering good wages, from what I hear."

"Then we need to have a word with this Iarko," said Gavril. "I'll go and investigate first thing tomorrow."

The boyars shifted uneasily at this suggestion, looking from one to the other. Gavril wondered what he had said to cause such a reaction.

"Forgive me, my lord," said Avorian crisply, "but it would be more appropriate at this stage to send someone else; the sudden appearance of the High Steward himself would doubtless cause consternation. Let me—or one of my clerks—go in your stead."

"Your carriage is here, Lord Nagarian," announced Lord Stoyan's portly steward from the far end of the chamber.

"Very well." Gavril, glad of the opportunity to escape the chamber, rose and the others rose too. "I'll leave the matter with you for now, Avorian; I'll look forward to your report. Good night, gentlemen."

I'd much rather walk back; the night air would clear my head. He rubbed his dry eyes as he followed his bodyguard Semyon into the courtyard. *Why must the boyars insist on overheating the council chamber? That fug stifles any kind of fruitful discussion; half the councilors were dozing off during the last petition.*

As Gavril stepped up into the waiting carriage, he heard the cathedral clock of Saint Sergius striking eight, each sonorous note resonating dully through the chilly spring evening.

Is it so late already? I forgot to send word ahead to Kiukiu and now the dinner will probably be spoiled. He sat back against the worn leather of the carriage seat as Semyon closed the door and took his seat beside the coachman. *I doubt she'll be pleased; she's still unconfident around the mansion servants.* He couldn't help a little grin at this thought. *I shouldn't tease her; after all, I'm almost as unused to being a noble as she is. What a strange pair we must make: an impecunious portraitist and a kitchen maid, playing at being lord and lady!*

He felt the grin fade as the carriage jolted into movement, the wheels bumping over the rough cobbles, as the coachman directed the horses out onto Azhgorod's main thoroughfare.

Have I asked too much of her? She's been so distant recently. And since Larisa started teething, neither of us has had enough sleep. Then there's been all this official business to deal with: endless problems with the customs office at the new harbor in Narvazh. I haven't spent nearly as much time with them as I'd planned to. And now there's this.

He checked inside his jacket to make sure he still had the paper Avorian had slipped him earlier that day.

The druzhina aren't going to like it. Not at all. How am I going to break it to them? And how will it affect Kiukiu?

The thick cloth of his jacket gave off a faint stale whiff of tobacco smoke and barley beer. He wrinkled his nose in disgust. *Too long cooped up in that stuffy chamber with the councilors; they like their pipes and mulled beer too much. Kiukiu will complain; she'll think I've been whiling the afternoon away in the tavern.* A little sigh escaped him. It seemed an age since his carefree student days when he had gone drinking with his friends and argued passionately over politics, art, and philosophy late into the night.

The carriage juddered as it went over a pot-hole, then slowed; he heard the coachman calling to the horses as he pulled on the reins.

But what will Kiukiu make of this Tourmalise connection? Whatever happens, it's going to open up old wounds that have barely healed. It could split Azhkendir in two again. And I can't let that happen.

Gavril leaned forward to raise the blind on the window. *We must be back at the mansion.* He could just make out the tall pillars of the gateway, lit by the ocher flare of torches, as the coachman guided the horses into the courtyard. The druzhina on guard at the gate saluted as they closed the gates behind them.

"Home at last." Gavril stepped out of the carriage as Semyon went on ahead to open the door for his master. He called it "home" but he was already missing Kastel Nagarian: he had been loath to leave just as the sharp, sweet scent of spring blossoms and rushing snowmelt from the mountains transformed his winter-bound domain. But Kiukiu and Larisa were waiting for him—and wherever they were, he knew he would always feel at ease.

He hurried after Semyon, eager to see them both and apologize for his late arrival.

Perhaps Larisa's new tooth has come through at last . . .

But before he'd reached the open door, he heard voices inside.

"So she isn't with Lord Gavril?" he recognized Sosia's shrill tones.

"He's been in council with the boyars all day," Semyon was explaining.

"What's the matter?" Gavril entered the hallway to see the members of his household huddled together in animated conversation. "Sosia?"

"I'm sorry, my lord, but it's just that my niece—I mean, my lady—hasn't come back."

"You mean Kiukiu?" Gavril, not understanding, looked from one anxious face to another. "She went out?"

"With the baby."

"Did she say where she was going?"

Sosia shook her head. "The only person who saw her leave the mansion was Ryska, the new scullery maid."

"And you're sure she hasn't left a note?"

"Her gusly's gone too."

Gavril's relief at arriving home turned to dismay. "No one called at the mansion, asking for her services?" Since she had become his wife, Kiukiu had given up practicing her calling as a Spirit Singer.

"Your druzhina would never let anyone suspicious past the gates, my lord." Vasili spoke up.

"I know that, Vasili." Gavril was trying to fight the rising sense of alarm; he knew he must try to stay calm in front of his household. "Did any of the boyars' wives invite her to take tea?" Even as he asked the question, he could sense Sosia's eyes on him; no one said anything, but everyone knew that his choice of wife had not pleased the boyars who had expected him to marry one of their daughters—or a foreign princess. His mind was racing, with all kinds of horrible possibilities scuttling in. He had made plenty of enemies, both here in Azhkendir and in Smarna. "We'll go out to search for them."

"But where shall we start?" Semyon looked blankly at him. "Azhgorod's a big city—and it's dark."

"Was it market day today?"

"There's a market every day, my lord; this *is* the capital city."

Gavril looked up to see Karsibor, the elderly major-domo appointed by his father to look after the Azhgorod mansion. Sosia tutted loudly, evidently offended that Karsibor had corrected his young master in front of the servants.

"Did you see my wife leave, Karsibor?"

"I regret to say that I did not, my lord. If I had, I would certainly have counseled her not to set out alone. It's not safe for a lady to wander unchaperoned around the streets at night."

"I am fully aware of that fact." Gavril forced himself to keep his voice low; to lose his temper now would accomplish little.

"If I'm not mistaken, my lord has not yet eaten supper—" began Karsibor, undaunted.

"I'll eat later. Something cold. Don't keep the kitchen staff up waiting to serve me." If Gavril had been hungry earlier, he had lost his appetite.

"I'll organize a search party, my lord," said Semyon.

"Give me a few minutes and I'll be ready." Gavril went up the stairs to the rooms he and Kiukiu shared on the first floor to change out of his formal clothes.

The dust sheets had been stripped from their bed and folded neatly, a fire was burning in the grate, and Kiukiu's nightgown was laid out on the blue and gold embroidered coverlet. A little wooden rabbit, carved lovingly by Semyon, lay in the baby's cot; Larisa liked chewing on the pointed ears to soothe her aching gums. He picked it up, absently stroking it, as if by holding it he might sense some clue to her whereabouts.

There was no sign of a struggle. No one had broken into the mansion.

There has to be a rational explanation. Kiukiu wouldn't just run away.

As he was standing there, lost in thought, Sosia came in.

"Forgive me for prying, my lord," she said in a confidential undertone, "but you haven't had some kind of falling out with my niece, have you?"

Gavril shook his head. Though even as he did, the specter of an old argument rose to haunt him. *I said some harsh things to her after that singer Khulan came from Khitari. But she was acting so strangely . . .and she's never really spoken about the months she spent traveling with Khan Vachir's caravan.*

"It's just . . . she doesn't seem to have been herself of late. Having a baby can change a woman. It might be that she's been brooding about poor Afimia."

"Her mother?"

"You know the story, my lord." Sosia's face looked drawn with worry in the candlelight. "Her parents were torn apart and destroyed by the clan war."

"But she used her skills as a Spirit Singer to bring their souls peace. She told me so."

"Don't tell me *you* haven't thought about your own mother a few times after Larisa was born." Sosia stared accusingly at him. "Becoming a parent alters how a person looks at the world."

"I've saddled up Krasa, my lord!" Semyon called up the stairs. Gavril hastily handed Risa's carved toy rabbit to Sosia and hurried past her. *I can't stay here.* Anything was better than pacing the empty room, waiting for news.

Chapter 30

Chinua stopped at a farmhouse up in the foothills and the farmer's wife (an old acquaintance of his and a loyal customer) offered them shelter.

Kiukiu, still in a daze, fed Larisa, gratefully ate hot, spicy cabbage soup and black bread, then fell asleep, wrapped in her cloak beside the blue-and-white-tiled kitchen stove with Larisa snuggled up close to her.

Next morning, she was awakened by Larisa's energetic wriggling. For one moment she lay blinking in the dull light of early morning, wondering where they were. And then the farmer's wife came in to open the shutters and all yesterday's fears came crowding back to haunt her. But Larisa, who had woken in a good mood for once, stretched her chubby little hands out to the farmer's wife and cooed a greeting.

"And good morning to you, little one." The farmer's wife smiled broadly in return. "What bright blue eyes you have! You must be hungry; how about some porridge?"

Only then did Kiukiu realize that she had fled the mansion with very little money in her purse—but Chinua paid their hostess with a couple of tea bricks, one green, one black, each stamped with a pattern of lotus flowers and cranes "for good fortune".

As they set out, fortified by hot porridge sweetened with honey and cinnamon, the raw spring morning air sharpened Kiukiu's dulled mind. She had slept fitfully, woken twice by Larisa's demands for a feed, and troubled by ominous dreams.

"If Gavril comes after us . . ." she began as Chinua led the pony and cart out along the churned farm track toward the road that led to the pass.

"If?" Chinua echoed softly, clambering up into the driver's seat. "Do you have so little faith in your husband?"

Gavril will come after me. and then what can I say to him? "Go away?"

Kiukiu felt the color flooding into her face. She lowered her head, ashamed.

"No. I'm the one who's at fault here. I've treated him horribly, running away, not even leaving him a message." Even as she said the words, she began to realize the enormity of what she had done. "But I don't know how else to protect Larisa. And Lady Anagini is the only one I can turn to."

"You haven't told him, have you?"

"I can't." Kiukiu stared at the stained boards beneath her feet. She felt numb. "I can't even talk about it with you. If I tell anyone the bargain agreed on between us, I'll—"

"I understand," Chinua cut in. "She's bound you and you're returning to honor your part of that bond."

But I'm also bound to Gavril. We took vows to stand by each other, no matter what happened. He may never forgive me for abandoning him like this. I just don't know what else to do.

As the damp morning mists lifted, the fresh green of the foothills was slowly revealed. The piping of little mountain birds: snow finches, and buntings, echoed shrilly overhead. Catkins trembled on the birch branches and the grassy verges were starred with glossy yellow celandines. After the drabness of an Azhkendi winter and the white pallor of the snowfields, Kiukiu was dazzled by the vibrant colors of spring flowers and unfurling new leaves.

And I was so looking forward to spending our first spring with Larisa at the kastel; we were going to clear the overgrown rose garden outside the summerhouse so that she could play there safely while Gavril painted.

Larisa grabbed a handful of her hair. "Ouch! That hurts!" Larisa looked up at her as she extricated the stray lock and let out a chuckle. "You want to play? You're bored?" She lifted her onto her knees facing forward so that she could see where they were going.

"Am I doing the right thing, baby?" she said, resting her chin on the top of Larisa's head. "Your father must be beside himself with worry." Every time she thought about Gavril she felt a hollow ache in the pit of her stomach. *He may never forgive me for abandoning him like this.*

Or suppose the vision Lady Anagini showed me was false? Is she manipulating me? No, surely she wouldn't use me so cruelly. Kiukiu swiftly dismissed the thought. *She's always helped me, as has Chinua. Chinua's stood by me. He's even shown me his true soul, his wolf form.* She stole a sideways glance at the shaman who was softly humming under his breath, eyes half-closed against the sparkle of the morning sun. *If he hadn't protected me, I'd never have survived those difficult months in Khitari.*

"It might be best not to draw attention to yourself," Chinua said as they traveled on up the winding track. "Don't use your skills as a Spirit Singer for a while. Every time you play your gusly to enter the Ways Beyond, whether to lay a wandering soul to rest or pass on a message from the living to the dead, *they* will be aware of you."

"Oh no." Kiukiu realized the wisdom of his advice. "I've already drawn attention to myself." Had they been aware, the Winged Guardians, that she was listening to them?

Taliahad. The Warrior sent by Prince Galizur to track them down and destroy her daughter had such a noble, beautiful name. The glimpse she'd caught of him had revealed a youthful face, almost painfully innocent and eager to do his commander's bidding. It was hard to believe that one so pure would be sent to kill a mortal baby.

How would he set about finding them? She gazed agitatedly around the tranquil valley, sensing no unnatural presence close by. *But he'd probably disguise himself. If he walked around with his wings visible, he'd draw far too much attention to himself. And even if he could hide his wings, with hair that color, ice-blue, he'd stand out.*

"How can they call themselves our Guardians," she said, still unable to comprehend the warning that Anagini had shown her, "when they're planning to take the life of an innocent child? Auntie Sosia taught me that angels are there to watch over us, and protect us."

"What do you think your grandmother would have advised?"

Kiukiu looked away, remembering what Malusha had said to her in the Ways Beyond.

"Accept that you've borne Larisa for Lady Anagini; she's always been the snake goddess's child and you're merely acting as her nursemaid until she's old enough to go back to her mother."

This is how it has to be. Gavril must stay in Azhkendir to carry out his duties as High Steward, and I will look after Larisa and serve Anagini at the Jade Springs. And as time passes, perhaps he'll forget about us and find someone else to love.

The brilliance of the sparkling spring morning blurred as her eyes filled with tears.

Chapter 31

After several hours fruitlessly searching the ill-lit streets of Azhgorod, Gavril returned to the mansion, tired and sick at heart. He picked at the cold supper served him by Taina, the housekeeper, but he had no appetite and pushed the plate aside, the roast fowl hardly touched.

He climbed the stairs slowly, unwilling to face the empty bedchamber again, yet knowing he must try to sleep to gain the strength to start the search again in the morning.

Kiukiu must have been abducted. Kidnapped. There's no other possible explanation. Soon there'll be a ransom note.

Taina had lit the candles on the mantelpiece and turned back the sheets on the bed.

They know. They know I'm just an ordinary man again. That I'm Drakhaon in name alone. The Son of the Serpent has no fangs.

He looked up, and caught sight of his drawn face in the mirror. He stared at his candlelit reflection, seeing the desperation in his eyes, and turned away, disgusted at his helplessness.

"Where *are* you, Kiukiu?"

Only then did he notice the little lacquer tea chest that Khulan, the Praise Singer, had brought as a Naming Day gift.

Kiukiu used to come to Azhgorod with Malusha to visit the market. "Grandma loved her tea," he remembered her saying with a wistful smile, "but the special Khitari blend from Chinua's shop was always her favorite."

He lifted the box and opened it; a faint, dusty scent escaped. Had it contained more than fragrant tea? A secret message, perhaps? Gavril had never fully understood the deep friendship that linked Kiukiu and the Khitari shaman merchant; all he knew was that Chinua had protected her on her long journey to the Jade Springs. Although he had always suspected that Chinua's shop was a front for other activities; the shaman was probably acting as Khan Vachir's eyes and ears every time he crossed the border to sell his teas in Azhkendir.

Yet in spite of his tapping and prodding, no secret drawer was revealed and he put the chest down again, frustrated.

Nothing for it but to go and look for Chinua's shop.

***

With directions from Taina, Gavril and Semyon set out for Chinua's Tea Emporium. But when they eventually found the little shop, tucked away in a side street off a leafy square, it was securely shuttered up. Gavril knocked but there was no answer; the place looked deserted.

"You're too late to buy tea," an elderly woman called out as she swept her doorstep. "Chinua left last night."

Gavril hurried over to her. "Left? Where has he gone?"

"Khitari, of course." She looked at him pityingly as if he was slow in the head. "He always goes straight back when the snow melts and the high passes open up."

Semyon came over to join him. "Don't speak to my lord so rudely, Grandma," he said.

"It's all right, Sem." Gavril preferred not to be singled out for special attention. "And when will Chinua be back?"

"Oh, not for a fair few weeks. He usually opens up again around midsummer's eve."

"Midsummer," Gavril muttered, wondering how easy it would be to trace a tea merchant across the high passes into Khitari without the benefit of wings. "You didn't see a fair-haired young woman pass by here yesterday afternoon? Carrying a baby?"

The old woman shrugged. "All sorts of folk pass by and at all times," she said and carried on with her sweeping.

"Do you think my lady's gone with Chinua?" Semyon said.

Gavril hardly heard the question. *If she went with Chinua, did she go willingly? And why didn't she leave word for me? She must have known I'd worry.*

"Let's go ask the guards at the Northern Gate." Semyon, ever practical, was pointing out the way ahead. "They keep a record of who goes in and out."

Gavril nodded, following Semyon. More people were already about, laborers hurrying off to work, women dragging reluctant children to school.

The piercing spring sunlight, leaking through clouds, made his sleep-deprived eyes ache. *I need coffee to keep me awake. But the good people of Azhgorod prefer a steaming mug of hot spiced ale on a chilly morning.* He drew one hand over his face, feeling the grate of stubble against his fingertips. *At least, unshaven and still wearing yesterday's rumpled clothes, I'm unlikely to be recognized as the High Steward.*

***

"The records of yesterday's travelers passing through here? You'd need an official permit from Lord Stoyan to see those, son. Next." The guard turned from Semyon to the next man waiting in line to leave through the Northern Gate.

"Now just wait a moment!" Gavril heard Semyon's raised voice and sighed. "I'm one of the High Steward's bodyguards. I'm here on Lord Nagarian's business." *Why must he always charge in like a wild colt? Will he never learn to be more diplomatic?*

"Official permit," repeated the guard, opening the papers presented to him by the next in line.

"My lord!" Semyon's cry of frustration made everyone in the queue turn to stare at Gavril. "He won't listen to me!"

So much for my attempt to do this incognito. Affecting as nonchalant an air as he could manage, Gavril strolled across to the guard post. Ever since the Tielen invasion, Lord Stoyan had introduced much more stringent checks at all eight city gates, often resulting in long trails of frustrated travelers and farmers on either side. And as he approached, he became even more aware of the intense—and furious—stares boring into him. *I must speak with Boris Stoyan about this; we need to deploy more guards so that the queues don't build up.*

The guard checking papers glanced up, his expression at once bored and hostile.

"There's a queue," he said. "Wait in line, like the others."

Gavril thrust his right hand in front of his face, displaying the ornate enameled signet ring of office that the Emperor had bestowed upon him. The guard blinked and then got to his feet, knocking over his chair in his confusion. Other guards turned around, alerted by the disturbance.

"Forgive me, my lord. It's just that we weren't told to expect an official visit."

"So I see." If Gavril had not been so worried about Kiukiu and Larisa, he would have taken some enjoyment in the man's embarrassment. "You'll be better prepared next time, I trust."

"Please come into the guardhouse, my lord. We keep the records locked in there."

Gavril followed him into the gloomy inner room in the base of the round tower, Semyon hovering at his heels. The guard lit an oil lamp and, gesturing to Gavril to sit at the wooden table serving as a desk, unlocked a tall armoire to remove a ledger, and put it in front of Gavril. "We use a different book for each day of the week," he explained, opening it up and turning to the previous night's entries.

"Were you on duty last night?" Gavril asked, finding it hard to decipher the inky scrawl with tired eyes. "I'm trying to trace Chinua the tea merchant."

"No, my lord; we change the guard at dawn and dusk and I'm in the dawn detachment. But I know Chinua; he comes and goes every two months or so."

He pointed at an entry at the bottom of the page. "There. He left the city at sunset, just before the gate was closed for the night. That's late for him to set out, even in the spring."

"Does it mention if he had any passengers?" Gavril asked. "I'm told he often gives lifts to farmers."

"He's got his regulars," said the guard, painfully eager to please now. "But we don't usually write down who goes on whose cart. Not enough time." He indicated the queue outside the window with his thumb.

A sigh escaped Gavril's lips; in spite of his determination not to lose heart, he was beginning to fear the worst. *I've made so many enemies.*

"My lord?" Semyon could read him too easily; the time they had spent together hiding from the Commanderie in Francia had forged a strong bond of understanding between them.

Gavril closed the ledger and rose. "I'll speak to Lord Stoyan about increasing the number of guards on the gate to ease your task."

"Thank *you*, my lord." The guard bowed low as Gavril made his way back out into the street.

"So all we know is that Chinua left the city last night." Semyon said, following close on his heels.

"And Chinua's got half a day's lead on us already." Gavril set out, heading back toward the mansion. "I'm going after him. Even if Kiukiu and Larisa aren't with him, he may know something."

"Let me ride on ahead," offered Semyon. "I can ask in the villages on the road leading up to the pass. If my lady's with Chinua, someone will have seen them. There's no way to cross into Khitari without going through Fire Falcon Pass."

"Very well." Gavril could not drop all official business and disappear into Khitari without notifying Lord Stoyan. "Wait for me there, at the mountain customs house. I'll follow with Vasili."

Semyon took to his heels and was soon out of sight; Gavril followed, trying to stop his imagination from conjuring up more and more alarming images.

It's not as if I've never been apart from her before. I survived that hellhole in Arnskammar Prison. Stripped of everything, even my name, I managed to endure by thinking of her. But if she's abandoned me too . . .

Chapter 32

The track widened as it wound on up the deep-sided gorge toward Fire Falcon Pass, named after the elusive birds of prey that nested in the highest rocks above. Their pinions and beaks were tipped with scarlet and they could sometimes be spotted, circling high above the lower peaks, the rays of the setting sun turning their feathers to flaming red.

Kiukiu could see other carts ahead of them, approaching the customs house. There was a queue and as Chinua called to his ponies to stop, she realized that it would be some while before their turn came.

They had almost reached the customs officials when she heard a man's voice, breathless from riding against the wind, asking in Azhkendi, "Have you seen Chinua the tea merchant?" Against the fading light, she saw the silhouette of a horseman bending down in the saddle to interrogate the other travelers.

Have we been found already? She shrank down in the seat, wrapping her shawl about Larisa, hoping no one would point them out.

"My lady?" The man dismounted and came hurrying over the rock-strewn path toward the cart.

She recognized the agile gait and untidy sandy-red hair. "Sem?"

"What on earth are you doing all the way up here?" cried Semyon, reaching the cart and leaning on it to gaze up at her, his face twisted into an expression of incomprehension. "Lord Gavril's beside himself with worry."

Kiukiu sniffed. "So worried that he sent you in his stead."

Semyon thumped the side of the cart, making her jump. "He's following on behind. He couldn't just abandon all his official duties and disappear without a word. As you did." The fiery light of the setting sun enhanced the look of accusation burning in his eyes.

"Are you telling me off, Sem?"

She saw him swallow hard. "I know it's not my place," he said defiantly, "but you shouldn't have given us all such a scare."

But what else was I to do? I have to take Larisa to a place of safety.

"And where's Larisa?" Larisa popped her head out of Kiukiu's shawl as if playing peek-a-boo and beamed at Semyon, showing off her new tooth. "Well, thank goodness you're safe—and little Risa's safe too."

"Why?" Kiukiu said sharply, pulling the shawl over Larisa's auburn wisps of hair. "Has anyone been asking for Larisa? Anyone . . . strange?"

Semyon gazed at her quizzically in the darkening twilight. "What's up, Kiukiu?" he asked more gently, dropping all formalities. "Has someone threatened you or the baby?"

She shook her head. *If only I could tell you, Sem. I want to share this burden so badly.*

"Come back with me. Lord Gavril will pay you generously, Master Chinua, for all your trouble."

"No!" Kiukiu said quickly before Chinua could reply. "I can't go back. I have to take Larisa to see someone in Khitari." She floundered, wondering what excuse would convince Semyon, let alone Gavril.

"Who?" Semyon looked blank.

"Someone with . . . special skills."

"A healer? Is Risa sick?" Semyon said anxiously, one hand hovering to stroke Larisa's head. Larisa cooed cheerily back at him. "She looks as lively as ever to me." And then he reached out and took Kiukiu's hand instead, pressing it between his horseman's calloused fingers. "Please come home," he said. "I've never seen Lord Gavril look so worried before. He was searching the city into the small hours. I don't know if you've had a falling-out and I know it's not my place to interfere, but I can't bear to see him so unhappy."

Gavril unhappy. Every word Semyon said made Kiukiu feel more torn until she tugged her hand free. "Stop it, Sem!" she said, her voice hoarse with the effort to hold back tears. "I can't go back yet. Tell Gavril that I'm really sorry—but I have to go alone."

"At least tell him so yourself." Semyon's steadfast gaze made her glance away. "Tell him to his face, so he isn't left without a proper farewell."

"Since when did you learn to speak such good sense, Sem?" she said, her words freighted with regret. "But I can't wait for him, can I, Chinua?"

Chinua gave a little shrug. "There's an inn up ahead on the Khitari side of the customs house. I was planning on us staying there overnight."

"You'd better stay too, Semyon," said Kiukiu, realizing that she could hardly make out his features any longer. "It's almost dark." The air was bitingly chill now that the sun had disappeared.

"I'll give Varnava a rest and grab a bite of supper at the inn," said Semyon. He glanced up at the clear sky overhead in which the first stars were beginning to glitter. "But the moon's almost full. I'll have moonlight in plenty to see me safely down through the pass. Just wait here a little longer for me to bring him to you." He stroked Larisa's cheek and turned back toward his horse which was contentedly grazing the sparse grass beside the track.

Kiukiu rested her chin on top of Larisa's head as she watched Semyon climb up into the saddle and ride away into the night. Her heart felt even heavier than before.

"Lord Gavril is not the kind of man to let his wife and child leave him without putting up a fight." Chinua shook the reins and the sturdy mountain horse obediently started off along the track. "What are you going to say to him? He may take Larisa away from you if you refuse to go back with him."

"Is there any kind of glamour you can cast to cover our tracks?" Kiukiu asked. "Some kind of barrier? Or disguise?"

"You mean the kind where the people we pass think they've seen two old farmers and their dog?" Chinua chuckled; he seemed amused at the prospect. "I might be able to conjure something of the sort."

Chapter 33

"And so I must leave the governance of Azhkendir in your capable hands for a few days until I return."

Gavril was just signing and sealing the letter to Lord Stoyan when he heard a clatter of hooves in the courtyard.

Is Semyon back? Has he found Kiukiu? He jumped up from his desk, abandoning the letter, and ran eagerly toward the hall.

"Where's Lord Gavril? I must see him!" Gavril recognized the deep rasp of the horseman's voice as that of Gorian One-Eye, Askold's senior lieutenant.

"Gorian?" he called, hurrying out onto the steps. "Is all well at the kastel?"

Gorian dismounted and handed the reins of his horse to Ivar. His face was glowing from the fresh bite of the wind.

"No; all's far from well." He was breathing hard and gripped the stone balustrade to keep himself upright. Gavril resisted the urge to offer a steadying hand, knowing that it would be proudly shrugged off.

"Come inside and have something to drink," he said, leading the way inside, wondering what new problems had arisen in his absence. "Taina, bring beer for Lieutenant Gorian."

Gorian sat down at the kitchen table and drained the mug in one long draught as, one by one, the other members of the household filed in.

"There are men on the Waste," Gorian said, wiping the froth from his lips with the back of his hand. "Several cartloads of them. They've set up camp and they've started to dig."

"Exactly how many cartloads?" cried Vasili. "And what d'you mean, 'dig'?"

"The Bogatyr said you should be informed straight away," Gorian said to Gavril, ignoring Vasili. "It looks to us as if they're mining."

"The Caradas Company." Gavril had been so worried about Kiukiu and Larisa that he had forgotten about the matter raised at the boyars' council the day before.

"You know about this, my lord?" Gorian said accusingly.

"Oris Avorian promised me he would look into it." *Just as I feared; matters have already overtaken us.* "I had no idea that work had started already. There is— as I'm sure you all understand—some legal dispute as to who owns the land."

"Well, this crew obviously don't care a fig for the law or lawyers."

"Caradas?" said Sosia."That's not an Azhkendi name. What are foreigners doing digging up your lands?"

"They're not strictly *my* lands—" began Gavril.

"You're Lord Volkh's son," said Gorian, thumping the table with his fist, making the crockery rattle.

"And Lord Volkh won those lands in battle for the clan when he defeated Stavyor Arkhel—"

The distant jangle of the doorbell echoed from the hallway and a few moments later Karsibor appeared to announce, "Maistre Avorian has arrived."

"Show him down here," Gavril said. "The druzhina need to hear what he has to say."

Karsibor's eyebrows rose in an expression of shocked disapproval.

"In the *kitchen*, my lord?"

"Very well." Gavril rose, suppressing a sigh of irritation. *Why now? I need to be looking for Kiukiu, not arguing about mining rights.* "I'll receive him in the morning room. But I want everyone there; this matter concerns us all."

***

"So, Maistre Avorian," said Gavril when all the members of his household had crowded into the morning room, "what have you discovered about the Caradas Company?"

Oris Avorian glanced around at the glowering faces and Gavril sensed considerable reluctance on his lawyer's part to share the news he had brought.

"I told you, my lord, that the claim was filed under the name of a certain Brigadier Denys, Baronet Caradas, of Tourmalise." He paused, drawing in a deep breath before continuing. "Lord Denys is dead, but his daughter, Lady Tanaisie is very much alive, as is her husband, Ranulph."

"Ranulph," Gavril echoed beneath his breath, remembering the Emperor's warning.

"Get to the point, man!" growled Gorian. "Why are these foreigners digging up our land?"

Avorian glared at him over his spectacles. "Lord Ranulph is no foreigner. He has a valid claim to dig in the Waste. In fact, he is the legal heir to the Waste and the Arkhel lands."

"Heir?" repeated Sosia, clutching at Gorian's arm. "How can he be? All the Arkhels are dead!"

"Lord Ranulph is Ranozhir Arkhel, Lord Stavyor's youngest brother who was far away in Tourmalise when Lord Volkh attacked and destroyed the Arkhel clan."

Avorian's last words were drowned as Gavril's servants and bodyguards began to protest until a sudden sonorous metallic clang rose above the angry voices. Karsibor was banging the dinner gong to quieten them down.

Such a predictable response. Gavril sighed, pressing one hand to his forehead, feeling the first warning throb of an imminent headache.

The major-domo glared coldly at the assembled staff and said, "Have you forgotten your duty to Lord Gavril and our visitor? Have the good manners to listen to what Maistre Avorian has come here to tell us."

"Gorian has just ridden over from the kastel," Gavril said. "He's brought a message from Askold, informing me that mining has already begun in the Waste. But now that we know this name 'Caradas Company' is merely a front for the Arkhel clan, this places us in a very difficult situation."

"Drive them out!" said Gorian, thumping the table with his fist again. "What right does Ranozhir Arkhel have to come back to stir up trouble?"

"Every right," said Avorian dryly. "Let me remind you that he is Lord Stavyor's youngest brother."

"Then we'll have to persuade him and his men to leave," muttered Gorian. "Drive 'em back to Tourmalise."

Gavril glanced at Gorian and saw from his ferocious expression that he had meant every word. *This revelation couldn't have come at a worse moment. The last thing I need now is the old hatreds between our clans stirred up once more, spreading like a contagion through Azhkendir.*

"How many have signed on to work for Lord Ranozhir?" he asked.

"Askold and I counted at least a hundred men, if you include the guards posted around the site. Armed guards," added Gorian, crossing his arms across his broad chest.

"A hundred?" This was considerably more than Gavril had anticipated; he found himself wondering how many of his own druzhina would be ready to fight if hostilities arose. "Lord Ranozhir must be investing a lot of his own funds in this venture to employ so many workers."

"Not to mention the office and warehouse he's opened at Narvazh to handle the export side of his business," said Avorian. "I hear his steward, Iarko, has already made an arrangement with a Tielen merchant captain."

"A business venture on this scale can't have been set up in just a few days!" Gavril was beginning to wonder if he shouldn't have investigated matters in the autumn when he received the warning letter from Eugene. "How long has Lord Ranozhir been in Azhkendir? And why didn't we know he was here?"

"It seems he set up the mining venture using his wife's name in late autumn. But no one in Azhgorod paid any particular attention to Ranulph Caradas, Baronet of Serrigonde. Why would they?"

"Do we know what he's mining?" Gavril asked Avorian.

"My clerk overheard Iarko warning the carters to move the casks with extreme care. He heard the words 'volatile' and 'explosive' used."

"That sounds like firedust." Gorian scowled as he pronounced the word; the druzhina had never forgotten being forced to mine for firedust when Tielen soldiers invaded Azhkendir.

"But how could the Arkhels know about firedust?" Sosia turned to Gavril. "The Tielens kept it secret. Who could have told them?"

Gavril was remembering the Emperor's last letter. "Lilias Arbelian," he said. *Why does this have to happen now—just when I'm so worried about Kiukiu and Risa? Is Lilias out to stir up the old hatreds between the clans?*

"*That* woman?" Sosia clicked her tongue in disapproval. "Don't tell me she's mixed up in this, Maistre Avorian?"

Avorian shook his head. "There's been no mention of Mistress Arbelian—thus far. Although she filed a claim last year in the name of her son, Stavyomir, to be officially recognized as the sole heir to the Arkhel estates—which makes her a rival claimant. But as she has no legal proof that she was ever married to Jaromir Arkhel . . ."

"First Kiukiu and the babe disappear and now that shameless hussy dares to meddle in our affairs again," Sosia muttered to Taina.

Gavril swung round to face Sosia. "You think there's a connection?" Why must she put the worst of his fears into words? "Yet there's still been no demand for ransom. I should have gone with Semyon."

"What's this about my lady?" Gorian asked.

"She went out yesterday afternoon with Larisa and no one's seen them since then," said Sosia. "We fear she may have been taken against her will."

"I've sent Semyon up to Fire Falcon Pass to look for her," Gavril said, slumping back down in his chair. The lack of sleep was beginning to tell on him. "I was about to set out join him when Gorian arrived." He rubbed his sore eyes. "Is there any more coffee, Taina?"

"I'll make a fresh pot right away." Taina bustled out.

"I can organize the search for Lady Kiukiu, my lord," said Avorian. "I have ears and eyes all over Azhgorod. In fact, I wish you'd contacted me sooner. Although," He bent down and murmured in Gavril's ear, "could we speak in private for a minute?"

Gavril rose. "Please tell Taina we'll take coffee in my study, Karsibor."

"You must forgive me for asking," said Avorian as soon as Gavril had closed the study door behind them, "but do you suspect there might be a third party involved?"

Gavril heard the insinuation in the lawyer's careful choice of words. "You think Kiukiu has a secret lover?" He heard himself begin to laugh incredulously at the suggestion and then stopped, wondering if it might be true. "It's true that we were apart a long time when she was in Khitari. She's never really wanted to talk about what happened to her there. And she began to act strangely after a singer from Khitari attended Larisa's Naming Day celebrations."

"In my work, my lord, I'm afraid I see this situation all too often."

"But Kiukiu's not like that—" Gavril broke off, shaking his head in vehement denial.

There was a tap at the door and Taina came in with a pot of coffee and cups on a tray.

"I've made it strong, my lord, Smarnan style," she said, serving Avorian and then Gavril.

Avorian stirred sugar into the little cup. "I'll send a messenger to you the instant I hear any news."

"Thank you." Gavril drank his coffee, relishing the smoky-sweet bitterness of the roasted beans, hoping it would revive his sluggish brain. "But I hope to have found her before then."

"You don't suppose that the Arkhels have secretly made contact with your wife?"

"Because she's the last surviving Arkhel Praise Singer? You think Lord Ranozhir might have set up a meeting . . . or even had her spirited away?" Gavril's troubled imagination had begun to conjure up yet more dire possibilities. "Her presence would confirm his status as rightful lord of the Waste—"

"My lord!" Karsibor called from the hallway. "Semyon's back!"

Gavril leapt up and flung open the study door. He spotted his young lieutenant in the hall, brushing the dust of travel from his clothes as Karsibor looked on disapprovingly.

"Sem!" Gavril hurried toward him. "Did you—?" And then he checked himself as he saw Semyon's expression, grabbing him by the arm and steering him into the study.

Semyon glanced uncertainly at Avorian who was calmly helping himself to a second cup of coffee.

"You can speak freely in front of Maistre Avorian," Gavril said. He was already dreading what Semyon was about to tell him, but any news was better than no news at all.

"I caught up with my lady at Fire Falcon Pass," Semyon said, his voice hoarse from travel. Gavril poured him coffee and handed it to him. Semyon drank it in one mouthful, grimacing at the taste, and continued, "She's in good health. So is your daughter. As you guessed, she's with Chinua, the tea merchant."

"So why is she going to Khitari?" Gavril didn't know whether he was relieved to hear that they were unharmed or furious that she had gone off with Chinua without a word. Chinua had adopted the role of tea merchant as a cover for his work as agent for Khan Vachir as it enabled him to come and go freely without anyone asking awkward questions. So was this some scheme of Vachir's after all?

"She said to tell you she's really sorry. But she has to take your daughter to someone in Khitari. And she said she has to go alone. I don't really understand why."

Gavril thumped his clenched fist against the desktop. His dominant feeling was one of hurt that Kiukiu had a secret that she had kept from him. But beneath the hurt and incomprehension, something else nagged at his mind, insinuating that maybe she was trying to shield him from some far greater injury.

"And there was something else," Semyon added. "She said, 'Has anyone been asking for Larisa? Anyone strange?'"

"Strange?" Gavril turned on him. "What did she mean by strange?"

Semyon shook his head. "I wish I knew. She wouldn't be drawn any further. And you know my lady, she can be quite stubborn when she chooses to."

That decided it. "I'm going after them," Gavril said. "I can be stubborn too." But there was one other matter that had to be resolved before he left. "Send Gorian to me, Sem."

***

Gavril was packing his saddle bag for the journey to Khitari when Gorian appeared. He handed over the sealed letter he had written to the Bogatyr, saying, "Take this to Askold. Make sure he understands my wishes. No one—no matter how bitter a grudge they bear against the Arkhels—is to act until I return. Keep up the patrols, as usual."

"Suppose they make the first move?" Gorian stuffed the letter deep inside his jacket. "Suppose they attack us?"

"Then do all that has to be done to defend the kastel until I return." Gavril heard himself give the order, yet the last thing he wanted was for the druzhina and the Arkhels to come to blows. "One more thing, Gorian. How are your sons? Are they still keeping watch over Morozhka's Round?"

Gorian heaved a sigh. "I'm worried about my lads. They're not themselves—not since they started this patrol."

"In what way?"

"They used to be laughing, joking all the time, chasing after the girls."

"And now?"

"They've got this distant look in their eyes. They don't hear what you say to them."

Gavril remembered only too well that distant look Gorian was describing. He wanted to find a way to break Lady Morozhka's hold over the twins—but that would have to wait until he had brought Kiukiu and Larisa back. "Have they reported any unusual activity up at Morozhka's Round?"

Gorian scowled at the mention of the name. "These Caradas workers or whatever they call themselves have been constructing some infernal contraption at the old copper mines near the Round. Pumping out water, making a mess, curse them."

So the Arkhels had begun to mine for copper close to Lady Morozhka's sanctuary. And the ownership of that land had been disputed territory for years beyond living memory. By rights any minerals mined there belonged to the Nagarians. This time it was Gavril who sighed, foreseeing lengthy legal proceedings while trying to prevent tempers from flaring and matters getting out of hand.

Semyon came in from the courtyard. "Krasa's all saddled up and ready to go, my lord."

"Then we'd better be on our way." Gavril picked up his bag and slung it over his shoulder. "Take care, Gorian—and keep an eye on your sons for me."

"Come back to us soon, my lord," Gorian said as Karsibor summoned the household to line up on the mansion steps to formally bid their lord and master farewell.

As Gavril turned Krasa's head toward the Khitari Gate under a threateningly cloudy sky, he wondered if he was betraying the trust that Eugene had placed in him by going in pursuit of Kiukiu just at the time when trouble was brewing in Azhkendir once more.

Chapter 34

". . . and to my charming companion Madame Lilias Arbelian, I leave a pension of five hundred gold coins a year until her death. If she chooses, she may continue to live in the West Wing—or if she prefers, she may ask my son Gavril to establish her in my mansion in the city of Azhgorod."

"Frankly, Mistress Arbelian, I'm surprised," and Maistre Avorian stared at Lilias through his pince-nez in a most unfriendly manner, "that you have the nerve to return to Azhgorod."

"What kind of a welcome is that for one of your clients, Maistre Avorian?" Lilias stared boldly back, determined not to be outfaced by the Nagarians' lawyer. "I've merely come to ensure that my legacy, the five hundred gold crowns a year, left me by Lord Volkh, is still at my disposal. The terms of his will stated that it is to be paid on the first day of the spring equinox. So here I am!"

Oris Avorian pressed his fingertips together, as though collecting his thoughts before speaking. "It is true that the late Lord Volkh left you a most generous settlement. But only because you led him to believe that you were carrying his child. And since the birth of that child, you have allied yourself with the Nagarians' rival clan and claimed that little Stavyomir is in fact the son of the late Jaromir Arkhel. My dear lady, you can't have it both ways."

"Are you—a reputable lawyer—saying that you're going to refuse me my rightful legacy because my child is not a Nagarian?" Lilias felt a sudden twinge of anxiety at the possibility that Gavril Nagarian might have instructed Avorian to stop her allowance. "There were no conditions attached!"

Avorian sighed. "That is indeed true. Yet the Nagarian estates have fallen on hard times. There is very little revenue coming in."

"Is that so?" Lilias did not know whether she was glad to hear that Gavril was in financial difficulties or alarmed that her only regular source of income might be about to dry up. "And where, precisely, does that leave me? I distinctly recall there was a codicil that allowed me to remain in the West Wing of the kastel—*if I chose to do so*," she added, staring directly at the lawyer, wondering what his reaction would be. "Or the Nagarian town house."

Avorian took off his pince-nez and ran one hand over his eyes. He looked weary. "Only if Lord Gavril gave his consent."

"And where is Lord Gavril?" Lilias asked, without even hesitating. To show any sign of hesitation at this stage of the negotiations would be fatal to her plan— even if the prospect of meeting him face-to-face was the last thing she wished to do.

"I suppose I could ask Lord Gavril to allocate you some land, a cottage maybe, in lieu of the five hundred . . ."

"Me? Live in some peasant hovel and grow cabbages?" Lilias was horrified at the prospect. *The Nagarians all loathe me. I wouldn't put it past one of them to arrange for me to suffer a tragic accident.* "But the will specifically states five hundred coins. There's no mention of land."

Avorian sighed again. "I may be able to find a way of arranging for you to receive a monthly stipend. But I can only advance you fifty crowns today."

***

Dysis was sitting patiently waiting for Lilias outside Avorian's office, her features concealed, as usual, by a black lace veil. "Well?"

"Let's talk outside," said Lilias, steering her maid toward the door.

"No funds?" Dysis said as they stepped out into the street. "How are we going to pay the innkeeper? He'll throw us out if the bill isn't covered by the end of the week."

Lilias was concentrating on trying to avoid the muddy pot-holes, lifting her skirts as daintily as she could without revealing too much petticoat or ankle. "Ugh. I detest Azhgorod in spring. It's filthy underfoot. We should have gone to Tielborg instead. At least they have pavements there."

"But we didn't have enough to afford rooms in Tielborg." Dysis stopped and turned to face her mistress. "Why is there no money?"

"'The Nagarians have fallen on hard times,'" said Lilias, mimicking Avorian's severe tones. "He's going to try to arrange a 'monthly stipend.'"

"That's better than nothing, I suppose."

"I think it might be time to pay Jaromir's uncle a friendly visit. We are family, after all. I understand that conditions are rather primitive out at the camp he's set up on the moors but—" Lilias realized that she was talking to herself. "Keep up, Dysis!" she began tartly but then, looking around, she saw that Dysis was standing in the middle of the street, trembling from head to foot.

"For heaven's sake, pull yourself together!" She marched back to her maid and caught hold of her by the wrist, shaking her. "Whatever's the matter?"

"The D-Drakhaon," Dysis managed to say between chattering teeth.

"Lord Gavril?" Lilias had been dreading this moment—but as she scanned the busy thoroughfare, she could see no sign of the young ruler or his tattooed druzhina. "Are you certain?"

Dysis nodded, pointing with a trembling finger to three horsemen who had just ridden past them at a brisk pace in the direction of the Khitari Gate.

"Then let's be on our way." Lilias pulled Dysis firmly along behind her, determined above all, that they should not run into Gavril Nagarian. Though it seemed unlikely that he should be riding through the streets of his capital city without any fuss or fanfare. But then, one could hardly call him a conventional kind of a ruler; given his liberal upbringing in Smarna, it would be just like him to go about incognito. She reached a coaching inn and dragged Dysis inside, forcing her to sit down. Dysis placed both hands over her veiled face.

Sarah Ash

"Francian brandy," Lilias called to the innkeeper, not caring about the disapproving stares of the red-nosed old men drinking their eau-de-vie near the tiled stove. "And be quick! My companion has had a terrible shock."

A serving girl brought over two glasses and poured a measure of the strong, golden-brown spirit into each one. "Will she be all right?" she asked, peering at Dysis.

"She'll be fine in a few minutes," said Lilias firmly. When the girl had gone, she raised Dysis's veil and lifted one of the glasses to her lips. "Drink," she ordered. Dysis obeyed, coughing as she swallowed.

"I'm sorry, my lady," she said in a hoarse voice. "Just seeing him—unexpectedly—brought back so many memories."

Lilias drank her brandy in one gulp, nodding. It was unlike Dysis to react with such emotion; her maid had kept calm when they had escaped from debtors and irate landlords, even when they had endured terrifying storms at sea. "Of course," she said, "neither of us has seen him since that terrible night when he broke into the kastel. And you were so brave, protecting my little Stavy."

Dysis reached out for the brandy glass and swallowed the rest of its contents at one go. "I can never forgive him," she said softly, "for what he did to me. Because of him, men look at me and shudder in revulsion. Women whisper words of pity. Children point at me and stare. My face is ruined."

"He's lost his daemonic powers, everyone says so." Lilias patted Dysis's hand awkwardly; comforting others did not come easily to her. "He will never hurt anyone again as he hurt you."

"But he can't restore my looks. He can't make up for the pain he caused me. Or know how difficult it is each day to go out among other people, looking the way I do."

Lilias was surprised to hear Dysis revealing her innermost thoughts. *She must have been bottling all this up since it happened; and now the brandy has brought out the bitterness she's been hiding.*

"I hate him," Dysis said with quiet vehemence. "Why should I suffer like this while he lords it over us all, basking in the Emperor's favor?"

"We'd better be on our way." The brandy had loosened Dysis's tongue a little too much; Lilias placed the coins to pay for the spirits on the table and helped Dysis to her feet. It wouldn't do to draw too much attention to themselves while Gavril was still in the city but she realized that the visit to Avorian had clarified matters. This poison eating away at Dysis's soul could be used to both their advantages—and Lord Ranulph's too.

"Listen to me, dear Dysis," she said in her ear as she guided her toward the door, "what I have set in motion will bring you all the satisfaction you could possibly desire and much more, besides." Even as she spoke the words, she felt a delicious frisson of anticipation. "Did you not see which gate he and his bodyguard were heading for? He's heading out— to Khitari. Which means the town house is almost certainly empty."

Dysis turned around. "You mean—?"

"The terms of Volkh's will were quite clear: I am owed four hundred and fifty crowns. *"Or . . . she may ask my son Gavril to establish her in my mansion in the city of Azhgorod."* As there is clearly no money in the Nagarian coffers, Oris Avorian will be obliged to honor the terms of the will. We will take up residence in the town house without further delay!"

Chapter 35

A gust of wind shivered through Fire Falcon Pass, setting the new green leaves on the overhanging trees and bushes trembling. The shadow of a bird of prey, high above the jagged rocks, skimmed across the sky. Kiukiu glanced up—but too late to catch more than a glimpse before it dipped suddenly out of sight.

Chinua was busy lighting a cooking fire at a little distance from the cart; Kiukiu and Risa sat on a brightly colored rug close by, Risa chewing furiously on a rusk of hard-baked bread.

"I've had this feeling all day." Kiukiu struggled to put her needling unease into words. "As if someone's watching us. Have you felt it too?"

Chinua nodded as the kindling caught alight. "Yet it's not the Winged Warrior that attacked the Magus. That one, Ardarel, had a fierce, fiery aura. This is more . . . elusive."

"Taliahad," Kiukiu said in a whisper, not daring to pronounce his name more clearly, in case *he* heard and took it as a summons. "He's a Guardian of Water, not Fire."

"Then we must be wary around any sources of water: ponds, streams, waterfalls. He might be able to use them to manifest an earthly form."

Risa chose that moment to let out a furious yell. Removing the rusk, she thrust it, dripping in drool, at Kiukiu.

"I don't want it! Let's give it to the birds." Kiukiu reluctantly took the slimy rusk between finger and thumb and threw it into the bushes. "Look at your poor red cheek. I hope this new tooth comes through soon."

Risa began to grizzle; Kiukiu gave her a hug, wincing as the baby bumped her sore gums hard against her shoulder. "So I've made up my mind. We can't wait any longer for Gavril. We have to go on."

"Even though you know that he and his men would lay down their lives to protect you if the Heavenly Guardians attack?"

"I don't want them to throw their lives away in a fight against impossible odds. I couldn't bear it if Gavril died trying to defend us." Even as the words left her mouth she felt guilty; it was as if she was making up excuses to justify her actions. "It's the only way to protect Risa." She had stayed awake worrying away most of the night and she could see no other solution.

"Ma. Ma!" Risa said, hearing her name. "*Ma!*"

"Yes, Risa, I know your gums are sore. Let me put some more of that salve on them."

But Risa pressed her lips tight shut, vehemently shaking her head. Kiukiu sighed. Risa was too clever for her own good. "I know it tastes bitter but it'll stop the ache until your new tooth comes through."

More head shaking. Kiukiu sighed; she would have to think up a new ruse to distract her red-cheeked daughter, just to earn enough time to pop her salve-smeared finger inside her mouth and apply the remedy.

"We need an escape plan, Chinua. Gavril can be very difficult to dissuade once he decides to do something. I wouldn't put it past him to bring the druzhina to capture us and drag us back to Azhkendir. Can you use your skills to spirit us away, somehow if things get difficult?"

Chinua stroked his chin slowly, pondering her suggestion. "I should have asked the Magus for a handful or two of his mirror-dust," he said. "That might have given us a few minutes to escape—but even then, on this winding track, we wouldn't get far. I fear I may have to resort to something more underhand."

"Underhand?"

"Tea."

"Tea?" Was Chinua making a joke? Kiukiu wrinkled her nose at him in disapproval; this wasn't a humorous matter.

"I have many different blends in my collection, some to stimulate and refresh the mind, a few to calm and relax. The soporific effects last for several hours. Long enough for us to reach the end of the pass where the road divides."

"Drug Gavril and his bodyguards? Won't they suspect?"

"We'll have to pretend to drink it too." Chinua said. "If I attempt anything more drastic and use my powers, it could cause a disturbance in the aethyr and draw unwelcome attention to ourselves." He gestured to the sky.

Kiukiu understood too well who he was referring to but did not name. "Very well." She could see no other alternative. "But they won't suffer any long-lasting effects, will they?"

Chinua gave a little shrug. "Nothing worse than a mild hangover. Trust me."

She had no choice but to trust him. She nodded, biting her underlip.

***

"I can see smoke further down the pass!" Vasili, excited, rose up in the saddle, pointing.

Gavril looked. A thin twist of blue woodsmoke was rising into the clear air above the tumbled rocks below. But he refused to allow himself to hope that they had caught up with the tea merchant yet.

"That could be anyone's cooking fire." Semyon sounded unimpressed.

"It means people to ask. We haven't met anyone since those fur trappers back at the waterfall."

The narrow track through the gorge, just wide enough to allow one cart to travel along it, was beginning to widen out. They must be coming to the end of the pass, Gavril realized. Some way beyond lay the wide grasslands of Khitari. He had flown over the green steppes when he and Khezef were one, the Drakhaoul's dragon form and powerful wings effortlessly taking them fast and far—

"I can see a cart down there, my lord!" Vasili's shout jolted Gavril out of his reverie. "Is that the tea merchant?"

Gavril looked further down the snaking track and saw a cart in a little dell far beneath them, a couple of stocky ponies cropping the grass alongside. The smoke that Vasili's keen eyes had spotted was rising from a cooking fire.

"Why have they stopped?" Semyon wondered. "It's not dusk for an hour or two."

"It's a good place to make camp for the night—and a good vantage point." Vasili might be something of a loudmouth but he had inherited his father Askold's practical nature. "It's off the track but you can see who's coming in either direction."

Including us. Gavril was already urging Krasa onward down the track, ahead of the two druzhina. He found it hard to accept that Kiukiu and Larisa were camping out under the stars rather than staying with him in the warmth of the Azhgorod mansion. *What's driven her to take to the road?* Suppose Chinua had inveigled them out of the city on some pretext, acting on the orders of his master, Khan Vachir? *I never really had the chance to get to know Vachir. And he—in Drakhaoul form—was the one who killed my mother.*

As Krasa reached the dell, Gavril saw a fair-haired young woman gently placing a sleeping baby in a little tea chest on the cart; an improvised crib, padded out with brightly woven fabrics in scarlet, saffron and grass green.

They're safe. He felt his knees go weak as relief overwhelmed him. As he dismounted and went running toward them, it was all he could do to keep from stumbling.

"Kiukiu!" His only thought had been to hug her, to hold her close but the forbidding expression on her face made him stop short. "What's wrong?"

"Didn't Semyon give you my message?" Kiukiu stared accusingly at him. "This is something I have to do. Alone. You can't help me, Gavril."

I can't help her? He couldn't believe it was Kiukiu who was speaking so coldly to him. "I was so worried." The words burst from Gavril in a torrent. "Have you any idea how I felt, finding you both gone? I thought you'd been kidnapped!"

"There wasn't time to explain," she said tonelessly.

"Why didn't you find a way to tell me? We vowed to share everything. *Everything.*" Gavril heard the harshness in his own voice and saw a sudden flash of fear in her eyes. *Am I sounding like my father?* The strength of his anger alarmed him.

"And please keep your voice down; Risa's teething and I've only just got her to sleep."

The tea merchant appeared from behind his cart and bowed low to Gavril. "Is all well, Kiukirilya?" he asked pointedly.

"It's all right, Chinua," Kiukiu said without shifting her gaze from Gavril's face.

"I'll show your men where to water the horses," Chinua said, retreating.

Gavril drew in a slow breath, willing himself to calm down, and asked more gently, "Why? Why did you run away?"

"Because I had a warning." She was on the defensive; her stance, feet apart, as though braced to counteract a blow, body tensed, expression defiant. "A warning that Larisa was in danger."

He was bewildered. "Who warned you? And what danger?"

"What was it that you said about the vows we took together?" Tears glittered in her eyes but she did not break down and cry. Seeing her so furious with him only bewildered him more. Wasn't he the injured party, the one deserted without a word?

"This is all to do with Khulan. Isn't it?" Kiukiu still not had answered his question and he needed an honest answer if he was to believe that she had not betrayed him. "Everything was fine until Khulan came to Kastel Nagarian. Was she sent to bring you back to Khitari? Were you forced into making a contract with Khan Vachir?"

So much must have happened to her in Khitari that she's never revealed . . . and the Khitari shamans are said to practice obscure and forbidden rituals. Did she make a secret pact with one of them, binding her to return?

"It's nothing to do with the khan or his family! Where did you get that idea from? Who planted that seed in your mind? I had a really horrible time when I was traveling with them." A single sob escaped, on an intake of breath. "Even after I healed the little prince, Grandma and I were still treated like dirt."

Had he forced her to confront painful memories she had tried to forget? All he wanted was to understand why she had fled.

"Kiukiu—" He took a step toward her, only to see her shrink away. Her reaction infuriated and alarmed him. He tried again. "Don't you trust me anymore?

Because all I want is for us to be together again: you, me and Larisa."

"It's not a matter of trust." She was twisting a fold of her skirt between her fingers, her face averted. "Look, Gavril, I'm sorry. I'm really sorry that I didn't tell you. But I knew that you would have done everything you could to stop me." She raised her face to his. "I need you to trust me," she said, her voice low, trembling but not breaking. "This is something only I can do. You have to let me go. That's just how it is."

"Let you go?" Gavril repeated. Was she telling him their marriage was over? Anger boiled up inside him, raw and uncomprehending. Why was she rejecting him? Again he forced himself to ignore the painful feelings she had stirred up inside him. *There has to be a reason.* "Are you leaving me?" But his voice broke as he asked the question he didn't want to hear the answer to.

"If that's how it looks to you . . ."

"How else could it look?" He could no longer hide his hurt. Every instinct was crying out within him to take her in his arms and hold her close, breathing in the scent of her skin, her hair—but the tension in her stiff, awkward stance, her averted eyes, all radiated such a strong message of rejection that he hesitated. He clenched his fists at his sides, forcing himself to pay attention to what she was saying, even though he didn't understand it. "Is it Lord Arkhel? Has he contacted you? Is he the one—"

"Lord Arkhel?" She was staring at him and he realized from her stricken expression that she did not know. "But he's dead."

"Lord Ranulph Arkhel. Stavyor's younger brother, Ranozhir. He's been abroad for many years. But now he's back and his men are mining for firedust in the Waste."

"Lord Ranulph?" she repeated, saying the name as if it were unfamiliar to her. "I thought they all died. Except Jaromir. I had no idea." Her response was so spontaneous that he had to assume she was telling the truth. So there had to be another reason.

"You've ridden a long way, Lord Gavril." Chinua reappeared, flanked by Semyon and Vasili. "You must be tired and thirsty. Why don't we all sit round the fire and have some tea?"

Kiukiu looked as if she was about to protest—but then she turned away. "I'll bring the bowls," she said over her shoulder.

"Can I see Risa?" Without waiting for her permission, Gavril went straight toward the tea chest crib.

"Don't wake her!" hissed Kiukiu, pursuing him. "I told you; she's teething again and she's been grizzling all day." Kiukiu hovered as he gazed down at Larisa who lay asleep tucked up in the bright woven blanket, one auburn wisp of hair twisted between finger and thumb. One cheek was bright red and shiny and she let out a halting little sigh that made him long to pick her up and cuddle her close.

"Are you sure it's just teething?" He looked at Kiukiu across their sleeping daughter. "Perhaps she's missing her daddy."

A strangely defensive look passed across Kiukiu's face.

I can't believe things between us have deteriorated so swiftly.

But before he could insist on his rights as a father, Chinua came past, carrying a black lacquered tray laden with tea pots and jars.

"Please invite your men to join us, Lord Gavril," he said, smiling. "I can offer you powdered green tea from the isles of Cipangu; bitter but delicious when consumed with these sweet bean cakes. Or there's a more robust black brew you might like to try from the northern hills of Serindher."

"Did you say cakes, Master Chinua?" Semyon called, rubbing his hands together. "I'm famished."

"You've got hollow legs, Sem." Kiukiu brought over tea bowls: glazed earthenware, plain and practical, which she set down on a brightly woven rug Chinua unrolled on the uneven ground.

Vasili, usually so loud and self-confident around his fellow druzhina, had suddenly become tongue-tied in the presence of Chinua. He sat down beside Semyon and drank his tea without a word. Gavril sniffed the bitter steam rising from his bowl; green tea was something of an acquired taste but one he had learned to appreciate from Kiukiu. He took a sip, aware that she was staring at him and wondered what on earth he could say that might make her change her mind . . .

***

"Ugh . . ." Gavril half opened his eyes. The daylight was piercingly, painfully bright and he closed his eyes again, feeling the sun's warmth on his eyelids. He was lying on dew-wet grass beneath a woven blanket of scarlet and saffron and the dawn sun was illuminating the little dell. His temples throbbed.

Was I drinking last night? He pushed himself up to a sitting position, gazing groggily around him. A little further off, Semyon lay sprawled asleep, Vasili next to him beside the ashes of the fire, lying on his back, mouth half open, softly snoring. There was no sign of Chinua, his cart and ponies—or his passengers.

Cursing, Gavril staggered to his feet and gazed around. He went unsteadily to the edge of the dell, gazing over the edge to where the track snaked on downward to the bottom of the pass.

"They tricked us. They've gone!"

Hearing his voice, Semyon stirred and sat up, rubbing his eyes like a sleepy child.

"Why didn't we hear them go?" he asked, his voice slurred. "Vasili; you were supposed to keep watch." When Vasili didn't reply, Semyon booted him in the side, none too gently. Vasili turned over, lashing out with an incoherent shout.

"Wake up."

"Ow. That hurt." Vasili reared up, still half comatose. "What's going on?"

"We were drugged," Gavril said. His tongue felt thick and the words came out slowly. "It must have been the tea. And while we slept, they went on their way."

He realized the two young druzhina were staring at him, mouths half-open, not knowing what to say. It was down to him to motivate them—although he felt so groggy he was struggling to think what to do next.

"The track divides at the end of the pass. We should split up."

"My lady seems pretty determined to go on alone," Semyon said.

"Determined enough to drug our tea," added Vasili, yawning till his jaw cracked.

"I don't need to hear that from either of you." But what his druzhina had said was all the more irritating because it was true. Gavril picked up the woven Khitari blanket with its flower-bright colors, feeling the rough softness of the wool. Kiukiu must have placed it over him to keep the night's chill at bay. An act of tenderness . . . or of guilt? Maybe both. He folded the blanket.

"I'm not giving up," he said. "They can't be too far ahead."

***

Kiukiu kept glancing anxiously behind her as Chinua's cart approached the end of the pass. She could see the track winding back up into the gorge but no sign yet of three horsemen. High overhead wheeled a couple of fire falcons, letting out shrill cries. Risa raised one hand toward them, flexing her fingers, imitating them with raucous little squeaks. At least she seemed to be enjoying herself, blissfully unaware of the problems she had caused her parents.

"We're not going to outrun Gavril. Even if they've only just woken up, the druzhina's horses are in good form."

"Don't fret," Chinua said easily. "I have a plan. We just need to make sure we're on Khitari ground for it to work."

"But I know Gavril. He'll be angry with us for resorting to such low tricks last night. He won't understand. How much further till we're in Khitari?"

"Trust me."

Kiukiu gripped the hard wooden seat with one hand, clutching Risa to her with the other as the cart bumped over pot-holes. She wanted to trust Chinua. But if Gavril caught up with them before they left the pass, she knew that she had run out of ways to stop him forcing her to return.

At last they emerged from the pass into open country. Kiukiu sat up, straining to see what lay ahead. The grasslands stretched away into a hazy distance, a lonely and empty vista that they must cross to reach the remote mountains on the far side where Anagini kept watch over the Jade Springs. *Still so far. Can we reach her in time before Galizur's envoy tracks us down?*

Chinua's ponies were sturdy and hard-working but there were only two of them and the cart was heavy. They plodded up a grassy incline. When they reached the top, Kiukiu saw that the track beyond divided into two.

"Time to call for a little assistance." Chinua said, pulling on the reins to bring the cart to a halt.

She glanced at him and saw that his eyes gleamed amber, no longer human but piercingly keen and wolfish.

"You're summoning your pack? But what about the ponies?"

Chinua clambered down from the bench and undid the harnesses from both ponies. He whispered in their furry ears and then gave each in turn a firm slap on the flank. To Kiukiu's surprise, they dutifully trotted away, soon disappearing among the trees at the entry to the pass.

"Where are they going? Won't someone steal them? Or eat them? I suppose you've done this before?"

Chinua replied with a brief nod. Then he flung back his head and let out a piercing howl that startled Kiukiu. She clutched Risa tight, certain that the baby would start to howl too. But Risa let out an excited chuckle and wriggled enthusiastically on her lap. It was then that Kiukiu heard a distant answering howl. She felt a chill at the back of her neck. *They* were coming. Chinua's wolven brethren had heard him and were speeding to their aid.

Risa gave a sudden shriek.

Hurtling toward them in a cloud of dust were Chinua's pack. Their eyes gleamed, unnaturally bright, even though it was day: orange and amber, stars in the gloom. To Kiukiu's amazement and Risa's delight, the creatures surrounded the cart, taking up the trailing ropes and straps in their mouths. She looked around for Chinua and realized that he had stealthily shifted to his wolf form for, leading the pack, was a large, shaggy male.

With a jolt, the steppe wolves began to pull the cart. Kiukiu gripped hold of Risa as the cart gathered speed. Soon it was bowling along far faster than the two ponies had ever managed to trot.

It was not until the green of the grasslands began to blur that she realized that Chinua was employing a powerful conjuration to put a considerable distance between them and Gavril.

***

Semyon dismounted, staring intently at the track. "Looks as if a herd's been driven through here recently. All this dust. Could be goats or those great hairy beasts they herd out here."

"Yaks?" offered Vasili.

"Except . . ." Semyon got down on one knee to look more closely. "It's hard to make out for sure but these don't look like cloven hoof-prints. More like . . . paws."

"Paws?" Vasili snorted with laughter. "A herd of mountain bears?"

"Or a pack of wolves." Gavril had not forgotten that Chinua was a shape-shifting shaman with powers almost equal to those of the Magus.

"Whatever they were," Semyon said, standing up, "they didn't pass through here that long ago. But the way they've scuffed up the earth, they've made it impossible to work out which way the cart went." He turned first to the track that led eastward, then to the other leading north, scratching the back of his neck in confusion.

Gavril was beginning to realize exactly how determined Kiukiu was to carry out this mission—whatever it might be—without his help. Still groggy from the drugged tea, he felt despair roll over him like rain clouds, sapping all the color from the morning.

She's left me. And I still have no idea why.

"This is something only I can do," she had said. *"You have to let me go. That's just how it is."*

"I'm not giving up," he said, as much to himself as to the two druzhina. "But I have to do this on my own. If I don't return in a couple of days, I want you go back to the kastel with a message for the Bogatyr."

"And leave you alone out here, my lord?" Semyon shook his head.

"Are you suggesting I can't fend for myself?" Much as Gavril valued Semyon's loyalty, he was reluctant to drag the two younger druzhina any further into Khitari.

"No, but—"

"Tell the Bogatyr to be on his guard in case the Arkhels try to stir up trouble while I'm away." And Gavril dug his heels into Krasa's flanks, speeding off along the northward track.

Chapter 36

The mountainside rang to the repetitive din of hammers and sawing. Distracted by a distant cry overhead, Gerard Bernay glanced up and caught sight of a snow eagle circling high above the ridge. He gazed at its widespread wings, marveling at the lazy elegance of its flight, the effortless way it skimmed on the breeze. *There must be so much more I could learn from observing it.*

"Careful with that beam!" The workmen's shouts and curses brought him rudely back from his reverie, drowning out the eagle's piercing cries. "Ingenieur; we're ready to lower this into place."

"I'll be right there."

Later, he promised himself as he turned back to help guide them to correctly position the heavy timber. They had already made good progress in making the mine entrance safe, and as another ox-wagon came trundling up the steep path with its load of machinery parts, he knew that he would be busy supervising the construction of the pump engine to start to clear the water from the mine. When the day's work was done, if the evening was fine, he would take his notebook higher up the mountainside and make sketches of the mountain raptors as they wheeled above the crags.

Gerard and his team had notched up six days working beside the old mine shaft and had created a makeshift camp in the ruins of the old miners' huts. The next job was to try to roof over what was left of the pump house and make the tall chimney safe.

But first there was a pump to install, machinery shipped in from Tourmalise to assemble; Rasse Cardin had been only too happy to supply the parts from the Iron Works at Paladur—for a not inconsiderable fee.

Mountain life wasn't so bad, Gerard reckoned as he walked briskly back to the camp; there was a waterfall nearby which provided clean water and a bracingly cold shower to rinse away the sweat of a day's hard labour. And watching the great birds in flight from so high up had rekindled his obsession; in rare idle moments, he had begun to make calculations and observations based on his sketches. His one regret was that to make the mine operable again, he would have to ruin the tranquility. Once the fires started to burn, the steam pump chugged into life, and they began to pump out the water flooding the mine, the wild birds' songs would be drowned out by the din.

As the workmen crowded around the wagon to start the unloading, he heard them raise a cheer. Hurrying over, he saw them rolling a couple of barrels alongside the hamper of provisions he had ordered.

"What's this?"

"Ale. My treat, Ingenieur." Kartavoi appeared, rubbing his hands enthusiastically. "The lads have worked hard all week; I thought they deserved a reward. It's a long time to wait for a relaxing jar or two till we return to the main camp."

"But after a jar or two up here in the mountains, a misplaced foot in the dark and—"

"These men can take their liquor. You worry too much." Kartavoi turned back to the wagon, laughing.

And who'll have to bear the responsibility if some drunken idiot falls to his death? Gerard bit back the response, knowing that Kartavoi would pay him no heed. With no way to vent his exasperation, he turned away, taking the path that led higher up, striding briskly away from the oblivious Kartavoi before the temptation to punch him became too strong to ignore.

"Who's there?"

One of Kartavoi's guards on lookout duty, suddenly appeared on a boulder above him.

Gerard found himself staring into the muzzle of a musket. He raised his hands. "You should recognize me by now," he said dryly to the guard.

"Ingenieur Bernay." The musket was lowered. "Sorry. There've been a few unexplained incidents today."

"Intruders?" Gerard could not help but remember the two Nagarian warriors who had threatened them before. "Uninvited visitors?"

The guard nodded. "Someone's been spying on us. Take care, Ingenieur."

"I'm just going for an evening stroll. Need to stretch my legs," Gerard heard himself saying airily.

Tracing the course of the mountain stream upward beyond the ridge, he found himself in a secret little valley, already half in darkness as the sun dipped down, illuminating the rocks behind.

A sudden intense shaft of late sunlight shone like a beacon into the little valley, blinding him. But not before he had seen them: tall figures, their faces masked, gathered together in a circle. Some wore horned masks, like mountain goats, others had antlers . . .

He blinked. At the heart of the grassy dell was a circle of standing stones.

For a moment I thought there were people standing there.

The stark contrast of evening light and shadow must have played tricks with his sight.

He rubbed his dazzled eyes and adjusted the wide brim of his hat to shade out the piercing brightness of the evening sun.

Not people but just ancient stones, set up centuries ago, probably to mark out a temple to the old gods of the mountain. Gerard had seen stone circles like this on the grassy downs that lay beyond Berse Heath in Paladur; local antiquarians had written treatises about their original purpose, even fancifully suggesting that they had been placed there long ago by their ancestors as a temple to the sun god. And Ryndin had made mention of some local deity, with much superstitious muttering about not disrespecting old customs and beliefs.

Gerard went up to the weathered stones and walked from one to another, examining them.

How did the ancestors transport them up here? Or did they hew them out of the mountain itself? But even so . . . to have the skill and knowledge to haul such massive objects into place and set them standing so sturdily upright . . .

He stopped and placed his hand on one, feeling the rough texture of lichen beneath his fingertips, closing his eyes a moment to listen to the silence.

It's as if time has stopped still here.

A thin whisper of breeze arose, stirring the grasses where he stood.

Murmur of voices chanting to the slow, muffled beat of drums; the rhythmic tread of many feet moving in time with the drumbeats.

Gerard opened his eyes, feeling the hairs prickling at the back of his neck.

He was, as his rational mind had assured him, alone on the edge of the circle.

I must have imagined it. And yet it had seemed so real, as if the dancers had brushed past him as they performed their ritual, weaving in and out of the stones.

The sun had almost sunk below the horizon and the shadows were spreading into a dark mist. He'd have to come back up the next day to continue his investigation.

Better get back to the camp before the sun sets— there's no moon yet and I didn't think to bring a lantern.

Gerard cast one last look back at the circle, each one a dark giant, looming out of the encroaching night. *Like silent sentinel warriors.*

As he made his way carefully back down the mountain path through the dusk, he caught voices rising in raucous song from the miners' camp below.

That blockhead Kartavoi must have broken open his kegs of ale. He grimaced. The prospect of trying to write up the day's accounts, let alone sleep in the company of drunken miners, was not an appealing one. *I hope to God they don't start picking fights—or stumble over the edge of the cliff in the darkness when they stagger off to relieve themselves.*

The miners had lit a fire and were comfortably sprawled around it, the orange glare of the flames enhancing the ruddy glow of their faces.

"Ingenieur!" Kartavoi hailed him. "Come and join us!"

It would look churlish to refuse. Gerard steeled himself and went over to join them, feeling the hot blaze of the crackling fire.

"Ale for our Ingenieur!" Kartavoi thrust a mug into Gerard's face, slopping a splash of ale onto his coat.

"Is there anything to eat?" Gerard was not eager to drink on an empty stomach. One of the miners passed him a bowl of steaming soup; Gerard sniffed it suspiciously.

"*Schi*: cabbage soup," said the man, grinning as he tossed him a chunk of rye bread. Gerard had become accustomed to *schi* over the last weeks: the base was cabbage and apples, but the cooks added anything they could lay their hands on, from mushrooms and carrots to salted meat. Sometimes it was delicious; at other times, barely palatable. Today, Gerard was hungry enough not to care and found soon himself holding out his bowl for a second helping.

"Tell me, Bernay." Kartavoi's face was already flushed. "What brings a clever young man like you all the way out into the wilderness, eh?"

Gerard stifled a sigh; he had learned that it was best to humor Kartavoi when he started drinking. "My boss, Master Cardin, sent me."

"Not gambling debts then?"

Gerard shook his head. *Unlike our employer, Lord Ranulph.*

"So you're still fancy free? Or is there a wife at home, waiting for you?"

"No wife," Gerard said.

"Sensible man!" Kartavoi burst into laughter. "I came up here for a bit of peace and quiet. Too much nagging at home. Peace and quiet and . . ." He gave Gerard a knowing wink.

Gerard did not follow. "And?"

Kartavoi wound one arm around Gerard, pulling his ear close to his mouth. "They say there's treasure buried on this mountain."

"They do?" Gerard tried to extricate himself from the heavy arm wrapped around his neck. Kartavoi had never mentioned buried treasure before.

"That's why the lads signed up for this job." Kartavoi took another swig of ale and belched loudly, enveloping Gerard in a cloud of foul-smelling breath. "Lady Morozhka's Hoard," he said in a confidential whisper. "No one dared to come and search for it while Lord Volkh was alive. But now we're all part of the empire, who's to stop us?"

"Doesn't this land belong to Lord Ranulph's family?" Gerard managed to extricate himself. "Was Lady Morozhka one of his ancestors?"

Kartavoi let out a chuckle. The idea seemed to amuse him. "Not as far as I know. Morozhka's the one who brings the snow. Lady Frost, the children call her."

"Ah yes; the Azhkendi goddess of winter." Gerard remembered Ryndin's warning. "*You don't want to anger*

407

Lady Frost up here in the mountains." And another memory came to mind from his time at Tielborg University: the students at the Department of Antiquities getting very excited over a treasure trove found in the grounds: the grave of an ancient warrior prince. Perhaps the stone circle concealed similar remains . . .

***

Dawn sunlight, rancidly bright, lit the tumbledown miner's shack where Gerard was sleeping, waking him. He lay there awhile, listening. The song of a little bird piping nearby brightened the early morning. But all the usual sounds of the camp stirring to life were absent: the men, coughing and grumbling as they forced themselves off their mattresses to go relieve themselves; the clash of metal pots and ladles as the cook made porridge. Sitting up, the warm blanket falling away, he realized that he was alone.

Gerard seized his coat and pulled on his boots. Hurrying outside, he saw that the mine works were deserted.

Where were they? Had they abandoned the work and gone back down the mountain?

He cupped his hands to his mouth and shouted out, "Kartavoi!" The sound of his own voice echoed back to him. And then the foreman appeared from behind the end shack where they'd rigged up a privy.

"Where are the men?" Gerard went over to him. "Did you send them off somewhere?"

"Search me," Kartavoi said, his voice thick. He was obviously suffering from the after-effects of the ale last night. "They can't have gone far."

Gerard was already fuming; Lord Ranulph wanted results—and he wanted to be done with this project. A delay like this would only extend his time in Azhkendir even further. "I'll go and search for them."

"I'll—be right behind you." But the foreman turned and staggered back toward the privy, so Gerard set off at a brisk pace on his own taking the path that led up to the stone circle.

Gerard swore. He had found his missing workforce.

The inebriated miners—and heaven knew how they had made their way up the steep path without coming to harm—lay snoring on the sun-warmed grass, some propped up against the ancient stones, others flat out on their backs, arms flung wide, utterly oblivious. Empty ale flagons were strewn on the ground alongside burned-out torches.

The tranquility of the remote mountain valley he had chanced upon yesterday had been desecrated.

But as Gerard strode out across the grass to rouse them, he almost tripped over a shovel half-hidden in a patch of young nettles. What had they been doing? Digging?

"*Buried treasure,*" Kartavoi had drunkenly confided in him the night before. And as Gerard drew nearer, he saw with a sinking heart that several of the ancient stones had been daubed with red paint, the same paint the miners were using to mark out the seams in the mine.

And there, beneath the red-daubed stones, was the evidence of their wanton vandalism: gaping holes excavated in an excess of ale-fuelled enthusiasm. As Gerard stood, staring down at the mess, speechless, one of the miners lying sprawled at his feet, let out a snorting snore and opened his eyes, squinting against the sunlight.

"Ingenieur?" he said in a voice thick with sleep. And then winced, clasping his hands to his head. "Wha— what time is it?"

"Time you were all at work," Gerard's voice was taut with fury. "Every hour you've spent snoring here is an hour's wages docked off your pay."

The miner sat up slowly and looked blearily around. He lumbered to his feet and stood there swaying. "Wake up, boys!" One by one, the other miners began to stir, groaning at the dazzling brightness of the sunshine. One of the younger lads, green-faced, wobbled to his knees, only to double up, vomiting into the grass.

Gerard could feel the righteous anger continuing to grow inside him, an unbearable pressure building behind his temples. And a sudden fierce gust of wind blew across the glen, shivering through the grass, even though the sky overhead was blue and cloudless.

"Look at the mess you've made." He gestured to the stone circle. He was so furious that he could hardly spit the words out. "I want all this paint cleaned off— and these holes filled in as soon as possible."

"What's the harm?" he heard one man mutter to another. "It's only a few old stones."

"A few old stones?" Gerard turned on him. "This is an ancient sacred site—which you have willfully defaced." Another gust of wind, fiercer than the first, surged across the glen. "For all we know, this circle could be a memorial to Lord Ranulph's ancestors." But all that his words earned him was a few hostile glances and more resentful muttering from the men. The sense of pressure in his head was increasing, made all the harder to bear by the need to keep his calm and not bawl the miners out; if he shouted at them, he'd lose what little respect he'd gained.

I've felt this pressure before.

Suddenly he was back on desolate Berse Heath, his mind filled with the wild banshee shriek of the wind as it tore across the scrubland toward him, fuelling his body with its raw and dangerous power—

"You lazy louts!" Kartavoi's voice rang out across the glen. "So this is where you've been hiding yourselves?" The foreman, mopping his shining face, appeared at the far end of the glen. "How are we to get the work done today with half a team?"

Then he saw Gerard and tugged off his hat in a deferential gesture, clutching it to his broad chest. "Ingenieur; I must apologize for the men's behavior; it's utterly inexcusable."

Gerard blinked. The wind had dropped and with it the feeling of unbearable pressure in his pounding temples. He turned his back on the stone circle and the unrepentant miners; as he passed Kartavoi, he said quietly, "And no more ale. Not till the work's finished and the mine's in working order. Understood?"

Kartavoi nodded. For once he didn't come back with a cheerful response.

***

Gerard left Kartavoi haranguing his workforce and set out down the track, his mind and body still tingling with the wind's shrill song.

It was as well Kartavoi came when he did. I have the feeling that I might have done something regrettable if he hadn't appeared. It was almost as if I'd somehow managed to summon the wind to do my bidding.

411

"No." He dismissed the ridiculous idea, shaking his head as if the movement would clear the lingering oppressive sensation. *There must be a logical explanation; a sudden drop in barometric pressure, most likely. That—or I must be going crazy up here, with only the miners and Kartavoi for company.*

The memory of Berse Heath had only served to remind him of Toran—and for some reason all he could think of as he came down the mountainside was how much he missed him; his lively conversation, his ardent enthusiasm for anything mechanical, the way his eyes lit up whenever he spoke of his grandfather . . .

Didn't I come all this way to give him the time he needs to mature and develop his talents? That was one reason why he had deliberately put so much distance between them. Although there was another darker, less noble reason too. *To give myself time to come to terms with my feelings for him. To forget.*

He had run away.

And then as Gerard turned a steep twist in the path, ducking beneath an overhanging boulder, he came out above the ridge where the mountainside fell sharply away, affording a breath-stopping view of the valley far below. He halted, gazing in awe. The thick coverlet of morning mist had burned off, revealing the moorland spread out in all the vivid colors of the Azhkendi spring that had burst through the melting snow: the tender green of new leaves unfurling, acidly bright against the muted purples of heathers.

But it was the cool kiss of the breeze that suddenly wreathed about his body that surprised him the most.

Almost as if some lithe, translucent aethyrial spirit had streaked past me, then returned to tousle my hair and stroke my cheek.

Chapter 37

Kaspar Linnaius opened the door of the mountain hut, peered out, and sniffed the morning air. There was a new softness to it, even a faint hint of sweetness.

"I can smell spring," he said.

At first, Izkael's wouivre kin had hidden Linnaius and Izkael in one of the caves high in the Sapaudian Mountains, close to the waterfall from which he drew much of his strength. But the winter's chill proved too harsh for Linnaius to endure and he had set out in search of the remote chalet in which he had learned his craft from his mentor, Izkael's sister, Eliane. Eliane had once been a wouivre, Elimariel, but had fallen in love with a mortal man and renounced her immortal shape-shifting form to live with him.

With the passing of so many years, the chalet was gone but he soon located a hut belonging to Bertran, a local farmer who used it when grazing his goats on the high summer pastures. Money was exchanged and Kaspar moved in, with a few books, plenty of firewood, a small cask of Sapaudian gentian brandy, and a few other necessities to see him through the bitter cold months. Most important of all, was the weaving of

413

impenetrable barriers to protect the two of them—or so he hoped—from the penetrating, vengeful gaze of Galizur's Warriors; Chinua had taught him a useful concealment trick or two used by the shamans in Khitari. And so he passed the dark days filling page after page of a ledger with his memories, trying to piece together the fragments that would lead him to his lost daughter . . . or her descendants. All the while, Izkael lay in a profound, strength-restoring sleep, slowly mending in the clean, cold mountain air that had given birth to him and his kin.

"But what use am I to Eliane and her children if I can't find them and protect them too?" Linnaius had written. "If the curse of the silver eyes has skipped a generation or two, there may even now be one of my bloodline awakening to their heritage, only to be hunted down and destroyed by Ardarel before I can warn them. Where to start? In Tielen?" He sighed and laid down his pen; to return to Tielen when he had retired from Eugene's service would lay all manner of temptations before him. He longed to see his imperial master one more time and even more so, Princess Karila; his talented young protégée, who must already be ten years of age and maturing too fast.

"No," he said aloud. "I said my farewells. Kazimir has taken my place. Alchymy has been superseded by science."

Linnaius went into the henhouse and collected the fresh-laid eggs while his hens tutted and squawked around his feet. Such simple, essential tasks were a daily pleasure: deciding whether to boil the eggs or make an omelette was probably the hardest choice he would have to make that day. "And I could grate some cheese into the mix; mountain cheese melts in such a satisfactorily gooey and appetising way."

But as he went back in, he saw that the dark interior of the hut was no longer lit with the wouivre's dull-silver glimmer. Carefully placing his eggs in a bowl, he approached the narrow bed on which Izkael, still in human form, had been lying for the past long weeks of winter.

The bed was empty.

I didn't sense him outside. Can he have recovered . . . and flown off without telling me?

Linnaius went back outside. "Izkael!" he called across the valley, his voice sounding deplorably feeble and agitated in his own ears. And then, when there was no reply, he called again, "*Azhkanizkael!*" using the wouivre's full name to formally summon him. The bond between them meant that the wouivre would be compelled to respond.

It was just then that he sensed it. Indistinct as the call of a distant mountain bird and just as fleeting. A mere vibration in the air. But a shiver of power so similar to his own that it made his skin prickle.

"Another wind magus." He closed his eyes, trying to divine the direction it was coming from. But it was no use and when he looked again across the valley, shading his eyes against the pale, intense brightness of the blue spring sky, the moment had passed. Wherever the wind mage might be, he was not close by.

The air vibrated as Izkael swooped down, sleek and graceful in his true wouivre form, to hover above his head.

"Don't run off like that without telling me first." Linnaius heard the tetchiness in his voice; he didn't mean to scold Izkael but his sudden disappearance after the long weeks of lying as one dead for so many weeks had troubled him deeply. Even though he knew that wouivres had their own way of healing themselves, to have to watch and wait at his bedside had been a test of his fortitude and patience.

"And I'm glad to see you well, too, Kaspar." A mischievous glint flickered in Izkael's brilliant eyes. Linnaius was relieved beyond words to see that his companion was restored to health but knowing the wouivres disdained being made a fuss of, he contented himself with asking, "So you sensed him too, Izkael?"

Izkael inclined his silver head. "Far away. But so clear, so distinct, his presence woke me."

"Can we be sure that this is the one?"

"One of your blood, Kaspar. The one you've been seeking. The one we both sensed before—but this time, the aura was so much stronger. He must be waking to his powers."

Linnaius nodded, trying to control the growing agitation building inside him. The realization that he could feel—even at a great distance—one of his descendants, maybe even Eliane's child, was almost too frustrating to bear. *If we come too late, how will I ever be able to forgive myself?*

"Can you take me there?"

"The very instant I rise from my healing sleep?" But Linnaius knew that Izkael's indignation was feigned, another mischievous dig. "And he's far away to the north from here. In Tielen, maybe."

"Tielen would make sense." Linnaius returned to his half-finished memoirs lying open on the table and frowned down at what he had written:

416

"A tall, narrow house, painted ocher, on a leafy little street in the university quarter of Tielborg, the faint scent of linden blossom in summer perfuming the air, floating from the trees in the nearby square."

A long time ago, he and Ilona had fled Sapaudia, taking the wouivres with them, and had sought refuge at Karantec in Francia where they both studied under Magister Hoel at the College of Thaumaturgie. But the desire for a normal life and children of their own drew them to the University of Tielborg, a safe haven for scientists and philosophers in liberal Tielen.

"The time you sent us away." Izkael had followed him inside. "The time you said you had no need of us." There was no censure in his voice, only a hint of sadness.

"I was trying to put my past behind me and lead a normal life as an academic." Linnaius closed the memoirs. "But my father was right: there's no escaping the curse of the silver eyes." He placed the ledger in a metal casket, locked it and hung the key on a slender chain around his neck. "Whoever he may be, this cursed child, he'll need to read what I've written. Bring him back here to Sapaudia, Izkael, if the need arises."

"The need?" Linnaius felt Izkael's translucent eyes pierce him, sharp and cold as icicles.

"You know very well what I mean," Linnaius said, more tetchily than he intended. "There are things he needs to know that no one else can tell him."

"Is there no way to trace him more accurately?"

Eliane's child. No, my grandchild. Linnaius was itching to be off—but first he had to make sure that the goats and hens that had sustained him throughout the harsh winter found a new home with his nearest neighbor, Bertran.

"Only if he uses his powers again." And one more unwitting use could be all it took to draw the vengeful Ardarel to obliterate him. There was no time to lose.

Chapter 38

The atmosphere at the copper mine camp was strained. The miners shuffled listlessly about their work, only stopping to shoot resentful glances at Gerard as he supervised the ongoing construction of the pump; gray-faced and unshaven, they were obviously still suffering from hangovers.

And serve you all bloody well right. You should be thanking me for not sacking the whole useless bunch for incompetence. Though Kartavoi should take his share of the blame as well.

"Until you can get that pump working, I'm going to use the traditional Azhkendi method of extracting the copper ore," Kartavoi said to Gerard. He seemed remarkably unrepentant. "We'll light fires in this seam to heat the ore and then, tomorrow, see what we can break out of the rock without risking blasting. Ruzhko and a few of the older miners are experts. By the way, where *is* Ruzhko?" he asked, wiping the sweat from his glistening forehead with the back of his sleeve.

"He went up the mountain with one of the apprentice lads to get dry firewood," said one of the miners.

"Shouldn't he be back by now?" said another, laying down his pick.

"You carry on with the preparations here," said Gerard. He was not convinced about the efficacy of this traditional Azhkendi method but until they could pump out the water from the second tunnel, there was not much choice; Lord Ranulph wanted results. "I'll go and find him."

He was halfway up the stony track to the hidden valley when he heard someone cry out. He stopped.

That's the scream of a man in pain. He'd heard just such a blood-chilling cry when one of Cardin's workmen had lost his footing and tumbled into the pumping machinery. The sight of his mangled body and the blood-splattered cogs and shafts had haunted his dreams for weeks afterward as he tormented himself with the thought that maybe there was something he could have done to prevent the accident.

He found himself running, feet sliding on the scree underfoot, grabbing at the jagged rocks to keep himself from slipping. The day was cloudy but as he reached the little glen at last, a shaft of watery sun suddenly illuminated Morozhka's Round. Bending over to break the sharp stitch stabbing his side, Gerard scanned the dell, seeing no sign of Ruzhko or his apprentice, only a flutter of little brown birds, fleeing into the distant bushes.

"Ruzhko?" Gerard's voice echoed back to him off the craggy rock face. When no one answered, he set out toward the stone circle. A day before, he had stood over the miners as they scrubbed the paint off. but a few traces still stubbornly remained, giving the disturbing impression that blood was oozing from inside the ancient stones.

And then Gerard spotted them. Ruzhko lay unmoving on his face at the far side of the circle; a few feet away sprawled the body of the apprentice boy, a bundle of firewood abandoned, next to him.

"What in hell's name—?" Gerard ran over to the miner, dropping to his knees beside him on the grass, reaching out to check for a pulse. And then he stopped himself, hand still outstretched. Blood had seeped onto the grass beneath Ruzhko's face, a glossy slick of rusty red. Now that Gerard was at close quarters, he saw the ugly gash in the side of the miner's head. Felled with one blow.

What happened? Did they argue? Did the boy attack his master?

Gerard pressed on the side of Ruzhko's neck; the skin was still faintly warm but Gerard could feel no throb of life beneath his fingertips. In spite of himself, he felt his stomach contracting and fought the growing urge to retch.

Was it his scream I heard?

Only then did he realize that he must have disturbed the murderers. And he had come up here alone, unarmed, never dreaming for one moment that he might be in danger.

The boy suddenly let out a low, guttural moan and tried to move his head.

Still alive . . . but only just.

"Easy there, lad." Gerard dug in his capacious pocket for the little metal flask of Tielen aquavit he carried for emergencies. He gently turned the boy over; causing him to let out another moan. "It's all right. I'm here." But even as he raised his head and shoulders against him, he saw the blood leaking from a deep gash at the base of his neck—probably inflicted with an axe. He tugged his scarf from around his neck and pressed it tightly against the gaping wound. But the boy's pallor and shallow breathing told him that his efforts might be in vain.

"What happened?" Gerard asked. "Who attacked you?"

The boy's graying lips moved and his wandering gaze fixed on Gerard's face. He whispered a few halting words in Azhkendi that were almost inaudible. But as Gerard leaned closer, he distinctly heard, "Dru . . . zhi . . . na . . ."

"Druzhina? Lord Nagarian's druzhina?" he repeated. "Are you sure?"

"What's happened here?" Kartavoi's voice, wheezily breathless from climbing, startled Gerard; he turned his head to see the foreman, followed by several miners entering the glade. "You're covered in blood, Bernay."

But before Kartavoi reached them, Gerard felt the boy let out a rasping sigh and his head lolled back against his chest. He laid him down gently on the grass and covered his face with his handkerchief. It seemed the only respectful thing he could do; inwardly he was seething with impotent rage that he had come too late to protect or save him.

"What in hell—?" Kartavoi stared down at the two bodies, eyes bulging with shock. "Who attacked my men?"

Gerard unstoppered his flask and took a mouthful of the rough local aquavit to calm his jangled nerves.

"Druzhina. Or that's what the boy said before he . . ." Gerard couldn't finish the sentence.

"God preserve us all. This is bad." Kartavoi held out his hand. "Give me a swig of that, Bernay. I need it."

Gerard passed him the flask.

"You know what this means?" Kartavoi said, wiping his mouth with the back of his hand before passing the flask back.

"The Nagarians want us off the mountain."

"Remember those two horsemen who threatened us? Bloody savages."

"We have no proof. Only the words of a dying boy. They might have been bandits in disguise."

"Ruzhko was a good man. A good friend. And the apprentice . . . he was only here to learn his trade." Kartavoi's voice had dropped to a low, troubled rumble.

"What do we do now?"

"I've a long memory, Bernay." Kartavoi's expression was grim, all traces of his usual good humor erased. "I don't want to see the old clan feud stirred up again."

"The Arkhels and the Nagarians have been at each other's throats for as long as anyone can remember." Toran's warning came vividly back to Gerard's mind.

"Has Lord Ranulph ever met with Lord Gavril?" Gerard began to wonder if he had unwittingly helped to reignite a generations-old vendetta. "Are we trespassing on Nagarian land? Does this land really belong to Lord Ranulph's family?"

Chapter 39

The tall, slightly lopsided house, painted in flaking ocher, looked sadly neglected and dilapidated. The linden trees in the square had grown taller, spreading a shady canopy over the cobbles but, so early in the year, had only just begun to unfurl leaves of the tenderest, palest green; there would be no honey-scented flowers for many weeks yet to come.

Linnaius, assaulted by emotions he had long forgotten, stared up at what had once been his home after he had fled to Tielen with his pregnant wife Ilona. A change of name (from Vernier to Linnaius) and a position at Tielborg University had earned them enough money to rent the ground floor of the ocher-painted house.

How could Anagini have taken all these precious memories from him?

It was my own doing, not hers; I made the bargain in full knowledge of what I was doing. And now I must take responsibility for my actions.

He steeled himself and went up to the tarnished doorknocker, rapping several times, then waiting even though there was little hope of finding anyone inside who remembered his family. It had all been so long ago and as he stood waiting on the doorstep and a breath of cold spring breeze stirred the lindens, he felt so frail that he could have closed his eyes and let himself be borne away on the breeze like thistledown.

"What is it?" The voice from inside sounded tetchy and tired. The door opened a crack and an elderly woman peered out at him. For a moment his heart skipped a beat, wondering—and then as her eyes narrowed in suspicion, he told himself that what he had hoped for could not be so.

"I'm looking for a family called Linnaius," he said.

"No one of that name here." She was just about to shut the door in his face when he put out one hand to stop her.

"Tivadar, then. Fru Tivadar." He used his wife's maiden name. "Or Vernier. Fru Vernier."

The woman shook her head emphatically.

"May I ask how long you've been living here?"

She shot him a mistrustful glance but said, "Forty-three years come this summer, if you must know."

Linnaius nodded, mutely accepting the information. As he turned to go, she called out, "Who was she, this Fru Tivadar?"

"My wife," he said, though more to himself than to her.

"Seems like you left it a bit late to come back for her." He could hear the undisguised disapproval in her voice. "Try the churchyard, old man."

Where did you go after I disappeared, Ilona? Each step dragged as he found himself instinctively walking toward the little parish church that stood beyond the square. *Did you try to track me down? Even if you had confronted me, bound by Anagini's spell, I would have been unable to recognize you and denied all knowledge of you.*

426

***

"Here are the parish records you requested." The pastor of Saint Klara's Kyrka pulled down a weighty leather-bound volume and tottered across to place it on the table in the little vestry. Linnaius watched, keeping his face devoid of expression, while within, a storm of conflicting emotions raged.

"Births, Marriages, Deaths and Burials. This volume dates back to the early years of this century; if the members of your family you're trying to trace lived in this parish, you should find them here."

The yellowing vellum pages were filled with column upon column of names and dates. Linnaius adjusted his spectacles and forced himself to peer at the spidery writing of past church clerks. He had no wish to face the inevitable but he owed it to his abandoned child and her descendants to do so. *It was so long ago. Why should Ilona return to haunt me now?*

And yet he saw his index finger tremble as he raised it to trace down the long lines of names. Page after page of the ordinary people of Tielborg: cobblers, seamstresses, apothecaries, bookbinders, pastry cooks, each life reduced to a brief entry in the register. *And I've outlived them all.* It was an achievement that brought him no joy.

Linnaius read on until his sight began to blur from weariness and his back ached from bending close to decipher the fading ink. It was always a possibility that Eliane had not borne any children of her own and his bloodline had been extinguished.

Then why did I feel that distant presence so strongly? Izkael felt it too.

The heavy mechanism of the church clock whirred in the tower overhead, then struck six. Linnaius sat back, knuckling his aching eyes. In spite of the long hours of daylight, he was finding it hard to focus on the hand-scribed entries.

If only I could devise a little glamor to search the text for me . . . but the presence of Saint Klara is too strong and my sight is failing..

Reluctantly, he closed the heavy volume and left the vestry.

"You're always so generous to the church, Maistre Bernay." The pastor was speaking to one of his congregation, a tall, gray-haired man plainly but neatly dressed: a doctor or a lawyer, Linnaius guessed.

"I'm merely carrying out my wife's wishes; she had a great affection for the church and the parish."

"She was such an gifted singer; we still miss her at services. I can't believe it's five years since she passed away."

"I miss Ilona every day, Pastor. But who am I to argue with God's will?"

Linnaius stopped abruptly, wondering if he had misheard. Ilona was not a common name in Tielen.

"And your son? Have you had any news?"

Maistre Bernay let out a curt sigh. "I believe he's in Azhkendir. He deigned to write several months ago, but he's a poor correspondent so I've heard nothing since."

The pastor caught sight of Linnaius, asking, "Have you been successful in your researches, Maistre Vernier?" Linnaius had thought it prudent to use his original name to convince the pastor of the validity of his search.

"Alas, no." Linnaius approached and saw Maistre Bernay look at him with suspicion. "But I couldn't help but overhear you mention the name Ilona, Maistre Bernay." He heard a slight tremor in his voice and made an effort to control it. "Your wife's family name—before she married—wouldn't have happened to be Vernier too?"

"No," Bernay said curtly. "That was her mother's maiden name. May I ask why it's of interest to you?"

It was only to be expected that Maistre Bernay would treat him with distrust. Linnaius cleared his throat and said, "Eliane Vernier was my daughter. I've been searching for her and her family for . . . a long time."

Maistre Bernay's stern expression did not alter. "You expect me to believe that? If you're after money, sir . . ."

Linnaius stiffened, offended in spite of himself. "I've been travelling overseas on the Emperor's business for many years. I was hoping that I might be able to re-establish contact with my daughter's family. We," and he hesitated, not knowing what words would convince the stony-faced Bernay, "had a falling-out."

"That must have been some falling-out. My wife's mother told us you were dead. She never even referred to you by name."

This was proving more dispiriting than Linnaius could have imagined. Even if this abrupt stranger was the man who had married his grand-daughter and sired his great-grandchildren, there was no way he could prove that they were related.

"I can understand your reluctance to accept my story," he said. "I merely wished to meet my great-grandchildren so I could make some provision for their futures," he added slyly.

"Then you'll have to travel far, Sieur Vernier. My son Gerard is in Azhkendir and my daughter Clémence has married a Francian."

"Azhkendir?" Linnaius repeated. That wild, turbulent country ruled over by Gavril Nagarian . . . *If I leave now I might be able to trace this Gerard Bernay by tomorrow.* He hesitated, torn between a desire to lay flowers at Eliane's and her daughter's graves and a nagging instinct that the sooner he found young Bernay, the greater his chance of protecting him. He realized that Maistre Bernay was still looking at him with suspicion and dug deep in his pocket, retrieving a handful of precious stones he had collected on his travels and which he often used for currency. He held them out, the crimson facets glinting dully in the shady interior of the church. "Perhaps you would give these to your daughter as a belated wedding gift from her great-grandfather. And please make a donation to the church on my behalf," he said nodding briefly to the pastor as he turned on his heel and strode toward the door.

"Wait! Wait a moment!"

Linnaius carried on walking, not once looking behind him, his footsteps echoing to the rafters of the whitewashed interior. The faint shades of the dead pursued him, whispering reproachfully, but he opened the heavy wooden door and went out into the daylight.

Forget dead Eliane and her daughter Ilona. Focus on tracing young Gerard. If only I can find him before Ardarel hunts him down.

Chapter 40

The sky above Swanholm Palace was overcast and there was a hint of drizzle on the breeze. The cadets from Tourmalise followed Colonel Lindgren down a wide white gravel carriageway that led past the neat parterres still bright with striped tulips. Toran noticed that the fresh morning air was smirched by a smell that was oddly familiar: it reminded him of the fumes and smoke that belched from the great chimney at Cardin's Iron Works in Paladur—yet the Emperor's palace gardens seemed an unlikely place to encounter such an industrial odor .

On the limpid waters of the Grand Canal he spotted two little pleasure boats, carved and painted to look like black-feathered swans. But as the cadets drew nearer, they heard a mechanical chugging and puffs of steam could be seen issuing from slender chimneys protruding from the decks.

"Do you hear that?" Toran said to Branville, unable to contain his excitement. "Those boats have been fitted with *engines*."

Branville scowled and shaded his eyes with one hand to get a better look.

"Professor Kazimir!" called Colonel Lindgren.

A slender, fair-haired man was talking with a couple of students at the water's edge. He glanced round nervously as the colonel approached them and the two exchanged a few words.

"So that's the famous Imperial Artificier they told us about?" Branville said in unimpressed tones. "He looks more like my father's tailor than a alchymical genius."

"Line up along the canal bank," Major Bauldry ordered the cadets. "We're here to observe. Don't get in the way."

Lorris exchanged a world-weary look with Toran. "As if we would..." But Toran's attention was focused on the nearest of the two boats as he took in all the details from the little paddle wheels to the slender metal chimney.

"Things to come," he said under his breath. He had a feeling that they were witnessing a trial that could change travel between continents forever. Already, in his imagination, he stood on the prow of a great iron-clad ship as it cleaved the ocean waves, its engines thundering below decks, powered by steam...

Colonel Lindgren returned. "Bear with us a little longer, Major," he said with a smile.

"What's this all about?" Bauldry demanded.

"Doctor Maulevrier's students have been busy installing engines into these little boats. The Emperor is keen to demonstrate that *aethyrite*—our new alchymical fuel—is safe and efficient."

"*Aethyrite*?" Toran echoed, eager to learn more.

"The fuel that you'll be using to power your flying machines."

"What the deuce?" Branville muttered but was quelled by a withering look from Major Bauldry.

"The students will take part in a little demonstration of what *aethryite* can do: a boat race along the canal."

Professor Kazimir started up the steep bank, slipping in his haste; the colonel grabbed him by the arm just as he slid back down the muddy grass, steadying him.

"Would you be so good as to tell the Tourmaline cadets about *aethyrite*, Professor?" Lindgren said patiently.

"Um—yes." Kazimir cleared his throat, visibly flustered. "I've been working to refine this fuel for some time, using the notes left to me by my predecessor, Kaspar Linnaius."

"Can you reassure us that it's safe for my cadets to use?" Major Bauldry said. "It's not so long ago, I recall, that there was a disastrous explosion at the Munitions Factory in Tielborg; the news reached us even in Tourmalise."

Toran saw a muscle in Kazimir's cheek twitch at the mention of the explosion.

"Can you tell us more about the fuel, Professor?" he asked, suddenly uneasy. "What are its components? How can you be sure it will work with our engines?"

Another twitch. "We are using two different strengths of the same fuel: both liquid, one not unlike oil in their consistency." He turned to gesture to the two boats. "The *Prinsessa Karila* on the left is using the more concentrated distillation and the *Prinsessa Margret* on the right, the diluted version."

"And the source?"

Kazimir cast a pleading glance at Lindgren. "I am not at liberty to divulge the source."

"And yet you're asking us to use this '*aethyrite*' to power our *Aiglon*?" Branville's dark brows drew together in a forbidding frown. His intimidating manner could be useful at times.

"Not without trialling it first. You've brought your prototype with you, as requested, I trust?" Colonel Lindgren turned to address Toran.

"We have," Toran said, wondering how the delicate mechanism he had fashioned so carefully with Gerard Bernay's help would perform. The two teams had each been given an empty stable block in which to assemble their craft, watched over by the imperial guard to ensure no contestant spied on the rivals' entry.

"Although it's one things to propel a pleasure boat along a canal and quite another to lift a sky-craft into the air," said Branville darkly.

"We'll give you and Doctor Maulevrier's team time to run the necessary tests—"

But at that moment a blast of steam erupted from the slender funnel of the *Prinsessa Karila* and the paddle wheels began to turn, churning the limpid canal waters. An answering blast came from the *Prinsessa Margret* as the students on board raised a cheer.

"I think they're ready to begin," said the colonel. He nodded to an adjutant on the bank who raised the blue-and-white Tielen flag he was carrying and then brought it down with a flourish to indicate the start of the race.

The *Prinsessa Karila* instantly took off, skimming down the limpid canal waters, leaving her rival black swan craft chugging stolidly but slowly onward toward the finish line. Another group of students were timing the competing vessels, consulting stopwatches, running alongside on the bank.

"As predicted," muttered Branville. "But can they control the speed?"

At that moment, the *Prinsessa Karila* veered wildly toward the bank, hit the side and capsized, spilling its crew into the canal, its paddles continuing to turn. As their peers hurried to the rescue, amid the splashing and shouting, the *Prinsessa Margret* calmly steamed past and reached the finishing line.

Toran leaned so far forward, straining to see, that he almost tumbled in. Branville grabbed him, hauling him back up. "Are you trying to drown yourself, idiot?"

Toran blinked, feeling the strength of Branville's grip burning through the rough cloth of his uniform jacket. Not so long ago he would have jerked his arm away, glaring in resentment at Branville. But now he leaned against him, regaining his balance, reassured by Branville's strength—and even grinned up at him. "Thanks." To his amusement, he saw Branville flush dark red as he hastily let go.

As Professor Kazimir rushed off to help rescue the floundering students from the canal, Colonel Lindgren turned to Major Bauldry. "Well, that decides the matter. Rest assured, Major, that we will *not* be using the concentrated distillation in the contest. I'll ensure that a small phial of the dilute *aethryite* is delivered today so that your cadets can test it with their machinery."

***

"Sorry I couldn't make the boat race this morning."

Kazimir glanced up from his work as Guy Maulevrier came into the laboratory, resenting the intrusion; he had been measuring out phials of the dilute *aethyrite* and Guy's unannounced arrival made his hands shake.

"I hear my boys took quite a dunking in the canal."

Kazimir winced. It was unfortunate that Maulevrier's students had ended up piloting the *Prinsessa Karila*—but the boats had been fairly allocated by ballot and no one could have guessed the outcome in advance.

"Just as well you conducted these trials in advance." Guy sat on a stool opposite him, grinning. "After all, we wouldn't want there to be any mistakes. There are men's lives at stake here."

Guy's observation was casually tossed aside, but Kazimir bridled, offended that Guy should even dare to imply that he would treat the contestants in such an irresponsible way.

"Now look here, Guy, I don't know why you think I might be so careless as to mix up the two fuels and risk killing the contestants," he said, "but I really must object—"

"My dear fellow, no offence intended, I assure you." Guy, laughing, raised both hands, palms outward as if to fend off Kazimir's response.

"All well, gentlemen?"

Kazimir started, hearing Colonel Lindgren's voice. Had the colonel overheard their exchange? Flustered, he began to protest as Lindgren came in that he would never make so basic an error as to mislabel the two strengths of fuel, especially after the morning's dramatic demonstration of the potency of the concentrate.

"It's true that we could have a problem on our hands, were the two strengths to be accidentally mixed up," the colonel said. "But it's a small problem that careful labelling will prevent. I know I can rely on you, Professor, to lock the concentrate safely away until the contest has taken place. Is all ready?" And he held out his hands expectantly. Kazimir, hands still shaking, handed over two slender stoppered phials.

"Excellent," Lindgren nodded his approval. "Will you accompany me, Doctor Maulevrier? I'm sure you and your team are eager to start testing the *aethyrite* in the mechanism that powers your flying craft. And then I'll make my report to his imperial majesty."

Chapter 41

"Two of our men attacked?" Lord Ranulph stared at Gerard, his amiable smile of welcome erased. "Murdered?"

Gerard gave a brusque nod. He was still shaken by what he had seen. "We've had no option but to halt all operations until we've reassessed the situation."

"Do you have any idea who attacked them? Where were they?"

"At Morozhka's Round. The miners got very drunk, no thanks to Kartavoi, and defaced the standing stones." Gerard could hardly keep the anger from his voice, agitatedly turning the brim of his hat round and round as he spoke. "I made them clean up, but the damage was done. And then I found Ruzhko and his apprentice—just a boy—"

"Any witnesses?"

"Before he died, the lad said just one word. 'Druzhina'."

"Druzhina." Lord Ranulph took a swig from his hip flask; as he put it back in his pocket, Gerard saw that his hand was shaking. "I hoped it wouldn't come to this," he said distantly.

A buzz of voices had begun outside and was growing steadily louder.

"Why would Lord Gavril send his druzhina to attack my men? It's Arkhel land."

"It's possible that the lad was mistaken," Gerard said, realizing that he was treading on dangerous territory.

"Iarko's employed men from families loyal to the Arkhels. They've had to lie low for years, nursing their grievances. Word must have got out."

"You can't mean it was the Nagari—" Gerard began, understanding what his employer was saying. "But we have no proof."

"Yet you were threatened, along with Ryndin and Kartavoi, weren't you? And—" A loud rap at the door made him break off. "Come in."

The door creaked open, bringing a gust of damp air and with it the protests of the miners assembled outside. Kartavoi came in, followed by Iarko and his son Temir, a tall, well-favored young man.

One glance at the Arkhel retainers' expressions told Gerard how volatile the situation had become. And another glance at Lord Ranulph—who had been entertaining two ladies to tea not half an hour ago—revealed that Toran's father had been away from Azhkendir for far too long and was utterly out of his depth.

"What's all this damnable racket, Iarko? Tell the men to be quiet."

"The men are loyal to you, my lord." Iarko's face was flushed. "They want to let you know that whatever action you choose to take against the Nagarians, they are ready to support you and defend the mine."

"What action do they think I'm going to take?" Lord Ranulph looked bemused. "I'm not going to attack Lord Nagarian. Although I'm prepared to meet him, face-to-face to discuss reparation."

"But this is a slur on your honor, my lord. It's an act of deliberate provocation. If the Nagarians want a fight, let's give them a fight."

"I came back here with one aim, Iarko," Lord Ranulph's voice hardened. "To mine firedust. And copper. Not to start another clan war."

Gerard looked at him in surprise. This was the first time he had heard his employer speak so decisively.

"Ingenieur," Lord Ranulph suddenly turned to Gerard, catching him off-guard, "I'd like you to go to Kastel Nagarian and set up a meeting with Lord Gavril. On neutral territory. Temir, pick a couple of reliable men and accompany Ingenieur Bernay."

"Me?" Gerard was taken aback; he had no wish to walk straight into the lion's maw.

"I'll write a letter." And Lord Ranulph sat down at the table, picking up his pen.

"But I'm just an ingenieur. I have no experience of mediation or negotiation—" Gerard began.

"You'd better take this." Temir came over and handed him a pistol.

Gerard instantly handed it back. "If we ride over armed to the teeth, they'll think we're coming to pick a fight."

Temir shrugged and stuck the pistol in his belt.

"Temir's a crack shot. Used to be my gamekeeper at Serrigonde." Lord Ranulph folded the letter, sealed it and handed it to Gerard, clapping him on the shoulder. "He'll look after you." Close to, Gerard smelled the brandy on his breath. *This incident must have reawakened memories that he'd rather forget.* He took the letter in silence and tucked it into his inner pocket.

***

What am I doing here wasting my time in Azhkendir? Gerard was still fuming with resentment as he rode behind Temir across the moors toward Kastel Nagarian. *If Maulevrier hadn't played me for a fool and stolen my designs, I could have been back at the university in Tielborg, lecturing, teaching, sharing my discoveries with like minds, exchanging ideas about the mechanical arts with the students, not caught up in some ancient barbaric blood feud.*

"We're lucky it's early summer," Temir said, jolting him out of his thoughts. "Long hours of daylight this far north."

Ahead lay a great forest, marking the eastern border of the moors and the Arkhel Waste. The meandering road they were on, little more than a stony track, would eventually lead them to the western entrance to Lord Nagarian's demesne. Gerard soon spotted a crenellated tower rising above the evergreens.

"Is that part of the estate?" he asked, pointing.

"That must be the western gatehouse," Temir said gazing up at the ivy-festooned tower, eyes narrowed in a frown.

"Did you grow up here, Temir?"

"No; I was born in Tourmalise. My father married one of Lady Tanaisie's maids. But he and Ryndin taught me the Azhkendi tongue."

"You seem to know your way around."

"Dad used to draw maps for me. Told me how it was in Lord Stavyor's time. The good days, he used to say. Before Lord Volkh—"

"If you were at Serrigonde," Gerard said, hastily changing the subject, "you must have known Lord Toran."

Temir turned round in the saddle and Gerard saw that he was smiling. "We used to play together when we were little. He loved the wolfhounds. Almost as much as he loved his granddad, Lord Denys." Gerard felt his mood mellowing; the image of a much younger Toran burying his face in the rough gray fur of the family hounds, laughing as they licked his face, made him smile too. "He was always sneaking out to his granddad's workshop, tinkering around with bits and pieces, making models. But why do you ask, Ingenieur?"

"I—" Gerard broke off abruptly as he spotted two horsemen riding toward them. Temir must have heard the thud of the hooves on the stony track too, because he swung around, gripping the reins with one hand, the other moving to grab the pistol in his saddle holster.

"Wait," Gerard said. "We're here to deliver a letter."

"They're not like you and me, Ingenieur," Temir muttered, "they're barbarians." But to Gerard's relief, he slipped the pistol back into its holster.

The horsemen drew near, one of them hailing them in the common tongue.

"What is your business here?"

"I bring a letter for Lord Gavril," Gerard called back. He wondered as they rode closer exactly what Lord Ranulph had written. He hoped it was nothing contentious. As they approached, he saw that the horsemen—although dressed in conventional riding attire—also had cobalt blue clanmarks tattooed on their foreheads, just like the two warriors he and Kartavoi had encountered near Morozhka's Round. The elder of the two looked very much the seasoned soldier; at closer quarters Gerard saw the pale rim of a scar running from his left eyebrow to his chin. Battle-hardened warriors, both of them.

"I am Askold, Bogatyr of Lord Gavril's druzhina," said the elder one. He spoke with courteous reserve but Gerard sensed that he was assessing them intently."And who might you be, gentlemen?"

"My name is Gerard Bernay," Gerard said. "I am an ingenieur from Tourmalise in the employ of Lord Ranulph, and this is Temir, my guide."

"I see." Askold and his subordinate exchanged glances; too late Gerard wondered if it would have been better not to have mentioned his employer's name.

"My lord is away in Azhgorod at the boyars' council and cannot receive you."

"But two of the ingenieur's men have been murdered," Temir burst out. "There's a killer on the loose. We can't let their deaths go unpunished."

"However, Lord Gavril is expected home in a few days' time." Askold extended his right hand. His scar-seamed face was impassive yet Gerard sensed the growing tension in the air. "I will ensure that the letter is safely delivered."

Gerard handed over the letter, all the while fearing that Temir, silently seething with repressed anger, might lose control.

Temir began to protest but Gerard gave a swift, terse shake of the head to silence him and without further exchange of words rode away from the watching Nagarians back toward the moors.

***

"So Lord Gavril's away from home." Lord Ranulph gave a little shrug. "Then my hands are tied until he returns." Gerard sensed he was relieved that the meeting had been postponed. And yet his employer's demeanor was not entirely that of a man who was weighed down by the responsibilities of his enterprise; there was a hint of sparkle in his eyes and an air of suppressed excitement, like a child bursting to share a secret. He kept glancing at a letter which lay on the table.

"If you have no further instructions for today—" Gerard began, suddenly overcome with weariness; it had been a long and disheartening day.

"You met my son in Paladur, didn't you, Bernay?" Lord Ranulph was beaming. "I've just received some excellent news."

Gerard had turned to leave; he stopped, his attention caught, in spite of himself.

"Here; read it yourself." Lord Ranulph, very much the proud parent, handed the letter to him. Gerard instantly recognized Toran's bold, somewhat erratic hand:

"Dearest father,

"Our adventure continues. After a terrible storm in the Iron Sea (Branville was seasick as a dog!) we've safely made landfall in Tielen at last and I'm writing to you from the port of Haeven. We're about to travel on to the Palace of Swanholm where the Emperor is hosting the contest. Major Bauldry has hired two wagons to transport our equipment and the parts of the *Aiglon*. We will be allocated outbuildings on the estate in which to reassemble our craft. The contest will take place—if the weather is fine—close to the festivities on Dievona's Night when the sun hardly sets."

As he read, Gerard could almost hear Toran's voice excitedly relating the events and could not help smiling. But then his smile froze as a desperate sense of frustration and longing arose within him. *I should be there at his side, not that arrogant boor Elyot Branville.* He realized—just as a ray of cold Azhkendi daylight pierced the looming cloud pall, revealing the landscape in startling clarity—that everything he cared about: flying machines, the elegance and beauty of the ingenieur's craft, had become somehow inextricably mingled with his feelings for Toran.

"We've just learned that the finalists will be using a new fuel especially created by the Emperor's alchymists." A new alchymical fuel? Unease spread like a feverchill through Gerard's body as he read. Surely the imperial military scientists wouldn't experiment on the contestants?

"Bernay?"

He realized that Lord Ranulph was looking at him expectantly, one hand extended to take back the letter, obviously waiting for him to comment on Toran's achievements. He handed back the letter. "Your son is a gifted ingenieur," he said with conviction. "I truly hope that his team wins the contest. And I wish I could be there to wish them well."

"But what would I do without you here?" Lord Ranulph clapped him genially on the shoulder. "You're indispensable, my dear fellow."

Bernay nodded. Up until that moment he had convinced himself his expertise was essential for the successful running of the enterprise, that—in helping Lord Ranulph restore the Arkhel family fortunes—he was, in his own way, helping Toran at a distance. Now his instinct told him to stop running away. It was time to gather up his meager savings and scrape a passage—even in steerage—on the next ship sailing from Narvazh to Tielborg. What would it matter if Maulevrier recognized him? He'd be going to support Toran and the cadets, not to accuse him of stealing his designs. Maulevrier could say what he damned well pleased.

"I'd like to take a look at the copper mine tomorrow," Lord Ranulph added. "Could you show me around? Our funds are running a little low, so it would be good to see some returns on our investment."

"With pleasure," Gerard heard himself answering. He had a certain ingenieur's pride in overseeing the construction of the pump at the copper mine. This would be the ideal time to hand over the running of the mine to Kartavoi, pump and all. The only problem was persuading the superstitious miners back to work.

But how long was it till Dievona's Night? He remembered from his student days drinking into the small hours with his friends to celebrate the end of the examinations on the night when the sun never set. Amorous couples would jump the bonfire embers, hand-in-hand, to win the pagan goddess's blessing on their union, a tradition frowned on by the pastors of the Tielen Church.

Gerard picked up the little calendar on the office table. Out here in the wilds he had lost count of the passing of time but Lord Ranulph had been keeping a record. The letter must have taken over a fortnight to reach the mine works.

Which meant there were only two days to go to the contest. The calendar dropped from his hand. He would never make it to Swanholm in time.

Chapter 42

Gavril reined Krasa to a sudden halt. A violent shiver coursed through his whole body as if the air temperature had suddenly dropped. The disconcerting sensation stirred up fragments of memory—and yet also felt alien and unfamiliar.

Is it a Drakhaoul? He scanned the empty plain but could see no sign of another living creature, not even a bird. *There's no way it could be.* All he could hear was the faint whine of the wind stirring the heather, rattling the spines on the gorse bushes. *Yet it feels so like Khezef, or Belberith...*

And at that moment a wave of yearning for his lost daemon overwhelmed him and the ache of loss was so strong he dropped the reins, clutching his arms to his chest, trying to hold in the grief.

What's the matter with me? The fusion with Khezef was destroying me, eating away at everything that made me human. At least I can honestly claim to have been myself—and myself alone—this last year.

The shiver caught him again, like a freezing wave breaking against the shore, then another, and another. The wind was growing stronger, blowing in gusts across the steppe until it whipped his hair into his face.

What is *it?*

Fighting the growing urge to kick his heels into Krasa's sides and ride like hell away from whatever was coming, Gavril dismounted.

I have to find out what this is.

He stroked Krasa's neck as much to calm himself, as to calm her.

It's here.

Slowly turning, Gavril saw a man where there had been no one before, walking directly toward him across the steppe, moving with an easy, determined stride, his feet scarcely seeming to touch the ground. But it was not just his swift progress that took Gavril's breath away, it was the piercing glitter of his eyes, his cascade of hair, the pale icy blue of a sunlit Northern sea . . . and the furled wings that sprouted from his shoulders.

"Gavril Nagarian," the winged stranger called to him. The voice was strong, yet light and youthful with nothing of Khezef's world-weary cynicism.

"What do you want?" Gavril tried to steady his voice, and yet his heart had begun to thud painfully fast against his ribs. *He must be one of the Heavenly Guardians.* "Have you come to punish me?"

Still the stranger came on, moving at a swift and steady pace, his bare feet scarcely touching the scrub. "We need to talk, Gavril Nagarian."

"Talk?" It had to be a trap. Or a stalling tactic, designed to lull him into letting down his defenses. Although what defenses did he have, now that Khezef was gone? He almost laughed out loud at the irony of the situation: if the Heavenly Guardians wanted to destroy him, he was utterly unprotected.

Krasa whinnied, jittering around nervously as the Heavenly Warrior drew closer, and Gavril took tight hold of the reins, speaking softly to steady her.

"My name is Taliahad of the Seven Seas," said the stranger.

Is this how Khezef looked once, before he followed Nagazdiel to this world and fell from grace? Gavril found himself wondering, overwhelmed by the beauty and nobility of the young seraph's features. There was an unsullied innocence in the directness of his piercing gaze and an appealingly earnest ring to his voice.

"Why now, Lord Taliahad?" Gavril's mouth had gone dry and the words were hard to get out. He realized that he was fighting back a fear so great that it threatened to unman him. The angel must have been sent to punish him. "Why have you waited so long to hunt me down?"

A look of incomprehension passed across Taliahad's bright face. "Hunt you down? That was not my purpose. I was sent to watch over you—and your daughter."

Gavril was so astounded to hear this that for a moment he had no idea how to react. "B-but why?" he heard himself stammer.

"When the Fallen Guardian Khezef left this world, he left you and your unborn child utterly unprotected. And there are many unscrupulous forces lurking in the mortal world that dearly desire to use your daughter for their own ends."

"Use Larisa?" All the fears that had been tormenting Gavril since Kiukiu and Larisa had disappeared surfaced again. "What do you know? Is she in danger? Am I too late to save her? *Tell me.*"

"Your wife, the Spirit Singer, has run away, hasn't she? Taking your daughter with her."

"How do you know that? And why should I trust you? How can I be sure that you're who you claim to be?"

"I told you; my task is to watch over you. It is my duty to know." Taliahad's gaze was so steadfast that Gavril glanced away, ashamed to have accused the young Guardian too hastily.

"So why has Kiukiu disappeared with Larisa?"

Taliahad sighed. "Has your wife ever told you what happened to her in Khitari? Or the price she was forced to pay to regain her lost youth?"

A cold, unsettling feeling began to churn in Gavril's stomach. He shook his head.

"Your wife is in thrall to Anagini, one of the Elder Ones. Some call her the Guardian of the Jade Springs, others the Snake Goddess, but she was here long before Nagazdiel's rebellion."

"The Snake Goddess," Gavril repeated under his breath, remembering the worn carvings on the tumbled stones of the ancient island temple where he and Kiukiu had made love. Images left long ago by some early primitive people: a full-breasted female divinity, half-woman, half-serpent, yet when Kiukiu had discovered them in the morning sunlight next day, she had reacted strangely. At the time he had wondered why—but events had overtaken them, leaving him no opportunity to ask her why she had been so troubled.

"Anagini's powers are rapidly diminishing—and so she placed a binding spell on your wife. The price of restoring her youth was the pledging of your firstborn child to her service. And if Kiukirilya ever breathed a word to anyone of this bond, she would instantly lose her youth and become an old woman again."

"But that's—that's blackmail." Gavril could scarcely choke the words out. No wonder Kiukiu had become so remote, so furtive over the last few months. Bearing this intolerable burden alone must have been what eventually drove her to run away. Now he felt ashamed at the times his suspicions and hurt, confused feelings had ended in arguments and hurtful silences. *But how could I have guessed? I assumed she didn't trust me enough to confide in me.*

"The Serpent Woman has bewitched your wife. Her poison has been working in her system for a long time. It will be very difficult to persuade her to believe you. But you must persist."

"Poison?"

"Anagini seals her bonds with her victims by biting them with her fangs. You'll find a mark somewhere on your wife's body: her ankle, her wrist, maybe even her neck. That snake-bite is the proof that her venom is still in your wife's body."

"There is a mark—I thought it an old scar—on Kiukiu's left ankle." Everything that Taliahad said made sense.

"As we suspected."

"So Anagini really is a snake?"

Taliahad gave a brusque nod. "Of the worst kind. One that preys on those whom she compels to serve and worship her."

"I had no idea." Gavril had wanted answers but now that he had them, they were hard to digest.

"We have to try to save your daughter before Anagini takes control of her." The Guardian took a step closer. "And that's why I've been empowered by Prince Galizur to break our centuries-old silence and give you our aid."

"Prince Galizur?" A shudder of a shadowy memory awoke in the recesses of Gavril's mind at the mention of that name. *Is that a warning Khezef implanted in my brain?*

"I was ordered to give you a choice, Gavril Nagarian. Accept our help and save your daughter— or risk losing her forever to Anagini."

"This Elder One, Anagini; why does she want my daughter?"

"You were still possessed by Khezef when the child was conceived. Your wife is a Spirit Singer. Your child is unique; she has inherited your wife's abilities to travel the Ways Beyond, and that, mingled with the daemon-imbued blood of the Nagarians, means that she is unlike any other."

Gavril could hardly take in the explanation. *I was still possessed by Khezef when Larisa was conceived. She is as much Khezef's child as mine? What did Khezef do to me that night? How did he use my body . . . and my seed?* "Unlike any other?" he echoed.

"She is a Key. She holds within her the power to open a gateway to the place where Khezef and his kin have gone. Anagini and the other Elder Ones intend to follow them there before their waning powers run out. But they need a Key."

"*That* place?"

454

A second doorway towers above the Drakhaouls, limned in molten silver. It opens and light pours out, translucent and pure.

Gavril would never forget. The place where he had said his final farewell to Khezef. The gateway beyond the Serpent Gate on Ty Nagar.

"But if the Elder Ones use my daughter to open that gateway—"

"The strain on her little body will be too great. She'll die."

Taliahad's blunt answer struck home, a knife-stab to the heart.

"I'll do anything to protect Larisa," Gavril heard himself saying. "And Kiukiu, if it isn't already too late. But what can you do to help me?"

"What is your greatest impediment? What's slowing you down in your search?"

"I need to find them as soon as possible." Gavril looked up, meeting the Guardian's penetrating ice-blue gaze. "Can you give me back my wings?"

"Your wings were Khezef's. Only he could give them back to you."

Mute with disappointment, Gavril nodded. His emotions were in turmoil; all he could see was Larisa's eyes staring trustingly into his when she stretched her chubby arms to him, asking to be picked up. *So innocent, so vulnerable . . .*

"I can give you new wings. Different wings."

Taliahad's words didn't make sense at first.

"But I can't restore Khezef's destructive powers."

"I don't want them." Even the thought of wielding Drakhaoul's Fire again horrified Gavril—as did the greater dread of having to pay the price in terms of physical cravings. "I don't want them ever again. I just need to find my wife and daughter."

"These new wings will not be so easily mastered. They will cause you agonizing physical suffering. Every wing stroke will hurt, because you will no longer be sharing the burden with your Drakhaoul. Are you still prepared?"

"Anything to save Risa from this Serpent Witch." Gavril didn't hesitate in replying. Khezef's child, his child, didn't matter; he loved her and would endure any amount of physical pain to protect her.

"Very well." Taliahad turned his head to gaze over his shoulder at his own furled wings. He paused a moment, as though steeling himself, then, to Gavril's surprise, tugged a feather from his left wing—and another from his right. A translucent ichor dripped, like blood, from the quill end of both feathers. Angel's blood? It must have hurt, for Gavril saw a fleeting look of anguish dull the icy brilliance of his eyes.

"Are you ready?"

Gavril nodded, wondering how Taliahad was going to conjure wings for him. Taliahad drew closer and, raising his right hand, suddenly plunged the feather he had plucked into Gavril's right shoulder-blade, passing through his greatcoat, shirt and skin, deep into the flesh beneath. The sudden blow pierced Gavril's body like a lightning blade, radiating pulses down his arm and back. He gasped with the shock and dropped to one knee, trying to regain his breath.

"Brace yourself." And before Gavril could recover enough to stammer out another word, Taliahad stabbed him in the left shoulder with the second feather, leaving him clutching his arms across his shuddering body, trying to hold in the bright agony.

As he crouched on the rough turf, feeling wave after wave of pain surge through him, he wondered dully whether Taliahad had merely been sent to punish him after all—and had indulged in this cruel deception just to increase his torment.

It feels as if those pale, pearl-sheened feathers are spreading filaments throughout my body, burrowing into every vein and sinew, weaving an intricate network of new connections.

Or is my body rejecting them?

And then the cresting waves of pain reached a climax so shatteringly excruciating that it almost wrenched him from his conscious mind.

Must endure this for Larisa. For Kiukiu.

Something burst from his shoulder blades. The propulsion threw him sideways onto the ground. Scrambling back up to his knees, he glanced behind him again to see an extraordinary sight. Slowly issuing from his throbbing shoulder-blades came blood-slicked feathers attached to a viscous blue membrane; first one, then another wing gradually emerged from his torn, protesting body. Shaking, he tried to stand, only to drop back to his knees.

"I can't get up; they're too heavy."

"Be patient; the fledging is not yet complete." Taliahad gripped him by the right shoulder, steadying him against himself. "The sun and the breeze will finish the process; as the ichor dries, the feathers will become lighter."

The furled, powerful wings were utterly different from Khezef's; they were feathered in shifting shades of soft, iridescent blues, a paler version of those sprouting from Taliahad's back.

"They're . . . magnificent." Awed, Gavril closed his eyes, concentrating on the newly-fledged wings, attempting to open and spread them wide. A searing pain shot through his back and down his arms.

"It may take you a while to master them," said Taliahad as Gavril dropped, gasping, to his knees. "You have no Drakhaoul to help you."

Gavril nodded, unable to speak for fear of disgracing himself and howling aloud. *It can't continue at this intensity, the pain will dull soon enough. God knows, I've endured worse before.*

He waited for what seemed an interminable time until the shudderings ceased."How can I go among other people like this? They're so . . . obvious."

Taliahad gave him a disdainful look. "I'll teach you how to conceal them. Though it won't be easy for you to master in a short while a skill that usually takes us many of your mortal years to perfect. Watch—and copy me." He gave a little shrug of his shoulders, folding his shimmering wings behind him but, as he tucked them neatly away, Gavril saw him falter.

Something's amiss. Could it be that he's not so different from Khezef after all?

"How is it, Lord Taliahad," Gavril asked softly, "that you've come to the mortal world without a body of flesh and blood?"

The keen icy light in Taliahad's eyes was dimming.

"I thought you aethyric creatures were unable to survive here for long without a mortal body to act as your host."

A look at once agonized and furious, passed across Taliahad's handsome features. Gavril realized he must have guessed rather too accurately what was ailing the young Guardian.

"We have to assume a physical form when entering the mortal world—but it's hard to sustain for any length of time." Taliahad's voice had lost its vigor; he paused, as though making a supreme effort to control of himself. "It drains our energies, forcing us back to the Ways Beyond to restore ourselves."

"So you would never do what Khezef was forced to do? Merge with one of us mortals to survive?" Gavril knew only too well what the Drakhaouls had undergone when they were stranded in the mortal world: outcasts from the Ways Beyond, summoned from their eternal prison by the priests of Ty Nagar and forced to do their bidding.

Taliahad shook his head. "That is forbidden. Galizur would send me to the Realm of Dust . . . if I transgressed." He sagged, dropping to one knee, the pearlescent shimmer in his wings dulling even as Gavril watched. Gavril could not help but feel concern for him; it was hard to see such a strong, beautiful aethyric creature fade so fast even as he looked on. Echoes of Khezef's sufferings resonated through his own body.

"I can manage on my own from now," he said. "Go back, Taliahad."

Taliahad managed to raise his drooping head to gaze at Gavril. "Are you sure? Are you strong enough . . . to confront Anagini?"

"You've given me this gift," Gavril said, gesturing to his wings. The burning ache in his shoulders was hard to bear but he was certain he could learn to endure it if it was for Risa's sake. "Thank you. If you hadn't come to my aid, I don't know what I would have—"

"Save your daughter." Taliahad seemed to rally a little. He forced himself to his feet, swaying alarmingly. "Forgive me, Gavril Nagarian. I have overstayed my time here." Slowly, shakily, he spread his wings and began to rise above the grasslands, the slow beats of his wings sending ripples through the dry grass like waves.

As Gavril watched, the pale sky above them split open to receive him.

"And don't forget—trust no one." Taliahad's voice drifted down from the clouds. "The wolf shaman Chinua is Anagini's servant . . . and he . . ."

"Lord Taliahad?"

This time there was no response. Gavril gazed upward, shading his eyes with one hand against the brightness. But the Heavenly Guardian had gone—leaving him alone to fathom out the mysteries of flight all by himself.

"I've flown on Drakhaoul wings more times than I can recall. I can do this."

The grasslands were flat, with no hills or prominences that would have provided a useful place from which to launch himself into the air.

He closed his eyes, concentrating. He slowly extended the wings. Flapping them created a breeze that rippled through the grasses, but every movement still sent shimmers of pain through his shoulder blades and down his back. He bit his underlip and dug his nails into his palms, forcing himself to keep

460

up the momentum. The faster the wings beat, the more intense the pain became—and still he was on the ground.

There has to be some knack to mastering this...

But the pain only increased, until it felt as if every sinew and bone was screaming in protest. He collapsed again, too close to Krasa, the great wings spread out around him like a pale blue cloak, brushing her with the feathers.

Krasa let out a terrified whinny and bolted.

"Krasa!" Gavril called after her as she galloped away, hooves stirring up a thin haze of dry earth. "Come back!" He put his fingers to his mouth and let out a piercing whistle, Semyon's foolproof trick for recalling a recalcitrant mount. But she didn't even hesitate, she kept going, heading back the way they had come until he could see nothing but a little cloud of dust marking her passage.

Gavril sat back on his heels, dumbfounded. His only reliable means of transport had fled, leaving him alone and without any means of escape—except for Taliahad's gift.

Chapter 43

Gerard slept badly. In his dreams, flyers skimmed over his head, engines whirring—and he realized he was at the Emperor's competition, searching eagerly for a glimpse of the *Aiglon*. Suddenly his attention was distracted by a puttering, choking sound. Glancing up, he saw the *Aiglon,* black smoke billowing from its engine, careering out of control. Unable to move, he watched helpless as Toran's flyer burst into flames and plummeted to the ground.

He woke with a dry mouth and thudding heart, his mind still scarred with the images of burning, broken bodies tumbling from the craft. Stumbling out of bed, he checked his almanac for the date of the contest, circled in red ink.

Tomorrow.

Gerard closed the almanac, wishing he could rid his mind of the horrifying dream images. He had believed himself to be a rational, practical man, not given to emotional reactions. But the nightmare had shown him what he had tried to forget in his waking hours: he cared for Toran and he was desperately worried that he would volunteer to fly the *Aiglon* himself.

"But what can I do?" he asked himself. "He's hundreds of leagues away. Surely Major Bauldry would never risk his cadets' lives by letting them pilot the flyer using the new fuel."

Dawn came early this far north and the miners' camp was usually noisy as the men prepared breakfast and loaded up the wagons for the day's work ahead. But although the sun was up, there was little sound of activity outside.

Opening the door of the hut, shading his eyes against the brilliance of the morning sunlight, Gerard gazed around in bewilderment, seeing only a few of the older miners stirring a pot of porridge over their campfire.

Today was the day he had agreed to show Lord Ranulph the pump at the copper mine.

"Where's everyone gone?"

***

"My father." Temir stared at the ground, not meeting Gerard's gaze. "He knew Ruzhko years back, when they were boys. He's taken his death hard."

Gerard grabbed Temir firmly by the shoulders, forcing him to look into his face. "What are you saying, Temir?"

"He's on his way to Kastel Nagarian with Ruzhko's crew. He's invoking some ancient Azhkendi law. He says he has the right to demand retribution. A life for a life. Two, in this case."

Gerard let Temir go. "But that's directly disobeying Lord Ranulph's orders. He told everyone to wait until he's spoken with Lord Gavril face-to-face." He seized his hat and coat. "We have to go after them. We have to stop them before the situation deteriorates any further."

Temir let out a derisive laugh. "Stop my father? Ever since he set foot on Azhkendi soil again, he's been a changed man. He's been itching for an excuse like this to get back at the Nagarians. You're wasting your time, Ingenieur. He's spoiling for a fight. And you could get hurt in the crossfire."

Gerard rounded on him. "We're talking of Lord Toran's inheritance here. I'm not prepared to let an ages-old grudge spoil Lord Ranulph's dreams." It was only when the words were out of his mouth that he realized what he had said. *So it's true. I've admitted it aloud. I'm doing this for Toran.* But if he couldn't persuade Iarko to back down to protect his young master's future, the cause was as good as lost.

"Temir," he said, "give me that pistol."

***

I thought Iarko had more respect for Lord Ranulph than to go against his orders. Gerard put his head down and rode into the keen wind that had arisen out on the moor, stirring the yellow gorse blooms. The flowers might give the impression of spring, but the wind was blowing directly from the jagged snowy peaks of the Kharzhgylls and it had a raw chill to it that made Gerard pull up the collar of his greatcoat with one hand, keeping the reins tightly gripped in the other.

The rawness of the wind matched his mood; the closer he drew to the Nagarian estate, the more his exasperation and frustration grew. How dare Iarko risk ruining Lord Ranulph's venture and, worse still, the Arkhels' good name?

He checked the pistol he had slipped into the holster in the saddle, but the feel of the smooth wooden grip only increased his agitation.

Temir's warning still echoed distantly at the back of his mind. It was true; he wasn't a fighting man and was only too aware of the danger that the pistol might misfire if he was obliged to use it. He was hoping that a well-timed shot into the air might cause enough of a distraction to diffuse a tense situation.

What makes me think they'll pay any attention to me? They've been harboring this grudge over twenty years.

But then another icy gust of wind buffeted him, stirring up the cold fury that was simmering in his brain, sweeping away every other rational thought.

And beyond the whine of the wind he thought he suddenly caught the sound of distant shouts and cries coming from the forest. His sturdy bay mare slowed, sensing, perhaps, that trouble lay ahead, wrinkling her nostrils, as though sniffing the air for clues.

Am I too late?

***

As Gerard followed the carriage road into the forest, he spotted the ivy-covered crenellations of the western gatehouse tower rising above the trees. The shouts grew louder and more aggressive. Urging the bay forward, he came around a steep bend into full view of the gatehouse.

The day before, he and Temir had been met there by two of the High Steward's druzhina. Today it was defended by a dozen warriors or so, ranged along the top of the battlements and armed with old-fashioned crossbows. A group of miners stood below, brandishing pickaxes as they chanted, "Hand them over! Hand them over!"

And leading the chant, pistol in one hand, punching the air with the other in time to the chant, was Iarko. It was obvious to Gerard—unless more druzhina lay in hiding behind the gatehouse—that the Nagarians were outnumbered by two to one.

"Break the door down!" Iarko waved his men forward and they began to hack at the great door, tearing the wood to splinters with their pickaxes.

"Stop!" cried Gerard, digging his heels into his mount's flanks to urge it forward. No one paid him any attention.

"Fire!"

The druzhina began to loose their crossbow bolts on the intruders. Most missed their target, thudding into the mossy ground—until Gerard heard a hoarse yell of pain. One of the miners had collapsed, a bolt protruding from his shoulder.

"Nagarian dogs!" Iarko, voice shaking with rage, aimed his pistol at the druzhina who had given the order to fire on the attackers.

"Iarko! *No!*" The cry rasped from Gerard's throat.

A shot rang out, echoing through the forest, and the Nagarian staggered, then fell from view behind the crenellations.

Gerard's horse, unused to gunfire, shied. Next moment, Gerard found himself tumbling out of the saddle. He hit the stony ground—hard. Winded, ears ringing, he tried to push himself up on to his knees.

His horse skittered away from him, nervously shaking her head, eyes wild and alarmed. Blood trickled into his eyes as he tried to make out what was happening. Through the red, he saw the miners push open the battered gatehouse door—Iarko waving them on—only to be met by the Nagarian defenders.

"No!" Gerard dashed the blood away with the back of his hand and got unsteadily to his feet, staggering forward. His pistol was still in the saddle holster. He was unarmed. But he had to stop the fight from escalating.

"*Iarko!*" No one could hear him; they were too intent on exacting their revenge.

Must stop them. Any way I can.

A fierce blast of snow-chill wind gusted through the forest, setting the tree branches writhing. Its keen edge was like a dash of icy water, reviving Gerard, clearing his head, charging his body with new energy.

Suddenly the air was streaked with silver wisps of wind that curled and spun around him, just as they had on Berse Heath, on top of the academy tower, and only a couple of days ago, at Morozhka's Round.

This sensation . . . so exhilarating. The mountain wind gusted about his ears, ruffling his hair, each buffet like the playful leaps and nudges of an exuberant hound.

Instinctively, Gerard raised both arms, reaching out to catch it and channel it through his outstretched hands, sending the full force of the snow wind hurtling toward the fighting men.

***

The distant cry, desperate yet fraught with fury, resonated through Kaspar Linnaius's mind like a sizzle of lightning.

The wouivres sensed it too, for Izkael turned his horned head.

"Did you feel that, Kaspar?" he cried even as the sky-craft sped onward through the clouds.

"It's him," Linnaius said. The unfamiliar voice sent a thrill through him: hope, terror and fear mingled in equal measure.

"Is this the one you've been searching for?" Instinctively, Izkael had changed direction, his siblings following his lead, heading toward the voice.

"It could be." Linnaius didn't dare to allow himself to believe that his long search might be over. "Whoever it is, they're in danger."

Had Ardarel and the Heavenly Guardians already tracked young Bernay down? The thought that he might come too late was almost too unbearable to contemplate.

His skin tingled. A shiver ran through him as he sensed that other wind mage reaching out into the aethyr again to summon help. And this time the presence was much closer—and much more desperate.

He's in danger.

Chapter 44

The sun, sinking in the far west, cast an eerie light over the empty steppe. Semyon felt a prickle of goosebumps and rubbed his arms, hoping it was no more than the chill of the oncoming night and not a presentiment of bad news. Another long day had dragged to its conclusion and Lord Gavril had still not returned.

He and Vasili had taken it in turns to patrol on horseback. They counted birds of prey overhead. They ate the last of their strips of dried meat, leaving only a handful of nuts and berries to sustain them until they traveled back through the pass and reached the inn at the border.

And to make matters worse, the gently undulating grasslands offered up no landmarks to help them mark their progress; whichever way Semyon looked, all he could see was grass and scrubby bushes. So when his keen eyes spotted the signs that horsemen had passed that way, he pointed them out to Vasili who instantly jumped down from the saddle to investigate.

"They're definitely the prints we made earlier on." Vasili looked up from examining the evidence: the scuffed grass, the hoof-marks in the earth.

"No one else has come this way since then." He straightened up, wiping the dirt from his hands on his breeches.

"Lord Gavril's never abandoned us before." Semyon dismounted and gazed out across the empty grasslands. He could see no hint of movement. Only the high keening cry of an eagle, wheeling high above their heads, broke the stillness. "He rescued me and Dunai when the Francian Commanderie abducted us. Snatched us right from under their noses." Semyon still found it hard to speak of those dark days; the mental scars left by the Commanderie interrogators had gone deep, lingering long after the physical scars had faded. "He was . . . magnificent. And terrifying. I've never seen him so angry."

"Was he in full Drakhaoul form?" Vasili stared at Semyon, wide-eyed.

"Oh, yes." Semyon, lost in the memory, saw the midnight glitter of dragon scales, the hooked claws, hard as slivers of sapphire, the furious gleam in burning-blue eyes. He snapped back out of the reverie. "Didn't your brother ever tell you?"

Vasili shook his fair head, in a way that reminded Semyon of his elder brother Dunai. Physically, Vasili and Dunai were strikingly similar, handsome young men with hair so blond it was almost white, but their personalities were diametrically opposed: Dunai had become the silent stoic, while Vasili remained resolutely cheerful and outward-going.

"Dunai doesn't talk about what happened in Francia," Vasili muttered. "Da said not to ask him. Said he'll tell us when he's ready. But when I saw what they'd done to his leg . . ." He gave a dry shudder of disgust. "Those bastard Francians."

Semyon cuffed him. "Don't let Lord Gavril hear you talk that way. They're our allies now."

"And Lord Gavril's lost his Drakhaoul powers." Vasili glared at him, rubbing his cheek.

"He'll be back," Semyon said staunchly, although he realized how hollow his words must sound.

"We should never have agreed to split up. One of us should have accompanied him."

Vasili was right which only annoyed Semyon even more. "But he insisted on going alone."

As the daylight faded to twilight, a wind began to sigh across the steppes, setting the grasses whispering. A faint whinny made the grazing horses raise their heads, startled.

"Did you hear that?" Vasili grabbed Semyon's arm. "Someone's coming!"

Semyon's heart began to thud. Lord Gavril hadn't betrayed their trust after all; he had kept his word. Eagerly, he scanned the darkening plain.

"Is that Krasa?" Vasili pointed at a shadowy shape moving toward them at an unsteady pace.

Semyon put two fingers to his lips and whistled encouragingly; he had known Krasa since she was a foal and had helped Ivar to break her in.

"That's Krasa all right," he said, starting out toward her, then halting when he saw there was no rider in the saddle. "But where's Lord Gavril?" He called softly, "Here, girl. Over here."

The roan mare approached warily until he was able to reach up and catch hold of her slack reins with one hand, patting her reassuringly with the other. Her coat felt greasily damp and her eyes stared wildly at him. "It's all right, Krasa," he murmured, "you're with friends now. But where's your master?"

Vasili came over, moving slowly so as not to spook the jittery mare. Both men looked at each other in the dwindling light across the mare's empty saddle.

"What d'you think, Sem?"

"No bloodstains." Semyon checked the saddlebags. "But no sign of a message."

"Has he fallen off?"

"Unlikely. Lord Gavril's a good horseman."

"But if they were attacked by those steppe wolves, Krasa could have bucked and thrown him."

The thought had occurred to Semyon too although he hadn't wanted to say it out loud, as if the very act of putting thoughts into words would somehow confirm the possibility they were true.

"Perhaps," he began slowly, "he's persuaded my lady to change her mind and they're on their way back. Or perhaps he's traveling with her deeper into Khitari to do . . . whatever it was my lady needed to do there." *But to just disappear . . .*

"So what do *we* do?" He heard the uncertainty in Vasili's voice. "Go back to the kastel without him?" He knew the young druzhina was looking to him to come up with a plan—and he had nothing.

"That's what he said. If he didn't return after a couple of days. We have to go back and tell the Bogatyr. Only it doesn't feel right, somehow."

"How will he travel without Krasa? On the tea merchant's cart?"

"Everything's still in the saddlebags," Semyon said. "Water, provisions, pistols . . ." He leaned his head against Krasa's sturdy neck, silently telling himself not to imagine the worst. He believed in Lord Gavril. There had to be a reason.

"The blood-bond," said Vasili. "Try the blood-bond."

Semyon had not wanted to resort to such a drastic measure as his lord had always insisted it was not to be used except in the direst of emergencies. And he and Vasili were not in any danger. To call to Lord Gavril when he had already told them to return to the kastel would be akin to disobeying his orders.

"But if he was injured, or worse," Vasili insisted, "how would we know?"

Semyon thought about this. "Lord Gavril gave us a message to deliver," he said slowly. "'Tell the Bogatyr to be on his guard in case the Arkhels try to stir up trouble while I'm away.'" He let out a sigh that vibrated through his whole being. "So we have no choice but to follow his instructions and go back to the kastel."

Chapter 45

The branches tossed and groaned as the gale tore through Kerjhenezh forest, stripping off leaves, pine needles and cones. It hit the Nagarian gatehouse with such force that roof tiles and loose stones were dislodged, raining down on the brawling men, along with a hail of forest debris. Some clutched their eyes as dry earth blew around in blinding dust clouds; others fell back as they were pelted with branches and debris. The roar of the wind was deafening as it lashed the trees but Gerard faintly heard Iarko bellowing, "Take cover!"

Have I stopped the fight? Half-blinded by swirling dust and grit, Gerard peered through streaming eyes to try to make out what was happening.

The cloudy sky was suddenly rent in two. Lightning dazzled Gerard—yet through the jagged rent he could just make out a figure emerging, cleaving the boiling clouds asunder with a fiery blade. Astonished, he stared upward, wondering if he was concussed and hallucinating.

Wings, each feather flame-tipped, unfurled from the figure's shoulder blades; they rose and fell in shuddering strokes, controlling his descent, like a mountain eagle swooping down from the high peaks. The Winged Warrior's hair was fiery gold, streaked with copper and crimson and his eyes burned like glowing coals as he scanned the ground beneath him.

An angel? It had to be some trick of the Nagarians to scare the Arkhels away, a kind of automaton designed to intimidate and confound attackers. But as the winged one came closer, Gerard felt a shimmer of heat issuing from his gleaming body.

Like standing too close to the blast furnace at the Iron Works. If this is some mechanical construct, it's very advanced . . . a flying automaton.

"Where is he?" A voice issued from the angel's mouth, brazen as the martial blast of a trumpet. "The wind mage?"

Gerard dimly registered that the guttural cries of the battling clansmen had ceased. All he could hear was the beating of the powerful wings and the clarion voice.

Wind mage. Who does he mean?

And then the fiery eyes fixed on him and he felt their heat searing into his mind.

"*There* you are."

Me? Gerard wanted to run for cover but his legs refused to move. Fear paralyzed him. Instinctively, he raised his hands and arms to protect his head. The silvery wisps of mountain wind swarmed to him, as if answering his silent plea for help. Even as the angel Warrior drew back the fiery blade for the final blow, he saw that they were not mere wisps of mist, they were translucent sky dragons, weaving in and out to create a barrier. Gouts of flame dripped from the angel's sword, swirling to make one dazzling, burning barb that sang through the air as it descended.

"Die, Magus."

The angel Warrior raised the fiery blade, bringing it down in a flaming arc that scored a slash of dazzling heat across Gerard's vision.

Half-blinded, he closed his eyes, waiting for the white-hot metal to slice through flesh and bone, severing the thread of his life in one agonizing slash.

He felt his legs buckle beneath him. There was nowhere to hide.

"Toran," he whispered. His heart ached with unfulfilled love and regret. *If only I could have seen you once more before* . . . He closed his eyes, bracing himself for the scorching blast of fire to obliterate him.

A tremendous gust of chill air swept through the glade. The temperature dropped as the fiery blast was extinguished in a sudden cloudburst. Gerard opened his heat-stung eyes.

The fiery angel turned his attention from him, swiveling around in mid-air to counter the new attack.

Swooping down through the storm clouds came a sky craft pulled by a great horned sky dragon. At its prow stood a stern-faced old man, one hand outstretched toward the fiery angel, white hair streaming behind him in the wind.

Chapter 46

The Emperor decided to wear his new uniform as commander-in-chief of the New Rossiyan Imperial Army to grace the final round of the competition.

The weather—thankfully for an unreliable spring in Tielen—was fine, with only the lightest of breezes blowing from the northeast. The sky above Swanholm was the palest blue, dotted with one or two innocent-looking white clouds as Eugene went out onto the wide viewing platform on the balustraded terrace above the gracefully curving double staircase overlooking the park. The fine morning only served to enhance his good humor: he had eaten some delicious local smoked herring with coddled eggs for breakfast and now he was ready to take the next step in promoting the new mechanical science of aeronautics.

The cadets from Tourmalise filed out in their dark blue uniforms to stand obediently to attention below as their team leader, a fearsomely mustachioed officer, inspected them. They looked painfully young and inexperienced alongside the rival team from Tielborg University, led out by Doctor Maulevrier, with Altan Kazimir hovering anxiously in the background. But

Eugene's attention was distracted by a ray of morning sun glinting in the hair of one of the cadets.

Arkhel gold.

He turned to Colonel Lindgren and murmured, "Who *is* that boy?"

Lindgren gave a start; he also had been staring at the contestants—but at Maulevrier's team.

"Which boy, majesty?"

"You have a list of the team members, don't you?"

"The list of competitors?" Lindgren beckoned one of his adjutants forward who presented an elegantly scribed document to the Emperor with a bow. Eugene scanned it, focusing on the names under the heading: Paladur Military Academy.

"Cadets Elyot Branville, Toran Caradas, Piers Lorris . . ." He stopped. The name Caradas was vaguely familiar but for the moment he could not remember where he had heard it before. He turned to summon Gustave to his side but heard the imperial palace band strike up the brisk, uplifting introduction to the New Rossiyan national anthem and was obliged, fuming, to stand to attention. The band master must have interpreted his gesture as the signal to commence the ceremony. This was instantly followed by the more sedate tones of the Tourmaline anthem which gave him longer to gaze at the cadets.

For a moment, I was convinced that Jaromir had come back. He blinked and stared again. *A trick of the sunlight?* But there was no doubt: the cadet had hair of the same distinctive bronzed gold peculiar to the Arkhel bloodline.

Another Arkhel born out of wedlock, like Stavy? Or could it be . . .

"Gustave," Eugene said softly, "find out for me who Toran Caradas is and where he hails from. Go ask the Tourmaline ambassador."

Gustave raised one eyebrow as if to say, "What, *now*?"

"I need to know."

***

Toran, dazzled by the clear Tielen morning sun and the austere grandeur of Swanholm Palace, stared up at the tall, broad-shouldered man on the terrace who, although flanked by high-ranking officers, ministers and ambassadors, drew everyone's gaze.

Emperor Eugene.

In his simple cloud-gray uniform, the Emperor exuded an air of calm authority and confidence as he took the salute of his household troops. Then, as Eugene turned to glance at the contestants, Toran felt for a brief moment as if he had been intimately scrutinized and assessed. Beside him, he sensed Branville tense; was he impressed too, in spite of his earlier disparaging comments?

We've travelled all this way, endured seasickness, weevil-ridden rations, and terrifying storms, just for this moment.

***

"Stop!"

Altan Kazimir skidded to a halt at the foot of the stair leading to Linnaius's laboratory as the two imperial guardsmen on duty blocked his way. "What's wrong?"

"Ah, it's you, Professor." They saluted and stood aside. "There's been an incident. Someone broke into your laboratory."

"They *what*?" Kazimir stumbled and almost fell up the stone steps in his haste to see what had happened. Righting himself, he ran on, wondering what awaited him.

There was no doubt about it; the lock to the laboratory door had been forced.

Kazimir stared in disbelief at the damaged metalwork and found himself wishing—in spite of his rational education—that he had been gifted with the same supernatural abilities as his predecessor Linnaius. When the Magus had been in residence, an invisible barrier kept the contents of his laboratory safe—and several mischievous and ingenious magical booby-traps had scared off the foolhardy who dared to try and enter without Linnaius's permission. He had even fallen foul of one of the Magus's cunningly devised traps himself and the memory was not a pleasant one.

And now the Emperor is waiting for me to bring the new fuel to the competing sky craft pilots so that the competition can begin. He's placed his trust in me. I can't let him down in front of so many eminent guests.

He gingerly pushed the door which opened with a low and sinister creak—and then froze on the threshold.

Suppose the intruder has left some unpleasant surprise behind? A booby trap?

"Are you up there, Professor?"

Kazimir let out a little squeak of surprise. He turned to see Guy Maulevrier ascending the stair, flanked by the two imperial guards who had been stationed at the foot of the stair.

"S-someone's broken in," stammered Kazimir.

"So these gentlemen of the guard have just informed me." Maulevrier looked vexed.

"Were you on duty?" Kazimir turned to the guards, more than a little intimidated by their height and the immaculate smartness of their brass-buttoned uniforms.

"We came to relieve the night watch, Professor," said one. "And it was only then that we noticed the door was ajar. We didn't want to disturb anything inside until you arrived."

"And the palace night watch heard nothing, saw nothing?" Kazimir raked his fingers through his hair, tearing out two or three strands in his agitation.

"They would have raised the alarm, if they had. The intruder must have been quite skilled at sneaking in and out to have slipped past them."

"Well, let's not dawdle," said Maulevrier. "The pilots are eager to make their craft ready for the race. We mustn't keep his imperial majesty waiting."

Kazimir shot him a resentful look. *As if I need to be reminded . . .*

Inside the laboratory, very little appeared to have been displaced or disturbed. Kazimir stared around at the books, still precariously piled high, Linnaius's treatise open at the place he had left it the night before. He had expected to find broken shards of glass beakers, spilled chymical potions, cupboards ransacked, the signs of an intruder's desperate search.

He hurried on toward the inner chamber where he had left the precious fuel in the locked cupboard specially reinforced with double metal doors in case of accidents "of the explosive kind".

That lock had also been broken.

"Oh no, no," Kazimir heard himself muttering aloud as he opened the double doors, fully expecting to find the phials of the precious fuel missing.

"Well?" Maulevrier was right behind him, peering over his shoulder, uncomfortably close.

Kazimir reached in. His fingers made contact with the sleek, cold glass of the stoppered phials.

"They're all still here," he said, puzzled. His suspicions were in no way allayed.

"Perhaps the thief was looking for something else."

Kazimir held first one phial and then the other up to the daylight, examining them. There was no evidence that they had been tampered with and the precious fuel he had spent so long refining from the volatile Azhkendi firedust crystal still gave off a faint glimmer, betraying its potent alchymical nature. He checked the labels. All was in order. The two phials left ready at the front contained the fuel used to power the *Prinsessa Margret*. The more volatile formula that had propelled the *Prinsessa Karila* into the bank of the lake had been moved to the very back of the cupboard.

"Or the thief was disturbed and made his getaway, empty-handed," he heard himself saying, although more in self-reassurance than rational explanation.

The click of military boots briskly climbing the stair made them both look round; moments later, Colonel Lindgren appeared.

"Is all well, Professor? The Emperor is very eager to get the competition underway while the weather holds fair."

Kazimir heard a hint of censure beneath the colonel's polite tone.

"Y-yes, Colonel."

"Then let's go."

Kazimir hastily followed him; in his agitation, he stumbled over the doorstep and felt Maulevrier steady him.

"Perhaps," Guy said easily, "it would be better if I carried the fuel, Professor? You've had a bit of a shock this morning."

"A shock?" To Kazimir's relief, Lindgren's keen ears missed nothing. The colonel stopped and turned around to confront the two academics. "Ah, but wait a moment, Doctor Maulevrier; you have a horse in this race—it wouldn't be right for you to be seen carrying the fuel. People might suspect . . ." And he held out both gray-gloved hands, nodding to Kazimir to give him the phials.

"Touché, Colonel." Guy gave a good-natured laugh as Kazimir, secretly relieved, handed over the volatile liquid.

"So—unlike the cadets from Paladur—you're not going to pilot your flyer yourself, Doctor Maulevrier?" the colonel said as he walked briskly back toward the contestants.

"Indeed no; I have a poor head for heights," Maulevrier said with a self-deprecating smile.

"So, who is the pilot? One of your students?" The question was lightly asked but Kazimir thought he detected a keen edge to Lindgren's affable tone. Surprised, he glanced at the colonel, wondering if he had detected something unusual in the composition of Maulevrier's team.

"My students are here to help fuel and maintain the craft; it's their pride and joy—after all, they built it. But my pilot is newly returned from the colonies; he's been involved in the spice trade and has plenty of experience of navigation at sea."

"And his name?"

"Lorens. Karl Lorens. Have you heard of him?"

Lindgren gave a terse shake of the head as they rounded the corner of the West Wing of the palace and came out onto the wide gravel carriageway where the competing teams were making their final checks and preparations. Maulevrier's students were busy, just as Maulevrier had said, tightening nuts and checking straps. The sea-faring pilot had his back to them, busy, no doubt, in checking the controls.

"Well, I must say these two sky craft make an impressive sight." Lindgren nodded in approval, first at the university team, then at the young men from Paladur Military Academy. He glanced up to the terrace; Kazimir followed his gaze and saw that the Emperor was beginning to show signs of impatience, fidgeting with his immaculately white gloves as he exchanged pleasantries with the ambassadors.

"I think it's time to get this contest underway," Lindgren said softly to Kazimir and gave a swift hand signal to the imperial military band. A crisp roll on the drums and a fanfare from the trumpets drew all the audience toward the balustrade.

***

"The winning craft must be seen to leave the ground and fly—unaided—the length of the grand parterre, then land near the Dievona fountain," Colonel Lindgren announced, making a gesture toward the distant landmark at the far end of the park. "The first to do so successfully will be named the winner of the contest and awarded the Emperor's gold medal."

Toran squinted into the clear sunlight, assessing the challenge. The green lawns, the grass clipped and watered, would make a soft landing if the *Aiglon* came down before reaching the finishing line.

"Professor Kazimir will now add the special fuel to the engines of the two competing crafts, observed by the impartial judges selected by the Emperor."

Branville stood, arms folded tightly across his chest, frowning as the Emperor's representative, Professor Kazimir, carefully poured the *aethyrite* into the *Aiglon*'s fuel tank. Toran watched, trying to quell a niggling sense of unease. Was it the glint of the spring sunlight or did the opaque silvery liquid exude a slight shimmer? He had not noticed anything unusual during the trials the cadets had conducted with his prototype—although its efficacy had necessitated many last-minute alterations and modifications to the cogs and pistons. And the assurance that the black swan pleasure craft that graced the palace canals were now safely using the new fuel to power their little engines was in no way reassuring.

The professor's hands shook as he tipped in the last drops, hastily wiping away the residue with a fine linen cloth. Colonel Lindgren, who had been looking on to ensure the procedure was carried out correctly, escorted him over to the rival craft which stood on the far side of the gravel drive. A shadow loomed over Toran and, glancing up, he saw Branville glowering down at him as he and Lorris carried out their final checks.

"Making us their guinea pigs," he muttered. "I don't like it. Not at all."

"At least our opponents are forced to comply with this condition as well." Toran nodded toward the rival flying craft. "We're up against the brains of the Tielborg University Faculty of Mechanical Arts. We must look like raw schoolboys to them."

Clustered around the rival machine were a group of students, all busily completing the final checks on their flyer, supervised by their team leader. The man who was to pilot their craft stood a little way off, observing the frantic activity with what seemed like detached amusement. He was tall and lean, with deeply tanned skin, and Toran could not help but think he looked more like an experienced sailor than an academic.

A sudden unwelcome sensation flared within him, setting his nerves jangling: fear of failure. He wished—not for the first time—that Gerard was there to support them.

"The contestants will shake hands," announced Lindgren. "Then they will start their engines. Princess

Karila will then give the signal for the race to commence."

Toran and Branville walked out to meet their opponents. The pilot introduced himself as Karl Lorens. Even though he said nothing other than his name, there was a distinctly devil-may-care confidence in the nonchalant way he sauntered back to his craft as its inventor came forward to acknowledge them.

So this was Doctor Maulevrier. *"When you get to Tielen, stay well away from Guy Maulevrier."* Bernay's warning echoed in Toran's memory. *"He's a man who doesn't like to lose. If he offers help—in the most charming of ways—just don't accept."*

He looked at the man who had called Gerard Bernay a cheat and had brought about his disqualification from the competition. He had imagined a sallow-faced fellow with a hungry, mistrustful gaze but found himself shaking hands with an affable-looking man in his mid-thirties, sandy hair cropped short in the military style favored by the Emperor.

"Two pilots? Your flyer can lift two men into the air?" The question was asked with the unmistakable inference that it could not. Branville shrugged and grinned back at Maulevrier. Toran knew that wolfish grin well by now; Branville was spoiling for a fight.

But his attention was distracted by the rival team's craft, fully revealed as the students stripped away the protective covers.

There was no doubt about it; the Tielborg University flyer, the *Svala*, bore a remarkable similarity to the one he had seen and studied in Bernay's plans. The one that had been disqualified. And Toran had no doubt in his mind as to which man had come up with the design the first. Faced with the indisputable proof that Gerard's hard work and ingenuity had been usurped, he heard himself saying out loud, each word cold and clear, "I've seen that flyer design before. On the drawing board in Gerard Bernay's office last autumn in Paladur."

"And how would you know Gerard Bernay, young man?" Guy Maulevrier's expression was unchanged, his confident smile as bright as before.

"Bernay's my mentor," Toran said, aware that Branville was scowling at him but carrying on, nonetheless. "He taught me a great deal. He's a very talented ingenieur."

"I can't argue with that fact," Maulevrier said lightly. "But I hope your instructors at the academy were aware that he left the university in disgrace."

"Disgrace?" Branville's shadow loomed over Toran; he had obviously been listening. "A scandal?"

"I'm afraid that Gerard Bernay's morals were in no way equal to his talents as an ingenieur." Maulevrier's voice dropped as though he were about to confide an unpleasant truth. "He forced himself on one of the younger students."

Toran heard the assertion but the violent and disturbing images it conjured up stirred first feelings of shock and then utter disbelief. "Surely not!"he heard himself saying. It had to be a lie. A false allegation. "The Gerard Bernay I know is not the kind of man to do such a thing."

"Ah, but how well do you really know him?" Maulevrier gave him a pitying glance. "The young man concerned was uncommonly good-looking, fair-haired, not so unlike you, now I come to think of it; Bernay obviously favors your type."

This was taking things too far; the sly insinuation made Toran clench his fists to stop himself from punching Doctor Maulevrier.

"And you, Doctor? What's *your* type?" Branville said with an unmistakable leer; he put one arm protectively around Toran's shoulders. "This one's already spoken for." Toran was so surprised that he didn't react to Branville's teasing as he would normally have done—with a shove and a string of expletives. Maulevrier's smile froze and his eyes narrowed. He gave a brief nod of farewell and turned away to return to his students.

Toran heard Branville swear under his breath and, gazing up at him, saw that his dark gaze was still fixed on the Tielen ingenieur.

"How dare he?" he heard him mutter, his fingers tightening on Toran's shoulder.

"You came to Ingenieur Bernay's defense," Toran said, still surprised. "I thought you hated him."

Branville swiftly withdrew his arm. "Let's show 'em what we can do, Arkhel."

And before Toran could reply, Branville grabbed him around the waist and hefted him into the front seat. Toran, caught off-guard, was so surprised that Branville was strong enough to sweep him off his feet, that he forgot to upbraid him for using his family name instead of Caradas.

"Start her up, Lorris!" Branville shouted as he clambered in behind Toran. Toran nodded to Lorris who had been hopping nervously up and down at the side, waiting for his signal. Branville's excitement was infectious; Toran felt a very different energy radiating from his co-pilot who was seated so close behind him that he could feel his breath, hot on the back of his neck. Branville was actually *enjoying* himself. After weeks of sullen moods and rude or disparaging remarks, Elyot Branville was revealing his true self. Toran sensed that he relished the challenge and the danger.

The engine shuddered once or twice then chugged into life. The whole craft vibrated in rhythm with the beats of the pistons

"On my mark, pilots!" said Lindgren, his voice sharp and commanding, as if on the parade ground. He drew his saber and positioned himself where both teams could see the blade glinting in the sunlight.

The Emperor's daughter, a slender, fair-haired girl, had appeared at his side on the terrace. *She looks just like Clarisse,* Toran thought, distracted by a sudden longing to see his younger sister again. But as Eugene turned to the princess and placed a white handkerchief in her hand, Toran pushed all thoughts of family from his mind, intent on listening to the hum and chug of his engine. He could feel every vibration and beat as if it was an extension of his own body and when the white handkerchief fluttered, his heart fluttered too.

Colonel Lindgren's saber slashed the air like a bolt of lightning.

"We're off!" yelled Branville in Toran's ear. Toran tugged on the lever that opened the throttle. Lorris gave a yelp and leapt out of the way as the *Aiglon* careered forward. The noise from both engines was deafening.

The wind—as they gathered speed—became a roar, drowning out the cheers of the onlookers.

They zoomed down the long drive over the white gravel. Toran risked a swift glance at their opponent and saw—to his astonishment—the rival sky craft lift into the air.

And they were still on the ground.

"Now, Toran!" Branville's shout startled him. His heart pounding, he pulled the lever that released more fuel into the engine. Branville adjusted the rudder so that the nose of the craft pointed toward the heavens and suddenly they were rising, skimming above the gravel drive, gaining on the the rival craft.

Toran let out a whoop of elation. "This *aethyrite*— it's amazing!"

"There's the fountain. I'll circle around toward that far lawn." Branville's voice was hardly audible above the rushing sound of the wind and the growl of the engine.

"Have we won?" Toran could see the wide bassin below, more a small lake than a fountain, could see their pale reflection in the rippling waters passing above the statue of the goddess like a white bird.

"Less power," Branville shouted. "Or we'll overshoot."

Toran employed the lever to reduce the steady flow of fuel to a trickle and slow the pistons. But still they flew on. The Dievona fountain was already behind them and the graceful curve of Swanholm Palace was dwindling into the distance. And an ominous puttering sound began to issue from the engine.

***

Nils Lindgren shielded his eyes against the sun as he watched both flyers rise into the air, and approach the finish line at the Dievona Fountain. Around him he heard the onlookers gasp in awe as the noisy engines chugged past, flying down the long white gravel drive.

It was a splendid sight. But something was bothering him, scratching uncomfortably like a claw at the back of his mind. Maulevrier's pilot. The name, Karl Lorens, was unfamiliar, but something about the man's stance and the lithe way he had moved as he leapt into the flyer, jogged a memory—and not a pleasant one.

Oskar Alvborg: his scourge and tormentor from military academy days.

It couldn't be. Surely he wouldn't dare break his terms of exile and risk execution.

Lindgren turned to gaze up at the Emperor and the princess; Eugene was following the competitors' progress through a nautical spy-glass and seemed not to have noticed; neither, it seemed, had the princess.

***

The *Aiglon* flew on—and so did the *Svala*.

Yet no matter how much strength Branville exerted into tugging back on the rudder to try to keep the *Aiglon* aloft, no matter how much Toran tried to regulate the flow of fuel powering the engine, the puttering sound grew louder and the craft began to lose height rapidly.

"Hold her steady!" Toran yelled above the hissing and rattling emanating from his precious mechanisms.

"What the fuck d'you think I'm trying to do here?" Branville was straining to steer the craft away from the tall pines looming ahead, the outer reaches of the vast forest that delineated the Swanholm estate's northern boundaries.

"We're coming down too fast!"

"D'you think I don't know that?" Toran heard a note of desperation in Branville's voice above the howl of the wind as the ill-controlled descent, nose-first, continued. "Do *your* job, Arkhel, and slow her down so I can do mine."

Branville's scared. Things must be bad. Are we going to die? Toran pushed the rising tide of fear away, forcing himself to concentrate on the practical. *What would Gerard advise?*

The engine was hiccupping and a dark plume of smoke had begun to issue from beneath the craft. With each erratic beat, the craft lost height. They were skimming the tops of the pine trees; branches scraped the undercarriage.

"Clearing up ahead," Toran shouted. "If I stop the engine, can you do the rest?"

"Can I hell?" came back Branville's grim reply.

Toran cut the engine.

The craft went plummeting down, the left wing scraping against the branches of a giant fir, skewing the angle of descent as they skidded onto the mossy green of the glade floor. But still the *Aiglon* kept going, bumping over tree roots, hurtling onward.

Toran heard, as if from far away, his own voice screaming above the rush of the wind.

And then the *Aiglon* crunched into the screen of trees at the far end of the clearing. There was a flash of searing white light and all sounds, all smells, all sensations abruptly cut out.

Chapter 47

"Out of my way!" The Winged Warrior's voice blasted through the roar of the wind and rain, its metallic timbre making Gerard's ears ring until he feared his eardrums would burst. The blast sizzling directly toward Gerard went wide, diverted by the newcomer's arrival.

The old man deftly steered the little craft around, placing himself between the Warrior and Gerard cowering below. The wet air shimmered with silvery sky-dragon scales as more and more flocked to the old man, filling the sky with their snaking, sinuous bodies.

In the roar of the gale, Gerard could not make out the words issuing from the old man's lips. But the fiery angel hesitated even as he was about to launch another blast of golden fire. The light in his eyes had dimmed. The crackling hum emanating from his flame-tipped wings diminished until Gerard heard the old man cry out in commanding tones.

"Be gone, Ardarel!"

A great rent opened in the clouds massing overhead. The angel retreated, disappearing into the swirling gray.

Gerard, mouth and throat heat-scorched, drew in a raw, ragged breath of rain-chilled air. He tried to stand up and fell down again. When he raised his head again, he saw that the old man had deftly steered his sky-craft to earth and was carefully disembarking.

"This wasn't quite the way I'd intended for us to meet," he said, turning to face him.

Gerard blinked, dazzled by eyes that were as silvered as his own, glittering with icy striations, piercingly intelligent in spite of the old man's weathered, lined skin and wild wisps of windblown white hair.

"Y-you have the advantage, Sieur," Gerard stammered, feeling as if he had just been intimately scrutinized. He staggered to his feet, slipping a little on the sleet-sheened grass.

"My name is Linnaius. Kaspar Linnaius." And the stranger held out his wrinkled hand to Gerard. Gerard, not certain that he had heard aright, automatically reached out and took the extended hand in his own, pressing it with warmth and profound gratitude. For there was something strangely familiar about the elderly man, even though he was certain they had never met; he would certainly have remembered encountering someone as charismatic as this before.

"Let me look at you." Kaspar Linnaius placed his other hand on Gerard's shoulder and gazed at him intently. There was an otherworldly air about him: his skin was translucent, as if too thinly stretched over his bones, lending an air of great age and frailty.

"Hmm," Linnaius said at length, "I see something of myself in you. My much younger self," he added wryly. "You're Gerard Bernay, aren't you? I'm your great-grandfather."

"My great-grandfather?" Gerard had only a hazy memory of his grandfathers, both long dead, so the appearance of an even older antecedent was a challenging concept to come to terms with.

"My hair was once that color too . . . and your profile owes more to the Verniers than the Tivadars."

"I beg your pardon?" Gerard had no idea what his self-styled great-grandfather was talking about. Still shaken from the encounter with the Winged Warrior and the clash of the clans, he gazed uneasily beyond Linnaius to the damaged gatehouse. The Nagarians— those that were still on their feet—had begun to shout, aiming their crossbows in their direction.

"We can't talk here," said Linnaius. He climbed back into the craft and beckoned to Gerard to join him. Gerard, not certain if he was awake or dreaming, hesitated and then as the druzhina began to run toward them, hastily clambered in.

"Izkael!" cried Linnaius and Gerard saw the long, lithe translucent dragon that had coiled itself, patiently waiting, on the ground, uncoil and dart upward. With a jolt that sent Gerard grasping at the side, the craft rose into the air. To his amazement, he saw other silvery sky dragons dart down to help lift the craft and bear it upward, deftly avoiding the shaggy overhanging branches of firs, until the druzhina below were as tiny as fallen pine cones and they were far beyond the reach of their crossbow bolts.

"Do sit down," said Linnaius who had settled himself in the stern of the craft, one hand on a rudder.

"You'll find it more comfortable—and there's less danger of you falling over the side."

Speechless, Gerard obeyed, cautiously settling himself on the rugs beside the old man, moving slowly so as not to disturb the balance of the little craft. He stroked the grain of the wood, wondering what kind it might be: ash or hazel, durable, yet light, more like a boat, expertly constructed by a master of the ship-building trade.

"What was that creature?" Gerard's sight was still scarred by flames; his mind still dazzled by the glare of the fiery blade. "You called it Ardarel. It looked like . . . an angel."

"Ardarel is one of the Seven Heavenly Guardians of the mortal world. Some people call him and his brethren angels."

Gerard's mother had instilled in her children a respect for the tenets of the Church and had kept a little statue of Saint Klara in a little niche in their house. But he had never once imagined that the angels in the luminous stained-glass windows in the parish church with their calm expressions could be anything other than benign protectors.

"What have I done wrong? Why did he want to punish me? I've really led quite a boring life." Gerard laughed but there was no relief in the laughter. Boring . . . but not chaste or sin-free in the eyes of the strait-laced Tielen Church. He even found himself wondering if this could be some punishment called down on him for making Edvin his lover.

"I'm to blame, Gerard. You've inherited the curse—or the gift—of the silver eyes from me. You have mage blood. And the Guardians have but one design: to destroy us."

The craft flew on; already they had left the forest behind and were skimming high above the moors. Gerard caught sight of the huts of the miners below and the raw earthen scars where they had been digging.

"But—but why? Do we pose such a threat to them?"

"We are the living proof that one of their kind transgressed. He fell in love and lay with a mortal woman and we are his descendants. The indisputable proof shows in our eyes and in our elemental powers— powers that mortals were never meant to possess."

Gerard tried to digest this information. To his rational mind, it was the stuff of legends. There had to be a better explanation . . . yet here he was, seated in a little flying boat, drawn through the air by wouivres, skimming over Azhkendir at a faster speed than he had imagined his flyer could ever achieve.

"Since then, Ardarel and his kin have pursued us relentlessly. They leant their powers to certain saints and convinced them that we should all be burned as sinners to purge the mortal world of our malign influence. Not surprisingly, there are very few of us left."

"Then why did Ardarel retreat just now?"

"Ha!" Linnaius let out a curt laugh, all the while keeping his eyes fixed on the skies ahead, one hand on the tiller. "Because the Guardians are aethyrial beings. They can't tolerate the atmosphere of the mortal world for long. It weakens them. Which is why they used the saints as their agents. They can only last here for a few minutes."

Gerard considered this. "So, even with all their powers, they haven't yet found a way to survive here?"

"There is a way. To take on—share—a mortal body. But it's anathema to them. They'd rather use other mortals to do their 'holy' work for them. They want to close the forbidden ways to and from the Aethyrial Realm which those with mage blood in their veins and certain crafty shamans have been using to slip in and out. And I fear they'll pursue us until they've achieved their goal."

Gerard had begun to shiver; the chill of the winds was numbing him, slowing his thoughts.

"Wrap yourself in the rugs," said Linnaius, thrusting one toward him. "You're not accustomed to traveling at this great height where the air is thin."

"Where are you taking us?"Gerard asked, pulling the rug tightly about him.

"To introduce you to my patron, the Emperor."

"Emperor Eugene?"

"Is there any other?" Linnaius gave him a stern look from beneath his wispy white brows.

And then Gerard remembered. "The flying contest."

"Eh?" It was his great-grandfather's turn to look confused.

"The Emperor is holding a contest. My protégé Toran has reached the final stage. The challenge was to design a sky-craft and fly it. "

To Gerard's surprise, Linnaius chuckled. "Just like Eugene," he said, more to himself than Gerard. "Still so impatient. These things take time. I've only been gone a year . . . And how, pray tell, are these sky-craft supposed to move through the air?"

"Toran made mention of a special fuel that would power the engines."

"A special fuel?" There was a note of disapproval in Linnaius's voice that disturbed Gerard.

"And yet the prototype *Aiglon* flew perfectly without the need of any special fuel. I helped in the manufacturing of the components. I know it works—"

"Well, of course anything that you touched would absorb something of your gift." Linnaius's reply was salted with an unmistakable tinge of exasperation. "But you were unaware of it, I suppose, so you can't be held responsible."

"You mean that any of the flying mechanisms I helped to construct would fly successfully because of the powers I've inherited from you?" Gerard was just beginning to realize the import of his great-grandfather's words and their implications. "But I had no hand in the construction of the full-scale *Aiglon*." He sat bolt upright, setting the craft shaking. "Dear God, that means those cadets are in danger. We all assumed the *Aiglon* could fly because of the design of the wings and the efficiency of the little engine and . . ."

He felt a hand on his shoulder and looking up saw his great-grandfather regarding him intently.

"When did you say this contest was to take place?"

"Dievona's Night. At the palace of Swanholm ."

"Today. Then we may still get there in time."

Chapter 48

The two competing sky-craft, airborne, reached the wide bassin of the Dievona Fountain. Eugene leaned forward, shading his eyes, eager to see which one had landed the first. The spectators all strained in the same direction, Major Bauldry training his spyglass on the distant craft which, like two white-winged cranes, flew onward.

Behind him he could hear Altan Kazimir agitatedly muttering under his breath, "It can't have been the fuel. No it can't have been."

"Lindgren!" Eugene turned to the colonel who was staring, mouth open. "Why haven't they landed? Where are they going?"

The sky-craft disappeared from view.

"I confess I have no idea." Lindgren seemed frozen; suddenly he blinked and addressed Eugene. "Permission to organize a rescue party, majesty."

"Granted."

As the colonel hurried away, calling for his adjutants, Eugene put one hand on Karila's shoulder to reassure her. It was only then that he realized that she was still staring fixedly into the sky; she had not even turned her head to follow the progress of the flyers toward the fountain.

"Kari?" he said sharply. She blinked and seemed to wake from whatever trance she had fallen into. Fears stirred within him from a time—not so long ago—when she had been inextricably linked to Khezef. The daemon-Drakhaoul had even called her his soul-child. Forgetting for a moment about the flyers, he gently cupped her face in his hands, tilting it up to his. "What's wrong?"

She gave a little shudder and he saw his own fear mirrored in her eyes. "It couldn't be," she said softly. "I thought . . . just for a moment . . . I sensed Sahariel."

"Sahariel?" Eugene echoed. His half-brother Oskar's Drakhaoul. The one who had kidnapped Karila. "But there's no way Sahariel could still be here."

At that moment, Gustave reappeared, pushing his way through the throng.

"Countess Marta," Eugene said, beckoning to Karila's governess. "Please escort the princess indoors and find her some refreshment."

"Will the cadets be all right, Papa?" Karila asked as the countess guided her away.

"Don't worry, my dear, we'll see to it that those brave young men don't come to any harm." He heard the easy reassurance in his voice and hated himself for lying to her. As he turned to Gustave, he was already wondering how he would make adequate recompense to the Tourmalise government, the Paladur Military Academy and the boys' families, if they did not survive the flight.

"Toran Caradas," Gustave said in an undertone as the other guests were ushered by the palace staff to the back of the terrace where punch and caraway cakes were being served, "is Jaromir Arkhel's younger cousin and only son and heir to Lord Ranozhir Arkhel. His mother's father was Lord Denys Caradas of Serrigonde in Tourmalise."

Stricken, Eugene gazed at Gustave. "So he's Jaro's cousin. And we may just have unwittingly sent the boy to an untimely death." The thought chilled him. He spotted Major Bauldry trying to rally the other cadets who were standing around looking confused. Doctor Maulevrier's students looked equally bewildered.

The sound of horses' hooves crunching on gravel made all the onlookers swivel their heads as Colonel Lindgren led a small detachment of imperial cavalry at the gallop toward the Dievona Fountain. Following behind was a small closed carriage which Eugene recognized as belonging to his physician Doctor Amandel; Gustave had prudently thought to anticipate all eventualities.

Jaro's cousin. Eugene was seized with an overwhelming impulse to accompany the rescue party. "Gustave, cover for me," he said and before his secretary could object, he hurried away, swiftly descending the sweeping staircase and calling to the sentries on duty for a horse.

∗∗∗

Beyond the gray-green Saltyk Sea far below Gerard spotted land: a rugged coastline with bays and inlets. As they drew nearer he could make out ports, harbors, the weather-boarded houses painted in the colors favored by his countrymen: red, blue, green, to brighten the long dark months of winter.

"Is this really Tielen?" He could hardly believe that they had traveled so far in such a short time.

"We're heading to the palace of Swanholm," Linnaius said. And then he leaned forward, resting his free hand on Gerard's shoulder. "Listen, Gerard, if anything happens to me, you must go straight to Enhirre. There's a hidden community of mages there. They'll train you and keep you safe from Ardarel."

"Enhirre?" Gerard repeated. "That's half a world away. And how will I track down these mages if they're in hiding?"

"I've written it all down for you and left the book with an old friend, Chinua. He's got it in safe-keeping for you."

"How do I find this Chinua?"

"The wouivres will take you to him. Although he's in just as much in danger from Ardarel as we are; he's a shaman with shape-shifting powers."

Instinctively, Gerard glanced into the sky, dreading to see the burnished gleam of fire-tipped feathers streaking through the clouds toward them, in pursuit once more. One question came to the fore of his mind. "Why?" he asked. "Why are the angels attacking us, not defending us?" He felt betrayed. He had always thought he was a rational man, a man of science who no longer believed in the numinous, let alone the stories from holy scripture he had listened to in church as a child.

"Because we represent rebellion and disobedience. Our existence threatens the order they were created to preserve and protect."

"And if he returns?"

"Our only defense is to outrun him until he tires again."

That was of little comfort to Gerard who was beginning to suffer from a delayed reaction to the tumultuous events of the day. He didn't want to reveal how he felt to his great-grandfather, fearing that Linnaius would see it as a sign of weakness. But almost as if he had read his thoughts, Linnaius said, "You must be hungry and thirsty after so long a journey. There's rye bread and cheese tucked inside that little basket beside you. And a bottle or two of cider; help yourself."

Gerard didn't hesitate; he couldn't even remember if he'd eaten that morning before hurrying in pursuit of Iarko and the miners. The provisions were wrapped in a red-and-white checked cloth. He unwrapped them and tore off a hunk of Tielen rye bread. It was hard to chew but the taste of caraway was nostalgic; rye bread was not baked that way in Azhkendir or Tourmalise.

"What about you?" he asked, turning back to Linnaius who shook his head with the faintest hint of a smile softening his austere expression.

After Gerard had eaten half the loaf and some of the salty cheese, washing it down with dry, cloudy Tielen cider, he felt less shaky.

"Down there." Linnaius pointed. Gerard craned his neck and saw the austere but elegant buildings of a palace constructed of light stone: two curved wings on either side of a main building set in a great green park, laid out with white-graveled carriageways radiating outward, the longest of them stretching down to a lake and a fountain supplied by a dark canal. "Swanholm."

"Where are the competitors?" Gerard squinted into the sunlight for any sign of flying craft or crowds of spectators. "Has the competition happened already and we've missed it?" He could not hide the disappointment in his voice.

"Horsemen." Far below a group of gray-uniformed cavalrymen were riding past the fountain, followed by a little carriage, pursued by a lone horseman riding at full gallop. "Dear me; what is the boy doing now?" Linnaius said under his breath with a perplexed little laugh.

Gerard looked at him questioningly. "You recognize that horseman from this great height?"

"That is the Emperor. My protégé and student before he succeeded his father. But as to what he's doing . . ."

But Gerard's attention was distracted; on the horizon two faint columns of black smoke were rising into the clear air. Beyond the parkland he could see moorlands stretching into the far distance, flanked by a forest to the west. One column of smoke was rising from the forest; the other was further to the east, above the moors. They could have been woodcutters' fires, but there was something about the darkness of the smoke that suggested burning oil . . . or fuel. What had Toran written to his father? "The finalists will be using a new fuel especially created by the Emperor's alchymists."

He gripped the rim of the sky-craft with both hands, leaning out perilously far as he tried to ignore the nightmare of burning flyers that had disturbed his sleep.

"Would a new alchymical fuel make smoke that dark?"

Linnaius narrowed his eyes as he stared toward the two columns smirching the air.

"Let's go and investigate."

Chapter 49

The foul stink of burning engine oil brought Elyot Branville back to semi-consciousness. He could also smell pine sap and his own sweat, rank with fear.

Burning. Smoke. *Danger.*

His dazed mind slowly registered that all these pungent smells were a warning. He tried to move and found, blinking through a haze of eye-stinging smoke, that he was lying across the nose of the *Aiglon*, still attached by his harness, as the sky-craft dangled from the wide branches of a pine tree.

"Damn it all to hell." *Must get out.* Some basic survival instinct awoke, forcing him to fumble for the sheathed knife in his belt to hack and saw at the straps as the smell of burning grew more pungent.

Suddenly the severed fibers broke under his weight and he tumbled to the ground, landing clumsily on his back. Black smoke was gusting from the sky-craft; he could see orange flames leaping higher.

Get clear.

Only as he righted himself did he remember that he had not been alone.

"Arkhel!" he yelled over the growing roar of the flames. "*Toran!*" His voice cracked as he strained to make himself heard. There was no answering shout. "Damn it, Toran, where are you?" Had he fallen clear before the craft hit the tree? He could be lying injured, unconscious nearby . . . or worse, he might still be trapped in the flaming wreckage overhead.

A sharp, crushing pain suddenly flared in Branville's chest as he staggered from beneath the burning wreck of their craft. He gasped aloud, clutching at his side. Had he cracked some ribs in the crash? There wasn't time to pay attention to the pain. For all he knew, the burning fuel in the *Aiglon* might explode at any moment. The black, billowing smoke was making it hard to breathe, let alone see.

And then he tripped over a body lying sprawled on the ground.

"Toran?"

He must have been thrown clear at the moment of impact. But was he still breathing? Heart thudding, he knelt down and turned him over. To his relief, he heard Toran let out a low groan.

He slung Toran's left arm over his shoulder and staggered away across the mossy clearing, dragging the barely conscious young man one slow step at a time.

***

Toran gradually became aware that he was being hauled over bumpy ground. His head throbbed with every movement and the air was filled with the noxious stink of smoke. Through half-open lids he saw that his rescuer was Elyot Branville. And there was something oddly reassuring in being supported against the older cadet's broad shoulders.

"S'you, Branville?" he heard himself saying, slurring his words drunkenly.

"There's a hut up ahead. We can rest there."

Tucked in beneath the trees stood a little stone hut with a shingled roof; as they stumbled closer, Toran saw that the place had a distinctly neglected air.

"Hallo!" Branville called. Toran heard desperation as his strong voice cracked. "Anyone at home?" He thumped the warped wooden door with his free hand. There was no response. He kicked it and it creaked inward; the darkness beyond smelled of damp and cold ashes.

"Must be a shepherd's hut. Or whatever they herd this far north in Tielen. Reindeer?"

Propping Toran up against the outer wall, he ducked beneath the low lintel and went inside. "Earth floor, fireplace, pretty basic but shelter," he called back.

Toran didn't care; he just wanted to lie down. His head was still spinning and his breathing and heartbeat refused to slow to a more regular rhythm. *I must be in shock.* He felt ashamed to show weakness in front of Branville, of all people. Later, he knew he would be subjected to merciless ribbing for being so weak. *If there is a "later" for us.*

"No one's been here for a while." Branville reappeared. "But there's firewood. We can light a fire."

***

"Sabotage." Toran looked wearily up at Branville. He was so tired he could barely enunciate the word.

"You think someone interfered with the engine?" Branville's dark eyes caught the firelight, gleaming through the smears of oil and smoke streaking his face.

Toran nodded. "That or the fuel. Someone who didn't care if we lived or died. Someone who wanted to win so desperately that they were prepared to risk everything in making it look like an accident."

"By God, when we get back, there's going to be hell to pay." Branville clenched one fist, holding it up to the firelight. "I'm not going to stay silent about this."

"It'll be almost impossible to prove." Toran could not stop shivering. "We have no evidence—just our narrow escape and a burned-out wreck."

"But if Maulevrier's craft won, we know who to suspect." Branville took a swig from his silver hip flask and passed it to Toran. "This'll warm you up."

Toran automatically took a mouthful and wheezed as the fiery brandy inside scalded his mouth. Trust Branville to carry neat spirits.

"Perhaps there's a farm nearby where we can ask for help in the morning. Maybe someone saw the flames or heard the crash . . ."

"Or maybe we're too far from anywhere. Surely anyone who saw the flames would have come to investigate by now."

In spite of the fire and the brandy, Toran's teeth began to chatter. He pulled his tattered coat closer to himself, tucking his knees beneath his chin. Earlier he had not felt anything but now his bruises had begun to hurt. *Must be the shock of the crash. I thought I was made of stronger stuff.* He didn't want Branville to see him in such a weakened and demoralized state.

"Are you all right, Arkhel?"

Toran swore; Branville had noticed. "J-just cold. And tired." He curled up before the blaze on the earth floor, feeling the fire's warmth on his face—but the shivering didn't stop. "I need sleep. It's been a long day. Too long."

Branville leaned forward and put another branch on the blaze, setting off a fizz of blue sparks. Toran heard him draw in his breath as he did so; he must be feeling his bruises too.

"Come here," Branville said. "You're shivering. Your teeth are chattering."

Toran saw him pat the floor beside him. He shook his head.

"I said: come here."

"I'm fine where I am."

"Then I'll come to you."

Branville lurched a little, sliding down, back against the stone wall, right next to Toran.

"You're not in your right mind. You must have taken a bump to the head when we crashed." The words came babbling out, but to Toran's annoyance the chattering of his teeth made them sound pathetically unconvincing.

"Why?" Branville said. "Why won't you look at me, Toran Arkhel? Why do you ignore me? Why can't you see me for who I really am?"

"How much brandy have you drunk?" Toran tried to inch away but Branville reached out and pulled him close, holding him against his own body, his arms crossed over his chest so he couldn't wriggle free.

"We should have died. We're too young to die. There's so many regrets."

"Regrets?"

"I'll be twenty next week. I'd like at least to have had the Emperor award us the gold medal and shake us by the hand for winning his contest fair and square. To recognize the craft and the skill and all the damned hard work."

Branville's voice had grown softer; it might be the brandy that had loosened his tongue but Toran was surprised to hear him speaking so candidly. The heat of Branville's body had begun to seep into his own, calming the involuntary juddering. The tightly restraining arms felt strangely reassuring. Toran's head began to droop against Branville's shoulder. It was too much of an effort to keep alert and on the defensive. Branville was still talking, half to himself, and his breath was warm on the back of Toran's neck.

Have I misread his moodiness and that infuriating bloody-minded attitude of his?

Have I misjudged him?

Chapter 50

Karl Lorens—Oskar Alvborg, bastard son of Prince Karl the Navigator of Tielen and unacknowledged exiled younger half-brother of the Emperor Eugene— lay on the stony ground, stunned, staring up at the sky. He wasn't quite certain how he had survived the crash. Kazimir's alchymical fuel had sent both of the competing sky-craft much further than the length of the grand parterre. The flight had been crazily, heart-stoppingly exhilarating. Until it ended in the engine puttering, then cutting out, sending the craft spiraling down, nose-first, out of the sky.

Just when he thought his time was up and he would crash into oblivion, shattering bone and flesh as the craft hit the ground, a rent appeared in the sky overhead and a bolt of fiery light pierced the clouds.

Something broke his headlong descent.

And I flew again.

He hadn't realized how much he had missed the sensation, the freedom, the sheer elation of skimming through the sky. Nothing in his life—not even being pleasured by the most celebrated courtesan of the Tielen court—had ever come anywhere near. Even if it had been bought at a terrible price: sharing his body, his mind with the daemon Drakhaoul Sahariel.

But Sahariel had abandoned him, leaving the mortal world, passing into a far and distant dimension. And then Eugene banished him—his own half-brother— for the many crimes the daemon had forced him to commit. An unjust banishment. How could he have resisted Sahariel's forceful will? Eugene knew, better than anyone, how hard it was to defy a Drakhaoul once they got inside your consciousness.

And I was so close to winning your damned competition, brother.

He had often fantasized about stepping up to receive the gold medal from the unsuspecting Emperor and at the moment their heads came close as Eugene bent down to place the ribbon around his neck, sliding a concealed blade into his grip and plunging it deep into his brother's throat. Bathed in a warm fountain of his blood as the horrified courtiers stared, too shocked to do anything to help their dying Emperor, gasping his last, gargling breath at his feet . . .

A breathless laugh escaped Oskar's throat—cut short as the pain from innumerable lacerations and bruises shot through him.

He kept fading in and out of consciousness. The impact—which had flung him clear and into a clump of cloudberry bushes—had left him miraculously alive but horribly scratched by the thorns.

Some way off, the sky-craft still burned, a black column of foul-smelling smoke smirching the clear air. Eventually, he reckoned dully, it would eventually attract a rescue party to these bleak moorlands. Or so he hoped.

"So this is one of them." A deep voice . . . but why did he have the strange sensation that it was resonating within his mind?

"Help me . . ." Oskar forced his eyes open to see if rescue had arrived but the effort was too great and they closed again.

"It doesn't work, Nuriel." So there were two. *"I've tried. Our bodies can't adapt to the air of this world."*

Each word set off little ripples of color in Oskar's head: flame-red, fading through copper to orange.

"If we are to carry out our assignment in the mortal world, there's no other way but to copy what Khezef and his kin did."

Khezef? He must be hallucinating.

"The Drakhaouls made free use of the mortal bodies of Artamon's descendants. They adapted them to host their aethyrial forms. We will do the same."

"And this is one of them. This is Sahariel's host."

"But he's injured. Broken."

"All the easier for us to take control of him and bend him to our will."

Oskar had the unsettling feeling that the unseen speakers were hovering right above him. Did they realize he could hear them discussing him? Or did they just not care?

"But that means we commit the same sin for which we punished Nagazdiel."

"His sin—which brought shame on our kind—was to forget his true nature. To become one of them. Even to lie with a mortal woman. I would never stoop so low."

Oskar could not help but smile. At any moment, he would come back to his senses and find that he was alone on the lonely scrubland, the martial voices just a figment conjured by his confused and injured brain.

"But if you possess this one, can you gain control of him in time to carry out Prince Galizur's mission? You failed twice before. Such failure is very costly—to you and your aethyrial powers."

"The two magi are close at hand. I won't fail a third time."

"Then . . ." and the one called Nuriel paused as though considering what was being proposed. *"I place my trust in you. Do what needs to be done and return."*

A golden, fiery warmth enveloped Oskar. For one panicked moment he was certain that the flames from the burning flyer had spread through the heather and he was about to be consumed. *Death by fire.* But the panic melted away as the gilded heat overwhelmed him in a soothing cloud. *Like sinking into the healing waters of a steamy hot spring.* The gnawing pain in his bruised and broken limbs ebbed away. The sensation was so pleasurable after the brutal reality of the crash that he felt tears welling up—a singularly unfamiliar sensation.

Distracted by his own confused feelings, he did not at first notice the slow, subtle infiltration until a voice murmured from within his mind, *"Don't be afraid, mortal. I have healed your wounds. Now I need to use your body to fulfill my mission."*

"Wait a—" Oskar began and then realized that the healing fiery warmth was coursing through his veins, energizing his body until he was pulsing with strength. For some reason he could not quite yet grasp he had been chosen to host this powerful being. "Who *are* you?"

"We cannot stay here." The being ignored his question. Next moment, Oskar felt himself rising—shakily—to his feet, propelled by the other's volition, not his own.

"Wait!" While he still had some control over his own body, he knew he must resist until he understood more of the being's purpose. "What is your mission? Why do you need me to help you?"

"Brace yourself, mortal."

"I have a name! Oskar Alvborg. Count of—" A sudden convulsive spasm pitched him off his feet and onto the dry heather again, face first. "What the hell?"

"It seems I have not quite understood how a mortal body works yet . . ." Not so much a reply as a puzzled musing, failing to include him in the conversation. *"Time to make a modification or two."*

Before Oskar could protest any further, he felt an extraordinary build-up of pressure in his back. Something seemed to have infiltrated itself beneath his skin and was trying to force its way out. This was not the way it had been with Sahariel. An involuntary cry of pain broke from Oskar's mouth, incoherent and raw. He sensed the being within him react as well, mirroring his own pain with surprise and confusion.

"I had no idea it would be so overwhelming."

"What . . . are you . . . *doing* to me?" Oskar managed to get the words out through gritted teeth.

"Granting your wish."

And then the unbearable build-up of pressure beneath Oskar's shoulder blades culminated in a rending, crunching sound as flesh and bone were torn apart and something, no, two "things" burst through.

Oskar's involuntary scream resonated back to him through the being's momentary stunned silence. He tried to get up but the new unfamiliar weight on his back forced him back down. Breathing hard, sweat trickling from his body, he tried again, determined not to be beaten, attempting to snatch a look behind at what the being had done to him, fully expecting to see blood and slime pulsing from the open wounds.

What he glimpsed robbed him of speech. Rocking on hands and knees to try to dispel the agony, he felt them slowly unfurling, flexing in the fresh air, as the being within him took control .

Wings. But not Sahariel's scarlet leathery Drakhaoul wings, these were formed of golden feathers, tipped with flame, that dazzled as they dried in the sunlight.

"You wished to fly again."

So the being had read his thoughts. Unless, knocked half-senseless, he had been babbling his delusions aloud to the empty moorland.

"But why me?" As the waves of shock gradually died down and Oskar was able to think more clearly, suspicions formed in his mind. "And what do you intend to do?" The being had not offered him a choice. He had just taken control of his body.

"You will help me complete my mission. And expiate some of the sins that Sahariel forced you to commit."

Oskar began to comprehend. "You're one of Them. The Heavenly Guardians."

The enemy.

He sensed a slight ripple of offense at his unspoken reaction. Though he had only been Sahariel's host for a brief time he still retained many of his memories and bitter resentments.

"My name is Ardarel. And now that the fledging is complete, we have work to do."

Before Oskar could protest, he felt Ardarel slowly ease him to his feet. For a moment he—they—stood still, listening to the sounds of the moorland: the hiss of the wind through the grass, the occasional warning tweet of small birds fluttering in and out of the spiny bushes. And through Ardarel's heightened senses, Oskar began to hear far-distant sounds and experience little tingles and disturbances in the air.

"Do you sense that too? That's what I've been sent to destroy. The interference in the aethyr caused by a powerful magus."

Oskar only knew of one magus in Tielen: Kaspar Linnaius. And that name evoked memories from his past he would rather forget of a disastrous mission to Azhkendir and his first encounter with Gavril Nagarian. Without Linnaius, Eugene would no longer be able to protect himself and his family.

"Destroy the Magus? That can only aid my cause." But even as he spoke the words aloud, he became aware that, without asking, Ardarel had taken control anyway. The wings unfurled, spreading wide to fan the air in a gilded ripple. The physical effort almost made Oskar lose consciousness but then he felt Ardarel flood his body with supernal strength and they were rising into the air, each powerful wing-beat propelling them higher.

Oskar let out a whoop of delight.

This was what he had been missing. The freedom. The sensation of being airborne, of leaving all the cares and disappointments of everyday life far below and just . . . soaring upward.

Chapter 51

The wouivres slowly spiraled down into the forest. They brushed close to the shaggy branches of larch and spruce. Gerard was still gripping the rim of the craft, his knuckles bleached white, when he spotted smoldering remains in the clearing below, black smoke rising upward from the charred, skeletal vestiges of a flyer, He forgot his own fear.

"The *Aiglon*." Dread at what he might find overwhelmed him: the pilot's body, broken beyond hope of repair or horribly burned in the ensuing inferno.

"Your student's craft?" Linnaius's question brought him back from his imaginings.

"I fear so." And Gerard vaulted over the side of the craft as soon as Izkael brought it to rest on the forest floor. He had to find out what had happened—no matter how horrific the sight.

The air of the clearing was tainted with the smell of burning, a vile chymical odor that made his eyes sting. All he could see was a tangle of cogs, gears and pipes, still emitting a dark vapor. He felt a painful tightening in his chest that was not caused by the fumes but the realization that he was looking at the remains of the engine of which Toran had been so proud and had spent so long constructing.

"Toran!" The cry racked his throat. *"Toran!"*

No reply. The thick canopy of branches seemed to absorb the sound of his voice. As he turned around, he noticed another wisp of smoke, blue-gray, almost translucent, rising from the stunted chimney of a little stone hut hidden amongst the tree trunks.

Woodsmoke.

Gerard set off at a run, almost tripping over knotted roots in his haste. He reached the hut and pounded his fists against the warped door.

The rotting wood gave way and the door creaked inward, revealing a startled pair of eyes staring at him from the smoky interior.

"Gerard?"

Toran, bruised and bloodied, sat slumped against another taller, broad-shouldered cadet whose arms were wrapped protectively around him, his dark head drooping against Toran's shoulder.

Gerard recognized the black curls of Toran's onetime bully and rival inventor.

"Branville?" What was the third year doing here, and why was he holding Toran so close? A flare of indignation burned through Gerard. "Get away from him!"

On hearing his name, Branville stirred and slowly raised his head as Gerard lunged toward him.

"No, Gerard!" Toran glared up at him so fiercely that Gerard stopped, surprised at the vehemence in his voice. "Branville saved my life. I owe him."

Branville was gazing at Gerard through half-closed lids, as if having trouble focusing. "That's right," he said, his words a little slurred but delivered with his habitual arrogance, challenging Gerard. "I saved him."

Gerard forced himself to ignore Branville's riposte and knelt down beside the cadets. "Are you hurt? Can you walk?"

"I'm fine." Toran nodded. "But how did you find us?"

"I'll explain later." Gerard knew from bitter experience at the Iron Works that an injured man might protest that he was fine and a short while later collapse, felled by some hidden internal injury. "Let's get you back to Swanholm." He stood, holding out his hand to help Toran to his feet.

**

Gerard emerged from the hut to see Linnaius inspecting the smoldering remains of the craft, sniffing at the fuel residue blackening the twisted metal.

"The cadets are safe," Gerard said. "But they're both badly shaken up; they may even have a broken bone or two. Can you take them back to the palace? I'll stay behind."

"Oh, Izkael can easily carry four people," Linnaius said airily. "The question is: do *you* want to reveal who you really are to them?"

There was no point in hiding the truth any longer. "Too late to pretend otherwise." Gerard turned to see Branville and Toran in the open hut doorway, propping each other up. "Your passengers are the Honorable Elyot Branville and Lord Toran Arkhel.

Cadets, this is Kaspar Linnaius, the Emperor's Magus and my great-grandfather." As the cadets limped toward them, they halted and Toran's eyes widened as he gazed at Linnaius.

"It's an honor to meet you, Magus," he said in awed tones. "My grandfather used to tell me about your inventions; he was very impressed by your ingenuity."

"So my reputation traveled beyond Tielen?" Linnaius gave a little nod of satisfaction. "I'm flattered."

"Is there any way we can mark this spot? It's the farthest we flew," Toran said. "If we beat the rival team, then it's proof that we won the contest fair and square."

"Even if they tampered with the fuel," Branville added darkly.

"The wreckage of the *Aiglon* is more than adequate proof," Gerard said. "And even if the saboteurs were canny enough to remove it, they'd have difficulty erasing all the evidence."

"I've taken a sample from your engine," said Linnaius as they slowly crossed the clearing. "A test or two should reveal any unusual ingredients; after all, I was the one who invented it."

Gerard helped Toran and Branville into the craft, silently observing Branville scowl at his outstretched hand—proudly ignored—and the ensuing wince of pain that he couldn't hide as he clambered in.

Toran was gazing around him at the craft and the sail hanging limply from the mast, as Linnaius climbed in.

"But how does this fly?" he asked, wide-eyed.

"Brace yourselves." Linnaius took his position at the rudder and said, "Take us back to Swanholm, Izkael!"

Izkael sprang into the air, tugging the craft behind him; the slack sail filled with the breeze and Gerard heard Toran's shout of amazement as they rose rapidly between the trees. Branville, white-faced, swore under his breath.

Gerard settled back, more than a little relieved that they were conveying the injured cadets to safety far faster than the imperial cavalry could have done. After so many shocks and alarms, perhaps he could afford to relax.

And then he felt it again, that faint disturbance in the aethyr: a distant shiver of golden fire, fine as the vibration of a lute string.

"Ardarel?" he asked in a low voice.

Linnaius gave a brief shake of the head. "Like . . . but different." He seemed perplexed, rather than alarmed.

"Another Guardian?"

"Maybe. Maybe not."

"Close by?"

"Not so close that we need to stop what we're doing. Let's just get your students back to Swanholm so that their injuries can be treated."

Gerard nodded but could not help glancing up into the pale sky, hoping not to see it rent asunder again by the Winged Warrior with the fiery sword.

***

The wouivre-drawn sky-craft sped back toward Swanholm Palace. To Gerard's relief, he soon spotted the cavalcade of imperial horsemen below, cantering out of the great gilded gates on the furthest northern boundary of the palace park. And, catching up to them, the lone horseman in the gray and gold uniform that Linnaius had identified earlier as the Emperor.

"Swanholm," said Gerard to Toran. "You're safe now."

He heard a rasping sigh and Branville slumped back against Toran. His face was pallid, mouth drooping slackly, a little trickle of dried blood at one corner.

"Elyot, wake up. Elyot!" Toran took the older cadet's hand in his, squeezing it hard. When Branville did not respond, Toran up looked at Gerard, eyes dark with concern. "He's been putting on a brave face. Suppose he's badly hurt?"

"Take us down, Izkael," Linnaius ordered.

And not a moment too soon, Gerard thought.

***

A shadow passed across the pale sunlit sky above the gilded park gates; Eugene reined his horse to a standstill and glanced up.

Flying toward him above the forest came a sky-craft. His heartbeat quickened as he recognized the white-haired pilot and he raised his hand to wave frantically.

"Magus!" he shouted with the full force of his lungs. The imperial cavalry lieutenant, hearing his cry, called the troop to halt and the coach driver followed suit. Everyone on the ground stared up into the sky to where the Emperor was pointing. The lodge keeper hurried out just as the Magus brought the sky-craft down to the ground, easing it to rest on the grass beside the white lodge house. But Eugene had already dismounted and was running over to greet his errant mentor even before the craft had come to a complete stop.

"Where have you *been*, Kaspar?" His breathless question came out in more of an accusatory tone than he had intended, revealing, he realized, how much he had missed the old man. And then he gazed at the three other occupants of the craft and recognized with relief the distinctive shock of Arkhel hair on the drooping head of the third. "Toran Arkhel and Elyot Branville—thank God you're both safe." Alive, he noted, but the two cadets were badly gashed and bruised, with scarcely enough energy left to register who he was or where they were.

"These cadets are in urgent need of medical attention," said Linnaius. "Is that Doctor Amandel's coach I see over there?" He had neatly sidestepped answering Eugene's question—but Eugene would not have expected any less of him. So he beckoned to Amandel's driver to bring the coach closer and stood aside while a couple of the imperial cavalry, under the doctor's instructions, carefully helped the two Tourmaline cadets inside, aided by the fourth occupant of the craft.

Who the deuce is he? Eugene stared at the unfamiliar passenger, noting with keen interest that he wore thick-lensed spectacles of the kind often adopted by magi to conceal the telltale glitter of their eyes. Was he another magus? *Kaspar has some explaining to do.*

***

Gerard busied himself with helping Toran and the groggy Branville into the dark, leather-upholstered interior of the doctor's coach. He was relieved to have something practical to occupy his mind so that he could block out the confusion of feelings surging through him.

The Emperor recognized Toran. Have they been introduced before? Perhaps before the race . . .

As he withdrew his arm from around Branville, Toran said, "Will you come back to the palace with us, Gerard? Guy Maulevrier is there."

Gerard frowned at the mention of his tutor's name.

"He stole your designs." Toran's voice was slurred; he seemed to be fading in and out of consciousness again. "There was no mistaking it. And your craft flew really well."

"He stole— " Gerard began. It was confirmation of his worst suspicions about Maulevrier – and yet he felt oddly detached. Everything that had happened in the last hours had so changed his view of his path in life that Guy's underhand act seemed relatively unimportant. He glanced over his shoulder at his great-grandfather. "I'll stay with the Magus. Please give my regards to Major Bauldry," he added, withdrawing from the coach to make way for the doctor. As he stepped back, he could not help noticing Branville slumping sideways, his dark head coming to rest against Toran's shoulder—and Toran not only failing to push him away but adjusting his own position to support him. No doubt about it; in the months since he left Paladur, there must have been a dramatic shift in the way the two interacted. And a wry sense of resignation settled over him like a fine drizzle dampening a bright morning.

Perhaps it's better this way. I'm not the same man I was back in Paladur. Anyone who stays close to me will be in mortal danger. Best I cut myself loose from all ties. But there was still a strange dull ache about his heart that no amount of rationalization could dispel; it would be hard to forget Toran.

The coachman shook the reins and the horses set off at a brisk trot, drawing the coach along the long *allée* toward the distant palace.

Gerard watched them go, listening with half an ear to the conversation between his great-grandfather and the Emperor, wondering if it was impolite to eavesdrop in the imperial presence.

"We spotted a second column of black smoke out on the moors. I'd venture that's where you'll find the other flyer—and, if the poor devil's still alive, the other pilot. We can lead the rescue party there in the sky-craft, if you—" Linnaius suddenly broke off.

At the same moment, Gerard sensed a vivid disturbance in the atmosphere. A shimmer of fiery gold resonated with such vibrancy that it sounded like the violent jangling of a steeple of bells in full clamor.

The imperial cavalry horses began to whinny and rear up wildly; several bolted in panic, their riders clinging on for dear life.

A flaming blade sliced a jagged rent in the pale blue sky and a winged figure emerged, spilling gouts of fire in its wake as it dived directly toward the Magus and the Emperor.

Ardarel.

"Look out!" Gerard yelled.

Izkael reared up, lashing his great silvered tail and unleashing a gust of stinging hail-stones.

Gerard peered at the Winged Warrior as it descended, sweeping Izkael's hailstorm aside with one sweep of the fiery blade.

Ardarel was . . . different. The angel's body was clothed in ragged, charred mortal clothes. His face, snarling, distorted, bore no trace of the inhumanly beautiful features Gerard had seen earlier, but looked oddly ordinary.

Has Ardarel broken the taboo and taken possession of a mortal body to enable him to carry out his mission?

It was only just above the rush of flame-feathered wings, the searing roar of a hot, dry wind that Gerard heard the angel cry out in a voice that was harsh with all-too human tones of hatred, "Eugene! At last, damn you, *at last!*"

In the same instant, Kaspar Linnaius flung himself in front of the Emperor, knocking him off balance. The flaming sword caught the Magus full in the chest.

Kaspar Linnaius toppled without a sound, the Emperor still shielded by his body.

Chapter 52

"Great-grandfather!" Gerard picked himself up and stumbled toward the Magus.

"Protect the Emperor!" The imperial cavalrymen rallied, some reaching into their saddle holsters for primed pistols and firing at Ardarel, others urging their horses forward to form a protective barrier around Eugene and Linnaius.

Ardarel let out a sudden, harsh cry. Gerard looked upward and saw that a patch of crimson darkening the angel's right shoulder. *He's bleeding? But how? I thought his body was made of aethyrial matter—and impervious to bullets?*

"Another magus?" Ardarel turned to stare at him and he felt the searing force of his gaze resting on him. "You *again*?" And he raised the dazzling blade, aiming it in his direction.

I'm done for. Unless . . . Gerard closed his eyes a moment, seeking for the elusive presence of wind as the cavalrymen continued to fire, creating a distraction. *If ever I needed you, zephyr, breeze, gale, I need you now.*

A sudden rush of power buffeted him, almost knocking him over. He tried to seize hold of it, wrestling with its wild, willful fury to direct it toward Ardarel as he hovered above them. The gust, as it passed through him, knocked him flat on the ground and hit the wounded angel with full force. Ardarel let out another agonized cry and the flames gouting from the fiery blade dimmed.

The rent in the sky gaped open once more and Ardarel retreated, disappearing from sight above the clouds.

Gerard listened. The gilded vibrations that emanated from Ardarel's wings and sword had ceased. He was winded—but unharmed. But as for the Emperor and his great-grandfather . . .

***

"Kaspar. Kaspar, can you hear me?"

The Emperor had raised the Magus's head and shoulders and was supporting the old man's body against his own as Gerard hurried over.

"Is he . . . ?"

As Gerard knelt beside them and reached out to take his great-grandfather's hand, Eugene slowly shook his head, indicating the scorch marks left by Ardarel's blade across the Magus's robes.

"He saved my life." Eugene's strong voice shook. "And now, I fear . . ."

The rattle of carriage wheels over gravel and the soft whinny of a horse cut across his words. A barouche had appeared from the direction of the palace, drawn by two elegant grays and was slowing to a stop outside the lodge.

"Magus!"

A pale, fair-haired girl jumped out of the barouche and flung herself down beside Linnaius on the grass, reaching out to caress his wrinkled cheek with slender fingers.

"Don't you dare die!" she said, her tone surprisingly fierce for one so young.

Gerard, still dazed from Ardarel's attack, wondered who she could be to his great-grandfather to address him in such a familiar way.

"Kari?" The Emperor sounded almost as surprised as he. "But how did you—?"

She glanced up at him. "The same way you did, Papa," she said. "I felt the disturbance when *it* broke through." So this was the Emperor's eldest child, Princess Karila.

"Karila," Kaspar Linnaius stirred and his hooded eyes opened.

"Yes, it's me."

"You've . . . grown." But the shrewd and piercing silver gleam had dulled and Gerard was obliged to lean closer to try to catch his halting words.

"Where have you been? Why did you leave us for so long?" Her voice cracked on the last question as tears spilled out and she added with a poignancy that touched Gerard's heart, "I've missed you so much."

"I was looking . . . for my own daughter."

Gerard saw a look of disbelief pass between Eugene and the princess.

"And did you find her?" the Emperor asked gently.

"No." Linnaius closed his eyes as if too weary to continue. But then a moment later, he opened them again to glance up at Gerard. Gerard tightened his hold on his great-grandfather's hand, realizing how chill it had become, as if warmth and life were ebbing away too swiftly. "Although I found my great-grandson instead. This is Gerard."

"*You're* the great-grandson?"

Gerard felt the full probing force of the Emperor's stare boring into him. Undaunted, he nodded, daring to hold the Emperor's gaze. "My name is Gerard Bernay," he said. "But until today I had no idea of who—or what—I really am."

The Emperor suddenly let out a little snort of amusement. "Those eyes certainly give the game away, Magus Bernay."

Magus Bernay? The title sounded strange—and yet not unpleasing—to Gerard's ears. And it had been conferred on him by the Emperor himself. Even as he was adjusting to the confirmation of his new identity, he felt a slight pressure on his hand and saw that his great-grandfather had closed and opened his eyes in tacit approval. And then Linnaius's gaze drifted upward, focusing on the skies above their heads. Gerard, feeling his skin prickle with a chill, new sensation, looked upward too to see the wouivres streaking toward them.

"What a truly wonderful sight," he heard the Emperor murmur.

"*You* can see them too, imperial majesty?" There had been rumors about the Emperor's dabbling in the hidden arts at the time that the Drakhaouls appeared in Tielen but Gerard had doubted their veracity . . . until now.

The wouivres slowly descended in an elegant downward spiral that set the air whispering and stirred up eddies of white dust from the gravel. Yet as they alighted, each one shrugged aside their glittering coils to emerge in human form. Gerard gazed at them, speechless; he had experienced so much beyond his comprehension in the last hours and yet this unexpected transformation was the most surprising of all.

His great-grandfather stirred again, making an effort to raise himself up; Gerard and the Emperor supported him into a sitting position. Gerard could feel how frail the elderly Magus's body was, bones as brittle as twigs beneath the papery wrinkled skin as thin as skeletal leaves; only Linnaius's indomitable will power must be keeping him alive. The princess snuggled closer, inserting herself in the crook of her father's arm with one hand placed protectively on Linnaius's shoulder.

One by one, the wouivres came forward, to kneel before Kaspar Linnaius. Clothed only in their long locks of floating silvery hair, their slender, insubstantial bodies were almost translucent, showing a tracery of glimmering veins. Each in turn raised their hands to him, whether in supplication or greeting, Gerard could not be sure. All he knew was that their presence resonated deep within him, stirring a feeling of loss and longing so powerful he feared it would utterly overwhelm him.

Linnaius slowly, tremblingly, extended his right hand toward them. Gerard could feel the supreme effort that it cost him to make even this simple gesture.

"Serapiel," he whispered. So he knew them all by name. "Nahaliel." As he brushed their extended translucent fingertips with his own, each wouivre in turn bowed their head. "Auphiel. Asamkis." And to the tallest one who waited until the last to kneel, Linnaius looked up and a smile curved his lips. "Izkael," he said, his fading voice touched with warmth. "How can I thank you for all these years of faithful friendship you've given me?"

Izkael. The name reverberated through Gerard's mind more strongly than all the rest.

"We knew this day would come," Izkael said. "Our sister warned us. You've lived a long life for a mortal. But we are grieving. Because we owe you our freedom. You set us free from the cursed Angelsnares of the Saint Knights of Sapaudia."

Gerard listened in amazement, hearing unfamiliar and mystifying names that suggested tales yet untold of his great-grandfather's long life—tales that he feared that he would never get to hear.

"And now you have to let me go." Linnaius raised his free hand to gently touch Izkael's bent head. Gerard sensed the immense effort it cost him as if will alone were sustaining him. "But I place my great-grandson in your care. Make a new pact with him, Izkael. Break the pact we made and protect him. With Ardarel and the Warriors on his trail, he's going to need your help."

Izkael said nothing.

"Well, if you won't, then I must." There was still the ghost of formidable willpower in Linnaius's voice. "I set you free, Azhkanizkael, from the pact that has bound us all these years."

Izkael's head drooped lower. "Our pact is at an end," he said haltingly. "Josse—Josselin Vernier—we are no longer bound together."

The name—Francian from the sound of it—was utterly unfamiliar to Gerard. And from the murmur of surprise that passed between the Emperor and his daughter, he guessed that something had been revealed that Linnaius had kept hidden even from them. *Vernier. The name of my grandmother before she married. Is that his real name?*

Izkael raised his head to stare at Gerard, fixing him with his unearthly eyes.

The significance of the moment sent a shiver of elation through Gerard's body. He had dreamed of dragons. He had modelled his flyers on the Drakhaoul dragons he had once glimpsed flying over Tielen. Now he was about to become bound to an elemental air dragon—for life. The realization that his dream was about to come true both thrilled and terrified him. Undaunted, he stared back into Izkael's inhuman eyes and said in as strong and clear a voice as he could muster, "Acknowledge me, Azhkanizkael."

Without hesitation, the wouivre replied, "I acknowledge you . . . as my new master, Gerard Bernier."

The Magus gave a little sigh and his head drooped against the Emperor's shoulder.

"Kaspar!" The Emperor's cry seemed to rouse him and his lids fluttered open once more.

"I'm rather tired, Eugene," he said in tones of tender irascibility. "I could do . . . with a rest . . ."

Gerard was shocked to hear his great-grandfather speak so familiarly to the Emperor but Eugene seemed used to such chiding.

"I left . . . my researches to that idiot Kazimir . . ." The Magus reached out to Eugene who caught his hand in his own. "But will you promise me . . . to protect Gerard? He has inherited the gift—and the curse—of the silver eyes. He'll need . . . to study. But with your patronage, I believe he will serve you and your heirs for many years . . . as I have tried to do . . ."

"You need have no worries on that account, Kaspar." The Emperor turned to Gerard and, again, Gerard felt the full force of his penetrating gaze, disconcerting yet inspiring at the same time. "I offer you my full protection, Gerard Bernay, in the hope that you will stay by my side and continue your great-grandfather's work."

Overwhelmed, Gerard lowered his head in gratitude. "I'll do my best to live up to his expectations."

Linnaius lifted his other hand toward him, as if to beckon him closer. His lips moved. Gerard leaned closer, taking his hand in his own, trying to catch what his great-grandfather was trying to say.

"The key . . . protect the key . . ."

A sudden chill breeze gusted across the parkland, setting Gerard's senses tingling. All the wouivres dropped to their knees, heads bent, their luminous eyes averted. As Gerard stared, he saw—or thought he saw—the shadow of a bird of prey, arise, hawk-like, from Linnaius's body and dart away, fading into the uncertain daylight.

And then all was still.

"Magus?" cried the princess.

But Gerard felt his great-grandfather's grip on his hand slowly relax and drop back to his side. Tears glimmered in Eugene's eyes as he and Gerard gently laid the old man back on the grass.

"Papa," whispered the princess.

"Farewell, old friend." Eugene leant forward and closed Linnaius's eyes.

Chapter 53

Gerard knelt by his great-grandfather's body, head bowed.

"Attend on us at the palace when you're ready," the Emperor said quietly as he helped his weeping daughter into the barouche and Gerard nodded automatically in reply. The imperial cavalrymen remounted to form an escort and the party set off along the drive toward the palace.

Even as Gerard watched over Linnaius, he sensed a subtle change taking place. The Magus's lined face was tranquil in death, the skin so translucently pale that it reminded him of the pearlescent discs of honesty seedpods that used to grow in his mother's garden. And then to Gerard's bewilderment, the features blurred as if a fine mist had settled upon them.

"What's happening, Izkael?"

The wouivre gazed at his dead master's body. "Ah. His mortal form is breaking down. He was very old, after all, in your terms."

"How old, exactly?" Gerard wanted to avert his gaze but his eyes were fixed on the horrifying yet oddly beautiful sight of his great-grandfather's bodily dissolution until the Magus's features suddenly disintegrated into a cloud of silvery dust and the body beneath the robes collapsed inward.

"Your kind live much longer than ordinary mortals," Izkael said. "It's a gift and a curse too. Or so he said, more than once."

And as Gerard stared down on the crumpled clothes and the fine powder that had so recently been his great-grandfather and the reality of his own mortality—even if he lived to anything like as great an age as Linnaius—filled him with dread.

Am I looking at my own death? Is this how it will end for me?

A sharp breeze suddenly swept across the parkland and began to disperse the dust. Alarmed, Gerard started up, wanting to preserve the last remains but he felt Izkael place a restraining hand on his shoulder.

"There's nothing you can do. Let the North Wind scatter his remains. It's as it should be."

"But what shall I say to the Emperor? He's probably planning a funeral ceremony already—"

"I'll take you back to the court. You'll be wanting to make your farewells."

"I will?" Gerard was still too numbed to think about what he needed to do next. A sudden shaft of sunlight fell on the empty tumble of clothes and he caught a glint of metal. Looking more closely, he saw a slender silver chain with a key attached; his grandfather must have been wearing it around his neck.

Izkael bent down and picked up the key, handing it to Gerard. "This is for you. He planned to give it to you himself."

"*The key*," Linnaius had whispered to him with his dying breath. '*Protect the key*'"

Gerard hesitated—it seemed a little like grave-robbing—and then closed his fingers around the cold metal. He wondered what the key would unlock and what secrets would be revealed. But as he turned toward the sky-craft, he found himself staring directly into Izkael's translucent eyes.

Rush of ice-chill waters, steaming as they tumble from high, jagged rocks into a mist-wreathed gray lake.

Gerard shivered. "What was that?"

"*Our home. The mountain waterfalls and lakes that we protect, far from here, the source of our life force.*" Izkael's deep voice resonated in his mind, the rumble of a storm wind heard on a turbulent winter night. "*I will take you there later, if you wish.*"

I am bound for life to this creature of wind and water. The realization was oddly comforting amid all the confusion raging in his mind. And then he remembered that he had not yet checked to make sure Toran was all right. *And that's another part of my life I have to renounce.* He nodded. "I do wish to go there, Izkael, with all my heart. But for now, I have urgent unfinished business at Swanholm." He clambered back into the craft and, without another word, Izkael shrugged off his mortal form, returning to his powerful wouivre body in a dazzle of silvered scales.

***

Why? Eugene asked himself over and over again as he and Karila rode back to Swanholm in the princess's barouche. He was still in a state of shock at the merciless way Ardarel had struck Linnaius down.

Why did that Winged Warrior have Oskar Alvborg's face?

It was possible, of course, that Galizur's Heavenly Guardians were able to show mortals what they most feared or hated, and Ardarel had read in his mind a suggestion already planted there by Karila. Or worse still—and he tightened his grip around Karila's shoulders—Ardarel had possessed his half-brother and used him to attack them.

And if that was so, somehow—in spite of Baron Sylvius's vigilance—Oskar had evaded all his agents and slipped back into Tielen.

He's failed in his first attempt to assassinate me. But who knows where he'll strike next if we don't stop him? He wouldn't hesitate to single out Astasia and the children . . . That thought alone stirred up such a storm of alarm that he could feel his heart thudding beneath the crisp gray cloth of his uniform jacket.

Beside him he heard a stifled sob escape from Karila. He realized that he was so caught up in his own worries that he was neglecting her. His daughter was making a supreme effort to restrain her tears— but she must be doubly traumatized by the death of her beloved Magus at the hands of Oskar Alvborg, the one who had abducted her and subjected her to a terrifying ordeal at the Serpent Gate.

"Kari," he said gently, giving her a reassuring squeeze.

"I'm sorry, Papa." She nestled closer to him. "You must be so sad too. The Magus was your good friend."

"He was," he said, touched by the fact that she was concerned about his feelings, putting aside her own sadness to console him. "I don't know what we shall do without him." He heard his voice falter and cleared his throat. They were nearly back at the palace and he could not allow himself to betray any sign of weakness in front of the court.

The barouche slowed to a stop by the double stair and an equerry came forward to open the door. Eugene hesitated, half in, half out of the barouche, torn between his own need to mourn for the Magus and his instinct to protect his family. The instant he stepped down from the coach, his courtiers would be looking anxiously to him to reassure them that all was well even when he knew it was far from being so.

"Are you all right, imperial majesty?" Gustave came hurrying down the left stair to greet them.

"We are unharmed," Eugene said in the most robust of tones. "Where is Countess Marta?"

"Here, majesty." The ever-dependable Marta appeared, arms extended, to welcome Karila who threw herself into her arms and hugged her tightly.

Gustave shot Eugene a questioning look as Marta led Karila away. Eugene said, *sotto voce*, so that only he would hear, "We have just lost the Magus."

Gustave said nothing but one eyebrow quirked inquiringly.

"I'd like to see Countess Lovisa," Eugene said. "Can you ask her to come to my study?"

Baron Sylvius was currently in Tielborg but his most trusted agent (and mistress) Lovisa, Countess of Aspelin, was keeping a watchful eyes on affairs at Swanholm in his absence.

As Eugene passed through the airy mirrored reception room on the way to his study, he seized a little glass of aquavit from one of the attendants' trays and downed it in one gulp. The sharp, stinging bite of the spirits revived him; he needed a clear head to deal with this new threat.

Eugene entered his study, a light and airy cabinet with views across the park, and sat down at his desk. At his right, just within easy reach, was the Vox Aethyria, arguably Linnaius's most brilliant invention, an ingenious combination of metal cogs and dials that had often confused the uninitiated into thinking it to be some new type of clock. But the crystal that powered it was dull with not even a trace of the aethyric spark at the heart of its many facets.

As lifeless as its inventor . . . Eugene blinked the blur of tears away again. Damn it, the last thing Linnaius would have expected of him was to mope about when there was work to be done. There would be time to mourn properly later. The network of linked machines Linnaius had established to enable Eugene to communicate instantly with his agents and ambassadors in the furthest, most remote corners of the empire, had ceased to function the year before, during the Great Darkness.

And without it, my single greatest advantage over my rivals and enemies is gone.

Eugene drummed his fingertips on the polished surface of the desk as he contemplated the broken machine. If the Vox Aethyria had been functioning, he could already have spoken with Sylvius in Tielborg instead of fretting as he waited for Lovisa to arrive and then sending out a small squad of messengers.

I wonder if young Bernay knows how to repair the Vox?

But before he could pursue this line of thought further, there came a discreet tap at the door and Lovisa entered. She was, as always, impeccably dressed; today's gown was in gray silk, embroidered at the collar in speedwell blue and silver thread to match the underskirt. He supposed she had chosen the colors to reflect the flag of Tielen and the uniforms of his elite household troops in honor of the occasion.

"How can I be of service to you, imperial majesty?"

"Let's drop the formalities, cousin; we're alone," Eugene said, rising to assist her into a seat.

"Then how can I be of help to you, Eugene?" There was a slightly frosty edge to her words as she rephrased her question. Her punctiliousness was one of the qualities he valued in her; it made her one of his most meticulous and reliable agents.

"I want you to interrogate Guy Maulevrier, the ingenieur in charge of the Tielborg University team. Find out how he came to employ the pilot. The one who's so conveniently disappeared. Find out everything you can about this 'Karl Lorens'."

"Shall I interrogate Professor Kazimir too? After all, he was responsible for developing the new fuel. "

Eugene waved one hand dismissively. "Kazimir may appear like a gullible fool, but I trust him. He's no traitor. The Magus would never have bequeathed his life's work to him if he hadn't felt the same way. But now we have a new Magus, Lovisa, one Gerard Bernay."

"A new Magus . . . ?" Her blue eyes widened in astonishment; she so rarely let her true feelings show but this news had startled her. "Then Linnaius is—"

"Dead." Eugene heard himself say the word aloud but still had difficulty believing it, even though he had held the old man in his arms until the last breath had left his frail body. "Bernay is his great-grandson."

"I see," Lovisa said guardedly.

"Linnaius died protecting me from an attack by Oskar Alvborg."

Her eyes grew even wider. "Alvborg is here? At Swanholm? He gained entry in spite of the extra guards we've placed around the estate?"

"He made his attack from the air." Eugene didn't want to complicate matters by trying to explain what he had witnessed; he didn't begin to understand it himself.

"Are you saying that Karl Lorens is Alvborg? In disguise? How did he get back into Tielen? Sylvius' agents have been on high alert at all the ports looking out for him."

"Someone has been negligent. Although . . ." He left the comment unfinished; there was little point at this stage in singling out and punishing any of Sylvius' agents for negligence if Oskar had—for reasons that baffled him—been selected by the Heavenly Guardians as their instrument of vengeance.

"Although?"

He realized that Lovisa was prompting him to complete his observation. "My main concern is that Astasia and the children are fully protected at all times."

"I will see to it at once. And I'll report back to you straight away." And then, never one to be less than blunt with him, she said, "I noticed that her imperial majesty was absent from today's contest. I hope this recent bout of ill health is not a cause for concern."

"Just a headache, nothing more." Eugene smiled at her. "But Astasia will be touched to hear that you inquired after her health." There was still a distinct touch of frostiness in the air whenever the two women met; it had been hard to dissuade Astasia that he and Lovisa had never been romantically involved, in spite of the slanders certain malicious tongues whispered at court.

Lovisa shot him an enigmatic look, then rose, curtseyed, and departed in a brisk swish of silken skirts.

Eugene remained at his desk, mulling over her final observation. He had wondered when one of the courtiers would comment on Astasia's absence—and, of course, it was the fearlessly frank Lovisa who was the first to do so. He was more than a little ashamed that he had not sent Gustave to find out if the empress was feeling any better, but the extraordinary events of the day had delayed him far longer than he had anticipated. It was true that Astasia had been looking more pale than usual since they arrived in Swanholm but he had attributed her pallor to the rigors of the journey. He longed to tell her of Linnaius's death and to share the grief that he could not afford to show in public. Only with her could he allow himself to reveal the ache of loss that he had suppressed to deal with the crisis. But if she was still feeling unwell, he was reluctant to burden her with his troubles.

***

Astasia was sitting up in the great swagged bed, propped up on pillows and cushions, her dark hair unbound about her shoulders, holding a delicate porcelain cup of tea in both hands.

Eugene hesitated, seeing how pale she looked, the skin below her violet eyes darkly smudged, but hearing him come in, she looked up from the tea and smiled, carefully setting the cup back on its saucer.

"I'm so sorry to miss the contest, Eugene." She beckoned him closer, patting the bed. "How did it go? Who won?"

He could see she was making an effort to conceal how she was feeling. *That's my girl.* He went to sit beside her and took her hand in his.

"I heard the band playing, then the chug of the engines. And all the cheers! It must have been so exciting."

"I hope the noise didn't disturb you too much."

"No; it all sounded far away."

"And how are you feeling now?"

"Oh, much better." She did not meet his gaze, picking at a loose thread in the sheet with her free hand. He was not convinced. "You still haven't told me who won. Was it the Arkhel boy? I do hope it was."

He had been pondering how best to report what had happened to her. "In truth, Tasia, the other pilot has disappeared and we haven't yet found his flyer. So we will award the cadets from Tourmalise the gold medals. And if you're feeling better, it would be a fitting end to the contest if you could help me make the presentation to the cadets in front of the court.

They're brave, enterprising young men and merit their reward."

"It would be a pleasure," she said. But she still seemed distracted and distant.

"Astasia," he said, leaning forward to stroke her face, tilting it toward him. "Is everything well with you? Is there something you want to tell me? I'm here, ready to listen, whatever it might be. I've asked Nadezhda to make sure we're not disturbed."

"Um." Still she did not meet his gaze. "Well. I didn't want to say until I was certain. It seems that I'm—we're—expecting another child."

This was not at all what Eugene had been expecting. He had come back to the palace, raw from witnessing the death of Linnaius and now Astasia was informing him that he was to be a father again. He felt tears burning a path down his cheeks as he reached out blindly and crushed her tightly to him.

"Eugene?" he heard her say, surprised, her voice muffled by his shoulder. "Aren't you pleased?"

"Of course I am. I'm—I'm overwhelmed." He blinked away his tears and kissed her. "So when is the baby to be born? When shall we announce the good news to the court?"

"Nadezhda reckons around the Feast of the Holy Veil."

"The Holy Veil?" Eugene gave her a puzzled look, suspecting this was one of the many holy days celebrated in Muscobar which the Tielen Church regarded as unimportant.

"Autumn." She laughed for the first time in a long while. "Harvest festival time."

"Ah." He was making mental calculations. "But we can't rely on Nadezhda's guesswork. We must summon the best medical practitioners in Tielborg."

"Good heavens, Eugene, I don't want to be poked and prodded by strangers, no matter how good their qualifications . A good local midwife will be fine. And Doctor Amandel, if needs must. I'm not ill, I'm merely with child. It happens all the time, you know!"

"Of course, dearest Tasia, whatever you wish," he said, kissing her again, unable to help himself. "Do you feel well enough to attend the medals ceremony? I'd like to present Toran Arkhel to you. It would be a good opportunity to introduce him to his little cousin Stavy."

"I'd love to meet him."

There came a discreet tap at the bedchamber door and Nadezhda's white-coiffed head appeared.

"Forgive the interruption but Count Gustave has urgent news for his imperial majesty."

"Urgent? You'd better not keep Gustave waiting," Astasia said.

"I'll leave you to rest." He helped her back onto the pillows and kissed her forehead. But as he left the bedchamber, a little voice nagged at the back of his mind, reminding him that perhaps it was not so usual for pregnant women to be laid low with headaches.

In the antechamber, Gustave turned to greet him, holding out a folded paper. Eugene opened it and read:

"Farmers on the edge of the northern moors reported seeing flames in the sky. We've found burned wreckage—but no human remains. We're collecting the debris and bringing it back for further investigation.

"Alvar Baryard, Captain, Imperial Guards"

Eugene nodded and handed back the paper to Gustave. He was determined not to let this news—disquieting as it was—spoil his pleasure on hearing Astasia's news.

"If I might be so impertinent as to make an observation," said Gustave, "but your majesty seems to have recovered your spirits."

Of course! Gustave knew him too well not to notice. Eugene grinned at his old friend. "Indeed so, Gustave. I've just received some excellent tidings from the empress."

Gustave's brows rose questioningly and then he smiled too and bowed. "May I be the first to congratulate you both?"

"Thank you." Eugene clapped Gustave on the shoulder, delighted to have gained his approval. "But this report from Captain Baryard only confirms my suspicions; the pilot survived the crash. Which means he's still at large."

Chapter 54

Airborne at last, Gavril was rediscovering the skills he had learned in his Drakhaoul form. Taliahad was right: even though the feathery wings were hard to master and control, his body had not forgotten how to fly. Soon he was using the up-draughts and air currents to soar and skim. And the sensation was so deliciously invigorating that it allowed him to ignore the repetitive, tearing pain triggered by each wing-stroke.

From the air, the trail left by Chinua's wolves dragging the cart and its precious cargo across the grasslands was ridiculously easy to follow. The wolf shaman must have assumed that Gavril and his men would not be swift enough to pursue them on horseback and had not bothered to cover their tracks across the steppe.

But after a while Gavril began to flag. Krasa had galloped off with his water and rations in the saddle bags. His throat was dust-dry and his empty stomach had begun to cramp. And he had not spotted a single traveler on the steppes below. If he didn't catch up with Kiukiu and Chinua soon, there was a real danger that he would exhaust the last of his energy and crash to earth, parched and starving. All he could do was flap doggedly onward, keeping the wolves' trail through the crushed grass directly below him.

They'll have to stop at some stage to feed Risa. There's no sign yet of the mountains or Lake Taigal, so I haven't crossed into the Serpent Woman's domains. There's still time to stop them before they fall into her clutches.

***

Oskar flapped slowly, raggedly onward, propelled only by the Guardian's failing strength. The peerless blue of the Tielen sky was hazed over with a crimson sheen as waves of faintness washed through him. His main aim was to get as far away as possible from Eugene's men and then, like a wounded creature, go to ground. But each successive wing-stroke sent fresh jags of pain through his body as blood slowly dripped from the bullet wound to the earth below.

"You . . . you didn't warn me." The words were Ardarel's but they were issuing from his own mouth, using his own voice. "I had no idea—that it would feel like this."

Oskar spiraled clumsily down to the open moorland far beneath, dropping the last few feet to tumble onto a patch of heather. The fall knocked the breath from his lungs and jarred the bullet-wound in his right shoulder. He yelled aloud as agony shot through him.

"Damn you," he whispered, curling in on himself. "You promised me freedom. All I get is a bullet in the shoulder. Can't you heal me?"

"Is this . . ." the angel whispered back, "what you call *pain*? This rending, tearing, burning sensation? You mortals are so fragile. You break so easily. You are vulnerable . . . in so many ways."

"Just heal me. Make me whole again."

"Don't tell me what to do, mortal. I'm not your servant. I'm a Warrior of the Second Heaven, second-in-command to Prince Galizur—" Ardarel broke off as another surge of agony rose, cresting like a storm wave.

"But you can't fulfill your mission without my help." Oskar managed through gritted teeth.

There was a slight pause as though the Guardian was reconsidering his options—and maybe even regretting his prideful outburst.

"Very well." Oskar heard him mutter. And then the gilded heat slowly enveloped them both in a fiery cloud of healing.

***

Oskar sat up, flexing his arm, then slowly rotating the damaged shoulder. The pain had gone; all that remained was a slight sensation of stiffness where the torn flesh and crushed bone had been re-fused.

"Amazing," he said under his breath. He had no idea how Ardarel had used his powers to undo the damage; the ball had passed right through his body,

"Now that your body has been restored, I have a question for you." Ardarel's voice resounded in Oskar's mind, keen and incisive as his fiery blade.

"Why did you override my instructions? You attacked the Emperor, instead of the two magi."

Oskar rolled onto his back. Laughter welled up inside him. The irony of his situation would make a fine church morality play, full of comedy and pratfalls. He flung his arms wide to the sky and laughed aloud until his throat and ribcage ached. "What does it matter? The foolish old Magus sacrificed himself for his Emperor. Your mission was accomplished." He sat up, the last residue of laughter suddenly gone. "Although it would have been so much better if I could have destroyed them both with one single blow."

"You are full of hate. I had no idea how powerful this emotion could be."

"So you high and mighty ones have no experience of mortal feelings?"

"We have no need," Ardarel said.

Oskar considered the response. "That must make it almost impossible to deal with us. You have no real understanding of what drives us. No wonder we mortals are such a big disappointment to you. We're so . . . unpredictable." A sudden pang of hunger gripped him and he clutched at his empty stomach. He could not even remember when he last eaten. There had been fresh-baked rolls, slices of cheese and cold meats, berry jams and jellies laid on by the imperial kitchens before the contest. Just remembering the smell, the texture of the bread, brought saliva to his mouth; the taste of white rolls, still hot from the oven, spread with jam, dipped in steaming coffee almost made him drool.

"What is this?" Ardarel demanded.

"I need food. I haven't eaten all day. I'm light-headed with hunger."

"How can you find some . . . food?" Ardarel pronounced the word as if it were utterly unfamiliar.

"Not out here in the wild. It's too early for berries. And I've no money." Oskar began to laugh again, overwhelmed by the ridiculousness of the sorry plight he found himself in.

"And if you don't find food—"

A distant ripple disturbed the aethyr, a chill, fresh watery sensation that briefly lapped at Oskar's mind with a wash of blue. Ardarel felt it too for he fell silent, listening intently.

"What's that?" Oskar asked, puzzled. It had stirred up yet more memories, frustratingly fleeting, and he could not be sure whose they were.

"What are you doing here, Taliahad?" he heard Ardarel murmur. "Have you traced the Key Child?"

***

A thin curl of woodsmoke wisped upward, gray against the cloud-sheened sky: the first sign of life Gavril had spotted all day. But if it was Chinua, where were the steppe wolves? Had Chinua posted them to keep watch? Relief that he had caught up with the fugitives mingled with the realization that a difficult confrontation lay ahead. And he was so tired and hungry that when the rhythm of his wing-beats began to falter, he was too exhausted to find the strength to regulate them.

Then—there it was: the tea merchant's cart far below, sheltered in a small hollow. Gavril felt his pulse quicken at the sight.

Kiukiu and Risa.

But there too was Chinua, tending a little fire, the source of the woodsmoke, with an iron pot suspended above. How would the shaman react when he saw him? If Taliahad was right and Chinua was working for Anagini, then he would use all his shamanic powers to prevent him interfering in her plan.

Distracted, Gavril lost concentration and began to spiral downward. As he tried to control his descent, he suddenly saw Kiukiu poke her head out of the back of the cart, looking up into the sky, as if she had sensed he was there.

"*Gavril?*"

And then he hit the ground, rather less gracefully then he had planned and fell headlong in a tangle of wings and limbs. When he extricated himself, winded and dizzy, she was standing over him, gazing at him aghast.

"What have they done to you?" She backed away, shaking her head. "No! What have you done to yourself?"

It took all his concentration to fold the cumbersome wings, tucking them away as Taliahad had taught him so that he could walk without overbalancing. As he struggled, he heard Kiukiu say, "Why? I thought you had more sense than to let yourself be seduced by . . . by one of *them*." And even though her words burned with anger, he caught a glint of a very different emotion in her eyes: fear.

And Kiukiu was one of the most fearless souls he had ever met.

"Why didn't you tell me?" He was not going to let her make him take all the blame. "About the pact the Serpent Woman forced you into?" The way she flinched as he asked the question only confirmed that Taliahad had not lied to him.

"You have to go, Gavril. The longer we're here arguing, the easier it will be for the Guardians to track us down. Don't you see? They're using you."

There it was again, that telltale glint of fear. Fear . . . and guilt. And the proof that she had been lying to him—and was almost certainly still doing so—was so painful that he felt as if a weight was pressing on his chest, slowly crushing him, making each breath an agony.

"What are you waiting for? Go." Her voice trembled, belying the vehemence of her words. "If you love your daughter, use those cursed wings the Guardians have given you and lead him away from here. Far away."

Taliahad had warned him that she would refute anything and everything he said.

The Serpent Woman has bewitched your wife. Her poison has been working in her system for a long time. It will be very difficult to persuade her to believe you. But you must persist.

"I can't just abandon you." Gavril was at a loss. He had never felt so useless before. Every instinct told him to stay with the woman he loved and their child—and yet she was still pushing him away, rejecting his help.

"*Go,* Gavril!"

"At least tell me why you think Taliahad's been lying to me. Why he wants to harm Larisa."

"Taliahad?" she repeated in a low voice, freighted with loathing. "The blue-haired Guardian? He's the one Galizur sent to destroy our daughter. I heard him accept the mission."

"How?" Just as Taliahad had warned him, Kiukiu was reacting irrationally. "How did you hear? Through the machinations of this Serpent Woman? Did it never occur to you that she might be deceiving you, spinning lies to divide us and steal Larisa from us?"

Kiukiu opened her mouth to reply—but Gavril saw her hesitate. A flicker of hope lit his heart. Had she begun to doubt the Serpent Woman's words at last?

"Is all well, Kiukiu?" Chinua appeared, carrying Larisa who was snuggled asleep against his shoulder, utterly oblivious to what was going on. The sight of the shaman cradling his daughter almost made Gavril lose control. He ached to snatch Risa from Chinua and hold her tight; she was *his* child, not some pawn to be haggled over.

"Gavril was just about to leave," Kiukiu said, staring pointedly at Gavril as she spoke. "Weren't you? It's best for us all if you go."

Gavril caught an enticing aroma wafting toward them from the cooking pot suspended over the fire as the evening breeze stirred the flames. He swayed on his feet, feeling the last of his strength draining away. The rigors of the flight and a long while without water or food since daybreak were taking their toll. "I haven't eaten or drunk anything all day," he explained, ashamed of this sudden weakness. "Krasa bolted with my supplies. If I could just—"

Kiukiu exchanged a look with Chinua. "And then you'll go?"

Gavril was not going to acquiesce that easily. Stalling for time, he said, not untruthfully, "I can't go anywhere until I've got my strength back."

She went over to the fire and spooned broth into a mug. "Be careful; it's scalding hot," she said, handing it to him. He sniffed the savory steam and felt his empty stomach contract, reacting to the enticing smell of herbs and stewed dried meat. His first instinct was to gulp the soup down to appease the pangs in his gut but he blew on it, not wanting to burn his tongue.

"And what are you doing away from the kastel, anyway?" Kiukiu was still in scolding mode. "Didn't you say there was trouble brewing at home with this Lord Ranozhir turning up? Shouldn't you be there to make sure he doesn't reawaken the old clan troubles?"

"He's been abroad for over twenty years. I doubt he can do much harm in a few weeks." Gavril risked a sip of the hot broth and then another; it tasted so good it almost brought tears to his eyes. Only then did he remember that she had drugged their tea in Fire Falcon Pass; he was so desperate for food that he had forgotten all caution. "You haven't spiked this, have you?"

She glared at him. "When did I have time to do that? You saw me ladle the soup out yourself. If it's drugged, then we'll all—"

She broke off abruptly, gazing upward. At the same time, Gavril felt the same icy shiver he experienced when Taliahad first appeared.

"Too late," he heard her whisper.

A ragged rent appeared in the cloudy sky overhead, like silk ripped with a keen blade. Even as Kiukiu ran to snatch Larisa from Chinua, Taliahad appeared through the rift in the clouds. No longer unarmed, he was gripping a scythe-like weapon with a long, curved blade that glittered as if it was hewn from clear ice.

"It's him!" Gavril heard Kiukiu hiss, retreating behind him. Larisa let out a sleepy growl of protest at being awoken so roughly.

"What are you doing here, Lord Taliahad?" Gavril stared up as the Winged Guardian descended in a rippling shimmer of watery light. "And why are you armed?"

"Give me your daughter so I can protect her, Gavril." The young Guardian's voice was hard and urgent, with no trace of his earlier compassionate manner.

"Protect her?" Gavril dug his heels into the rough ground. "From whom?" Behind him he heard Larisa say in tones of delighted surprise, "Da!" as one sticky fist reached out and thumped him in a friendly way on the back of the head. "Did she just call me 'Da'?" he asked distractedly. The first time she had addressed him directly and it had to be now.

"You idiot, Gavril."

"Da. Da!" Larisa caught hold of a strand of his hair and tugged it hard, giggling.

"She wants me to pay her some attention," he said, wincing as she tugged harder.

"Let me take her," Taliahad said, coming closer, his free hand extended.

"Take her where?" Kiukiu demanded.

"Away from here. Before—"

"Hesitating again, Tal?" A strong voice, seared with sarcasm, cut in.

"Look out!" Chinua flung himself in front of them as a bolt of fire sizzled from the sky to char the grass at his feet. The wolf shaman staggered and went down on one knee.

"Chinua?" Kiukiu whispered his name but he seemed not to hear her, slowly sliding forward onto the grass, his human body melting away to reveal his wolf form as he collapsed.

Gavril looked up to see a second winged figure descending through the rent in the clouds. In one hand it brandished a sword whose blade dripped gouts of flame. But it was the taunting tone that Gavril recognized with a feeling of loathing and dread.

How can it be?

And as the newcomer approached, Gavril saw— not the noble features of one of Galizur's Heavenly Guardians—but a face he remembered only too well. The last time he had seen that arrogant, mocking smile, furiously defiant even on the brink of annihilation, was on Ty Nagar at the fall of the Serpent Gate.

"Oskar Alvborg!" The human host of Sahariel, the headstrong rebel among Khezef's brethren. But who had taken control of him this time? The fire-flecked wings and flame-bright eyes reminded Gavril of Sahariel but Oskar Alvborg's transformed body had taken on a form more angelic than daemonic; there was nothing of the scarlet-scaled Drakhaoul about this new fusion.

"Ardarel?" Taliahad found his voice. "What have you done?" He was staring at his fellow Guardian, clearly as shocked as Gavril.

"I'm merely using this mortal to help me fulfill the mission."

"You're committing a sin. Galizur will punish you if he finds out."

"Galizur only cares that we carry out his orders. You should do the same."

Taliahad gave a curt shake of his watery locks.

"You're fading already," said Ardarel callously. "Haven't you realized yet? The more time you spend in the mortal world, the weaker you become."

"But I returned to the Second Heaven to replenish my strength. I don't understand."

"It doesn't work that way. No matter how many times we return home, our aethyric bodies can't adapt to this atmosphere."

As the Guardians argued, Gavril murmured to Kiukiu, "Now. While they're distracted." She nodded and thrust Larisa into Gavril's arms.

The sudden movement caught Ardarel's attention. Down he swooped, hand extended, to snatch Larisa. Gavril unfurled his wings with a flourish, creating a violent gust, powerful enough to knock the Winged Warrior back.

Larisa began to chuckle. She wasn't frightened by Taliahad or Ardarel; she seemed to be enjoying herself hugely. With one flap of his wings that almost wrenched his shoulders from their sockets, Gavril was airborne. Risa gave a shriek of delight which almost drowned Kiukiu's anguished cry from below.

"Wait!" Taliahad cried as Gavril rose above him. "You'll never outfly Ardarel."

Ardarel darted forward, flaming blade raised. Gavril felt the intense sizzle of heat even as he tried to dodge; it slashed close, too close to the baby's head.

A cool glitter of ice sliced the air. Taliahad had placed himself in front of Gavril and Risa, blocking the sizzling blade with his scythe. Sparks exploded like a shower of sparkling frost flowers.

Gavril clutched his daughter tight even though she wriggled to get free, squawking her annoyance at being restrained.

"What's this?" Ardarel, thrown back through the air by the strength of Taliahad's parry, righted himself. "Are you defying me, Tal?" There was no hint of mocking laughter any longer.

"This is my mission." Taliahad insisted. "I'll do it my way."

"Don't trust them, Gavril!" Kiukiu's desperate shout reached Gavril as he hesitated. "Just *go.*"

But now he was trapped, with Ardarel on one side, Taliahad on the other

It was only then that Gavril realized that Taliahad's bright form was fading, just as Ardarel had predicted. His defiant words belied his stance. Even the watery shimmer of his hair had dulled.

Suddenly Taliahad hurled himself toward Gavril with such speed that Gavril had no chance to make any kind of evasive move. The white shadow of Taliahad's wings enveloped him and his squirming daughter.

Caught off-guard, Gavril realized Taliahad's intentions too late. This was how it had happened the

first time the Drakhaoul had possessed him. And yet—
as his consciousness fought to repel the intruder —it
was also utterly different. Then it had felt as if he was
drowning in swathes of shadow. Now his body was
flooded with a cool sensation that tingled through
every pore and vein until he was convinced his whole
body must be gleaming, translucent as ice or snowmelt
tumbling off a high cliff into a mountain lake.

The invasion happened so swiftly that it was
done before he could blink. The protective cocoon
of feathers melted away, absorbed into his body. His
sight sharpened, his hearing too. He felt the strength
of Taliahad's aethyrial wings infuse and reinforce his
own, keeping him effortlessly aloft.

"Lord Taliahad," he managed to whisper. *"Don't—
hurt—Risa."* Taliahad might have taken control
of his physical body but he still fought to keep his
consciousness free for as long as it was possible.

"Down here! Gavril!"

Gavril became vaguely aware that Kiukiu was
running along beneath them, reaching up, inviting him
to toss Larisa to her. But since the moment Taliahad
merged his aethyrial form with his body, he had lost
control of his own actions. Yet all he could sense from
the alien being within him was surprise—and utter
confusion.

"What . . . should I do?"

A fiery sword-slash half-blinded him. Peering
through flame-dazzled eyes, he saw Ardarel bearing
down on them.

Chapter 55

"Don't you dare harm Risa!"

Somewhere at the back of her mind Kiukiu wondered if it was a mother's instinct: this passionate compulsion to defend her child, no matter what the cost. The intensity shocked her; she had cried out on impulse without thinking.

The fiery Winged Warrior turned and gazed down at her. Terrified, she found she could not move. He raised his sword.

"Get out of the way, Kiukiu!" Gavril's warning shout penetrated her panicked mind. She heard the sizzle of the flames flickering along the length of the blade, felt their heat. She knew she should run.

Her own powerlessness, faced with two such formidable adversaries, shamed her.

I'm just a Spirit Singer. I'm no use to Risa. All I can do is sing the souls of the dead into the Ways Beyond. And now it's my turn. But who will sing for me when I'm gone?

As the fiery blade came slicing down, she squeezed her eyes shut, making a last, stumbling attempt to dodge, waiting for the searing heat to envelop her.

She tripped and fell, sprawling forward on the rough grass.

A harsh metallic clash shivered across the steppe. She dared to open one eye.

I'm still alive?

Her knees, chin and hands were scraped and smarting from the fall, but otherwise she was unharmed. Above her head, Gavril—or Taliahad, she could not be sure who was in control—had blocked Ardarel's blow with his ice-crystal scythe. She heard him grunt with the effort as he not only deflected the blade but used his strength to push Ardarel back. The brightness of the flame-tipped feathers faded as Ardarel seemed about to fall from the sky.

Then Ardarel righted himself, laughing.

"You've improved, Gavril Nagarian. But I have the advantage." His callously mocking tone made her shiver. "That scythe is frozen water, and fire melts ice."

Kiukiu pushed herself up to her knees. Was Ardarel right? Was the scythe really an inferior weapon?

There must be something I can do.

"Are you sure, Alvborg?" Gavril's retort, breathless but still defiant rang out above her head. "Water can also quench fire."

I sing the souls of the dead into the Ways Beyond. Could I send these Bright Ones back with a Sending Song too? They've come from that selfsame place. Those ancient melodies can open a pathway between this world and the next.

She began to crawl toward the cart where her gusly lay wrapped in a cloth beneath the front seat, hoping that Gavril could distract the fiery angel from what she was about to attempt.

The Golden Scale. Malusha had used it when they trespassed far into the Second Heaven to speak with the Blessed Sergius. If only she could remember the complex sequence of notes correctly . . .

She drew out Malusha's gusly, unwrapping it as she cowered in the cart, gently touching each string in turn to check the tuning, her ear close to the instrument. Fear made her fingers tremble so much she could hardly slide the metal plectra onto the tips.

But play she must, plucking one string after the other to create a pathway of sound.

"Think of weaving a rainbow bridge—in which each of the seven colours is a different pitch." Malusha had been a severe tutor but Kiukiu would never forget all the Guslyars' ancient melodies her grandmother had dinned into her. *"Spin out those filaments of sound, let them vibrate and create new pitches as they resonate and clash, one with the other, strengthening the pathway that links the mortal world with the Ways Beyond."*

—

"You blocked Ardarel." Gavril's last remaining tactic was to keep Taliahad distracted. "Why?"

A confusion of images and feelings swirled around his brain. Taliahad was struggling to assimilate, yet still failing to overmaster his human host.

"Must destroy—no, protect—Risa."

Gavril felt the Guardian's conflict raging through him, wave after wave of contradictory messages keeping him hovering indecisively

"*Must—carry out—the mission.*"

"Then just let go of the Drakhaoul's child." Ardarel's order, barked out in Alvborg's cynical tones sent a chill of revulsion through Gavril. "A fall from that height will kill it."

"No." Taliahad said aloud. "Prince Galizur told me to take her to him."

So Galizur wanted Larisa? Somehow this information was even more alarming than Ardarel's callous command. But before Gavril could react, a cascade of plucked notes rang out.

The gusly.

Surprised, Ardarel swung around, mid-air, searching for the direction the melody was coming from. Somberly dark, yet infused with a golden timbre, Kiukiu's voice resonated across the grasslands in a song Gavril had never heard her sing before. There was no mistaking the power emanating from the singer and her instrument: Kiukiu was pouring all her skill as the last Guslyar into spinning a numinous chant, capable of opening a rift between the worlds.

The air seemed to glow with the richness of the sound until there was only the intense throb of each note, as warm as rays of evening sunlight, penetrating the clouds in a glory of bronze and gold.

Larisa cooed with delight, recognizing her mother's voice. Taliahad paused, listening. At the same moment, Ardarel focused his attention on the cart where Kiukiu was hiding.

"*There* you are, Spirit Singer."

***

So he's noticed. Kiukiu forced herself to concentrate, maintaining the slow, stately progression of notes and, taking a deep breath, matched her voice to the rich, deep pitches.

A jet of flame sizzled close to the cart. It took all her will power not to falter; once the song had begun, she must keep singing or the spell would disintegrate.

It's working.

***

As Ardarel turned, Kiukiu felt the heat of his flaming sword, heard the feathery shudder of his wings as he launched himself toward the cart. Shaking, terrified, she forced herself to sing on.

The cooing issuing from Larisa's little mouth was growing louder and more insistent.

Is she singing too?

Kiukiu's fingertips stung. Without the metal plectra for protection, every note that she plucked from the wire strings burned into her sore and tender flesh; she could feel the blood oozing from the broken skin, making the instrument slick and harder to play with the accuracy the Golden Scale required.

But she forced herself to ignore the pain and kept playing.

And the clouds overhead were slowly parting, rolling back to let the light from another world shine through, illuminating the grasslands with the intense, clear brilliance that comes after a violent rainstorm has washed the ground beneath.

"You were warned once before, Spirit Singer." Kiukiu was momentarily blinded by the glorious light issuing from the rift she had created. "Never use the Golden Scale again." As she stared upward through half-closed eyes, she glimpsed a winged figure descending, one whose countenance was so bright she could not distinguish the features, only the searing power of its piercing eyes. "Now you must pay the price for your disobedience."

Only then did her dazzled eyes make out the flaming arrow he was pointing directly at her from his gilded bow, the bowstring pulled taut.

Her fingers ceased their plucking, the song dried in her mouth and the last phrase hung, unfinished, in the air.

**

Gavril sensed Taliahad react as the golden apparition appeared. And in that moment's distraction, he also saw with terrible clarity what the third Winged Warrior intended.

"*Kiukiu!*" The warning cry issued from his throat, raw and desperate.

And in that instant the Winged Warrior let loose his fire-tipped arrow at the gusly. It streaked through the sky to hit the gusly. The discordant clang and crash as the instrument burst asunder, splinters of painted wood and lethally sharp wires snapped, twanged and spiraled away. Behind the jarring explosion of the disintegrating instrument, Gavril heard Kiukiu's scream and then—

Silence.

Chapter 56

"Sehibiel," Taliahad whispered. The name sent a chill throughout Gavril's body, as if he had been drenched in a sudden wintry downpour.

At the same instant Gavril saw Oskar Alvborg pause in mid-flight, looking upward as the third Winged Warrior hovered above them, a low rhythmic thrum emanating from his rose-gold wings.

"Ardarel. Taliahad. You have broken our sacred code. You will return with me at once." Sehibiel extended one hand, pointing at each in turn. Gavril felt an immense pressure forcing him down to earth. He landed and dropped to his knees in the grass, wings splayed out, still clutching Risa to him. His only thought was to get to Kiukiu but even though he strained with every muscle to move forward, Sehibiel's power held him pinned to the ground.

After a moment's stubborn resistance, Alvborg was forced to the ground too.

"You have disobeyed our laws. You have corrupted your aethyrial bodies. You've become polluted by mortal flesh, blood and bone." Sehibiel made a sudden sweeping gesture. Gavril felt Taliahad being drawn out of him, a viscerally disconcerting, disorienting sensation.

As the watery shimmer of Taliahad's aethyrial form suddenly appeared beside him, Ardarel materialized too, the flames of his burnished wings dim and faint. Both Guardians were fading fast.

"You will both come back to the Second Heaven with me to be cleansed of these mortal poisons," Sehibiel said.

"But I have still to complete my mission—" began Taliahad.

Risa let out a squeak of surprise, pointing at the two hazy figures.

Her cry was enough to draw Sehibiel's attention; he turned his golden gaze full upon her. Gavril held her tight, glaring defiance at the Guardian, yet knowing he could do nothing to protect her from the Guardian's fiery arrows.

"So this is Khezef's child." Sehibiel's stern voice softened. "So small, so young, so pitifully vulnerable."

"Please spare her." Gavril heard his voice shake with an intensity of feeling that overwhelmed him. *My daughter. Not Khezef's.* He had no idea if Sehibiel would pay the slightest attention to what he was asking but he had nothing left to bargain with but his own life. "If there is a price to be paid for Khezef's crimes, then punish me. But not Larisa. She's innocent."

Sehibiel's penetrating gaze shifted to Gavril. Gavril forced himself to endure the intense scrutiny, knowing that he was being assessed—and judged.

"Your wife was under a powerful curse," Sehibiel said at last. "She was in thrall to Anagini of the Jade Springs. And you are still in thrall to her sister,

Morozhka." He pointed to Gavril's left wrist where the slash made by Morozhka's ice blade still burned. "Your task is to keep Khezef's child away from the Elder Ones." His gaze darkened. "We can't let them use her for their own selfish ends. The Elder Ones chose to come here and here they must stay. Until they cease to exist."

Gavril was growing increasingly angry. Sehibiel's words had only confused him the more. "All I want is for my daughter to be left alone—to grow up an ordinary, happy child."

"Hold out your left arm."

Gavril hesitated. "What are you going to do to me?"

"What I did to your wife." Sehibiel put the fiery arrow back in its quiver and slung his bow over his shoulder. "I'm going to break your contract with Morozhka."

"You broke Anagini's curse?" Suddenly Gavril began to wonder if he had completely misread the Guardian's actions. "You've set Kiukiu free?" He dared to glance over toward the cart—and saw that Chinua had reached Kiukiu and had propped her up against one of the wheels. Even though her head was drooping, he noticed that the shaman was holding a water bottle to her mouth. Perhaps she had just been stunned by the Guardian's attack.

"Your left arm," repeated Sehibiel.

It was hard to hold on to the wriggling Risa with just his right arm but Gavril did as he was bidden. Sehibiel came closer, so close that Gavril could feel the cloud of heat emanating from his body—yet it was not the fierce, intense burn of Ardarel's fiery feathers but a more gentle warmth. Gavril steeled himself as Sehibiel reached out and grasped him by the injured wrist.

Heat flowed from the Guardian's fingers into the jagged slash. At first the sensation was unbearable and Gavril instinctively tried to pull away—and then it felt as if the warmth was spreading up his arm and on into his whole body, soothing and healing.

Gavril looked down as the Guardian released his wrist and saw the raw, rough edges of the wound fading even as he watched, the skin healing over, becoming smooth and whole again. He looked up in astonishment, meeting Sehibiel's gold-striated eyes for the first time, and realizing that their frank, penetrating expression was not hostile, as he had initially thought, but merely questioning and curious.

"Thank you," he said dazedly.

"I am also known as Sehibiel the Healer," the Guardian said. He placed his hand on Gavril's shoulder, the gilded warmth flowing once more from his fingertips into Gavril's flesh and bone. "But, even with my skills, I cannot take away the wings Taliahad has given you without damaging you beyond repair. I can feel that the filaments have knitted themselves so intricately into your flesh and sinews that they are now an integral part of your body. "

"I see."

"I'm not sure you do, Gavril Nagarian. I'm telling you that you must not use them again—except in the most desperate of circumstances."

"Not use them?" As the healing warmth slowly faded, Gavril's mind began to clear and he realized that Sehibiel was delivering a warning.

"Flying with these wings puts an intolerable strain on your mortal body. They drain you of your energies, both mental and physical. It's your choice, of course. But know that you and Ardarel's mortal host," and he pointed to where Alvborg lay, "will shorten your lives considerably if you take to the air again."

"But how can I protect Larisa from the Elder Ones? Suppose they—"

"If you want to see your daughter grow up, then you will need to find other ways to protect her."

"You're saying that I'll die?"

"Your task is to keep Khezef's child safe from Anagini and Morozhka." Sehibiel withdrew his hand and the golden aura emanating from him melted away like morning mist at sunrise. He rose into the air, beckoning Taliahad and Ardarel to accompany him. "If you fail, we shall have to intervene." As the heavens opened to let them through, Sehibiel's words drifted down to earth. "We can't let them use her for their own selfish ends."

Chapter 57

"Ma! *Ma!*" The insistent high voice penetrated Kiukiu's consciousness. She came back to her senses to find Gavril kneeling beside her with Larisa in his arms.

"Is that you, Risa? Did you call me?" she said wonderingly as Risa leaned out from her father's grip to cling on to her affectionately with warm, sticky fingers.

And then she remembered. The golden Guardian, the flaming arrow, the terrifying moment it had struck home. Looking down at her lap she saw nothing but splinters of charred wood clinging to the linen of her skirt and littering the ground around, alongside fragments of the metal pegs and curls of broken strings.

"Malusha's gusly. The last—the only—thing I had to remember her by." She stood up unsteadily, the fragments falling from the folds of her skirt. And then she burst into tears and sobbed like a little child. On seeing her mother's tears, Risa broke into a wail too, her little face puckering up, then turning red as she howled in sympathy.

Gavril put his arms around them both and hugged them close.

"I thought we were all going to die," Kiukiu said incoherently into his shoulder.

"But we're still here," he said, resting his cheek against the top of her head. She clung on to him, torn between thumping him hard with her fists for risking his life so rashly and letting herself surrender to the comforting warmth of his embrace. "And Sehibiel broke the curse laid upon us by the Elder Ones."

"He did?" She released her grip on him, drawing back so she could look down at her left ankle. Anagini's mark—the serpent's poisoned bite that had sealed the curse laid upon her—had vanished. Her skin was smooth and unblemished. "He broke the enchantment?" She could hardly believe that the long nightmare was at an end; she must still be in shock as she felt no joy or relief, only numbness.

"You're free. Anagini has no hold over you—or Risa—any longer."

"But the gusly . . ." There had been a high price to pay and as she gazed around her she saw the inescapable evidence of Sehibiel's retribution. Strewn all over the grass were the charred fragments of wood and tangled wire that had once been her most prized possession: Malusha's exquisitely painted instrument, handed down to her by her mother, the Spirit Singer's bridge to the Ways Beyond. She had always dreamed of handing it on to Larisa when she was old enough to learn the Sending Songs Malusha had taught her and now . . .

The Sending Songs. As the warmth of Sehibiel's healing fire slowly faded away and she tried to remember the first Sending Song Malusha had ever taught her, her mind went blank. Not a single note resonated in her head. It felt as if her brain was filled with a fog of white clouds and all pitches, all sounds muted. And the more she tried to remember, the more elusive the melodies became, like a fluff of dandelion seeds, drifting far from her grasp, borne away on the breeze.

Perhaps it was a temporary loss of memory, brought on by the shock of Sehibiel's attack.

"I've made some tea." Chinua reappeared, beckoning them round to the other side of the cart, away from the scattered fragments of the gusly. He had regained his human form but was walking unsteadily, as if not yet fully alert.

"Are you all right, dear Chinua?" Kiukiu asked, concerned. The wolf shaman had been knocked unconscious by Ardarel and she had never seen him look so frail.

"I'll mend," Chinua said, pouring out strong black tea, and stirring in plum jam to sweeten it. He had even found some rice biscuits for Risa to chew on. But as they sat in shocked silence around the little fire, cradling the bowls of hot, sweet tea in their hands, staring into the flames, the impact of what had happened began to sink in.

"Well, this is nice. Tea and biscuits around the camp fire." The dry voice startled them all; glancing up, Kiukiu saw that Ardarel's host was awake and lurching unsteadily toward them. His wings were concealed. "Is there none for me? How inhospitable. I'm famished."

"You're not welcome here, Alvborg." Gavril stood up, placing himself in front of Kiukiu. "You just tried to kill me and my child. Or have you forgotten?"

"That was Ardarel's doing. Frankly I couldn't care less what becomes of you and your precious family." There was something about the man's tone that made the hairs rise on the back of Kiukiu's neck.

"I'll make another pot of tea," Chinua said and she caught a slight inflection in his voice, so slight that a stranger would not notice it.

"The same special blend you served me and my men back at the pass?" Gavril asked. So he had understood Chinua's intention as well.

"I believe there's some left in the cart."

"I'll fetch it." Kiukiu rose. She moved slowly, still not entirely certain she had fully regained consciousness.

In the cart, she found the box containing the "special blend" and as her fingers closed around the dark lacquered wood, the dusty scent arising from the contents triggered a memory from Larisa's Naming Day. Khulan had brought the gift of tea from Chinua— but it was that same tea that had triggered the visions that had convinced her to flee with Larisa to protect her from the Winged Warriors.

Can I really trust Chinua? The thought that the wolf shaman might have betrayed her to Anagini was so painful she dismissed it. No, it must have been Khulan who had tampered with Chinua's gift, adding some somniferous substance that had opened her mind to Anagini's influence when she drank the tea and inhaled the steam.

Which meant that Khulan was Anagini's agent. And Anagini could have already dispatched Khulan to find them.

We can't stay in Khitari.

When Kiukiu returned with the box containing the "special blend" that Chinua had prepared in case of unwelcome visitors, Oskar Alvborg was cramming rice biscuits into his mouth, choking them down as if he had not seen food for a week. Risa, now safely on Gavril's knee, was staring at Alvborg in awe. For a moment Kiukiu almost felt a pang of pity for him; he looked oddly vulnerable in his tattered, blood-stained clothes, his wings concealed, by the same artifice, she supposed, that Taliahad had taught Gavril. Without a word she passed the box to Chinua who proceeded to measure out the tea into the pot and to add hot water.

**

Gavril, only too aware of the presence of Alvborg— and remembering how unpredictable the Tielen's moods could be—tried to think of a way to distract their uninvited guest as the second pot of tea brewed.

"Don't worry," Alvborg said dryly, almost as if aware of what he was thinking. "I won't impose on your hospitality any longer than I have to."

"But how—?" Gavril stopped as Alvborg, with a glint of a grin, revealed a fiery shimmer of feathered wings before concealing them once more. "Wait! Didn't you hear what Sehibiel said? If we use the wings again, we shorten our life spans."

"Ha!" Alvborg almost spat out his response. "He would say that, wouldn't he! That's what he wants us to believe."

For a moment Gavril heard Sahariel's voice crackling with furious malice. He stared up at

Alvborg, half-expecting to see the daemon's crazed fire-flickering eyes staring back.

"Don't be so naive, Nagarian."

"But it's a risk—"

"A risk I'm prepared to take. Don't forget; Sehibiel and his Warriors were once our jailers."

"*Our*?" Alvborg had spoken as if still possessed by Sahariel.

"Don't tell me you've forgotten? Don't tell me you don't still wake at night, your dreams filled with *their* memories."

Gavril held his gaze. "So, you too." For a moment he almost felt some kinship with Alvborg, saw a shadow of his own nighttime torments in the Tielen's pale eyes. He began to wonder if Alvborg had gained any insight into the memories left in his mind by Sahariel that might be of help. Then he pushed the thought away, determined not to let himself be drawn into sharing any of Khezef's memories.

"Will you take jam with your tea, my lord?" Kiukiu asked, carefully carrying a steaming bowl across from the fire.

"Why not?" Alvborg raised his hands to take the bowl of tea. "When traveling in foreign lands, one should always adopt the practices of the natives."

Trust Alvborg to treat their hospitality with his habitual condescension. Gavril bit back a retort, knowing there was no point arguing with the Tielen. He tried not to watch too closely as Alvborg sipped his tea, in case the Tielen became suspicious. He just hoped that Chinua's special blend would work as effectively on Alvborg as it had on him and his druzhina.

***

Larisa had fallen asleep at last, snuggled in her tea-chest bed in brightly-colored blankets of red and blue. On the other side of the camp fire, Alvborg lay sprawled in drugged slumber, defenseless. It was time to make good their escape. Except that Kiukiu was exhausted, both in mind and body. She sat staring at the sparks rising from the fire. This was not the time to sit around moping; perhaps when she awoke the next day, the lost songs would return? And yet the emptiness in her heart and mind told her that they were gone for good, seared away by that single golden shaft of fire

Gavril moved to sit beside her. "Alvborg's out cold. Are you ready to leave?"

She nodded—and realized that tears were running down her cheeks again.

"What's wrong?" he asked quietly.

She wiped the tears away on her sleeve. "Sehibiel broke Anagini's spell. But the songs are gone. I can't remember a single note. Not one. And there's no one left alive to teach me now that Grandma's dead. Is this the price I have to pay?"

"I fear it is." He took her hands in his. "For both of us."

"Both of us?" She looked up and met his gaze, seeing her own sense of loss mirrored in his eyes.

"Sehibiel has severed the blood bond. I can't hear the druzhina anymore, nor they me. I think he did it to protect Risa from Morozhka."

"Oh, Gavril . . ."

"And the further we travel from Azhkendir, the more I see that I'm no use to them anymore. They need a strong leader."

"But the Emperor placed his trust in you." She squeezed his hands reassuringly. "He believes you're the best man to oversee Azhkendir."

"I'm just a painter at heart, Kiukiu. I have no skills as a strategist or a warrior. Semyon and Vasili must have returned home to the kastel by now. They'll have told Askold that I'm missing. And the moment Sehibiel severed the blood bond it would have felt like a death to them. *My* death. So now I have to stay dead—and never go back." Even though he spoke quietly, she heard the resolution in his words. "We just have to go elsewhere and make a fresh start, somewhere no one knows who we are. For Risa's sake."

"But where can we go? Nowhere is safe anymore." A slight sob escaped again.

"Somewhere far from Anagini and Morozhka. Risa deserves to grow up like a normal child."

"But we have nothing. No money, no jewelry to sell, just the clothes we're wearing."

"I still have this." He showed her his ring of office, bestowed on him by Eugene with the title of High Steward.

"Isn't that a betrayal of the trust placed in you by the Emperor? If you try to pawn that, questions will be asked."

"In Azhkendir maybe, but not this far north."

"Sapaudia," said Chinua suddenly from the other side of the fire, making them both start.

"Where?" she asked. The name meant nothing to her.

"Sapaudia. It's a remote canton of Allegonde, high in the mountains but it used to be a separate kingdom once. It's where the Magus was born."

"But it's so far away." The prospect of traveling so far to a country where they knew no one filled Kiukiu with apprehension.

As if he sensed her uncertainty, Gavril put his arm around her shoulders. "It won't be easy. But if it means that Risa can have a normal childhood . . ."

It was the first time in so long that she had felt she could rely on him. She had been carrying the burden alone for so long yet now they would be going forward together, a family once more. She let her head rest against Gavril's, grateful beyond words that he was there and they were reconciled at last.

***

Traveling across the Khitari steppes at speed pulled by Chinua's wolves was proving a unique and terrifying experience for Gavril. As they rattled across the grasslands in a little cloud of dust, he risked a glance at Kiukiu and Risa and saw that they seemed to be almost enjoying the bumpy, dusty ride. Yet he was clutching the side of the cart with one hand, his knuckles white, unable to let go, the other hand clamped on Kiukiu's shoulder.

"It's all right," Kiukiu said to him, patting his knee reassuringly. "You can trust Chinua. And he says it's the only way to get to the northern coast."

Chinua had told them that merchant ships from Francia regularly called at the northern port in summer; the journey by sea would be a long and uncomfortable one, by passing Tielen, but they often took passengers. Gavril felt a slight involuntary twitch of his concealed wings beneath his shoulder blades as the thought it would be so much easier to fly floated through his mind, tantalizing, yet forbidden.

And, at that moment, he sensed a presence high overhead. All his senses alert, bristling with alarm, he looked up and saw Oskar Alvborg flying above them, his great feathered wings catching the sunlight. Kiukiu looked up too and drew her cloak over the sleeping Risa protectively.

"The drug's worn off. Is he going to attack us?" she whispered.

"He may have wings but he has no other powers." Although even as he tried to sound reassuring, he prayed that Ardarel had not also gifted Alvborg with his fire-wielding abilities.

"So there you are, Nagarian." The words came drifting down. "You and your lovely little family. I see you've taken up with wolves."

"Do you have a death wish?" Gavril cried. "Didn't you hear Sehibiel's warning?"

"I have unfinished business with my brother in Tielen."

Alvborg's reply sent a chill through Gavril. But he ignored the bait. "Flying with those wings will shorten your life. You'll die."

A burst of laughter echoed back across the empty steppe.

"What do I care? There's no one left to cry for me." And he flapped onward toward the north.

Kiukiu let out a sigh. "Thank goodness he's gone. I thought he was about to take it out on us for drugging his tea."

"I think he has other more pressing matters on his mind." Gavril was still on edge, even though Alvborg was out of sight. "If only there was some way I could warn Eugene." Yet Tielen was far away and if Sehibiel's warning were to prove true, Alvborg would exhaust his strength flying over the Saltyk Sea and plunge to his death in its icy waters. "We have to think of Risa now. We have to create new names, new identities for ourselves. It's just the three of us from now on."

Kiukiu snuggled closer to him. "We'll make it work. At least we're together. And Anagini and Morozhka have no hold over us any longer. We may have lost our gifts but we'll manage. We just have to learn how to be ordinary again."

Chapter 58

"I made a promise to your great-grandfather. And I intend to keep it, Magus Bernay." The Emperor's clear gaze rested on Gerard, as piercingly intense as Linnaius's. "I will protect you."

Gerard, still profoundly shaken by what he had experienced in the last couple of days, was not sure that he was ready to be called "Magus" yet; the title felt unearned.

"Work for me and I will do all in my power to ensure your safety." Eugene placed one hand on Gerard's shoulder. "I loved your great-grandfather. He was my tutor and mentor. He was more like a father to me than my own father."

Surprised to hear a tremor in the Emperor's firm voice, Gerard looked up and saw that Eugene's gray eyes were bright with unshed tears. *So it's true. He's not just saying this to console me; he's been hit hard by Linnaius's death.*

"The least I can do," Eugene continued, clearing his throat, "is to ensure his heir has my full support and protection. If that is what you wish, Ingenieur?"

What I *wish?* "Y-your imperial majesty does me too much honor." Gerard found himself stammering out a lame reply, wishing he knew what the correct protocol was in such a situation. "But I'm just a simple ingenieur; I don't yet understand what it is to be a magus. And," he hung his head, "I was dishonorably dismissed from Tielborg University."

"I've had Baron Sylvius look into your dismissal already," Eugene said airily. "It seems you were most unfairly accused. 'Stitched up' is the phrase I believe Sylvius used. Silvius has uncovered some evidence of collusion between Edwin Stenmark's family and Doctor Maulevrier. A very generous endowment made to the faculty." The Emperor handed Gerard a document. "And it seems that your one-time tutor has also disgraced himself at the competition. We suspect that he and his pilot tampered with the fuel. Such blatant cheating has brought disrepute on the university and his students. So Maulevrier has been removed from his position at the university and threatened with legal action if he contests the case. We've suggested that he might find suitable employment overseas in the colonies. For some years. We may even have placed him on a merchant ship sailing to Serindher to oversee a project in the Spice Islands."

Gerard caught the slightest hint of a roguish twinkle in the Emperor's eyes. He realized his mouth had dropped open and hastily closed it.

"But won't my presence here draw Ardarel back again? I can't place your majesty and the imperial household under such a threat."

"Ardarel?" The hint of mischievousness vanished from the Emperor's eyes, to be replaced by a steelier look. "That's a problem I will take care of myself or, rather, his human host." He spoke with such conviction that Gerard was in no doubt that he would carry out his threat. "In the meantime, here's a mystery for you to solve. Have you ever seen one of these before?" Eugene removed a mulberry velvet cloth from an object on his desk. Gerard stared at it, perplexed.

"Is it some kind of clock?"

"This is a Vox Aethyria. Possibly your great-grandfather's most remarkable invention."

Gerard, intrigued, came closer and gazed down at the mechanism. Beneath a glass dome was an intricate array of cogs, dials and levers, all connected to a crystal whose many facets were dull, not reflecting any light. A small horn resembling the bell of a trumpet was linked to the device, protruding upward, almost inviting the observer to place their ear against it.

"What is its function?"

"This was the pride of the empire. This Vox was connected—via the Aethyr—to others in each of the Tielen embassies. My generals had one in their command tents. It's a device that enabled the operator to exchange information over many hundreds of miles instantaneously."

Gerard stared at Linnaius's invention in awe. "What a remarkable machine." There was a catch in his voice. If only he had had more time to talk to his great-grandfather; their meeting had been so brief. "Your majesty said 'was' connected. Is there a problem?"

"Unfortunately the whole system stopped working the day of the Second Darkness; the crystals lost their luster and the machines went dead, all at once."

"So it's the crystals that powered the mechanism." Doubly intrigued, Gerard reached out, itching to touch the dull facets. As his fingertips brushed the cold surface he felt a slight tingle and for a second he thought he saw the briefest of flickers of light at the heart of the stone.

Eugene must have seen it too for he leaned forward eagerly with an intake of breath.

"You're the first with mage blood to lay hands on this machine since that day."

Gerard tried again and felt once more a tremor of energy that set his senses tingling.

"Why does it respond to me?"

Eugene glanced up and grinned at him. "Because you, Gerard, are your great-grandfather's true heir and the magus who's going to save the empire by making it work for me once more. What do you say?"

Overwhelmed, Gerard opened his mouth to reply, longing to accept. And then he remembered. "I'd like nothing better than to serve you—" he began. "But before I'll be of any use to your majesty, my great-grandfather told me I have to go to Enhirre to learn how to use my gift."

"Enhirre?" Eugene repeated the name as if it left a bad taste in his mouth. "Be on your guard out there. The Francians are still regarded with hate and suspicion after the atrocities committed there by the Commanderie and, judging by your name, you have Francian blood in your veins."

Gerard nodded. "My father—although he became a Tielen citizen when he married my mother."

"Before you go, you must see your great-grandfather's laboratory. Altan Kazimir is working on the sky-craft fuel there at the moment; I'm sure the two of you will have much to discuss! I'll get an equerry to show you the way."

***

Gerard's first impression on entering the laboratory was of a great disorder. One bench was strewn with open ledgers; papers spilled out of folders, as if someone had been frantically leafing through them. Another bench was covered with glass phials, test tubes and all the mysterious paraphernalia of the alchymist's art. A strange chymical odor tainted the air that made his eyes sting. But there was no sign of Altan Kazimir.

"Professor Kazimir?" he called.

Someone let out a cry. Startled, Gerard realized that there was a door at the far end of the main laboratory and that the cry had come from that direction.

"Professor?"

The door opened and a fair-haired man peered out at him warily, spectacles perched precariously on top of his head.

"Who are you?"

"My name is Gerard Bernay—"

"The great-grandson?" Kazimir ventured out, approaching with one hand tentatively extended, as if unsure whether to shake Gerard's in greeting or make a welcoming gesture. Gerard saw that the hand was trembling.

"Are you all right, Professor?"

"I've just made a rather alarming discovery," Kazimir said. He sank onto one of the lab stools. "You see, there was a break-in at the laboratory just before the competition. At first I thought someone had tampered with the fuel. But it's worse than that. Far worse."

"Worse?" Gerard echoed, not really understanding.

Kazimir raised pale eyes to his. "Your great-grandfather's notes. My research. The formula we devised to make *aethyrite*. It's not here."

"You mean someone stole the formula?"

Kazimir nodded. "There wasn't time before the competition to check if anything was missing. Everyone was waiting. What shall I tell the Emperor?"

"It's not your fault." Gerard wondered if he would ever be able to work with this nervous, unconfident man. "And surely it would be best to tell him as soon as possible. His agents might be able to apprehend the thief and retrieve Linnaius's notes."

"But the implications!" Kazimir mopped the sweat from his face with a crumpled handkerchief. "In the wrong hands, it could be used against us. It's a very powerful, volatile combustible substance."

"All the more reason to report the theft straight away. The Emperor won't blame you—unless you keep the news a secret from him till it's too late to catch the thief."

"You're right." Kazimir tottered a little as he got to his feet and Gerard instinctively put out one hand to steady him. "Would you mind if we postponed our talk until I've made a report to his imperial majesty?"

"Not in the least."

***

Gerard came out from Linnaius's laboratory to stand on the terrace, glad to breathe in the fresh air and feel the breeze on his face. He felt overwhelmed by the weight of responsibility he had just assumed or, more accurately, that he had been skillfully persuaded into accepting.

I am not Kaspar Linnaius. How could he ever hope to live up to the Emperor's high expectations? Yet there was something about Eugene's frank, open manner that had won him over. Would he be letting the Emperor down if he admitted he felt in no way ready to accept his invitation?

He leaned out over the balustrade gazing across the empty cobbled courtyard below toward the leafy haze of trees in the parkland beyond, instinctively checking the sky for any sign of Ardarel. He didn't yet trust his senses to identify accurately that faint fiery shiver of heat that presaged the Heavenly Guardian's presence.

I can't stay here.

The sound of laughter, carefree and infectious, broke the silence as a group of young men came hurrying out from the rooms above the stables. Gerard recognized the dark blue uniforms with a catch in his throat: Toran, Branville and their fellow cadets were crossing the courtyard below, chattering together enthusiastically. They must be on their way to receive their gold medals from the Emperor.

He wavered, torn between staying a little longer to see Toran rewarded by the Emperor and receiving the congratulations of the imperial court. But as he looked on, he noticed Branville reach out to hook his arm possessively around Toran's shoulders and Toran briefly glance up at him affectionately with a familiar little smile.

That decided him. It was time to leave.

***

As his great-grandfather's sky-craft rose higher into the air, all the weight of disappointment and heartache seemed to lift from Gerard's shoulders, like morning mist evaporating in the first rays of sun.

As Izkael slowly circled over the elegant palace of Swanholm, the slate roofs glinting in the cloud-sheened light, Gerard stared down, marvelling that such a busy imperial court, peopled by so many important politicians and nobles, home to the most powerful ruler in the hemisphere, looked no bigger than a dolls' house and, from that height, just as insignificant as a child's toy.

"This must be how the Heavenly Guardians see us," he said. "All our concerns, rivalries and machinations appear so small and unimportant when glimpsed from this distance."

He had left a letter for the Emperor, his new patron, promising to return as soon as he had fulfilled Linnaius's last wishes. His hand rose to touch Linnaius's silver key on its slender chain around his neck and he felt a thrill of anticipation. He had no idea what it would unlock—or what secrets he would discover along the way but he was ready to dedicate his life to keeping his promise to his great-grandfather.

Protect the key.

CAST LIST

AZHKENDIR
Gavril Nagarian, High Steward of Azhkendir
Kiukirilya (Kiukiu) Nagarian, his wife
Larisa, their baby daughter
Bogatyr Askold (leader of the druzhina)
Gorian One-Eye, Askold's second-in-command
Semyon, lieutenant
Dunai, Askold's son (steward of Kastel Nagarian)
Vasili, Dunai's younger brother
Vartik, Ilsi's younger brother
Tarakh and Radakh, Gorian's twin sons
Ivar and Movar, grooms
Ilsi, housekeeper of Kastel Nagarian
Sosia, Kiukiu's aunt
Ninusha, housemaid
Kion, Ninusha's baby son (by Lieutenant Andars of Tielen)

Lord Boris Stoyan, boyar of Azhkendir and governor of Azhgorod
Oris Avorian, the Nagarian family lawyer
Abbot Yephimy of Saint Serzhei's Monastery

TOURMALISE
Lilias Arbelian/Arkhel, an adventuress from Muscobar
Dysis, her maid and companion
Lord Ranulph Arkhel
The Hon. Lady Tanaisie, his wife (Tansie) nee Caradas

Toran Arkhel, their son and heir
Fleurie and Clarisse Arkhel, Toran's younger sisters
Ryndin, Iarko, Temir, retainers
Captain Montpelier, Master of Ceremonies at the Sulien Pump Room
Aristide Touchet, bailiff

Cardin's Iron Works in Paladur
Gerard Bernay, ingenieur
Rasse Cardin, owner of the Iron Works
Mahieu, foreman of the Iron Works

Paladur Military Academy
The Hon. Elyot Branville, Second Year cadet
Lorris, Aubin, Morsan, First and Second Year cadets
Colonel Mouzillon
Major Bauldry

KHITARI
Chinua, tea merchant, shapeshifter and shaman (his name means 'wolf')
Khulan, praise singer to Khan Vachir

TIELEN/ROSSIYA
Emperor Eugene
Empress Astasia
Crown Prince Rostevan (their baby son)
Princess Karila
Stavyomir Arkhel, Lilias's young son, the Emperor's ward
Count Gustave, private secretary to the Emperor
Baron Sylvius, imperial spymaster

Chancellor Maltheus, chief minister
Colonel Nils Lindgren
Lovisa, Countess of Aspelin (Eugene's cousin)

Tielborg University

Professor Altan Kazimir
Doctor Guy Maulevrier

SAPAUDIA (canton of Allegonde)

Kaspar Linnaius, the Magus
Azhkanizkael, Nahaliel, Serapiel, Auphiel and
Asamkis, his wouivres

In Exile in Serindher

Andrei Orlov, the Empress's brother
Oskar Alvborg, the Emperor's illegitimate half-brother

Guardians of the Second Heaven (Raquia)

Prince Galizur, Ruling Prince of the Second Heaven
Ardarel, Angel of Fire
Taliahad, Angel of Water (of the Seven Seas)
Sehibiel, Angel of Healing

A modified version of the Prologue and Chapter 8 first
appeared as "Song for a Naming Day" in the anthology
Anniversaries edited by Ian Whates and Ian Watson
(2010) Newcon Press

ACKNOWLEDGMENTS

My thanks to my editor, Colin Murray for his attention to detail and asking those essential questions every writer needs to be reminded of!

For the breathtakingly beautiful cover art, my thanks go to Edward Miller (and Les and Val Edwards)

For the distinctive wouivre chapter header my thanks go to the ever-creative Marcelle Natisin

And my thanks to Chantal Chevalier and all at eBook Partnership too!

The Arkhel Conundrum is dedicated to all those kind readers who liked **The Tears of Artamon** enough to ask me what happened next to Gavril, Kiukiu, Eugene and Kaspar Linnaius. The tale is far from finished... and will continue in Book 5...

Sarah Ash
www.sarah-ash.com

Moths to a Flame
Songspinners
The Lost Child

The Tears of Artamon Trilogy
1/ Lord of Snow and Shadows
2/Prisoner of the Iron Tower
3/Children of the Serpent Gate
4/ The Arkhel Conundrum

Alchymist's Legacy
1/ Tracing the Shadow
2/ Flight into Darkness

Tide Dragons (2014-16)
1/ The Flood Dragon's Sacrifice
2/ Emperor of the Fireflies

Scent of Lilies 2019 (published by Manifold Press)

Made in the USA
Middletown, DE
06 September 2024

60449467R00368